UNRINGING THE BELL

JUDY HIGGINS

GOSSART
PUBLICATIONS

Books by Judy Higgins

The Lady
Unringing the Bell
Bride of the Wind
Call me Mara, the Story of Ruth and Naomi Available November 2018

To receive publication notifications,
Sign up for Judy's Newsletter at:
http://www.judyhigginsbooks.com

First Gossart Publication Edition, March 2018

Published in The United States in 2018
Published by
Gossart Publications
900 Brown Street
Washington D.C.

Photo Credits
Cover: Nat Jones
Author Photo: Studio Walz

First Gossart paperback edition March 2018
First Gossart e-book edition March 2018

Printed in the United States of America

Judy Higgins
Unringing the Bell: a novel/Judy Higgins

Summary: "Jacob Gillis becomes inadvertently mixed-up in a murder investigation and must outwit an ambitious DA in order to save his career and reputation."—Provided by publisher

ISBN 978-0-692-99885-4

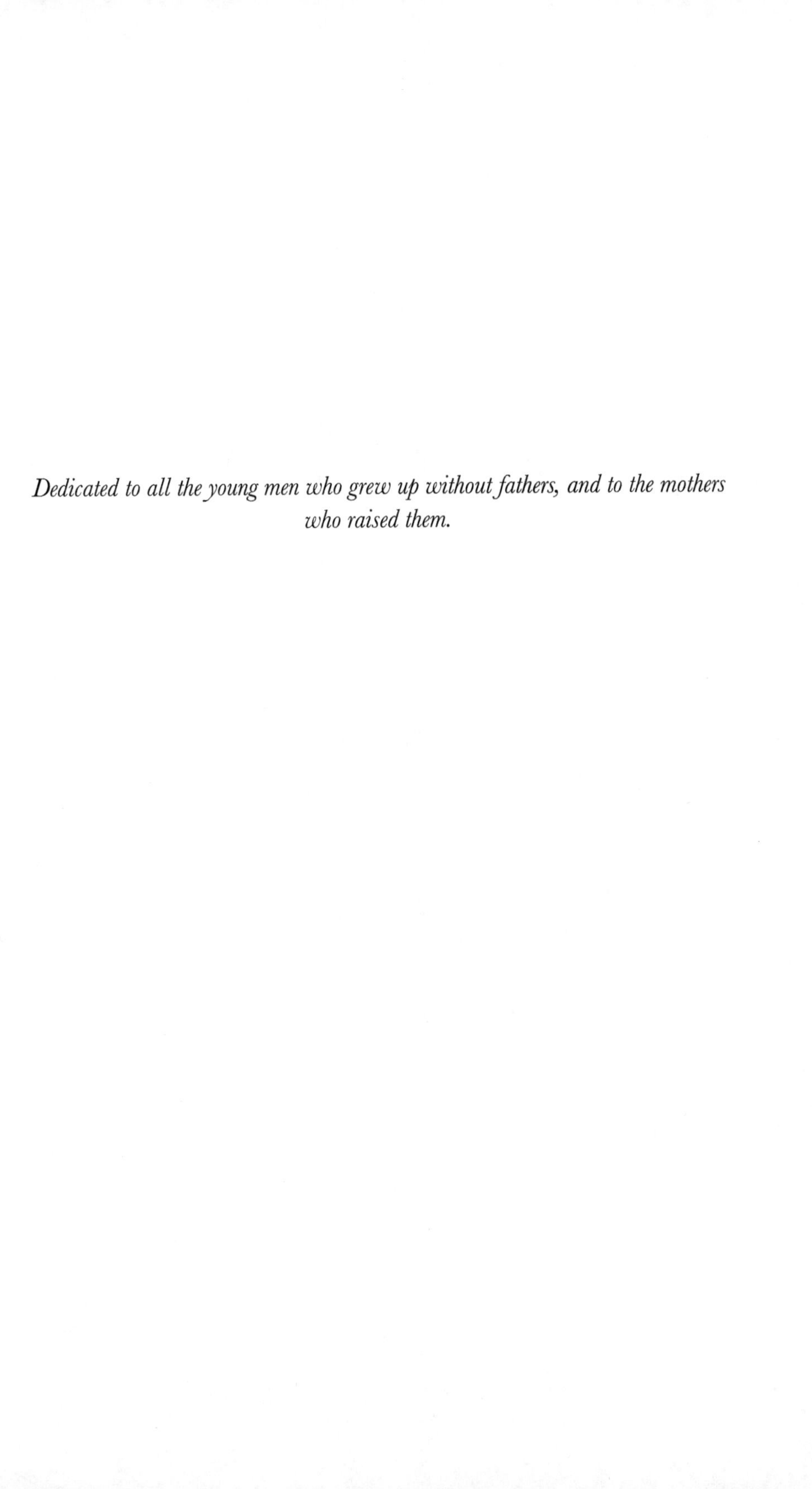

Dedicated to all the young men who grew up without fathers, and to the mothers who raised them.

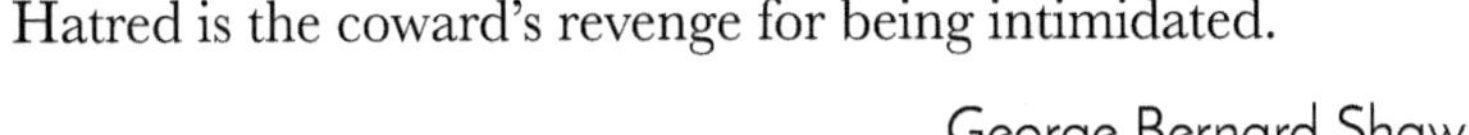

Hatred is the coward's revenge for being intimidated.

George Bernard Shaw

Chapter One

____

Monday, March 3
Bucks County, Pennsylvania

When Jacob Gillis was twelve years old, he burned down the town of Goose Bend, Pennsylvania. The fire didn't actually consume the entire town—only two blocks of the four-block business section went up in flames—but when the folks in Goose Bend spoke of the incident, they persisted in saying that Jacob Gillis, abetted by his friend Charlie Garrett, *burned down the town.*

"Two blocks is *half* the town," Jacob grumbled to himself late on a Monday evening, returning for the first time since high school graduation. Tired, stiff, and excessively thirsty, thanks to his twenty-hour journey, he wasn't in the best of moods as he turned onto Main Street, the scene of his infamy.

With night setting in, Goose Bend looked much the same as it had nineteen years ago—no people, no traffic, and no sign of life. In other words: dead. Except for the Pennston Hotel on his right. While the rest of the street slept in darkness, relieved only by a sliver of moon, a few faint stars, and several widely-spaced street lights, the ramshackle Pennston Hotel glowed neon and thrummed with the din of loud music, shouting, and laughter. Jacob was almost tempted to park and go inside for a quick beer to relieve his thirst, but his mother's commandment, *Don't you ever set foot in the Pennston Hotel,* haunted him from two decades before.

The only traffic light in Goose Bend brought him to a stop at the intersection of Main and Sixth. He closed his eyes and propped his head on the steering wheel. God, he was tired. His destination lay two miles beyond the eastern town limits, so only a few more minutes, fifteen maybe, surely no more than twenty, and then bed.

The chimes in the Lutheran Church steeple jolted him awake. About to pull forward, he thought he saw something move near the old telephone booth. He squinted at the dark shape of the cubicle, saw another flickering movement, and then . . . nothing. He rubbed his eyes. It must have been his imagination. After the marathon of a trip, they'd gone fuzzy and were simply trying to say goodnight.

He continued along Main Street, passing through Old Town and then New Town where he imagined he could still smell ashes, seared roof tiles, and burnt rubber. Even after all his adventures, and there had been plenty, coming home threatened to reduce him in spirit to a guilt-ridden twelve-year old. He'd faced down shifty-eyed industrialists in the International Court at The Hague, persuaded governments to conform to international treaties regarding rivers and wildlife, and dealt with bureaucrats and leaders of every race, religion, and political persuasion, yet in Goose Bend he was back in *Guilts-ville.* The town had more or less forgiven him when he was a high school senior, but one lucky toss of a football didn't even begin to make up for what he'd done.

His body, still on Rwandan time where it was already four in the morning, cried out for a jolt of caffeine so he pulled into the Texaco at the edge of town. Bleary eyed, he trudged inside, filled a large cup with Columbian Intense, tossed a bill and some coins on the counter, and started toward the door, but stopped when a big-boned, fleshy man with faded red hair blocked his way. A corner of Jacob's mouth curled in a wry smile. First ten minutes back and who should he run into but the police chief? Not that Bump Herrington had held the fire over his head. Not after the whole thing was settled as an accident. Still . . .

"Speak of the devil; it's Jacob Gillis." Bump slapped Jacob on the back, sloshing his coffee. Then Bump grabbed the hand that wasn't dripping with Standard Brand and shook it vigorously. "They told me you were moving back." Bump seemed genuinely glad to see him.

"It's good to see you, Chief."

"When did you get in?" Bump was dressed in his off-duty uniform of blue plaid flannel shirt, corduroy trousers, and brown and yellow Gander Mountain hunting jacket, all of which reeked of cherry-vanilla pipe tobacco.

"Just landed a couple hours ago," Jacob said. "How did you know I was moving back?"

"You must of forgotten what a small town's like; everybody knows everything including what God had for breakfast this morning."

"And that was?"

"Grits and scrapple. A concession to both ends of the Atlantic seaboard. Nah, I heard about your uncle leaving you his property. You're looking right good." He gave Jacob an affectionate punch on the shoulder. "How's that throwing arm these days?"

"A little out of practice." He knew the chief was being optimistic about his *looking right good*. His cheeks bristled with two days growth of stubble; his uncombed hair, badly in need of a trim, had turned "dirty blonde" during the long flight; and he probably gave off a little too much manly smell; not to mention his jeans needed a good wash.

Sipping his coffee and fighting sleep, he listened with amusement as Bump launched into local gossip. Who had died, divorced, been fired or newly hired. How the local teams were doing. He assumed the Chief was on his way into the Texaco for coffee, too. Only his would be loaded with cream and sugar. Etched indelibly in Jacob's memory were the five miserable hours of interrogation he and Charlie endured as Bump tried to determine if the infamous cigarette had been dropped accidentally. Desperately wanting to turn back the clock and undo the accident, Jacob had fought back tears and shaken with fear over how he and Charlie were to be punished while Bump drank cup after cup of loaded coffee. Now, Jacob felt a sudden fondness for the man. Once the incident was put to rest, Bump never brought it up again.

"Nobody in this town has ever forgotten what you did," Bump said, cramming his hands in his pockets.

Jacob cringed. And he had just thought . . . .

"It hurt like hell. We were so close. And then to lose." He shook his head at the painful memory. "Down by three; thirty seconds left."

Jacob let out a long breath. Bump was referring to the football game.

"Then you threw that pass. Lord a'mighty, I thought the bleachers were going to collapse with all the jumping and stomping."

Jacob shrugged. "It was just a Hail Mary."

"A Hail Mary! Bullshit. That was the longest pass I ever saw from a high-school kid. Right into Charlie's hands. I was standing down near the end zone. Charlie had the biggest shit-eatin' grin on his face as he strutted across the goal line. God! That was a beautiful moment."

Jacob grinned. It *had* been great. The first and only time Goose Bend High won the state championship. Ironically, the same six fire departments called in from surrounding towns to quell the blaze sent their engines to flash their lights and sound their sirens in the victory parade.

"We haven't . . . ." Bump stopped, pulled his buzzing phone from his breast pocket, and put it to his ear. "What's up?" A frown creased his brow as he listened. "All right, all right," he said finally. "I'll check it out." He hit the end button. "Crap. Can't even manage a cup of coffee around here. The night watchman at the Pennston Hotel thought he heard a gunshot. Just some kids playing with firecrackers, no doubt, but I have to check. I'll catch you later." Shaking his head, he left.

Fire crackers? Jacob smiled as he headed toward his car.

Imagine that; he and Charlie weren't the only naughty kids ever to be born. Or maybe it *was* a gun shot, he mused, remembering the movement near the old telephone booth. Someone hiding there? Then he dismissed the thought. Things like gun shots in the night didn't happen in Goose Bend.

Chapter Two

Detective William Laskey of the criminal investigation section of the state police squeezed his eyes shut for five seconds. Then for another five. This was always hard, especially when the victim was a young, beautiful woman lying face up in the middle of her dance studio, a puddle of blood over her heart, her blonde hair unfurled around her head. The blonde hair . . . almost an identical picture of . . .. He touched his fingers to his forehead. No, he wasn't going there. He took a steadying breath and opened his eyes.

He bent over and examined the body for signs of violence but saw nothing that indicated a struggle. The victim's black leotard, matching black leggings, and pink pointe shoes were neither torn nor in disarray. A spent cartridge lay a few feet from the body. There appeared to have been one clean shot and nothing more.

Straightening, he looked at Bump Herrington, Goose Bend's police chief, who stood off to one side, his face tight with shock. At least the chief had had the good sense to keep everyone away from the crime scene. A second police officer stood in the stairwell, holding the crime team at bay until Laskey gave the okay.

"Her name?" Laskey asked Bump.

"Ama Hunter."

"You know the family?"

Bump nodded.

"Have they been contacted?"

"John Jr., her husband . . . her ex-husband . . . . . Well, I mean her soon-to-be ex-husband . . ." Bump swallowed. "I tried calling, but he didn't answer. I sent someone around to where he's living but no one answered the door. You don't have to worry about him. The Hunters are one of our finest families. John wouldn't . . ." Bump squeezed his forehead.

Laskey knew the name. John Hunter Sr. headed up enough committees and organizations in the county that his name had to be familiar to anyone who read *The Doylestown Intelligencer.* His son, whose wife lay sprawled on the floor with a bullet through her heart, also sat on the board of several organizations. The family, one of the wealthiest in Upper Bucks, owned a shirt factory and an accounting firm.

"Gotten hold of anyone else in the family?" Laskey asked.

Bump shook his head. "Ama has no relatives other than her mother who's in a nursing home. I didn't even try calling her because she's in the last stages of senility. Or maybe she has Alzheimer's. John's parents are on a cruise. And his sister, Kate . . .. Well, I couldn't reach her either."

Nodding, Laskey averted his eyes. "I'll just take a quick look around." Turning away from Bump, he kept his face expressionless.

He did a circuit of the studio which consisted of nothing more than a large room, empty of furniture except for one chair. Barres stretched along two walls. At one end of the room, a row of windows overlooked Main Street. Mirrors covered the wall opposite the landing, doubling everything: the dead woman, Bump, the single chair, him. Opposite the windows, a short hall led to a powder room on the left and a small office on the right. The hall itself ended in a blank wall.

Seeing nothing unusual, Laskey returned to the landing and, after instructing the officer there to keep a security log, looked down the steps to where his team and the coroner waited, and signaled them up. While they set about their business he'd have Bump fill him in on Ama Hunter. Motioning to the police chief to follow, he moved to the hallway outside the tiny office.

He pivoted around to face Bump. "So, the husband isn't answering his phone, nor is he at home?"

Bump broke out in a sweat. "Noooo, noooo." He shook his head. "John Hunter would never do this." He propped one arm against the wall and covered his eyes with the opposite hand.

"I wasn't accusing him, but if he isn't guilty we need to rule him out."

"Look, I'll tell you up front . . . ." Bump straightened, pulled a handkerchief from his pocket, and wiped his forehead. "They were in the middle of a nasty divorce, and Ama was trying to skin John for everything he was worth. She was livid when he moved in with someone else, but that doesn't mean . . .."

"Who is the other woman?" Laskey held his pen and pad ready.

"Nancy Bolen. She lives out on the edge of town." The lines etching Bump's face grew deeper. "I got hold of her parents. Nancy's up in Scranton for a bridal shower." He tilted his head back and closed his eyes. "I can't believe this. The Hunters are pillars of the community. Law-abiding, church-going. Things like this shouldn't happen to people like them."

"Things like this shouldn't happen to anyone." Laskey turned and headed back to the dance floor.

A flash blinded him. After the click of the camera, the room subsided into silence for a few seconds, and then there was another click, and another and another as the photographer snapped the body from every angle. Rubbing his eyes, Laskey moved away.

"Anything?" Laskey asked the coroner who sat in the chair, scribbling.

"There appears to have been only one shot. No sign of rape. At least not without further examination. No sign of struggle."

Laskey nodded, acknowledging the information. No sign of struggle was a good indication that the perpetrator was someone she knew. He stood for a few moments watching a fingerprint technician dusting the door frame leading into the office, while a second one took care of the area around the landing. A bit heavy-handed with the powder, he'd splotched his black sneakers with white. A third technician drew a diagram of the scene, using a tape measure, to determine how far the body was from the wall, the size of the blood puddle on Ama Hunter's chest, the distance from the stairs to the body.

A noise from outside drew Laskey to the windows. He peered down at the group of men gathered on the sidewalk below, the red light of the ambulance flashing intermittently in their faces.

Bump had followed him. "It's darts night at the hotel," he said. "Every Monday evening a bunch of guys comes to play darts and drink. Maybe one of them . . ."

Laskey studied the men below. Sometimes he knew who he wanted to question based on stance, or the way a person fidgeted or twitched his lips, or the way he shifted his eyes. He couldn't see eyes or lips from the second story, especially at night, but he saw postures and body movements. An old man stood at the edge of the group leaning against a bicycle with an attached cart full of something that looked to be . . . Laskey squinted. Soda cans?

"Who's that?" he pointed to the man.

"Jimmy Q Haskell, the town's kook. He barely knows what day of the week it is."

"Can you have someone get their names?" He tapped the window pane.

"Sure thing."

What would be in a dance studio to tempt a thief, Laskey wondered as he turned back to view the scene through a screen of dust motes. Money, if it was pay day. Most teachers billed at the end of the month which would have been the previous Friday, and since most payments usually came in the form of checks, theft was unlikely. They would examine the body at the morgue, but it didn't look like rape. There were other possibilities, something drug-related, a random act of violence, a hate crime, but who would hate a dance teacher enough to kill?

He headed back toward the studio office, stopping when he came even with the landing. The officer stationed there held the security log on his knees, clenching it like it might fly away if he let go.

"You know John Hunter?" Laskey asked.

"We were classmates in high school."

"Were you in school with Jacob Gillis, too?"

The officer nodded. "All three of us were in the same grade." Then he looked at Laskey in surprise. "You know Jacob?"

"He's my godson." Disappointment flickered through him. For weeks he'd been looking forward to reuniting with Jacob and celebrating his return from Africa, but now he wouldn't be able to grab more than a few minutes with him until this murder was solved.

***

DURING HIS FIRST LOOK AROUND, Laskey hadn't paid much attention to the pictures on the walls of the office, but now he stared into a pair of eyes almost as black as the dancer's costume. He recognized the character of Odile, evil sorceress in *Swan Lake*, aka Ama Hunter, murder victim. The Odile portrait was one of two which were larger than the several dozen other framed pictures covering the wall. In the second of the pair, Ama, as Queen of Swans, was garbed in white, arms posed above her head, eyes looking off to the side. He wondered if any of the technicians recognized the portraits to be from *Swan Lake*, but he wouldn't ask. The fact that his interests extended beyond baseball, politics, and trout fishing concerned no one other than himself. He guarded his extracurricular interests almost as closely as his darker secrets.

Behind him, Albert, his assistant, was going through the bottom drawer of a desk. Tearing his eyes away from the portrait, Laskey turned around. "Anything?"

"Top drawer contained a check book and address book. I put them in the bag." Albert gestured to one of two plastic bags sitting on the floor next to him. "Not much else of significance. A few pictures similar to those." He swept his hand around, motioning to the photos hanging on the walls. "There was a bunch of miscellaneous stuff in the middle drawer. Magic markers. Empty file folders.

Pens. Paper clips. Post-it notes. Class schedule. Books for recording payments. They're in the bag, too. I left the sheaf of blank bills and envelopes in the drawer. Her purse is in the other bag. There was sixty-seven dollars and some change in it along with a Platinum American Express and an HSBC Visa card."

"What about that one?" Laskey nodded at the bottom drawer from which a whiff of grated citrus peel perfume rose.

"Going through it now. Mostly stuff you'd expect to find in a woman's desk. Make-up containers, spilled perfume, tampons, a nail file. There's shoe rosin and a roll of dance tape. The tape is used to wrap around feet." He shrugged, adding, "My daughter takes ballet."

"Keep digging."

Laskey turned back to the photos. Most showed Ama Hunter in different ballet positions, but three were of a handsome young man with dark, wavy hair and heavy brows. A former dance partner? An old boyfriend? Not someone from around here, he guessed. He was pretty sure no man in Goose Bend would be seen in a pair of tights.

"There were some cotton balls smeared with make-up in the waste paper basket beside the toilet," Albert said. "I wish I'd invested in the make-up industry back in the beginning."

"Yeah, me too." Laskey grinned. "Only that would have been a few thousand years ago. You bagged the cotton balls?"

"Of course."

He took one last look around, and then, about to leave, he glanced again at Odile and a shiver ran down his back. Her eyes had followed him. He moved to a different place. Again, her eyes followed.

"You ok, boss?" Albert gave him a quizzical look.

He pointed to the picture of Odile. "Just observing how her eyes follow you wherever you move."

Albert grinned. "She's trying to tell you something. Maybe you should go to a séance for help on this case."

Laskey gave him a dismissive wave and left the room. It was coming up on eleven P.M. Where was John Hunter?

Chapter Three

Tuesday, March 4

Jacob awoke to the smells of an old stone house: mold, mildew, soot, and the odor of two dogs belonging to the previous occupant. His uncle had lived in a nursing home up until his death seven months ago, renting out the property to a widower with two labs.

He groaned and sat up. Too tired to blow up the air mattress, he had crawled into his sleeping bag and slept soundly without benefit of pad, rug, or anything softer than a wide-plank oak floor. "The good news . . .," he said to the empty room as he looked at his watch, ". . . . is that I was too tired to wake up on African time." It was seven-thirty, well past his normal wake-up time in Rwanda where it would now be three-thirty in the afternoon. Between passing clouds, the sun blinked through the window.

It was time to check in. His mother was on a plane returning from a trip to England with Aunt Zuela, unreachable for the moment, but Meg was probably stewing because he hadn't called last night. A goose swept past the window as he reached for his phone. The faint hum of a tractor and the screech of a rooster came from a nearby farm.

Meg answered on the second ring. "You got in too late last night to call, little brother?"

"Five bloody hours late, to be exact. Twenty hours after leaving Kigali. Thirteen flying. Seven waiting at Schiphol because of a mechanical problem. And guess what?"

"What?"

"My luggage is still at Schiphol." He folded back the top layer of his sleeping bag.

"Rotten luck. Where did you spend the night?"

"At the house."

"You're kidding. You don't even have a bed."

"I have a sleeping bag."

"You could have come here first and relaxed a few days. Mike and the kids would love to see you."

"And I'd love to see them, but I want to get settled ASAP." He paused before adding, "I'm off to see Charlie first thing. He's been pestering me non-stop." For the past few days, emails had flown back and forth, Charlie insisting that Jacob come by as soon as he got back in town.

"Hmmmm. For better or worse, usually for worse, Charlie always had a knack for luring you into situations."

"Not this time."

"What about Laskey?"

"Dinner tonight. He's taking me to his latest most favorite restaurant. Wherever that is. Before I forget, thanks for having my stuff moved into the house. I owe you." His *stuff* consisted of nothing more than a few sticks of furniture and a couple dozen boxes packed haphazardly with the contents of his law school apartment.

"You sure do owe me, and I'll be collecting. Count on it. By the way, that house needs a bunch of work. I don't envy you."

"Guess I'll be busy. Got to go. Charlie has a meeting later, so I have to be on time. Talk to you later."

He clicked the off button.

Charlie this morning; Laskey this evening. He had six weeks to settle in before beginning his new job, and that included all the repairs the place needed, so in between seeing his best friend from high school and having dinner with the man who had become a father-figure to him, he needed to start unpacking the twenty-something boxes stacked in the dining room and kitchen.

JACOB STEPPED out of the shower, thankful that Meg had remembered to turn on the hot water heater and equally glad that the heater still worked. He fastened a towel around his waist and then scrambled through his dopp kit for his razor and shaving cream.

A crack in the mirror bisected his face from hairline to chin as he shaved. Add "mirror" to list of things to take care of, he noted. Repair, replace, repair, replace—he expected to be doing a lot of that in the next six weeks in order to make the old house livable. Stopping mid-stroke in the swipe of razor across cheek, he frowned. From the urgency of Charlie's emails, he knew his friend wanted something that threatened to eat into his time. But what?

He lowered the hand holding the razor to rest on the edge of the sink. It had been nearly nineteen years since he and Charlie had perched on the edge of that sawdust pile behind the hardware store. Sometimes he blamed Charlie for being most at fault because he furnished the Marlboros and Bic lighter. It was Jacob, though, who had been the first to light up. After an over-eager drag, he coughed so violently that the cigarette flew from his mouth. He ground the dropped cigarette into the sawdust with his heel and lit another. Then he and Charlie walked off, coughing and choking, not realizing the first cigarette was smoldering in the dry sawdust. That wasn't the only trouble he and Charlie had gotten into. There had been a long list, but everything else was minor in comparison, and their mischief had stopped after the fire. Mostly. They still managed a few misdemeanors, like skipping school for the opening day of trout season and inventing harmless pranks on Halloween. Funny thing was, Charlie seemed to have gotten over the incident in a way that Jacob never had.

***

JACOB LOCKED the back door and then headed for the Rav4 he'd rented at the airport. Now that Charlie had abandoned Goose Bend and moved to Doylestown, he had to drive ten miles to see his friend instead of running down to the end of the block. Ten miles to say *no* to whatever Charlie was about to ask of him, and then ten miles back home to unpack. Sounded like Charlie owed him a drink, or several.

He was about to climb into the SUV, but stopped when an old Toyota Sequoia swung around the side of the house and rattled to a stop beside him. With a surge of pleasure, Jacob went to greet the man who had stepped in to fill some of the loneliness when his father died.

"Jake!" Laskey said, springing out of his vehicle and throwing his arms around him and squeezing.

Jacob hugged him back.

When they finally let go of each other, Laskey grasped Jacob by the shoulders and leaned back for a better look. "You don't look any worse for wear after five years in Africa." Laskey had the kind of voice that sounded like it erupted from a tympanum.

"And you don't look a day older since I last saw you." At sixty-five, Laskey was the same age Jacob's father would have been had he lived.

"There's a little more salt than pepper on top these days." Laskey brushed his hand across the top of his head.

"Makes you look distinguished. I'm told women like it. One got her hooks in you yet?"

Laskey, legendary for his dedicated bachelorhood, shot him a contemptuous look.

"I'm still pissed at you for not visiting me in Africa," Jacob said.

Laskey shrugged. "I'm afraid of lions and tigers."

"Yeah, right." Laskey, otherwise logical, had a phobia about flying.

"I'm sorry, Jake," Laskey said, digging his hands into his pockets, ". . . but I have to cancel dinner tonight, and I only have thirty seconds now." Frowning, he blew out a little puff of air. "There was a murder last night, and I'm on my way back to the scene."

Harnessing his disappointment, Jacob was about to ask where the murder had occurred, but Laskey gave a brief shake of his head. "So, when can we get together for more than thirty seconds?" Jacob asked instead.

"Breakfast in the morning? Here? I want to check out this house your uncle unloaded on you."

"Sure. I'll whip up something." He had a frying pan. Somewhere. He'd grab eggs and scrapple on the way home from Doylestown and then set about unpacking until he found plates and eating utensils.

"It's good to see you, boy." Laskey studied Jacob through narrowed eyes. "You look more like your father every year. If it weren't that your hair's blonder, I could swear I was looking straight at him." He looked down at his feet and swallowed. "Still gets to me sometimes. Even after all this time. It's been . . . . what? Twenty-three years now?" He swallowed again as he turned to go. "I'll be here at the crack of dawn tomorrow."

Jacob watched Laskey walk back to the Sequoia, his limp barely detectable, and for the thousandth time he wondered why his friend kept what had happened to his foot a secret. But there were some places Laskey didn't go—formidable Laskey with his gruff manner and hard-muscled body. He was a private person and sometimes a grizzly bear, but he had a goose-down heart which he tried like heck to hide. But Jacob knew.

Chapter Four

"Appreciate it," Laskey said, accepting Bump's offer to walk him over to John Hunter's office.

"John's in shock," Bump said as they set out. "I don't think he knew what to do or where to go after I told him, so I left him sitting paralyzed at his desk. John senior and Gwen are down in the Caribbean on a cruise." Bump's voice came out as a croak, and he swiped at the sweat that kept popping out on his forehead. "John did manage to tell me he spent the night in Doylestown at his aunt's house. He came back to Goose Bend early this morning, went home to change clothes, and then drove to his office not knowing what happened."

Laskey wondered if the police chief was worried that the husband might be the culprit in spite of the Hunters being pillars of the community. Right now, a cloud of suspicion a mile thick hung over John Hunter.

"I guess John didn't want to leave the office and go to his parents' house since its empty," Bump said as they crossed over Fifth. "Can't say that I blame him. Although, I expect people will start showing up there soon enough. For obvious reasons, he wouldn't have wanted to go to Nancy Bolen's where he's been living for the past few months. I'm checking Nancy's alibi right after I walk you over."

"What time did John show up at his aunt's last night?" Laskey plunged his hands into the pockets of his jacket; nasty gusts of wind lashed at him.

"She said she was out for the evening. Playing bingo. When she got home a little after twelve-thirty, John was there, sound asleep."

"So we have no idea what time he got to her house? Or why?"

"He probably went for a home-cooked meal what with both his parents and Nancy being away. Since his aunt wasn't home, I'd be willing to bet he ordered a pizza, watched a little TV, and then went to bed."

They crossed over Main. "What kind of car does John drive?" Laskey asked when they got to the other side.

"Lexus."

"Maybe one of the aunt's neighbors saw it parked there. Any other relatives around?"

"Just his sister, Kate. I expect he'll go over to her place as soon as the shock wears off." Bump shook his head. "This is going to be a mighty big blow for John senior and Gwen when they find out. My office manager is trying to get through to the ship. Maybe she already did. It's mostly John junior that's running the accounting firm and the shirt factory now." He pointed to the intersection ahead of them. "This is where we turn."

They walked in silence until they came to the Hunter offices, located two blocks from Main, and then stood for a few minutes while Bump explained that John's grandfather built the Queen Ann Victorian-style building as a residence. He'd turned it into offices years later when he constructed a more elegant home on Boxwood. The grandfather had passed five years ago, so the senior Hunters now occupied the house on Boxwood. "John and Ama own a sizable brick Colonial on Maple," Bump said. "And this place . . . .." Bump nodded to the Queen Anne, ". . . . is used only as offices now. The accounting firm is located on the first floor and the business offices for the shirt factory on the second floor. The factory is . . . .."

Laskey let Bump ramble on. Laskey knew the shirt factory stood at the edge of town on the road to Doylestown, but sometimes vital information leaked from such ramblings.

Finally, the chief blew out a long *whooooooo* and shook his head. "I don't envy you having to question John. And I sure don't envy him. Poor guy. I guess I better get going and do what I have to do."

Laskey gave a cursory wave and then turned to examine the building.

The mint green of the outside walls and the white of the wood-work—gables, scrollwork, and trim—appeared to be freshly painted. A turret anchored the left top of the building, and a gable the right. Ama had been fighting for half the business and assets, according to Bump. Goose Bend real estate prices didn't compare to areas like the Main Line or even Doylestown, but still, the two businesses, the Hunter investments, and the real property must add up to an envi-able fortune for a dance teacher.

Laskey entered to the smell of roses and seven pairs of eyes staring at him. Four men in business attire and a gray-haired woman dressed in a navy linen suit were standing around, tight-faced and with drooping mouths, while a young woman sat behind the recep-tion desk, dabbing at her eyes with a tissue. An older woman dressed in what looked to be a cleaner's uniform sat on the sofa.

"Detective William Laskey," he announced to the group and held out his ID. "I'm here to see John Hunter."

"I'm Beatrice, the office manager," the gray-haired woman in navy said, stepping up to him. Her hand went up to nervously finger the pendant of her necklace. "Can I help you?"

"Thanks, but I need to speak to John."

She nodded and pointed to the hall. "First door on the right. Kate's with him. They asked to be alone." She let go of the pendant.

"Do you know who did it?"

He shook his head and then headed into the hall. Something about the bowl of roses on the desk irritated him. Probably just that bright yellow seemed out of place in the midst of a tragedy.

The first door on the right was closed. He rapped, and then stared at the engraved plaque with John Hunter's name on it as he waited. There was nothing on the plaque to denote John's position or credentials, as though Mr. John Hunter was too important to advertise his title on the door.

When no one answered, Laskey eased the door open. John sat at a massive mahogany desk, head propped on hands, face hidden so that only his black, wavy hair was visible, but then, looking up, he let his hands slide down to reveal his face. A woman, same black wavy hair and appearing to be past the midpoint of her twenties, stood beside the window. She'd been leaning her forehead against a pane but jerked her head up to stare at Laskey.

"I guess you didn't hear me knocking. I'm Detective William Laskey." He stepped across the threshold and onto a thick carpet. The room smelled of leather and Old English Furniture polish.

Slowly, John straightened. "Can I help you?" he asked, his voice barely audible.

"I'm sorry about your wife." Laskey paused. He knew the percentages. Wives killed by husbands. Husbands by wives. Lovers by lovers. "Do you have any idea what might have happened? Or who did this?"

Kate moved away from the window and took a few steps in John's direction, while John stared at him with blank eyes. Laskey waited. The less he talked, the more likely John was to talk, or at least that was usually the case. He took in John's gray, pin-striped Hugo Boss suit; his Paul Frederick's shirt, its collar properly stiff; his perfectly centered navy Hermes tie imprinted with white fleur-de-lis; the silver pin attached to his lapel. Except for his mussed hair, John could have been on the cover of a men's fashion magazine. Laskey reached up to check his own tie, wondering if he had put on the shirt with the frayed collar he should have thrown out five years ago. Not that he cared. It was just an automatic reaction. As a former FBI agent, he'd had his days of having to get all gussied up, spiffed, and polished; the days when it was his business to recognize what ilk of clothes people wore, Hugo Boss, Hermes, and otherwise. He missed many things from his former profession, but not the dressing up part.

He threw a fleeting glance at Kate. Her eyebrows drawn severely together, she met his glance head-on.

"Did Ama have enemies?" he asked John.

John picked up a Dunhill pen that lay on his desk. "None that would kill her." He tapped the pen nervously a few times and then set it down. A bead of sweat trickled down his brow.

"It was someone from that dump of a hotel," Kate sniped.

Laskey turned to study her. "The Pennston Hotel?" he asked at length. "Why do you think that?"

"Who else would have murdered her? Go take a look at the people who hang out there. It had to have been one of them."

"Why?"

She shrugged and wiped the back of a hand across her eyes.

"Money for their next drink. . . Because they're crazy. . . I don't know."

Those were always possibilities. Crazy people. Thirsty people. He stepped closer to the desk, close enough to trail his forefinger along the edge and to smell John's Marc Jacobs cologne. "Where were you yesterday evening?"

John's expression froze. "I spent the night at my aunt's in Doylestown," he said after an interval.

"What time did you get there? . . . . Where were you before that?"

"I didn't kill my wife."

"John?" Kate took a step forward. "Tell him."

John shot his sister a look of . . . . Laskey couldn't quite decide what the look meant. Warning? Kate raised her palms in a question, but then thought better of it and lowered them.

"I didn't kill Ama," John said, his face reddening and his hands clenching into fists.

"I'm not accusing you. Just tell me what time you got to your aunt's, and where you were before that, and then I'll be on my way. As painful as it is, I have to ask."

"I didn't kill her."

"What was Ama's routine?" Laskey tried a different tack.

"How the hell should I know?" John's voice rose. "I haven't been with her in five months."

"Surely you know how she spent her days."

"Yeah. She got out of bed every morning. She said nothing. She didn't eat breakfast and barely ate lunch. She went to her studio and taught her classes. When she finished arabesque-ing and pliè-ing, she went home and sulked. When I came home, she didn't talk; she went to bed. Then she got up the next day and did it all over again."

"John . . . ." Kate looked at her brother with pleading eyes.

"I didn't kill her," he shouted, banging his fist on the desk and half rising from his chair. "I didn't kill her."

Laskey pursed his lips. He wasn't going to get anywhere with John right now. He took a couple steps toward the door, but then stopped and twisted around to look at Kate. "Miss Hunter, where were you yesterday evening?" She stiffened. "It's just routine," he said with what he hoped was a disarming smile.

"I was at a book group." The pitch of her voice had risen. "Surely, you don't think I . . .."

"No, not at all."

Chapter Five

Jacob zipped past the law library on the ground level of the county courthouse in Doylestown, bounded up the stairs to the mezzanine and, after stepping into the elevator, pushed the button for the fourth floor where the District Attorney's office occupied the entire space. Charlie, the youngest person in Pennsylvania ever to be elected DA, supervised thirty-four attorneys and God knows how many paralegals. Jacob grinned. Not bad for his fellow arsonist.

He knew the layout of the DA suite—Laskey had given him the tour when he was a teenager—so when the elevator doors opened, he forged through the reception area where there was no receptionist in sight, and then through the common room. A couple of paralegals—one pretty enough she might be worth getting to know—looked up as. He smiled, pointed his finger toward the hallway in the rear indicating he knew where he was going, and swept past them.

In the anteroom to Charlie's office, he came to an abrupt stop.

A woman, sixtyish, and with auburn hair waving around her cheeks, looked up from the document she'd been frowning at, removed her tortoise-frame glasses, and pinned him with her blue-grey eyes. She was twenty pounds past slim and wore a red dress—an authoritative deep shade of red.

"Since you stormed in unannounced, let me guess. You're the infamous Jacob Gillis."

He shouldn't have barged in, he realized.

"Ha! I guess Charlie didn't tell you I bark but don't bite." She cocked an eyebrow and gave a crooked smile. "Get used to me, Huck. And to set your mind at ease, I already know everything about you." She rose and extended her hand. "Glad to meet you. I'm Maureen."

"I'm glad to meet you, too," he said, relieved.

She turned and called out, "Charlie . . . . .."

But Charlie was already through the door. "Jacob." He threw his arms around his friend and gave him a tight hug. "Am I ever glad to see you."

Jacob squeezed back. "It's good to be home."

Pulling away, Charlie looked at Maureen and winked. "You have no idea what kind of history we have."

"You've divulged some of your reprehensible past. Shameful. What I'd like to know is which of you was the instigator." She shifted her eyes from one to the other. "Or maybe you share equal blame. But while you catch up on your checkered past, somebody needs to work." She gave a dismissive wave, sat back down at her desk, and flitted her eyes at Charlie. "Don't forget you have a meeting in thirty minutes."

"She's a ballbuster, but she keeps me in line," Charlie said, leading Jacob into his office. "Man, it's good to have you back in the land of the free and the home of the brave. Have a seat." He waved at a chair and then perched on the edge of his desk, one leg dangling.

Jacob sat down and studied his friend with affection. Charlie no longer smelled of fish bait and football stadium mud, and he sported a respectable Brooks Brothers suit instead of tattered jeans and a Phillies baseball cap. But he still retained the devilish glint in his eyes. He had a triangular face, freckles splattering his pale skin, and brows so light they appeared to be white. His ginger-colored hair was marred by two cow-licks. His signature feature was his extra-large hands. "The better for catching a pass," Charlie bragged when anyone commented on his oversized mitts, and Jacob had to agree; between his passing and Charlie's receiving, they'd had one hell of a team. Girls had flocked to Charlie in high school, attracted by his exuberant personality. Being co-captain of the football team hadn't hurt either, Jacob surmised.

"Do I need to bow and scrape to my fellow conspirator now that he's the new District Attorney of Bucks County?" Jacob clasped his hands behind his neck and stretched out his legs. "What platform did you run on? *Been there done that, so I understand the criminal mind?*"

"Hey, we were a little high-spirited. That's all. Delaying the start of school with a few potatoes stuck in the tail pipes of buses hardly qualifies as a crime."

"I'm not sure Mr. Meecham would agree with you. Not after he spent an hour trying to figure out what was wrong with his bus. My mother sure thought we'd committed a crime."

"Yeah, mine, too." Charlie grinned.

"I sure am impressed with your new office here. Great decorations." He swept his hand around, indicating the unpacked boxes, the books stacked on the floor and desk, the unhung pictures leaning against the wall. "Looks like my place."

Charlie shrugged. "Too busy to organize my things." He paused for a few seconds, pursing his lips together and swinging his dangling leg back and forth. "Remember when we decided we wanted to go to law school and be partners someday?" he asked finally.

"We could have called our firm *The Arsonous Duo*, but since you're tied up here, and I have the perfect job, I don't think it's going to happen." The mention of their working together was the prelude to something, Jacob knew, but he was mystified as to what.

"We can still do it. In a few years, when we've established our reputations, we can make our exits and set up our own firm."

"We established our reputations when we were twelve years old."

"Touché." Charlie sat down in the other chair in front of his desk. "You start with WARPA in six weeks?"

"Yep. In six weeks."

"Sooooo . . ., what have you been up to?"

"Hmmmm, let's see." Jacob rubbed his chin. This was so like Charlie, sidestepping an issue until he found the right moment to pounce. "Since our last email exchange forty-eight hours ago, I boarded a plane in Kigali, flew to Amsterdam, waited in the airport for seven hours, and then flew here. This morning I got up, shaved and showered, and then drove to the office of the new District Attorney."

"OK, smartass." Charlie glanced at his watch.

"You obviously don't have much time, so why don't you just come out with it."

"I need you. You have no idea how much I need you."

"Can't do. Sorry."

Charlie got up and went to lean against the window frame. He rubbed his forefinger across his brow, and his expression grew serious. "I know you won't take a job in the DA's office, but . . . . Well, I'm so overloaded with work I need thirty-six hour days." He threw up his hands. "It's like a crime wave hit Bucks County just to test the new DA. Then to top it off, the attorney I hired a couple months ago, broke his pelvis in a skiing accident. He's flat on his back for another six weeks."

"Crap. That's bad luck."

"Yeah." Charlie shifted from foot to foot. "I was thinking . . . . maybe . . . . a small favor?"

Jacob knitted his eyebrows. Small favors scared him. "What do you have in mind?"

"Since you're not starting at WARPA for six weeks, you have a bunch of free time. You'll be bored to death out there in that old stone house, all alone, doing nothing but unpacking."

Bored? Jacob didn't think so. The house needed a shitload of work. Stone pointing. New fixtures in the bathrooms and kitchen. Floor sanding. Wall repair and painting. And God knows what else.

Rotten flooring in the attic? A leaky basement? At least the roof didn't leak. Not yet, anyway. No, he wouldn't be bored.

Charlie cleared his throat. "We have a big case pending, and it's right up your alley. A company down in Philadelphia bought a farm along the Pumqua River about five miles outside Goose Bend. Turns out the name on the deed is an invented name. They're looking for a place to dump their commercial wastes."

Jacob sat up straight. "No!"

"Yes!. . . . They're messing with our river and you, with your background, could pull up the test cases and regulations in a fraction of the time it would take me. I can try the case, if you prepare it for me."

"Bloody bastards." Were people idiots? Poisoning water, the air, the ground?

"Truth is . . .." Charlie paused and rubbed his chin. "Well . . ., sometimes I feel like I need to do something to make amends for the fire. This might be our chance—yours and mine. You know how people in Goose Bend hate Philadelphians trying to put one over on them. Remember the incident with the swimming pool?"

Jacob nodded. When he and Charlie were in high school, the city had bused hundreds of Philadelphia kids to Goose Bend to swim in the municipal pool, leaving no room for the locals who had paid for the pool.

Charlie moved around to stand behind his desk. "Together, we can scorch the crap out of this company and make Goose Bend happy. You can use the office we set aside for Barker. Come in and work whenever you want to take a break from stone pointing and carpentry. What do you think?"

It wasn't a difficult decision since he harbored the same desire as Charlie: he wanted to redeem himself by doing something good for the town. "I'll do it."

"Hallelujah."

A conspicuous throat clearing drew their attention to Maureen standing in the doorway, pointing to her watch.

"We have a new consultant," Charlie said to her, a note of

triumph in his voice. "Will you set him up in Barker's office? And he'll need an ID so he can access the files in the library."

"Are we safe with the two of you in the same building?"

"You're not funny, Maureen." Grinning, Charlie started for the door. "I'm off. The judge is a little touchy about tardiness." He stopped and turned back to Jacob. "Did I tell you how glad I am you're back? In case I didn't, I'm glad you're back." Then he was off.

A few minutes later, eager to hurl his expertise at an evil-intentioned manufacturer, Jacob paced the office that would have been occupied by Chip Barker if not for a ski accident. As a boy, he'd wanted to follow in Laskey's footsteps and become a detective. The vision of solving crimes sent tremors of excitement all the way down to his toes. But that was before he decided prosecuting criminals intoxicated him even more. His interest in taking down murderers, thieves, and embezzlers, however, took a turn during his first semester at the University of Vermont Law School. He realized what he wanted most was to take on the really big criminals: the corporations that stole people's retirement money; the organizations that endangered lives by withholding research or lying about the results; the manufacturers that poisoned the air; and most definitely, the ones that released toxic wastes into rivers and lakes. And that included the Pumqua River. He'd start tomorrow, jet lagged or not.

On his way out, Maureen, a phone pressed to her ear, raised a finger to detain him. Jacob stuck his hands in his pockets and waited.

"Did you know the dance teacher in Goose Bend?" she asked finally, hanging up.

"No. Why?"

"They found her in her dance studio this morning, shot through the heart."

A coldness hit him at the core. He'd seen, or thought he'd seen, a movement near the old telephone booth. It only been a few minutes later when a gunshot had been reported.

"What was her name?" he asked.

"Her students called her Miss Ama. That's all I know."

Chapter Six

L askey parked in front of the white Victorian-style house belonging to John Hunter's aunt, Isabel Cord. The house, four blocks from the center of Doylestown, stood in an older section lined with similar houses, all of them magnificent with mansards and turrets, spindles and knobs; all of them well-kept and surrounded by tidy lawns and properly spaced and pruned shrubbery.

He tucked his umbrella under his arm just in case the mass of dark clouds that had blown in during the night erupted, and then he climbed out of the Sequoia, made his way up the walk, and knocked on Isabel's front door. She knew he was coming, so he expected her to have her story primed and prepped, ready to cover for John. She'd been playing bingo at the Presbyterian Church down the street until a few minutes past 12:30 on Monday night, so he couldn't imagine what she'd concoct to get around that.

The door swung open to reveal a woman with white hair pulled back in a bun and a face almost as pale as her hair. Rimless glasses sat low on her nose, and she wore a lilac kaftan embroidered with flowers.

"Detective Laskey?" She touched her fingers to her cheek and shook her head as though to say *what a terrible thing this is.*

"Sorry to bother you." He held out his ID.

She waved him in. "Do you have any idea who did this? I'm in such shock. I can't believe there's been a murder in our family. And Ama . . . . who would . . .?" She inhaled deeply and then let out her breath in a long rattle. "I'll have Mabel bring us some coffee."

"I'd appreciate a good cup. Thanks." And hers would be good, he judged, looking around at the fine furnishings. No cheap brew for Aunt Isabel.

"Have a seat in the living room." She nodded to the room on the right. "I'll just step back to the kitchen and hurry Mabel along."

She slipped away, leaving him to wander alone into the room where none of the furniture looked comfortable. He chose a high winged, tufted love seat upholstered in rose-colored velvet, set his umbrella on the floor, and perched on the edge.

A few seconds later, Isabel returned and sat down opposite him. "This is just too, too awful."

"John spent the night here, I understand."

"Yes. He does that every now and then when he's in Doylestown for a late appointment. Or when he wants to get away."

"Get away?"

She shrugged. "Things haven't been easy for John lately." She picked at something on her kaftan. "Ama was being greedy. And that Nancy Bolen . . . I don't understand what he sees in her." She looked up, her eyes wide. "This is a bad dream, isn't it? I'm going to wake up in a few minutes and discover it was just a nightmare."

"You played bingo until after midnight, so you don't know what time John got here?"

"No." She gave him a helpless look.

"Is there someone who might have seen him arrive?"

She frowned. "I doubt it. This isn't exactly a swinging neighborhood. Do you really need to know?"

"I need to know where John was so I can mark him off the list."

"Of course. But I can't think who might have seen him. Oh dear."

Mabel appeared with a silver tray containing a coffee service and set it down. Isabel poured and then handed Laskey a cup. "There's sugar and cream, if you need it." She indicated the cream pitcher and sugar bowl.

"Just black, thanks." Laskey took a couple swallows. "Where was John on Monday before he came here?"

"At a meeting of some sort. Maybe it was an appointment with one of his clients. I'm sure he can tell you where he was."

Could, but wouldn't. He drank half the coffee in silence before setting the cup down. "I'd love to know more about Ama."

She settled back on the sofa. "What do you want to know?"

"What first comes to mind when you think of her?"

"That John should have married someone else."

He raised his eyebrows.

"Oh, don't get me wrong. Ama had a lot of things going for her. She was beautiful and talented. She danced with The New York City Ballet, you know?"

"I saw the pictures in her studio."

"When she met John, she was an up and coming star. At least, according to her. But she threw it all away when she married him, and we were all quite aware that she regretted it. To make matters worse, I don't think she had any real friends here. Except for Kate."

"Did she keep up friendships in New York City? Dancers at the ballet? People she went to school with?"

Isabel tilted her head. "I never heard her mention anyone."

LASKEY PAUSED on the sidewalk in front of Isabel's house and looked up and down the street, guessing that these grand houses would be occupied by an older generation not given to late night walks or any other activities where they might notice visitors during the evening. But you never knew. He'd assigned someone to question the residents but harbored little hope of finding out anything. At least the aunt hadn't tried to cover for John, he thought as he climbed back into his Sequoia. There'd just been a vague reference to a meeting or an appointment.

John was hiding something. Guilty parties usually invented an alibi. *I was home watching TV. I was out at such-and-such bar. I went to church with my mother.* But John had made no attempt. Just: "I didn't kill her."

Chapter Seven

Jacob avoided the center of town and the crowd he expected to have gathered around the town's first murder scene, and took the road that looped around the west end of Goose Bend. The road, which ascended to the crest of a row of hills, took him over the old railroad tunnel he'd escaped to as a boy whenever he wanted to sulk or be alone. The tunnel had been off limits to him and most of his friends after a child had fallen on the rusty tracks and gotten a serious case of tetanus, but Jacob had gone there occasionally despite his mother's rule. He'd hated the cramped Cape Cod, where someone always seemed to be no more than twenty feet away. The tunnel gave him several hundred feet of privacy.

He turned right onto Sky Drive when he reached the summit and traveled along the northern boundary of town. Groves of trees and thickets on both sides partially hid houses set on eight- to ten-acre lots. Only two businesses had managed to slip in and squat successfully between the residences: The Silver Spoon Diner which lay a quarter mile past the eastern city limit and The Bait and Bottle Tavern whose parking lot provided the only break in the forestation allowing a view down onto Main Street.

The tavern didn't open until late afternoon, so the lot was

empty. He parked and went to stand at the railing along the back edge. From there, he had an unimpeded view of four blocks of rooftops descending into the center of Goose Bend. Dark clouds, kicked by the wind, scudded across the sky, darkening Main Street with flickering shadows. Two police cars blocked the street in front of Lacy's Mercantile, flashing their red lights, illuminating the several dozen people who had gathered to stare at the crime scene.

He remembered that a dance studio had been located on the second floor above Lacy's and tried to recall the name of the teacher—he must have heard it from some of his female friends—but his mind was blank, and the name *Miss Ama* didn't ring a bell.

The people gathered around the scene weren't much more than matchsticks from his perspective. One person stood apart and appeared to be leaning on something rectangular. Jacob squinted. "Good God, Jimmy Q Haskell is still alive and kicking," he said aloud, recognizing the rectangle as Jimmy Q's bike with attached cart. The old man used the cart to collect soda cans to sell for whiskey money. Night and day, seven days a week, he rode his bicycle around town, scavenging until he had enough money to restock his liquor supply. Then Jimmy Q would disappear for several days to drink himself into oblivion. When he recovered from his binge, he'd slink back out to begin collecting anew. Jimmy Q had been "old" when Jacob was in high school, but almost everybody had been old then. Even his twenty-nine-year-old geometry teacher. No one knew what the "Q" in Jimmy's name stood for, but people had lots of fun guessing.

That had been another thing on his mother's list: *You absolutely will not make fun of Jimmy Q Haskell.* Mom had strict rules about making fun of anyone, but particularly Jimmy Q. Old as Methuselah, and dirty and unshaven unless it was monthly bath day, Jimmy Q was rumored to hear "voices." He lived in a second-floor room of the Pennston Hotel and was the butt of endless jokes. Even if his mother hadn't threatened Jacob with weekend incarceration, he wouldn't have made fun of Jimmy Q. Something about the man's absolute freedom, the way he thumbed his nose at convention and blazoned his disdain for worldly goods and status intrigued Jacob.

And maybe he really did hear voices. Who was to say? Fifty years ago, people would have labeled as crazy anyone who predicted the time would come when you could tap a few keys on a computer keyboard and within seconds find out what color outfit Kate Middleton was wearing or how much the average kangaroo weighed. Magic abounded.

He crawled back into the SUV and continued east along Sky Drive, the heavy feeling that hit him upon first hearing of the murder grown heavier. Living in Rwanda had taught him at least one survival skill, though. *You can't live everyone's misery, or you'll break.* During a one-hundred-day period, twenty percent of the country's total population, including seventy percent of the Tutsi, were slaughtered in the genocide. Every family lost someone. Often, multiple members. Surrounded by broken families, orphans, women purposefully infected with AIDS, he'd learned to box up tragedy and keep a tight lid on it.

A mile and a half past the eastern town limits, he turned onto a winding road that led to the bottom of the row of hills. Another turn, and then a quarter of a mile farther he came to the lane of the old stone house he'd inherited.

He stopped at the head of the drive, rolled down the window, and caught a whiff of manure. His neighbors, at least the ones who still farmed, were getting ready for planting season. The air smelled of rain which was good since his nine fallow acres lay brown and prickly as a hedgehog. The sooner it rained, the sooner the fields would come alive, greening his fiefdom. The wind picked up, rattling the branches on the sugar maple at the intersection of his lane, and driving the clouds eastward toward the Delaware River. Fickle March's sun winked at him from behind a cloud, and then winked again. Some of the dark mood slipped away, and a hint of euphoria tugged at him. He was home.

During the past five years, he'd climbed mountains, traipsed through jungles, stood within a few feet of Dian Fosse's gorillas, negotiated the labyrinths of Asian cities and the grime of African ones, mastered the art of bus travel in places where people rode on top with their chickens, learned to avoid stray camels on the roadways of desert countries, and attended weddings where dowries consisted of cows and goats. But all he wanted now was to be here, planting his roots, enjoying his job, seeing Mom and Meg. And Laskey. And Charlie. And Aunt Zuela. A murder had dampened his homecoming, but in a day or so it would be solved and, thank God, it wasn't anyone he knew.

JACOB THREW his car keys on the kitchen counter and began ripping open boxes, piling the contents on counters and on the dining room table since he had no idea where to put things. He'd unpacked only a few boxes when the phone rang.

"Jacob." Charlie's voice shook.

"Yeah?"

"The victim was John Hunter's wife."

Jacob leaned one-handed on the counter, jolted like he'd been hit by a two-hundred-fifty pound tackle. John Hunter had been their classmate, their teammate, their friend, president of the class three years in a row, student council president.

"Are you still there?" Charlie asked.

"Jeez, that's bad news."

"Did you ever meet Ama?"

"No. I got an invitation to their wedding, but I was on my way to Africa. Do they know who killed her?"

Charlie paused. A little too long. "No idea," he said at length.

Jacob closed his eyes tight and squeezed his forehead. He knew what was coming next.

"You know the husband is always a prime suspect," Charlie said.

"I know. But John wouldn't . . . ."

"Of course not. But still, he'll be a suspect until he's cleared. I'm sure he must regret it like hell, but they're saying John made remarks around town about shooting the bitch."

"He's not the first husband to say things like that."

"Nor will he be the last, but that doesn't do him any good right now. I have to go. Just wanted to let you know."

The news stung every fiber of his being, and, for a few moments, he remained motionless, barely breathing, a crushing weight descending on him. One minute the world is this way, and the next it's that way, irrevocably changed, only this time it was someone else's world that had changed. He knew the statistics of murders. More often than not, it was a spouse or someone else close to the victim. But John wouldn't . . . .

The heaviness morphed into frenetic energy. Grabbing a packing box, he ripped it open and began tearing away bubble wrap. Soft things clothes, towels, linen, underwear—grew in a heap on the counter near the refrigerator. Dishes and utensils landed near the sink. Books beside the dishes. Miscellaneous items on the dining room table. He unpacked box after box.

He should go and see John. Did you tell an estranged husband you were sorry that the wife he was fighting tooth and nail with was dead? But it wasn't really the discomfort at not knowing what to say to John that made him hesitate. Truth was he didn't want to run into John's father. *Oh, hi, Mr. Hunter. It's me, Jacob Gillis. Relax. I haven't smoked a cigarette since that day.*

Juvenile court ruled that the fire had been an accident, but the judge decided community service was in order and turned the arrangements over to the town council. Mr. Hunter, president of the council, took charge. Jacob shuddered at the memory. He and Charlie had stood there awaiting their fate until Mr. Hunter, his spiteful face folded in frowns and mottled with red, read out their sentence. Two years of community service doing whatever the town council decided needed doing. Eight hours every Saturday with a twenty minute lunch break. They would pick up trash in the park, clean the school yard, sweep streets before parades, sweep streets after parades, dispose of Halloween litter, remove old election posters, clean up church grounds after carnivals. Whatever the town council dreamed up. And it had been plenty. For two years he and Charlie missed Saturday football games, Boy Scout campouts, fishing trips, while their friends, on the way to where he and Charlie wanted to be, taunted them, calling out from bicycles or poking their heads out of car windows as their parents chauffeured them to their destinations.

He'd thought their Saturday purgatory would never end, and not just on those days when rain seeped through the necks of their raincoats, turning their clothes to a smelly, miserable sop, or when freezing cold sliced through mittens and bit through socks. The crisp, sunny days were worse – the days when the weather was perfect for fishing or playing ball or just hanging out. He would have sold his soul to sleep late on those Saturdays. Or to crawl out of bed and, still in his pajamas, watch *Outer Limits* or *Aaahh!!! Real Monsters*.

He and Charlie finished their penance, but Mr. Hunter's hostile face still haunted his dreams.

He threw a stained pot holder onto the soft pile and then drummed his fingers on the counter. In spite of Mr. Hunter, John had still been a friend. Not one of his best friends, but a friend. John even enticed him to the occasional party in the Hunter's basement rec room. Mr. Hunter was usually off working, but there were a couple times when Jacob found himself wishing he could sink into the floor as he sidled past Mr. Hunter's beady eyes and slack-jawed glare.

He ripped open another box and found the coffee pot at the bottom. He glanced out the window as he placed the pot in front of the outlet near the sink. A breeze rippled the surface of the triangu-lar-shaped pond just beyond his backyard. The pond wasn't much more than an over-sized puddle. A willow trailed its fronds across the surface at the pond's apex, and a mass of reeds grew along the left bank. A quarter-mile of fallow field edged by the wavering line of a shallow forest lay beyond the pond, and a few hundred feet into the forest, the Pumqua River meandered easterly on its journey toward the Delaware.

Jacob felt the magnetic pull of the river. He'd considered it his sacred duty to be standing on its shores each year on the opening day of trout season, and he'd performed that duty with thorough-ness. His mother, strict and uncompromising in everything else, managed to forget when opening day came, metaphorically turning her head and ignoring the phone calls from school regarding his absence. What she didn't know about was all the other days he decided fishing was more appealing than sitting in a butt-punishing school desk. And now, someone wanted to poison the Pumqua.

He brushed aside the pull of the river and opened a box containing books. He could easily use his recent return to the country as an excuse for not paying his former classmate a consolation visit on the death of his wife. *Just got back in the country and didn't know right away,* he could say. But face it, he told himself as he tossed a couple books on the counter, Mr. Hunter isn't the only reason you don't want to see your former classmate. He tried to banish the other thought. But it was there. If he saw John, would he be looking into the face of a murderer?

Chapter Eight

"Do you want an attorney present?" Laskey stared down at an ashen-faced John Hunter. John sat hunched on Kate's living room sofa, hands dangling between his knees. His hair was sticking up in tufts, and his left cheek had red streaks where he'd rubbed it raw. The Hugo Boss jacket hung over a chair arm, one sleeve dangling on the floor.

"Do you want an attorney?" Laskey asked again.

"I don't need an attorney; I'm not guilty."

"Attorneys are here to protect the innocent as much as to prosecute the guilty."

John clamped his lips together, and his eyes glazed over.

"Any time you want one, speak up. Where were you yesterday evening between eight and midnight?"

"I didn't kill her," John hissed between clenched teeth.

"Did she have enemies?"

"Not that I know of."

"Did she do drugs?"

"No."

"Never?"

"She was a dancer, for Christ's sake. She didn't smoke. She didn't drink. She didn't eat. And she didn't do drugs."

"Was she having an affair?"

John gave him a look that Laskey interpreted as *Are you kidding* and then hung his head so Laskey could no longer stare into his face. Laskey studied the top of his head instead. What was John hiding?

Clasping his hands behind his back, Laskey paced a few steps and saw the source of the faint whiff of turpentine he'd noticed when he first entered the house. A canvas which appeared to be freshly painted leaned against the wall next to the arch between living and dining rooms. He examined the landscape containing a single tree, but oh, what a tree. He turned to look at the living room walls covered with paintings. Even in the darkness of a curtained room, the paintings glowed with color and movement. When he stepped closer, he saw that each piece had the name *Kate* scrawled in the lower right-hand corner.

He walked into the dining room to view the works there. There were several excellent paintings, but a portrait caught his attention. An older woman with silver-streaked dark hair and piercing black eyes scowled at him from the frame. Her lips were drawn in a tight line, and she had a deep cleft in her chin. *Not someone I'd have hanging on my wall,* shot through his mind.

But the art tour would have to wait. He strolled back into the living room where John still stared at the floor. "I'd like to talk to your sister," Laskey said.

John sat back and crossed his arms. "Kate isn't here."

"Where is she?"

"Taking care of funeral arrangements."

"When will she be back?"

John shrugged.

Laskey started for the door. "Since you refuse to tell me where you were yesterday evening, I have to assume you murdered your wife."

"I did not," John shouted. Springing from his seat, he faced Laskey with clenched fists.

"Then you need to talk to me. Let me know when you're ready." He lifted his hand in a goodbye salute and left.

JOHN LISTENED to Laskey's uneven plod, one foot coming down heavier than the other, until his footsteps faded away. The detective was gone. At least John *thought* he was gone. Right now, his paranoia made all things possible including Laskey's returning to spy on him through the window. Even though the blinds were closed, making it impossible for Laskey to see in, John still had the impulse to go and see. But he was too exhausted. Tired beyond all reason. So tired.

Exhausted or not, however, he had to do it now. Kate would be back soon.

Breathing slowly, he tried to steady the beating of his heart and to bring some order to the chaos in his mind. He grabbed a scarf Kate had carelessly flung across a chair and swiped at the sweat on his forehead. Then, throwing the scarf aside, he dragged himself to the stairs.

He withdrew a briefcase from beneath the bed in the guest bedroom. Treading softly, he went to the door, stopped, and listened. Something creaked in the attic and the voices from the perpetual soccer game that went on in the back alley murmured through the window panes. Nothing else. The coast was clear.

In the kitchen, he pulled a chair over to the stove. Kate stored the baking paraphernalia she never used in the cabinet above the stove, which she also barely used. He removed cake pans, muffin tins, and pie plates, and shoved the brief case onto the shelf, and then returned the cookware, arranging it to conceal his secret.

Chapter Nine

"**P**sssst."
Bump, hurrying down Fifth Street toward the Seven-11, stopped and muttered one of his rare imprecations. The reek of filthy clothes and body odor proclaimed who had snuck up behind him, and Jimmy Q was the last person he wanted to deal with right now. Laskey had scheduled a meeting for exactly twenty minutes from now, and Bump wanted to grab a bite first. It was late afternoon, and his only meal had been a bowl of Raisin Bran at the crack of dawn. The walls of his stomach were about to collapse against each other, not to mention that he had a headache to end all headaches.

"Pssst, pssst."

Bump turned wearily around, shielding his eyes against the sun which had sunk three-quarters of the way down the afternoon sky. "Go away, Jimmy. I don't have time for you."

"But I seen something. You better take me to that detective man so I can tell him."

"You didn't see anything, Jimmy. Go away." Bump gave him a dismissive wave and trudged away. *Crazy old man.* Last month, Jimmy

Q had tried to warn him that the Lenni Lenape were floating up the river in their war canoes, and a few weeks before that, that the Pumqua was full of alligators.

Chapter Ten

Wednesday, March 5

The nasal *hwaaaannnhhh, hwaaaannnhhh* from a skein of Canada Geese swooping past Jacob's window, jarred him awake. He knew the sun was about to rise by the dull red glow on his window panes and because his only two pieces of bedroom furniture were emerging from darkness into recognizable shapes. The country-style French wardrobe that had belonged to his grandmother anchored the far wall, and a hand-me-down Victorian marble top table stood next to his sleeping bag. The table wasn't his style, but it was furniture. Actually, he didn't have a *style*, but if he did, he was sure it wouldn't be Victorian.

He'd managed to sleep through the night again instead of waking at three a.m. "One giant step against jet lag," he mumbled into his pillow, pulling the covers around his ears and burrowing in the warmth but failing to enjoy it. He needed to buy a bed. The sleeping bag was fine for a few nights, but not for long.

He'd spent the previous evening unpacking while the TV blared in the background. *Murder in Goose Bend. Former member of New York City Ballet shot in her studio. No suspects.* Pictures of Ama Hunter flashed across the screen: Ama on her toes, arms raised, dressed in a white tutu as the Queen of Swans. Her platinum hair was pulled back and her eyes focused to the side. The most striking picture showed her as the Sorceress in a black costume staring into the eyes of the viewer. Thanks to his grandmother, he was familiar with Swan Lake and knew about Odette and Odile. Other than that, his knowledge of ballet was on a par with his knowledge of Greek.

John had also been mentioned in the broadcasts. *Graduate of Goose Bend High School and Lehigh University. Class president. Student Council president. Football player. Head of Hunter and Son Accounting Firm. Owner, along with his father, of Hunter Manufacturing.* A darker tone weighed the voices of the newscasters when they mentioned that John and Ama had been in the middle of a bitter divorce.

Braving the cold, he crawled out of his nest and fumbled around in his suitcase which had arrived late the previous afternoon. He pulled out jeans and a sweatshirt and put them on and then donned a plaid flannel shirt over the sweatshirt. He scrunched his feet into his running shoes without bothering with socks. Shivering, he went downstairs to the kitchen. In spite of the temperature being in the low fifties, he'd opened the windows before going to bed to rid the house of smells.

The kitchen was a long rectangle, one end comprising the actual kitchen, while the other served as a sitting area with a large fireplace in front of which he'd placed his two rocking chairs, another bequest from his grandmother. A breakfast nook was formed by an ell which projected out the back of the house from the fireplace end of the room.

He spooned coffee into the DeLonghi and set the dials so that all he had to do was push the "on" button when Laskey arrived. Laskey hadn't said what time he'd come. Just, *early.*

Jacob stuck plates, mugs, and utensils under the faucet to give them a more thorough rinse than he had yesterday, and then set them on a paper towel to dry.

Outside the kitchen window, the rising sun cast tentacles of yellow and orange over the pond. If Laskey arrived in the next few minutes, Jacob mused, he would see a fine painting done by Mother

Nature. Before joining the state criminal investigation brigade, Laskey had been an FBI agent. When the agency discovered he'd grown up with an art teacher mother, they assumed he must know a little about art, so they sent him to liaise with the Philadelphia Police Department when they needed help with fine art and museum theft.

Jacob still wondered what made his godfather leave the FBI. Something to do with his refusal to carry a gun, maybe. Laskey was a half-breed—his father a Presbyterian and his mother a Quaker—which sometimes left Laskey with ill-defined and vacillating personal beliefs. Jacob guessed that Laskey's foot injury came from his time with the FBI, but it was only a guess. Maybe someday, Laskey would open up and tell all.

Jacob gave a little laugh. Lasky must be relieved that he no longer assumed the role of detective helper. He'd been spending the weekend with Laskey when Laskey had been called out on several occasions. There had been a kidnapping and then a bomb in a church, followed by arson at a car dealership, a newborn taken from the nursery of a hospital, and two murders. Apologizing for having to leave him alone, Laskey had forked over money for Jacob to order pizza, supplied him with DVDs, and given him free reign with his books which included complete sets of Sherlock Holmes and Perry Mason. Each time Laskey returned from his sleuthing, Jacob barraged him with endless questions and then offered his own solutions to the crimes. Laskey always pretended interest even though Jacob could see how tired he was. But in the end, as exciting as solving the puzzle of a crime was, Jacob had chosen Perry Mason over Sherlock Holmes, though if truth be known, his pulse still fluttered over the possibility of working out a riddle.

Sherlock, aka Laskey, would be here shortly, so he'd better get moving. After swiping at the plates and utensils to dry them, Jacob laid knives, forks, and spoons on the card table in the breakfast nook: forks on the left of each plate, knife and spoon on the right, knife blade toward the plate. One of Laskey's eccentricities—and Laskey had a whole list—was that he expected the table to be properly set even if he were only eating warmed-over Chinese. Laskey's persnickety-ness must be a result of growing up in a family with four sisters, Jacob surmised.

He'd forgotten to buy napkins, so he tore two sections from a roll of paper towels and folded them. Laskey used cloth napkins: checked ones, plaid ones, plain ones, and some with monograms and/or flowers embroidered by one or the other of his sisters. Never paper napkins. But Laskey had a cleaning woman to do his washing and ironing. Jacob didn't. His friend would have to rough it with paper towels this morning.

Done with preparations, he returned to the window and watched the geese splashing in the pond like a gaggle of happy kids, except for the irate gander that waddled back and forth at the water's edge, straining his neck and thrusting his head toward his merry companions, directing nasty *hwaaannnhhhs* at them. Without warning, the gander lunged at a flotilla of geese, whipping the water around him, but stopping short when the objects of his anger floated off, ignoring him. The gander returned to shore and limped away. Simon Legree, Jacob named him.

A blast of cold air buffeted through the window. He reached up to close it but then remembered if he did, they'd be eating scrambled eggs seasoned with the smell of labs and mildew. "I'll build a fire," he said aloud and the sound reverberated through the long room devoid of carpets and curtains to soften the edge of noise.

He'd just set the logs and kindling in the hearth when he heard the rumble of a vehicle. He listened to the car slogging down his lane, metal clanking against metal as the car bounced over potholes. He smiled. Laskey had to have cloth napkins, properly folded, yet he drove an old SUV marred with scratches and one dent, and he wore a jacket that should have been donated to Good Will years ago.

He stood up, brushed bits of bark from his pants, and went over to start the coffee. His finger was aimed for the "brew" button, when he glanced out the window. Instead of Laskey's Sequoia, a Subaru with faded green paint and a gash along the length of one side pulled into the back yard. The Subaru jerked to a standstill with a cough and shudder, but then lurched a few inches before the engine cut off.

He watched a woman wearing gray slacks and a gray fleece jacket climb out. His breath caught. What was *she* doing here? At six o'clock in the morning, no less.

Kate Hunter, rubbing her hands together, stood beside the car and looked around as though trying to decide what to do. A breeze tousled her dark hair, blowing a strand over her face. She brushed the hair back and then, shivering, crossed her arms high on her chest and snuggled her hands in her armpits.

He tensed. He was sorry—very sorry—that John's wife had been murdered, but he meant to keep his distance from the Hunters and let other people do the consoling. Yet, here was a Hunter standing in his backyard for some unfathomable reason. He breathed a sigh of relief when she turned abruptly back to her vehicle as though about to leave. "Go, go," he whispered. If he didn't know what to say to John, he *really* didn't know what to say to John's sister. Especially considering their past. Or rather, their lack of a past.

She stood with her hand on the door handle for a few seconds but then turned around, stuck her hands in her jacket pockets, and marched toward his backdoor.

"Kate Hunter," he said, opening the door a few seconds later. *Kate Hunter.* Now that was a brilliant thing to say. Not "Good morning." Or "How are you?" Just her name with his voice cracking and his adrenaline spiking. Shades of high school.

"Do you have a minute?" She looked at him, the sparkle he remembered in her eyes gone.

Reluctantly, he motioned her inside. How had she known where he lived? Ah, yes, small town, he thought bitterly. He caught the gingery smell of Ivory soap and a whiff of something else—turpentine?—as she walked past and then turned around, waiting for him to tell her where to go. He held his palm toward the kitchen, inviting her to go ahead of him. He followed, suddenly aware of the bits of grass and leaves he'd trailed in. The Hunter house had always been squeaky clean.

"If you go straight through the kitchen . . . ." his voice tapered off as his fingers plowed rows through his hair. He couldn't even begin to fathom why she'd come but, hopefully, whatever had brought her here at this ungodly hour wouldn't take long. Laskey would be here soon. "We can sit over there," he said, nodding toward the rocking chairs.

He placed himself behind a chair, hands resting on its back, while she sat down in the other. Too tense to sit back, she leaned forward, shoulders tight and hands pressed between knees.

"I came to ask for help," she said breathlessly. The look in her eyes was raw and pleading.

He hesitated for a few moments before he moved around and sat down. This couldn't go anywhere good. "I don't think . . . ."

"Hear me out," she shot back, sparks flashing from her eyes.

He clamped his mouth shut. In high school there had always been a place to escape from her—the gym, boy's bathroom, his next class—but here there was nowhere to hide.

"You know about . . . ." She stopped and swallowed.

"Yes." He felt contrite. He needed to forget what went on years ago because right now she was a woman in pain, although he was still mystified over what that had to do with him. "I'm so sorry, Kate. I can't imagine how horrible this must be for you."

"You know what some people will think." She looked at him as though she expected an acknowledgement of the truth, not a palliative lie.

He nodded. There were those who *would* think John Hunter had murdered his wife, and the longer the mystery went unsolved, the more people would wonder, the more reporters would harry her brother, and the more Laskey would pester John with questions and more questions.

"John won't hire an attorney because he thinks that will make him look guilty." She tightened her hands into fists, loosened them, tightened them again. "Schapiro, over in Doylestown, is representing him in the divorce, but Schapiro's away for a couple weeks. We thought . . . . Well, since you aren't officially working with a law firm yet, not for a few more weeks, we were hoping you'd agree to be the spokesperson for the family. That would give John the benefit of an attorney without having one officially. We'd pay you, of course, but under the table so no one would know we'd hired a lawyer. Everyone would just think you were doing it for an old friend."

No, he wasn't getting drawn into this. He'd returned to Goose Bend with the intention of staying as far away from trouble as possible and that included someone else's trouble. He was willing to offer sympathy, send flowers, deliver casseroles, and say a few kind words, but to get mixed up in this—no way.

"I don't do that kind of law," he said. "I'll be glad to ask around and recommend someone." He wouldn't be glad, and he imagined she detected his lie.

"I'm not asking you to defend him. It won't come to that." Blinking back tears, she raised her eyes to look at the ceiling. "It's been more than twenty-four hours since . . . . they found her, and they been more than twenty-four hours since . . . . they found her, and they don't have a suspect. Mom and Dad were on a cruise, but they're getting off the ship in Kingston and flying back as soon as they can book a flight. They think Ama died in an accident. We'll have to tell them what really happened, but by the time they get back, hopefully, the police will have arrested someone."

She rubbed a thumb over the fingernails of the opposite hand, and he noticed her short, ragged nails and stained cuticles. Her mother's nails had always been perfectly manicured, but Kate had good reason to have chewed her nails ragged in the past few hours.

"Jacob, are you listening?"

"Yes. I'm listening." He fidgeted with his ear, pulling at the lobe.

"Will you talk with John?"

"I'm sorry, Kate, but I don't think that's a good idea."

"Not a good idea?" She looked bewildered. "You don't care what happens to an old friend?"

"Of course, I care, it's just that . . . ."

"Just what?"

"Why don't *you* call an attorney for him?" He realized he'd snapped at her.

She scowled. "You never did like me, did you? But you can relax. If you think I'm chasing after you like I did in high school, especially for that stupid prom, you're wrong." She gave him a cold look. "You brushed me off like I was dirt. So I'm here, Jacob, not because I ever wanted to see you again. I didn't. But because John refuses to leave the house. He sent me. He needs help."

Didn't like her? She didn't have a clue what the real problem had been. And nothing had changed; her father was still her father. But as much as he despised Mr. Hunter, senior, he hoped the man didn't have to hear that his son had committed murder. He blew out a stream of air. At the age of thirty-one, even on a bad day, high school proms were trivial, and murder made them beyond trivial. "I thought you understood why I couldn't invite you to the prom."

"I didn't understand at the time. I was humiliated." She shivered and drew her jacket tighter around her. "If you won't help John now when he really needs you, then. . . ." Her voice had dropped, dwindling to a near whisper.

Jeez. She knew how to plant guilt. As a matter of fact, she was quite an expert at it. He truly did feel for her. How could he not? But getting involved was not something he intended to do. The plumbing clunked, and for a split second he thought Laskey had arrived.

"You were in Africa," she said, rubbing her arms to warm them and looking toward the unlit logs in the fireplace.

He shifted uncomfortably. From the monotone of her voice he knew she didn't really care about his having been in Africa. That subject was a decoy. She'd talk about something else, get him off guard, and then come back to what she wanted. And he was irritated that she knew so much about him. Where he lived; that he'd worked in Africa; that he planned to take a few weeks off before beginning a new job. What else did she know? The color of his underwear? His brand of tooth paste? Worse, she showed no signs of leaving; she was digging in.

She turned away from the fireplace where decades of soot coated the stones and let her gaze roam over the kitchen, studying the stone-age appliances, the nicked cabinets, and the counters piled high with the contents of boxes. He was sure the culinary department of the Hunter house still looked like a model for *Architectural Digest*.

Finally, she looked back at him and raised her eyebrows to signal that he hadn't answered her question.

"Yes," he said. "I was in Africa for five years, but business took me to Asia fairly often."

"You lived in Rwanda?"

"Only the last two years. I spent some time in Liberia and, before that, Uganda."

"Who did you work for?" She actually seemed curious.

"INECE. The International Network for Environmental Compliance and Enforcement."

"Oh. . . . . So . . . . you were doing something having to do with the environment?"

"In the beginning, mostly water, but in Rwanda I worked with a group advising the Rwandan government on international treaty issues related to animal life."

She stared at him. He couldn't tell if she was considering what he said, or if her mind was working out her next appeal.

"I'm afraid I have to cut this short," he said, rising. Judging from her intake of breath, he realized he'd been curt. He rubbed his forehead with his forefinger. "Actually, I'm expecting someone right now, and . . .."

"You're still an asshole, Jacob Gillis. Some things never change." She jerked up out of her seat, shot him a poisoned look, and stormed off through the kitchen and the mudroom and out the back door, slamming it behind her. When he heard the Subaru start and then throw up gravel as she shot away, he closed his eyes and let out a long breath.

Crap, he'd been rude, barely remembering to tell her he was sorry about her sister-in-law, and tactless about not talking to John. And she'd been half frozen; the least he could have done was light the fire or close the window, or both. Or offered her coffee. Maybe he *was* an asshole.

He punched the on button on the coffee maker harder than he needed to and jerked open a drawer for matches. He felt rattled. Well, hell, he *was* rattled. A girl he hadn't seen for thirteen years shows up first thing in the morning. The sister-in-law of the murder victim. Maybe even the sister of . . . . No, he wouldn't think that.

He lit the kindling and then sat back on his heels, watching the flames flicker to life. She had turned into a gorgeous woman, not that that was any surprise; she'd been a gorgeous teenager. But she wasn't his type. Not then. Not now. Rich girls who grew up in houses with perfect kitchens were probably too afraid of getting their hands dirty to do the things he liked to do. Nope, those girls weren't for him. And definitely not girls whose fathers served on the town council and issued public service sentences to juvenile arsonists. Why was she even still in Goose Bend? She'd be …. What? Twenty-nine? Or thereabouts. Whenever he glanced at her left hand it was covered by her other hand, or lay clenched in her lap so that her ring finger was hidden, so he had no idea if she was married or not. Not that he cared. Although, he could have been polite and asked.

Chapter Eleven

"**D**amn woman nearly drove me off the road." Laskey set a Clemens Grocery bag down on the counter.

"What woman?" Considering the huff Kate left in, Jacob could guess.

Laskey shrugged. "How should I know? Some crazy woman driving an old Subaru." He jerked his thumb at the grocery bag. "Bagels and cream cheese. I didn't trust your grocery supply. Good lord, it's freezing in here." He zipped up his Woolrich jacket. "Why do you have the windows open?"

"Getting rid of smells." Jacob opened the refrigerator for cream. "That fossil of a jacket doesn't keep you warm? They've come out with ways to make warmer coats in the last century, you know."

"*Hmmph*, my jacket is fine. It's only twenty-five years old."

Jacob nodded toward the fireplace where flames had begun to pop. "Go get warm. I'll bring over some coffee." He grabbed two mugs. "And thanks for the bagels."

A few minutes later, they sat beside the fire with coffee while scrapple sizzled in the frying pan. "Do you know anything yet?" Jacob leaned toward Laskey. "At least anything you can tell me?"

Laskey shook his head. "It wasn't a pretty sight—a young

woman sprawled in the middle of a dance studio with a bullet through the heart."

"No idea who did it?"

"Nope. Her purse was on top of her desk in plain view with money and credit cards still inside. I guess there's no harm telling you that since half the town knew by suppertime yesterday. Her driver's license was missing. That doesn't mean anything, though. She might have kept it somewhere else." He took a sip of coffee. "We have the ballistics report, but no murder weapon." He fixed his gaze on the hearth where a log had broken in two, sending sparks shooting up the chimney. Staring at the fire, he continued as though talking to himself. "The bottom drawer of her desk was a jumble. Nothing unusual about that. Everything else was neat and orderly, except for a few cotton balls smeared with makeup in the powder room wastepaper basket." He looked up at Jacob. "Do women use cotton balls to put makeup on or take it off?"

"Come on, Laskey. You may not have taken the plunge, but I'm sure you've seen a woman use make-up. You have four sisters. Don't they wear make-up?"

"No, they're beautiful without it."

Jacob threw another log on the fire. "I have to turn the scrapple. Be right back."

"How well did you know John Hunter?" Laskey called to his back.

Jacob considered his answer as he turned the scrapple and added bacon to the pan. He remembered John lolling in his classroom desk like he hadn't a care in the world; sauntering down the hallway in a slow, easy shamble while everyone else rushed to class; affecting an air of indifference when his classmates got excited over one thing or another. There were a couple times, though, when John had exploded—once, over a referee's call at a game; another when someone accidently hit him in the leg with a missile from a slingshot. John's rage hadn't been a pretty thing to behold.

"I knew him fairly well, but I also didn't know him well," he said finally.

"What's that supposed to mean?"

"How well does anyone know anyone? We all wear a bit of a mask, don't we?" He flipped the scrapple again. "John and I were in classes together. We spent our afternoons on the football field or in the training room. We went to the same parties. Or to some of the same parties. But we didn't hang together like Charlie and I did. John was . . . ." He paused to find words for what he felt about John's personality.

"John was what?"

"He didn't seem to have much of a real interest in anything. No hobbies. No passions. No favorite subjects." Jacob laid the spatula down next to the frying pan. "Well . . ., he did have *one* passion."

"Which was?"

"Blondes, brunettes, redheads, and everything in between."

"You knew he and Ama were getting a divorce?"

"Yeah, I heard."

"She was trying to take John for everything she could get, including half the businesses. They say John was pretty bitter."

Recognizing the conjecture in Laskey's tone, Jacob felt a jolt shoot through him. For him to wonder for a brief moment about John's guilt was one thing, but to have Laskey consider it. . . . He took a deep breath. Of course, Laskey would consider it. That was his job. "You don't think . . . .."

Laskey was leaning over, his forearms propped on his thighs, his hands wrapped around his mug, ostensibly studying it. "I don't think anything, right now."

When they were done eating, Laskey frowned at the paper towel filling in as a napkin but wiped his mouth without saying anything, and then pushed back his chair. "Are you going to give me a tour?"

"Come on, I'll show you where all my money is going for the next ten years."

"More likely for the next fifty," Laskey groused back.

———

"I'D STAY and help you clean up, but duty calls," Laskey said when they had finished the inspection and returned to the kitchen.

"Don't worry, I've got it."

"Well, then, I have a house warming present for you. Hold on while I get it from the car."

Jacob regarded him with surprise. Laskey wasn't given to presenting gifts.

A couple minutes later Laskey returned with an open cardboard box. He set it down on the floor of the mudroom.

Puzzled, Jacob looked down at a bunch of old towels inside. "What . . . ?"

"It's not a mongoose," Laskey said, squatting beside the box. "I know you would have preferred that." He pushed the towels aside to reveal a kitten and then scooped up the mewing bit of silver fluff and held it out to Jacob.

"Laskey, what in the world?"

"Don't you know a kitten when you see it? This is Daisy Mae. She's a Siberian Forest Cat. Every old stone house needs a cat to keep the mice away." He held Daisy Mae close to Jacob's chest, forcing him to take her. "I got her a couple days ago. I was going to wait until she was house broken to present her, but with this murder . . . . Well, you're going to have to do the training yourself. Got to get to work now. Thanks for breakfast." He headed toward the back door.

"Wait," Jacob called after him. "What am I supposed to do with this kitten?"

"Feed her. A bit of kitty litter would help, too." He gave a little wave and slipped out.

Chapter Twelve

————————————

"**A**re you in there?" Maureen tapped Jacob's forehead.

"What?" He had walked into her office so preoccupied with Kate's visit that he'd forgotten where he was.

"You look like you're on another planet."

"Sorry. My mind was somewhere else."

"No kidding. Charlie told me the victim was your friend's wife. She was pretty." She motioned to the newspaper lying on her desk, folded to reveal a picture of Ama Hunter. "A little unusual, though. Eyes that dark don't usually go with platinum hair." She propped her hands on her hips and gave him a teasing look. "You were so anxious to get to work you couldn't wait until Monday, or did you come in just to enjoy our company?"

"Just to enjoy your company, Maureen." Truth was there was something about bad news that made him want to be around other people. He still couldn't quite grasp that the wife of his high school friend had been murdered.

"Did you meet the special prosecutor yet?"

"No. I didn't even know there was one."

"Charlie has too many ties to Goose Bend, so he called in a special prosecutor from the state attorney general's office. I'm sorry to say, the *someone* has already shown up." Her mouth drew into a taut line.

"Judging by the look on your face I'm guessing you're not pleased with him."

"He didn't make a great impression." Frowning, she sat down, pulled a document from one of the files next to her computer, ran her finger down the page until she came to what she was looking for, and then ran a pink highlighter through the section. "Jerk," she muttered.

"That bad?"

She rolled her eyes.

"Why is he here? There isn't even a suspect, much less an arrest."

"Who knows. I left some papers on your desk. Charlie is out. He'll be back in a couple hours." She began typing.

Jacob shifted from foot to foot.

She stopped typing and raised her eyebrows at him. "Is there something you want?"

"Just curious about the special prosecutor. What's his name?"

"Lester Norman Inglehook. Who would name their child Lester Norman, of all things? Not to mention his last name sounds like a brand of wine. He's rude. He's a boor. He complained about the coffee. He sniffed when he saw the mess in Charlie's office and asked if he'd heard correctly that the new DA for Bucks County played football at Rice. Then he sniffed again and made some comment about football players lacking organizational skills."

"Yep, I guess we're all dumb jocks."

"He's a nerd, so he's jealous of you guys with a little muscle on your bones. And to add insult to injury . . . ." A red flush began at the base of her neck and crept upward until it hit her hairline, ". . . . he drilled me about my procedures and then gave me unwanted, unneeded, and unwelcome advice."

Jacob burst out laughing. "I sure hope I never piss you off, Maureen. You look like a viper about to eat her babies."

She gave him a withering look. "Charlie is going to have to set him straight about what I do, and what I don't do around here."

She pulled off her glasses and narrowed her eyes. "If Ingleshit thinks I'm going to be at his beck and call, he needs to rewire his thinking."

"Maybe Charlie could assign one of the assistants from the pool to work exclusively for him while he's here."

"That's a brilliant idea, Jacob Gillis. You just earned my eternal respect and whatever piddly amount of money Charlie plans to pay you. But I have work to do." She fluttered her fingers in a good-bye wave.

At the door, he turned back to Maureen with a grin. "If Norman Lester—or was it Lester Norman?—is rude to you again, tell him Charlie and I will take him on."

She gave him a slow, wicked smile. "I can see the headlines now. *"District Attorney and Friend Beat the Shit out of Special Prosecutor.* Now, that would be fun, wouldn't it?"

Jacob booted up the computer and logged in. Despite having slept through the night, he still felt the lingering effects of jet lag, but he didn't want to wait for his body to settle into Eastern Standard Time before taking a look at the case. What the corporate culprit was about to do to the river, or maybe had already begun to do, gave him the same feeling he had when he accompanied a UN inspection team into the jungle of the Volcanoes National Reserve in Rwanda where they'd discovered a dead Mountain Gorilla. Its hands had been cut off and the body left to rot. He had had to fight to keep from vomiting, not because he was squeamish—he wasn't—but because he recognized the gorilla as an older male that he and a guide had followed for most of a day a few months previous.

Now, a river close to him, both in space and spirit, was being threatened with chemical death. He'd fished in that river. Swam in it. Floated down it in a canoe. Tubed down it. Goose Bend's drinking water came from a lake, but there were two towns to the west that got theirs from the Pumqua, and even though Goose Bend didn't need the river's water to drink, they valued the river for fishing, boating, and in some spots, for swimming. People picnicked beside the river; the township had built hiking trails along its shores; and many loved the river just for its views.

Someone was in the hallway, talking about the murder. He cocked his ears to listen, but the conversation turned out to be nothing more than a couple questions from one voice as to whether or not anything new had been discovered. It had not, the other voice replied.

He pulled up the files on the river case but Kate Hunter's image kept inserting itself in front of the computer screen. Not in a million years would he have expected her to show up on his doorstep at the crack of dawn. She'd been a thorn in his side in high school, turning up on the sidelines after football practice, in the hallway at school, at the next table over in the library, at the adjacent table in the lunchroom. She schemed to grab a seat next to him at Student Council meetings. She was hot, so it hadn't been easy to ignore her, and had things been different . . .

But they weren't. There was no way he was having anything to do with the daughter of the man who sentenced him to two years of hell.

The chase ended when Kate tried to entice him to invite her to his senior prom. She was a sophomore. He and Charlie had hatched a scheme to make sure every girl in the senior class got invited to the prom. It hadn't seemed fair for the guys to invite girls from other schools and from lower grades but leave their female classmates sitting at home. Not that he would have gone with Kate anyway. But she, not knowing what they were up to, stalked him in the hallway one Friday morning after second period. He was dialing the combination on his locker when she waltzed up in her short denim skirt and bright pink, knit blouse with a neckline so low he practically needed a neck brace to keep from staring. She leaned on the locker next to his and smiled up at him. Silver hoops dangled from her ears and a silver chain necklace with a pearl pendant hung around her neck. The pendant reached to her cleavage, nestling enticingly between two perfect breasts. His blood raced and he felt a tightening in the crotch of his jeans. Frantic to subdue his reaction, he concentrated on opening his locker and scrambling through the detritus, looking for his calculus book.

"Who are you taking to the prom, Jacob?" she asked when he

flashed a glance at her.

He swallowed and turned his attention back to rooting for his text. Good God, she had gorgeous violet eyes and the longest lashes he'd ever seen on a human being. The thought of being in the back seat of a car with her had sent his pulse skyrocketing.

"I don't have a date," she said.

He stopped his mad scramble for the calculus book. Didn't she have a list like he had? *Don't set foot in the Pennston Hotel; Don't make fun of Jimmy Q; Don't this . . . .; Don't that . . . .* And especially, *Don't ever go out with that Gillis boy.*

"Thanks, but no thanks," he said. He slammed his locker shut, and took off for class. Minus his book. Even if he'd wanted to take her, which he didn't, he couldn't imagine showing up at the Hunter's house and Mr. Hunter answering the door with that look on his face. *My daughter is going out with Jacob Gillis, the town arsonist?*

He'd been a bit short with her that day at the lockers. Well, rude actually. There was no reason he couldn't have been polite and explained why he couldn't take her to the prom. And he could say the same thing for what happened this morning: he'd been pretty damn brash. He should apologize.

He gave up on the work he'd meant to do. Only forty hours back in the U.S. and he was trying to concentrate? He was tired from a marathon trip that touched three continents, and his mind was ping-ponging, one minute feeling guilty over his encounter with Kate, and the next, wondering if John Hunter had shot his wife. As hard as he tried to make himself think John couldn't have committed the heinous crime, the possibility still reared its ugly head in the back of his mind.

He needed a distraction. Taking a few minutes to get to know some of the personnel in the DA's office should do the trick, especially the pretty paralegal. His brain would right itself soon enough and, hopefully, John would be exonerated in another day or so, and if he apologized to Kate he could put that inglorious episode out of his mind and go back to mostly forgetting about the Hunters like he'd done for the past thirteen years.

He found a phone book in the desk drawer, searched out the

Hunter's phone number, and rang. When the answering machine came on after seven rings, he hung up and was about to close the directory when he noticed that underneath the Hunter entry was a separate listing for Kate. He tapped in the number.

"Hello." She sounded exhausted.

He swallowed. The right words had stalled somewhere in his primitive brain. He should have planned what he was going to say. Hell, he was an attorney. Weren't attorneys supposed to be reasonably good at expressing themselves? Words ready and waiting, sitting on the tips of tongues, raring to jump out?

"Hello," she said again, a note of irritation in her voice.

"Kate?"

"Yes, Jacob. It's me."

"You recognize my voice?"

"I've heard your voice more than a few times." Hers sounded like an ice cube.

"Uh, well. . . . The reason I called . . . ." he paused.

"Yes?"

"I'm sorry. I didn't mean to be an asshole this morning. It's just that you were the last person I expected to see. You took me by surprise, and I really was expecting someone else at any minute. Can we try again?"

She hesitated. "I guess."

"I'm tied up this morning. Can I drop by this afternoon?" She'd said Mr. and Mrs. Hunter were on a cruise and hadn't gotten back, so he was safe on that score.

"This afternoon, then," she said, finally. "Do you know where I live?"

"The same place you always lived?"

"No." She gave him an address.

Relieved, he hung up. He would apologize for his behavior and, after wishing her and John well, leave. That should satisfy his conscience. He'd do that as soon as he finished lunch with Aunt Zuela. He smiled. Now, *that* should be a distraction. And he'd bet Aunt Zuela could fill him in on everything he'd ever wanted to know about the Hunters and then some.

Chapter Thirteen

Bump stood near the open window several feet away from where Jimmy Q sat at the conference table. The only way to get the old man off his back, Bump had realized, was to give him a few minutes.

"So, you saw someone *suspicious* sitting in front of Lacy's Mercantile on the night of the murder?" Bump kept his face turned in the direction of the breeze blowing through the window. Jimmy Q was overdue for his monthly bath. They'd need to call a fumigator when he left.

Jimmy nodded. "Yep, I seen somebody."

"Tell me everything you did Monday evening. Step by step. Every detail."

"Well . . . first, I had a couple drinks." He grinned up at Bump as though telling a joke.

"At the Pennston Hotel?"

"Yeah. I done told you that." Jimmy pulled a packet of tobacco papers from beneath his belt.

"You can't smoke in here."

"I ain't smoking."

"Then put those papers away."

"There ain't no law says I can't hold them."

Bump took a deep breath and tried to control his temper, but it was hard: he was tired; he was frazzled; he was worried. "What time were you at the Pennston Hotel Bar?"

Jimmy shrugged. "Don't know."

"When did you leave?"

"Don't know."

"But you left?"

"I guess if I ain't there now, I must've left." Jimmy's fingers played with the cigarette wrappers. He tapped them on the table, pressed them to his forehead, ran the package across his face making a scratching noise over his unshaven cheeks.

"Put the wrappers away." Bump's demand burst out as a shout.

Startled, Jimmy examined the chief briefly and then tucked the packet back underneath his belt.

Bump felt a morsel of contrition for yelling at the old man. Jimmy Q couldn't help who he was, but this murder was tearing Bump apart. He would so love for Jimmy to actually be telling the truth about a man sitting in front of Lacy's. Perhaps a drifter looking for a bit of money and willing to kill for it. Maybe a boyfriend from Ama's past who wanted revenge back for being dumped.

He pulled a notebook from his breast pocket and opened it. "Let's see . . .." He examined a page. "Your room in the Pennston Hotel is across the alley from Ama Hunter's dance studio. You threatened her on several occasions because her music was too loud." There was nothing written in his notebook, but Jimmy Q wouldn't know that. "You didn't shoot Mrs. Hunter, did you?"

Jimmy Q's eyes widened. "I ain't never shot nobody."

"Then explain what you saw last night. You were so anxious to tell, go ahead. Tell me about leaving the bar."

"I left twice."

"Where did you go when you left?"

"I had to piss."

"You went to the men's room?"

"No."

"You went up to your room?"

Jimmy Q looked down at a blackened thumbnail and murmured something.

"Speak up. I can't hear you. Where did you go to piss?"

"The alley," Jimmy Q shouted and then made a face.

"You pissed in the alley?" Bump threw up his hands. "Why am I not surprised? After all, why would you go to a perfectly good restroom in the bar, or to the one up in your room when there was an alley to piss in? Why, in God's name, didn't you use the facilities in the hotel?"

"Somebody else were in there."

"And you couldn't wait? Why didn't you go to your room?"

"Didn't want to climb stairs."

Bump clasped his hands behind his back and paced along one side of the table and then back again.

"Who did you see when you were in the alley? Did you see girls going up to their dance class? Girls leaving?"

"I seen Miz Hunter leave."

"But she didn't leave. Somebody shot her. Remember?"

Jimmy Q looked confused. "Right," he said finally. "I guess it were last week when I seen her leave."

"Did you piss in the alley then, too? Has that become your personal toilet?"

Jimmy Q became engrossed in his fingernail.

Bump let out an exasperated sigh. "Who did you see Monday night?"

"That man."

"What man?"

"Don't know. He were sitting on that bench down in front of the Mercantile."

"Did he look like anyone you know?" Bump narrowed his eyes. "What size was the man? Would you say he was about the same size as . . .?" Bump corrected himself. "Was he as tall as me?" He shivered. He'd been about to ask if the man had any resemblance to John Hunter. John wasn't guilty, so why had he even thought of asking?

"Jimmy Q?" Bump put his hands on the table and leaned onto his arms. "Have you seen this man before? Did he have on a suit?"

"I seen him a couple times. Here and there. A while back, I guess. He didn't wear no suit." Jimmy Q raised his brows in a knowing look. "You want to know if it war John Hunter, don'chu? Well, it warn't Mr. High and Mighty. The man I seen was a great big man. Bigger'n Mr. Hunter. Bigger'n you. And he had on red cowboy boots."

"Were you drunk?"

"Naw, I weren't drunk. Just had a few, that's all, and I ain't talking no more."

Bump didn't try to stop him when Jimmy Q scraped back his chair and sidled out. People in Goose Bend didn't wear red cowboy boots. At least no one he could remember.

Chapter Fourteen

"Hellooooo," Jacob called as he stepped inside Aunt Zuela's bungalow.

His only greeting was the aroma of veal stew and the clank of lid against pot from the kitchen in the rear of the house. He took a few moments to savor being back in the old, familiar place. It had been five years, but everything looked the same: *The New York Times* folded to reveal the crossword puzzle on the seat of a worn, red upholstered chair; her Uggs slippers beneath the chair; a hodge-podge of furniture ranging from early attic to fine antique filling the living room as well as the dining room, visible through an arch.

"Eclectic," Meg once called it.

"Not sophisticated enough, my dear, to be called eclectic," Aunt Zuela had responded. "Shabby professorial is a better description."

Shabby professorial described perfectly the overflowing shelves that stretched floor to ceiling along one wall of the living room. One shelf was stuffed with worn notebooks containing Aunt Zuela's lectures.

She wasn't actually his aunt, but rather his mother's best friend. They'd moved from the flower farm into town after his father's death, and the Cape Cod they'd settled in stood two blocks away from Aunt Zuela's. When his mother had a late faculty meeting or evening parent-teacher conferences, he and Meg scooted over to Aunt Zuela's for food, hilarity, and advice on matters of life, death, and sex. A professor specializing in Shakespeare, she commuted three days a week to Philadelphia to teach classes at Temple. And heaven help anyone who didn't pronounce her name correctly. "Zoo-eeeeela," she emphasized to people who made the mistake of pronouncing her name Zoo-ELLA.

"My name sounds like one of those creepy things that swim around with the fish. Eeeeeee for eels!" she'd say.

He pulled off his jacket and threw it over the rocking chair he'd always claimed as his, and wondered if his gum was still stuck underneath the seat.

In the dining room, instead of a china cabinet, an antique, mullioned glass-door book case stood against one wall. Its shelves contained her collection of Shakespeare books: commentaries, several different editions of the plays and sonnets, and her doctoral dissertation on imagery in *The Merchant of Venice.*

"I'm here," he called out when he heard the clunk of a knife on a cutting board.

"Come on back," a gravelly voice responded. A clatter of dishes and the thud of something falling was followed by an expletive.

Still, the posture of a queen and the mouth of a whore, he mused as he strode into the kitchen. She was almost as tall as he and had short gray hair and penciled brows. She put down the knife she'd been using to slice cucumbers, took two steps forward, and threw her arms around him.

"It's about time," she said.

"About time for what?" he asked, grinning and hugging her back.

"For you to come home." She stepped back and looked him over. "Well, you don't look any the worse for wear after spending five years in Africa. Lunch is almost ready. As soon as I chop up some tomatoes we can eat. I'm starved."

"You're always starving, if I remember correctly."

"Some of us are just lucky, I guess." She motioned to a teapot on the counter. "All I have to drink is Earl Gray, but help yourself. I made a rush-rush trip to the grocery store this morning, but forgot to buy cokes." She turned on the faucet and doused two tomatoes beneath the gush of water.

"How was your trip to London?" He undid his tie and threw it across the room to land on a dinette chair.

"Great. Your mother and I both might decide to turn sixty-five again next year so we can plan another glorious trip as a birthday present to ourselves." She flicked the tomatoes, spattering drops of water on the floor and counter tops.

He looked around at the all-white cabinets and the gray countertops. Otherwise, anything that *could* be red, was red—pots, tea pot, bowls, napkins. "Nothing much has changed here, has it?"

"I moved a stack of books in the living room from the sofa to a chair. That's about it." She began peeling a tomato, but then stopped and twisted around to face him. Bits of pulp dropped to the floor. "What an awful thing to come home to. A murder. I don't suppose you're going to tell me if that detective friend of yours has a suspect in mind, are you?"

"If he has anyone in mind, I don't know about it." He took a glass from the cupboard and filled it with ice from the automatic freezer dispenser and then poured tea from the teapot into the glass. "Why do you call him *that detective friend of mine*? You've met him."

"Barely. The only times I ever ran into Laskey were when he was picking you up or dropping you off from whatever it was you two were doing." She shrugged. "Anyway, yesterday as soon as I hit town, I had my hair done. I didn't even unpack my suitcase first; you know what it's like after a trip and a long flight. That was *the* topic of conversation at the salon. *Do you think John did it?*"

"And what do people think?" He held the glass up and watched the ice melt in the hot Earl Gray.

"A couple people whispered that they think John killed her." She tore the peel from another tomato, quartered it, and threw it in the salad shaker.

"What do *you* think?" He knew she'd have an opinion. She always did.

"John Hunter doesn't have the balls."

"You know him well enough to say that?"

"I used to play bridge with his mother."

"And you got to know John by playing bridge with his mother?"

"You're as sassy as ever, aren't you?" She shot him an affectionate smile, as she jiggled the salad shaker, clunking the cucumbers against the top. "Another minute, and we can eat." She opened the container and began dishing salad onto pottery decorated with red tropical birds.

Jacob relaxed with the familiarity of it all. It felt like home. Or rather, his second home. Or was it his third because Laskey's home felt like home, too?

She carried the salad plates to the dinette table in the corner and, after setting them down let out a little huff. "Kate is the only member of that family who has balls. Gwen Hunter had us all thinking they were the perfect family. Not a speck of dirt in her house; dust, dirt, and grime fall off like magic as soon as their shoes touch the door steps. Husband never strayed. Kids behaved and made good grades. Always enough money to pay the bills. Probably the only place that family ever had a flat tire was in front of a service station. But there can be cracks in perfect families." She motioned to a chair. "Sit. Sit."

He moved over, stood behind a chair, but didn't sit down. He'd had quite enough of sitting during the past few days. While she ladled out stew, he wondered how she'd reached the conclusion that Kate had balls.

"Unless you're going to eat standing up, have a seat," she said as she set down two bowls of stew. She sat down and flapped her napkin in the air to unfold it.

He wanted to pursue the "cracks" in the Hunter family, but she launched into a description of the nasty tour guide who wouldn't let her and his mother bring food on the bus during their day trip to Windsor and Stonehenge.

Jacob listened patiently until he could no longer stand it. "Aunt Zuela, please, I'll take you to dinner one night soon, and you can tell me every detail of your trip. Maybe Mom will drive over and I can take you both, but *pleeeease*, right now I want to hear about the cracks in the Hunter family."

"Hah. I wondered how long you'd let me carry on without interrupting." She rested her forearms on the table, leaned toward him, and told him about the rumors of John cheating at Lehigh, a DUI bought off, a pregnant waitress up in Bethlehem. When she finished, she shrugged and said, "No idea if any of it is true."

He didn't want to believe it. In small towns rumors had a way of igniting from a single phrase or look, and then blazing out of control, and like every other hamlet in America, the citizens of Goose Bend were excellent at fictionalizing. They probably even made up stories about him; he just hoped they invented something exciting like an escapade that had him escaping from cannibals in the Congo or a story about him spending a week camping out with gorillas.

"What about Kate?"

"She's an artist, you know?" She forked a tomato.

That explained the smell of turpentine and the stained cuticles. "Being an artist means she has balls?"

"In her family it does."

He waited while she chewed and swallowed.

"Gwen and John Hunter Senior are as conventional as a church pew," she said finally. "John became an accountant like they wanted him to do, but Kate turned out to be a renegade. They expected her to marry and become a respectable wife, which, I imagine, includes enduring a weekly manicure and bridge game, certainly not going around with stained fingernails and paint-smeared jeans."

The senior Hunters must be living in some century other than the twenty-first, he decided.

"Kate graduated from Skidmore, you know?"

No, he didn't know. Or maybe he did, but had forgotten.

"Then she wanted to go Florence or San Francisco to study art. They wouldn't let her."

"How could they stop her?"

"By not giving her any money." Aunt Zuela slid back her chair, went to the spice rack, and came back with a bottle. "Needs more garlic," she said and, after sprinkling her stew, she set the bottle down in front of Jacob and sat down again. "Gwen told us that Kate has a trust fund from her grandmother, but her father locked it up until Kate turns thirty-six. He wanted the money properly invested instead of dribbling away while she flitted about painting pictures. Thus sayeth Gwen."

A feeling of empathy for Kate surprised him. He imagined the same spiteful man who issued harsh punishment for him and Charlie lashing out at his only daughter with something like: *You're not going to turn into a damn Bohemian on my watch.*

"Kate teaches art at the high school," Aunt Zuela said, scooping up a piece of veal. "Local gossip has it that she's saving money to finance her own studies. They arranged for John to have access to his trust fund when he married. How fair is that? Especially when it was John's money they should have worried about." She stuck the meat in her mouth and chewed. "If Ama hadn't died . . . ." Zuela looked at him questioningly, ". . . could she have gotten part of his trust fund in a divorce settlement?"

"Probably not. Is Kate married?" He tried to sound disinterested.

"No. Just a string of boyfriends over the years, ranging in age and wealth. None that Gwen approved of. So Ama wouldn't have been able to get part of John's trust fund?"

"I don't think so."

"Well, she was trying. The funeral is on Saturday morning. You're going, of course."

"No. I don't like funerals."

"Pick me up at ten. I'll fix you lunch afterwards. Besides . . . ." She leaned toward him. "You know what they say?"

"What do they say, Aunt Zuela?"

"That the murderer often attends the funeral. Maybe we'll see him . . . . Or her."

Chapter Fifteen

The cheap row house Jacob was parked in front of bore the same number and street as what Kate had given him. Either he'd gotten it wrong, or she'd played a joke on him. The houses on both sides of the street had identical gables, sagging porches, cracked sidewalks, and peeling paint. No Hunter would live in a place like this.

He sighed, got out, and headed toward the house he presumed *wasn't* Kate's. At least he had a great excuse for not showing up. He'd knock on the door, and then when someone else answered, he'd go home and call her. *I'm sorry, but I wrote down the wrong address.*

School had just turned out. Kids rode past on bicycles or ambled along with book bags, kicking at rocks, stopping to whisper in each other's ears or taunt each other. A couple houses down, a boy with stringy blonde hair—a first grader?—slung his backpack in anger at a couple of older boys and then ran into his house crying. His tormentors laughed.

When he turned onto the walkway that led to the front door, the hair on the back of his neck bristled when he realized he was being watched from the windows of two news vans parked along the street, both with cameras aimed in his direction. He was in the right place after all. He lowered his head. He didn't want to make the news ever again in this town. His accidental arson had been quite enough.

Two women gazed unabashedly at him from the porch to the right, and on the one to the left an older woman with a long gray pony tail paused in the act of watering geraniums to stare. He bounded up the steps and crossed the porch in three strides. This is what it would be like for the Hunters now, everything observed and dissected, comings and goings discussed, visitors noted. He raised his hand to knock, but the door swung open while he still held his hand suspended in front of the knocker.

Kate moved aside and then quickly closed the door behind him, plunging the room into a dark gloom that smelled of stale air. Drapes were closed and blinds drawn. The only light filtered in through four tiny panes framing the top of the door—red, blue, yellow, and green.

He tried to remember the apology he'd prepared, as Kate turned on a table lamp and then flicked the switch for the hanging fixture in the adjoining dining room.

"Have a seat." Stone-faced, she motioned toward the sofa.

About to sit, Jacob heard someone scurrying up the stairs in the back of the house. With a quick intake of breath, Kate darted a glance in the direction of the sound. His gaze followed the same path as hers, through the archway separating the living room from the dining room, and toward the stairs which he knew to be situated next to the kitchen. In high school, he'd had a couple friends who lived in houses with the same floorplan.

When the person reached the top, Kate turned to him. "Can I get you a drink?"

"No thanks. I'm sorry . . . ." He stopped, struck by the brilliant splashes of color springing from stark white walls. Paintings of all sizes filled both living room and dining room, mostly oils, but also a few watercolors and pastels, and one pen and ink. His gaze traveled from piece to piece. When he finished the first cursory look around, he stepped up to each painting, examining it in detail, exploring the kaleidoscope of hues and tints, the juxtaposition of shapes, and finally, the signature in the lower right hand corner. *Kate.* An almost insolent *Kate.* He wondered how a signature could be thought of as insolent, but he couldn't imagine a better way to describe her bold scrawl.

"I had no idea," he said finally, raising his hands in a gesture to indicate his surprise. "Aunt Zuela told me you were talented. But you're . . . . gifted. Do you know what kind of art I like?"

"I didn't even know you liked art."

"I like color." He swept his hand around in a motion encompassing all the paintings. "Big, bold swatches of color. Like we had on our flower farm every spring when the flowers burst out in every hue you could possibly imagine and some you couldn't. I'd climb into my treehouse and sit there feeling like I was in the middle of a gigantic painting." He held her eyes for a few moments. "Why are you wasting your time teaching when you paint like this?"

"Is there something wrong with teaching?"

"I just meant . . ." He'd said the wrong thing again, forgetting that Aunt Zuela had already told him why Kate had taken a job at the local high school.

She gave him a wistful smile. "I have to live, don't I? Eventually, I'll save enough money to . . . ." She rubbed her hands together. "Can't I get you something to drink?"

"No thanks." Ignoring the fact that he seemed to be making her nervous, he wandered into the dining room. She was the one who had come at the crack of dawn, pleading for him to talk to her. He was here now, to talk, . . . well, actually to apologize, but while he was here he might as well enjoy her work.

He studied two large landscapes and then turned to a still life showing three pomegranates on a table, a glint of light flaming the fruit crimson. A knife lay on a draped napkin beside the pomegranates, and an arrangement of mixed flowers stood behind. Other objects lay in shadows, blending into the dark background.

When he turned to view a portrait at the end of the room nearest the kitchen, he stopped short. The subject—a woman, in her sixties perhaps—had eyes so stern he almost flinched. She sat with shoulders drawn stiffly back and mouth pulled in a taut line.

Streaks of gray needled her black hair which had been twisted into a loose knot. Her head was tilted back, and her eyes peered down at the viewer in a look that seemed as uncaring and rigid as a drill sergeant.

"Mrs. Petrowsky," Kate said, coming to stand beside him. "Ama's mother."

"She looks . . . ." He was about to say "controlling" but left his sentence unfinished.

"If you were going to say she looks like a martinet, you're right. She was strong-willed, to put it nicely."

"Was? She's dead?"

"No. She has early onset dementia. Sometimes she knows what's going on. Sometimes not."

Jacob did the math. According to the paper, Ama was twenty-six, which would normally have made her mother in her fifties or very early sixties, much too young for dementia. The woman in the portrait looked older. She must have borne Ama when she was well past normal child-bearing years.

"Does she understand what happened?"

"I don't know."

"How are the other members of Ama's family taking it?"

"There aren't any. Ama was an only child, and her father died a few years ago. At least there aren't any other family in this country. The Petrowskys escaped from Poland, and none of their other relatives made it to America."

"That sounds like a story."

"It *is* a story." She crossed her arms. "Why were you so rude to me?"

He swallowed. "I know it's no excuse, but I was taken off guard, and I didn't know what to say to you." He gave a little shrug. "I never knew what to say to you, even in high school."

"Am I some sort of ogre?"

"No, it's just that you're pretty, and your family has white sofas and thick carpets, and they drive a Mercedes, and I was the kid who burned down the town."

"The sofas were cream-colored, not white." Her lips curled in the semblance of a smile.

His shoulders loosened. Had she smiled at him like that in high school instead of always trying to hook him like he was a damn fish, he might have forgotten who her father was. For a few seconds, anyway.

"I hated those sofas," she said. "We got to sit in the living room only if we took a bath, put on clean clothes, and underwent a dirt inspection. Dirt horrifies my mother. I envied kids who were allowed to play in the mud. You got to play in the mud, didn't you?" A spark of humor lit her eyes.

"All the time. Mud is a great toy. Mothers have different opinions, of course, but now they're saying dirt helps you build up resistance to diseases. I probably have lots of resistance."

"I wish I'd been your playmate. Anyway, the fire was an accident. Did you think people would hold it against you forever?"

"Yes."

She rolled her eyes. "Get over it."

"As easy as that?"

She put her hand on his arm. "I'm sorry, Jacob. I guess no one gets over things that easily. Ignore me. Are you finished with the art tour?"

As her hand slid away, he wanted to grab the hand and force it back to the spot it had warmed. While he struggled for something to say, he caught sight of a small painting full of geometrical shapes, the style inconsistent with Kate's other work. He took a step closer and recognized the artist from his art appreciation course in college.

"You have a Diego Rivera?"

"It's a copy." She moved over to stand beside him and brushed a finger over the lower part of the frame, stroking away a speck of dust. "I did it when I was a student at Skidmore."

He leaned over, looking more closely. "But his signature is here."

"If I can copy the painting, I can forge the signature."

Someone dropped something on the floor above. He glanced at Kate.

"I'm sorry, Jacob. You have to go." She squeezed her eyes shut for a few seconds, shaking her head slowly. "This is really hard," she whispered, and then opened her eyes. "John is staying with me for now."

So it wasn't a boyfriend. As quickly as relief swept through him, he doused it. She was nothing to him, nor would she ever be. She still had the same father, and she still grew up with white sofas. Nor did he have any intention of being on intimate terms with a girl who had a dirt-phobic mother who probably abhorred boys who grew up on flower farms and played in the mud.

"John thinks he's less visible here," Kate said. "He doesn't want to talk to anyone. Or see anyone. This morning when you refused to help, he changed his mind about wanting you to. He asked me not to let you in."

She made him sound cruel and heartless. Still, he felt guiltily relieved that he didn't have to talk to John. What do you say to a friend whose wife has been murdered? *I'm sorry* seemed inadequate. *Did you do it?* didn't work either.

"I don't know what to do." She choked back a sob. "Half the people I run into won't look at me. I know they're wondering if John did it. The other half stick their faces in mine and rant about there being a murderer on the loose." Her voice broke. "I'm sorry," she said, regaining control. "I shouldn't have gone to your place this morning. This has nothing to do with you. You came to apologize, but I'm the one who needs to apologize. It's just . . . . . I thought you might be the one person I could talk to. I didn't think you'd stare at me the way everyone else does." She hesitated a moment. "I'm not explaining it very well. But it's like being marooned on a distant planet."

It had never occurred to him that someone from the high and mighty Hunter family might feel isolated. When his father died, people came. So many people. They brought love, food, support. Where was her support? Were people staying away because they thought John was guilty?

"You need to get away for a little while."

"And where am I going?" She propped her hands on her hips.

"Name a place where I can forget for two minutes." Her voice was bitter.

"What if we go someplace for an early dinner where no one knows you? Not that you can forget, but at least it would be a break."

Relief flooded her face. "Thank you, Jacob. You can't possibly know what that means to me."

He nodded. "You name the place, but let's drive separately. Your neighbors are taking note of everything."

Her face reddened. "Why can't they just go away and leave us alone?" She took a slow breath, regaining her composure. "What about Odette's in New Hope? That should be safe from prying eyes."

Chapter Sixteen

I t was a good thing he slept long and well, and woke up each morning relaxed, otherwise, Laskey might have lost his temper, or at the very least made a snappish remark that would come back to haunt him. Still, he needed a few minutes to calm himself. He pulled into the parking lot of the Goose Bend Lutheran Church and parked at the far end where he was unlikely to be disturbed, and where an ancient oak shielded his eyes from the sun's glare. For obvious reasons the office at the police station which Bump had made available to him wasn't exactly quiet and peaceful right now, nor could he sit there for more than two minutes without being disturbed, and he needed more than two minutes to un-ruffle his feathers.

He switched off the engine, lay his head back on the head rest, and let his gaze go soft. His talent for falling immediately into a dead sleep no matter what was going on was a gift, and he valued it. Yesterday, after a late afternoon meeting with the Goose Bend police department and an even later meeting with his crime team, he had reviewed his notes, grabbed a Philly cheese steak, and zonked out almost before his head hit the pillow. This morning he rose brimming with energy, ready to track down a murderer, and after breakfast with Jacob, he was at it again. Interviewing. Interviewing. Interviewing.

Until Inglehook chased him down.

Laskey had heard about prosecutors showing up at the crime scene and hovering over the police force. Most of them, however, waited for evidence to make its way to their desks. Inglehook was his first personal encounter with a hoverer. The special prosecutor had appeared at the Goose Bend police station, where he had no business being, and pulled Laskey aside.

"I assume you'll be making an arrest soon," Inglehook had said in an undertone. "I predict that trying the football hero, class-president son of the richest man in town will get the attention of Anderson Cooper and all the rest, so . . ."

"We have no suspects at this time," Laskey interrupted.

Ingle hook gave him a conspiratorial smile. "Yes, I understand. No official suspects. But don't forget how much attention some cases have gotten. So get the details straight, Laskey. I want this trial to go off without a hitch. In other words, perfect. P-E-R-F-E-C-T." Inglehook had then looked Laskey up and down before adding, "Maybe you'd like to get a new suit. You want to look good on television."

Prick! Laskey slapped the steering wheel. He always got the details straight. If he didn't have exact knowledge of something, he admitted it. And he bloody hell didn't care how he looked on television.

He knew gossip circuits were buzzing. With no suspect and no discernible motive other than anger over a discarded wife trying to pluck her errant husband down to the last penny, how many people, Inglehook included, thought John the culprit? Especially, when they heard that money and credit cards were still in her purse. And word had gotten out. Before the meeting yesterday afternoon, Laskey had caught one of the Goose Bend police officers talking to a local about the cotton balls in the waste paper basket.

Could there have been something valuable in the studio? Laskey dismissed the idea almost as soon as it entered his head. A dance school wasn't exactly the place to house a treasure. Unless, of course, you hid something there for the very reason that no one expected a treasure to be hidden there.

Had Ama seen something she shouldn't have? A drug deal? According to Bump, she usually parked her white Mustang in the alley between Lacy's and The Pennston Hotel. She could have walked out one evening after her classes and witnessed an exchange. The men gathered around the night of the murder had been questioned at least twice, some three times, but none of them appeared to have anything to do with trafficking. They all claimed to have been at the hotel bar from six o'clock until some point past midnight participating in the weekly darts tournament. For whatever it was worth, the bartender verifed their alibis and they verifed his.

As for the murder weapon, it could be anywhere in the U.S., or in the world for that matter, since there was always the possibility the murderer came from Ama's past. She had no relatives other than her mother, and no close friends in the area in spite of having lived in Goose Bend for seven years. Her phone records showed four calls to the same person during the ten days before her death: a Marek Molnar, with a New York City phone number. So far, Laskey hadn't been able to reach him.

But what to make of John? There had been mixed messages. Yesterday, his insistence that he hadn't killed his wife seemed genuine, but that indecipherable look between brother and sister had branded itself in Laskey's mind. What had that been about? Was John hiding something or protecting someone? Why else did he refuse to come up an alibi?

Laskey stirred uncomfortably as Inglehook fouled his mind again. Over the years he had dealt with people who jumped to quick conclusions without corroborating evidence, but something about Inglehook made his skin crawl. It hadn't been three full days since the body was found, and the prosecutor was already planning the trial along with his TV debut. Laskey had a bad feeling. Like that first little churn in a stomach before full scale vomiting breaks out.

But he had to carry on in spite of the premonition that nagged at him. His foot found the gas pedal, and he cranked up the Sequoia and backed out. Nancy Bolen was back in town and had taken refuge at her parents' house. First, he'd question her, and after that he'd try to catch the one person he hadn't managed to pin down for more than a few minutes. Kate Hunter, too busy with Ama's funeral arrangements, had managed to elude him for anything other than a cursory conversation.

LASKEY HAD CHOSEN to remain standing, while Nancy Bolen sat on an ottoman in her parents' living room, looking more like a Sunday School teacher than the *other woman*. Her mother sat in a chair across the room.

"I don't know what John did on Monday evening," Nancy said, finally answering Laskey's question. She lifted her big, blue eyes, feverish with worry, to gaze at him. "I was in Scranton. My friend from college is getting married, and we gave her a shower."

"You didn't ask what John was going to do? That's sort of a common question for people living together, isn't it? *What will you do while I'm away?*"

"I did ask, and he said he had nothing planned. *Nothing planned* usually means an evening in front of the TV watching some game or other." She gave her mother a helpless look.

"I invited him for supper," Mrs. Bolen said, ". . . but he said he'd had a long day and planned to turn in early."

Laskey wrinkled his brow, pretending to think, but instead, taking in the room, and the people in it. Why the term *Sunday School* kept popping into his mind perplexed him. Maybe it was Nancy, angel-perfect with her oval face, flawless complexion, and blonde hair falling in short, loose waves. Her figure was rounded in the right places and slim where it should be slim. Or maybe it was the perfectly ordered room which looked like it had been bought in a furniture store, furnishings, pictures, and knick-knacks included. Maybe it was Nancy's mother with her ramrod straight back, legs crossed at ankles, and hands clasped together, although he knew her rigidness was probably meant to hide nervousness. Everything was boringly perfect. Possibly, boredom was what John wanted after Ama.

Ama had been blonde, too, but her blondeness reminded him of ice and snow. Cold and unforgiving. And instead of Nancy's blue eyes that shimmered like summer lake water, Ama had dark, piercing eyes that followed him when he moved from one place to another. If photographed eyes did that, then how did the real ones make John feel?

He went to the window and looked through the vee of the curtains at the birdbath outside. Both Nancy and her mother, worry lines engraved in their foreheads, had besieged him with questions about *who did it* when he first arrived. When he'd been unable to give them any answers, they'd fallen into silence.

"I understand you're a paralegal," he said, still looking at the birdbath.

"Yes, I work for Smith, Larson, and McCelvey in Doylestown."

He turned to face her. "Tell me about Ama."

She reddened. "I have nothing good to say about her, so maybe you shouldn't ask."

"Tell me anyway."

"She was a bitch."

So, Nancy wasn't wholly *Sunday School*, after all. "I imagine Ama gave John a hard time when he moved in with you."

"She gave both of us a hard time. We went to St. Lucia in January. When John tried to pay our hotel bill, they told him his card had been suspended. He called the credit card company, and they said Ama had reported the card stolen and canceled it. He tried his other cards, and the same thing happened. I didn't have enough credit available on mine. John had to call his parents to pay the bill." She let out a huff. "When we got home, there was a 'For Sale' sign in front of my condo, and Ama had filled out one of those forms to change John's address. He has no idea what important mail he's missed."

"Just awful," Mrs. Bolen chimed in. "I hate to talk about the dead this way, but Ama could be an awful, awful person. She wasn't nice to her mother, either."

"What did you do about Ama's harrassment?" Ignoring the mother, Laskey addressed his question to Nancy.

"John went orbital. He had it out with her, and she sort of left us alone after that."

"So, Ama was being Odile, not Odette."

"Excuse me?" Nancy looked at him in confusion.

"Never mind. So she did nothing nasty after that?"

"No, but . . . well, I was always afraid she was planning something really awful." She let out a long shaky breath. "I guess we're safe on that count now."

He moved toward the door. "Thanks for your time. If I have more questions, I know where to find you."

A bitch, he thought a few minutes later as he climbed in his vehicle. It sounded like Ama Hunter not only had a talent for ballet, but one for inventing nasty ways to get even.

Chapter Seventeen

H alfway to New Hope, Jacob's phone rang. He wrestled it from his jacket pocket and tapped the "on" button.

"Want to grab a bite?" Laskey's tympanum voice boomed through the earpiece. "I'm in Goose Bend. Meant to talk to Kate Hunter, but she's slipped off somewhere.

". . . . Jeez, ... I'd wish I'd known earlier, Lask. I'm on my way to New Hope to meet a friend. I'm free the rest of the week so let me know when you have a few spare minutes. How's the investigation going? Anything new?"

"Not a damn thing. I wanted to question John's sister about Ama's background. John clams up when I ask. About all anyone else seems to know is that she danced with the New York City Ballet."

"You think someone from her past might be involved?" Jacob stopped for a red light, rolled down the window, and propped his arm on the ledge. The afternoon had warmed to light- jacket-and-open-windows temperature.

"Just another stone to look under. The question is: Was Ama Odette, or was she Odile?"

"Sounds like a deep philosophical question." He drummed his fingers on the steering wheel as he waited for the light to change.

Funny coincidence: he was meeting Kate at a restaurant named *Odette's*.

"You know the story of *Swan Lake?*"

Jacob gave a single, grim chortle. "My grandmother took me to see it one summer when I visited her in Boston. For the record, I went unwillingly. I was twelve and about as eager to see a ballet as I was to muck a horse stall." The light changed, and he eased through the intersection. "Why are you asking about *Swan Lake?*"

"There are two pictures of Ama in her studio. Actually, there are lots of pictures of her, but two caught my attention. In one, she's Odette, and in the other she's Odile. It's the weirdest thing. In the Swan Queen picture she's looking off to the side, but in the Odile picture her eyes follow you around."

"She's trying to haunt you, Lask." He pulled into the passing lane to sweep around a puttering Honda.

"Don't make fun of me, boy, or I'll sic Inglehook on you."

"The special prosecutor is getting under your skin, too? I have to meet this douche bag."

"You will soon enough. I'd better let you go. I've been trying to get a call through to South America. Want to try again."

So who was in South America, Jacob wondered.

THE SUN WAS DIPPING below the horizon when he reached the outskirts of the village of New Hope. He slowed and drove along Bridge Street, so named because it ended at the bridge that spanned the Delaware River. On the other side lay Lambertville, New Jersey. Street lights flickered on, as he drove past the New Hope Inn – one of the five oldest in the United States. "The Inn is built in Colonial Kitchen-Parlor Style architecture," Aunt Zuela once explained to him. He still didn't know what Colonial Kitchen-Parlor Style meant.

He turned onto Mechanic Street, which ran parallel to the river, and crept past the Parry Mansion and then Gerenger's Ice Cream Shop. Judging by the people going in and out of the brightly lit shop, Gerenger's still did a lively business. Maybe after dinner Kate might agree to have ice cream. A few hundred feet beyond Gerenger's, stood the Bucks County Playhouse, built from one of the old mills for which the town was named. When the original mills burned, the new ones were referred to as "our new hope," and what had been the town of Wells Ferry became New Hope.

Tourist-oriented novelty stores had taken the place of many of the art studios and antique dealers that had once been almost the sole enterprises in the village. He noticed that the remaining antique shops still bore No Children Allowed signs. He and Meg had had to wait outside many a time while his mother and Aunt Zuela rummaged around inside, his mother searching for the antique hairpins she collected, and Aunt Zuela foraging for whatever her latest interest had turned to. One year it was old muffin tins; the year before it had been salt spoons. At various times she accumulated antique wine glasses, paper weights, Wallace Nutting prints, African carvings, and old corsets. What she did with all her purchases was a mystery to him since he saw little of it displayed in her house. When they finished with their shopping, Mom and Aunt Zuela took him and Meg to Gerenger's to reward them with ice cream cones for waiting patiently—chocolate for him; strawberry for Meg. Although, sometimes their waiting had been anything but patient, including the time Meg pushed him into the Delaware during an argument. They didn't get ice cream that day.

Odette's stood just beyond the village on a sliver of land between the canal and the river. Built in typical Bucks County barn-like style, the restaurant teetered near the towpath where horses once pulled barges loaded with coal along the canal. Jacob pulled into the parking lot, got out, and stood for a few minutes looking through the trees and their tangled mass of long shadows, to where the setting sun glinted off the Delaware River. He would have preferred to stand there longer, enjoying the peace, the quiet, the smell of a river, but he needed to get a table. He let out a little snort. It had taken a murder for Kate to accomplish what she'd tried so hard in high school to do: spend an evening with him.

HE RESTED an arm on the table, his gaze drifting to the river, now a deep navy, and watched the dark waters of the Delaware tumble and eddy on their way to the Delaware Bay. He imagined himself in a kayak, traveling with them. Once, he and Charlie had built a raft out of old wood they found stacked behind Charlie's garage. They'd launched it on the Pumqua and spent many happy hours drifting along before their contraption finally fell apart under the onslaught of friends who wanted to use it as a diving platform. The following summer he and Charlie decided tubing was more fun, and the summer after that, Laskey had dug up from somewhere a double-seater kayak for them. He'd loved the ragged, rough, bare-footed-ness of those glorious summers, building rafts and tree houses, rooting through the woods, fishing, tubing, kayaking.

A raven-haired waitress with a tattooed dragon stretching from wrist to shoulder yanked him from his reverie, asking if he wanted anything to drink while he waited. He ordered a glass of water and requested the wine list.

He looked around absently. It was still early, and only a few tables were occupied. There were three groups of women having tea and an older couple sitting at the table nearest him. When the man looked up and glimpsed Jacob, he stopped talking to his wife, smiled, and nodded. Jacob nodded in return and then looked away. The man, with his fringe of white hair, white sprouting eyebrows, and salt and pepper mustache, looked familiar, but not wanting to suffer the embarrassment of talking to someone who seemed to know him, but whose identity he couldn't fix on, Jacob pulled out his phone and studied it as though checking texts.

A sudden doubt that Kate might change her mind and leave him sitting there alone needled him, but quick on its heels came a feeling of relief. He hoped she did stand him up. For a few minutes this afternoon he'd forgotten who she was, but now he remembered. Loud and clear. What had possessed him to meet her here this evening? He felt trapped. And when this was over, when someone had been arrested for the murder of her sister-in-law, and this cloud no longer hung over her, would she leave him alone? He shifted, uncomfortable as a new thought struck him. Had she been attracted to him in the first place because she'd been a rebel, not only now with her doggedness about being an artist, but even back then, wanting to rile her family? Who to do that better with than the lowly town arsonist? "And all this time I thought it was my good looks and personality," he mumbled.

Muted voices, the occasional laugh, the clink of a glass from a nearby table, the smell of cinnamon and almonds, cucumber-cream cheese sandwiches, and smoked salmon lulled him into tranquility. Once again, his gaze drifted to the river. What was it about water that comforted? Its motion, its sound? Both? Then he realized he was mistaking tranquility for sleepiness. His body was still on East African time where it was four A.M.

The waitress clunked a glass of water down in front of him. "Here's the wine list, sir," she said cheerily, holding it out to him. "Can I get you anything else while you wait?"

"Not now, thank you."

He ran his finger down the list: Rombauer, Brunello di Montalcino, Caymus, Cakebread, ... Was Kate a connoisseur? He took out his phone and punched in Meg's number.

"Well . . ., I'm glad my charming brother found time to call. Is your house livable yet?"

"Not by a long shot."

"Need help?"

"I could use a whole lot of help. I've been waiting for you to ask."

"If you'd called sooner, I would have offered sooner. You get a D minus in the calling department, brother."

"What d'you mean? I called you first thing yesterday morning. But right now I have a question."

"Yeeeessss?"

"Can you give me some quick help ordering wine? In Rwanda we didn't keep up with wines. We drank other stuff. What are people drinking these days?"

Meg didn't respond immediately. When she did, he heard the ring of curiosity in her voice. "Where are you?"

"I'm meeting an old friend at Odette's, and I thought I'd try to act more worldly than I really am by having a great wine waiting."

"What friend?"

"I don't think you know this one," he lied. "But I need an answer in a hurry. I don't want to be talking on the phone when he gets here." He glanced up and saw Kate gliding toward him. "Quick. My friend is coming."

"Try 'The Prisoner.' If they don't have that, try . . ."

Jacob disconnected, whipped the phone into his pocket, and rose to pull out a chair for Kate.

She wore a pair of light gray slacks, a turquoise sweater, and a multi-colored scarf with two silver chains draped over the scarf. A David Yurman bracelet hung from her wrist. He and Meg had caught his mother admiring a David Yurman bracelet once and saved their money for almost a year to buy one for her Christmas present only to discover they probably couldn't even afford the box the bracelet came in.

The waitress had followed Kate to the table. "Can I get you something to drink? The drink of the day is a green Bloody Mary."

"I'll have water and whatever kind of wine my companion here . . ." She motioned to Jacob, ". . . is about to choose. You're caressing that wine list like it's precious," she said to him, "So I assume you're ordering wine."

"Do you have a preference?"

"Whatever will make me forget. I'd like to think for a few minutes that what has happened is only a nightmare."

He ordered *The Prisoner, Blindfold White* thinking it might have been a good idea to first find out what it cost. It would be six weeks before he began his job, and four more after that before receiving a paycheck. He needed the money he'd saved from Africa to live on between now and then and for house repairs. And for a bed. But it was too late. The waitress was walking away.

So what did they talk about now? When Kate flitted her gaze at him and toyed with her knife, wiggling the blade from side to side with her forefinger, he decided she must be wondering the same thing. He leaned back and studied her. What would she be like separated from the Hunter name, a heritage of white sofas, and a murder in the family? At sixteen, he'd been beguiled and aroused by her lively expression and animated voice, the wiggle in her hips, the soft mounds of her breasts, the way she swiveled her eyes to look at him, searing him with flashes of heat. Ignoring her had been difficult.

"This place is one of my favorites," she said then, and they fell into polite, desultory conversation until the waitress reappeared, poured the wine, and rattled off the specials.

He watched Kate's face, her eyes minus their former sparkle, and missed most of the recitation, hearing only the occasional item—pasta with crab and asparagus, filet something-or-other, mushroom risotto. Kate ordered. He asked for the same and then realized he had no idea what she chose because he'd been too busy basking in her allure.

Talking became easier. He explained how he landed the job with INECE which had sent him through much of Asia and parts of Africa; how he came to be part of a team presenting a case at the International Court in The Hague; how he'd gotten a position with the Water and Air Resources Protection Agency and come back to live in Goose Bend.

Would he allow her to paint his pond, Kate wanted to know then.

"If you want to paint water surrounded by stubble and goose droppings, be my guest."

"I do." She looked down and began drawing circles on the tablecloth with her finger. "I've taken a leave of absence from school until this horrible thing is . . . ." A crash from a neighboring table stopped her. She turned to look at the glass shards and the puddle of water on the floor, and then raised her eyes to him. "Well then, I'll slip over one day with my paints. I won't disturb you."

He was about to say she wouldn't disturb him, but she changed the subject, and they fell once again into easy conversation, speaking of old acquaintances and why she remained in Goose Bend.

"I was offered a job at the high school," she said. "I tried living with Mom and Dad, but Mom turned up her nose when I wore my paint clothes to meals. *How can we enjoy our food, dear, when you smell like turpentine? Your nails need attention, dear. Wouldn't you like to have a manicure? Don't you want to look nice when Daddy comes home, dear,*" Kate mimicked. "Besides, she kept harping about me getting married. So I moved out."

The waitress appeared with their food. "Another bottle of wine?" she asked as she set dishes in front of them.

"We can have another bottle, can't we, Jacob?" Kate's cheeks were flushed.

"I like this. You chose well."

Jacob nodded, surprised that they had already drunk an entire bottle without his being aware of it, and hoping two bottles of 'The Prisoner' wouldn't gouge too much from his savings. Then he looked down at the food in front of him, happy to see they'd ordered the pasta dish.

He noticed that the man with the white eyebrows and his wife had risen and were preparing to leave. They nodded at him as though to say goodbye, but before he could respond, they turned their attention to Kate. Oblivious to their stares, Kate had begun eating as though famished. Finally, the man put his hand on his wife's elbow to guide her out, flashed another glance at Jacob, and then the pair left.

Kate lowered her fork to rest momentarily on the side of her plate. "This is the most I've eaten since . . .." She gave him an imploring look. "It's going to be alright, isn't it? Tell me it is, Jacob."

"It will be." But he wondered. Wrath and bitterness because of a failed marriage, and the affliction of having to live with Mr. Hunter, senior, might drive even a saint to lose his balance, and John was no saint.

"Tell me about Mrs. Petrowsky," he said, changing the subject.

"Why?"

"No particular reason. Except that she looked like a virago."

"Wow. Did they teach you that word in law school?"

"Yep, that was in . . .." he closed one eye and squinted the other. "Hmmmm. I think we learned about viragos in a course called 'Bitches that Sue.'"

"Right. I need more wine." She held her glass toward him. "Ama called her mother a bitch fairly often."

"They didn't get along?" He filled her glass. "Or was Mrs. Petrowsky actually nasty?" His hand was still around the bottle when, reaching for her glass, her hand brushed his. He tried to ignore the warm fluttering that pulsed through his fingers, up his arms, and down his torso. Jet lag wasn't hindering some things.

"I found her tolerable. But I didn't have to live with her. Josephine Petrowsky was so religious it was like swimming in a sea of righteousness when you were around her." She shuddered. "Whoops. Sorry. I keep forgetting I need to keep my mouth shut in a town full of Mennonites, Baptists, and Lutherans. Are you religious?"

"Mom and I fought big time when I was in junior high. She tried to make me dress up in good clothes for church. I wasn't about to. My friends wore jeans, so I wanted to wear jeans. The issue was resolved when I refused to go to church period. I didn't win many battles with my mother. That was one of my infrequent victories."

"Sooooo, you didn't really answer my question, but that's ok. It was rude of me to ask. Back to Josephine Petrowsky. She tried to control everything Ama did. For all I know, she decided when Ama and John had sex. Although sometimes I question how often that actually happened."

Jacob steepled his hands in prayer position and raised his eyes to the ceiling. "Lord, save me from such a mother-in-law." He brought his hands back to the table. "Surely, you jest."

"About the sex, yes. But then, what do I know?" She shrugged. "I never met Ama's father. He died before John and Ama married."

"You said the Petrowskys immigrated from Poland."

She nodded. "During the Iron Curtain era. Josephine and Tadek went through Hungary and escaped into Austria using the bridge at Andau. And if you're doing math in your head, yes, that made Josephine old when Ama was born—one of those menopause babies. Menopause baby. Menopause baby," she chanted, her voice rising. She burst out laughing then. "God, I'm getting silly. I'm not used to drinking this much. I bet this is the last time you invite me to dinner." She interlaced her fingers and stared at him, challenging him to answer. "That's ok," she said when he didn't respond. "I'll live. I lived when you shunned me for the prom. I really am being silly, aren't I? The prom. High school stuff." She leaned her chin on her hand. "But I'm curious. If you and Charlie hadn't come up with that hare-brained idea to get the senior boys to invite the senior girls instead of inviting outsiders, would you have invited me?"

"No."

"You didn't like me?"

He detected a flicker of hurt in her eyes. "It had nothing to do with that."

"Then what?"

"I didn't want to be a trophy date. You didn't like me; you just liked that I was co-captain of the football team."

Her mouth fell open in surprise, but she recovered quickly. "That's what you thought?" She studied him for a few moments. "How did you decide who would take which girl?"

"Poker game."

"You guys actually ran a poker game to choose which girls you'd invite?"

He related how they decided it didn't seem right for the guys to invite dates from Quakertown or Lansdale, or from the tenth grade, while leaving female classmates, most of whom they'd been in school with since first grade, sitting at home. Instead of drawing names from a hat, they chose a more fun way to decide who went with whom by playing poker. Several girls, after graduation, had confided their appreciation that all the girls got to go the prom, not just the pretty and popular ones.

"Well, that was noble, I guess," Kate said. "I wasn't so noble. I spent a lot of time trying to think of nasty things to do to you in revenge for humiliating me. But don't worry, the need for revenge has passed." She gave a little wave of her hand and then looked down and began picking at the tablecloth, pinching it into pleats. "Ama's mother made her miserable. John made her miserable. She grew up thinking she was going to be a famous ballerina, but instead, she married my brother." She sighed. "Josephine probably thought a man with money was a better bet than uncertain fame. Sort of like a bird in hand is better than two in the bush." She took a large gulp of wine and then tapped her glass against his. "You choose good wine, Jacob. Or did I say that already?"

Her cheeks were crimson and her eyes starting to glaze. Would she remember tomorrow what she said tonight? To keep her from finishing off the bottle, he filled his own glass almost to overflowing.

"Tell me more about the Petrowsky's." He brought his glass to his lips, inhaled the aroma, and then set the glass down without drinking.

"They smuggled two triptychs out of Poland. The Communists were destroying religious art, so priests tried to hide Church treasures. They had people smuggle things out of the country whenever they could." She raised her eyebrows. "Do you know what a triptych is?"

"Yes. Amazingly enough, I made an A in Art Appreciation." The instructor had talked about triptychs endlessly during the first part of the course, so he knew they consisted of three panels hinged together with paintings exciting enough to set you in orbit. Like the Virgin Mary, as ugly as sin, holding a stiff green baby painted by an artist who never went into the nursery to see what a real baby looked like. Disciples, with long faces. Jesus looking more like a Swedish accountant than a Jewish carpenter. He raised his eyebrows back at Kate. "I bet you thought a former quarterback didn't know anything about art."

She rounded her lips. "Ooooh, I'm so proud of you." She gave him a slap on the arm with her fingertips. "It sounds like a typical case of Art Appreciation 101 that missed the appreciation part. I'll have to give you a course in that sometime."

"Marvelous idea."

"Some triptychs are beautiful. Not to mention valuable." She reached for her wine and quaffed the remainder. When she drained the last drop, she held her glass toward him. "You're not drinking yours. Share." She spoke slowly, making an effort to enunciate.

Gently, he pushed her hand away. "Nope. I'm going to drink it all myself." He took a sip.

"You're a prick." She held up her empty glass, examining the way the light refracted through it.

"What happened to the triptychs?"

She shrugged. "I suppose they must still be in Josephine's house."

"Are they valuable?"

"No idea. Most of the old ones have some value; a few are very valuable." She sighed. "I'm tired. I want to go to bed."

She didn't comment when he guided her to his car instead of hers. She'd have to find someone to bring her back tomorrow to retrieve the Subaru, although from the looks of it she'd be lucky if someone stole it. She was too far gone to fasten her own seat belt, so he did it for her and then went around to the driver's side. When he opened the door, she murmured something.

"What did you say?"

Her cheek rested on the back of the seat, and he saw she was about to fall asleep. "John was in Doylestown Monday evening at the time of the murder. Ama asked him to meet her at the Cockle Burr Inn to negotiate." She yawned.

He slid in the car, closed the door, and touched her lightly on the arm. "Did anyone see him there?"

"Claude McGonigle knows he was in Doylestown." Her mouth barely moving, her words came slow and indistinct. "Claude is the director of the Reilly Foundation, in case you don't know. John does their books." She blinked, trying to keep her eyes open. "John met with Claude that afternoon. . . . Claude had a board meeting . . . . . in the evening. . . . ." Her eyes closed.

He waited a few moments and then touched her arm again.

She fluttered her lids. "John won't tell anyone that Claude McGonigle

He waited a few moments and then touched her arm again. She fluttered her lids. "John won't tell anyone that Claude McGonigle knows he was in Doylestown . . . . Don't know why." And then she was out.

Chapter Eighteen

Thursday, March 6

Jacob arrived as Laskey was inserting the key into the door of his Doylestown office.

"I see you didn't bring breakfast," Laskey said. "I thought you might have read my mind and come with offerings of bagels and sausages." He pushed open the door, flicked on the lights, and motioned Jacob inside. After pocketing his keys, he set a file folder that he'd been carrying under his arm down on his desk. "I'm starving. All I had in my pantry was pickles. Let's go next door to Danny's."

A GUST of warm air bearing the smells of bacon grease and onions gusted out as they entered the old train car which had been converted into a diner.

"It's about time you showed up, Mr. Detective," a buxom redhead called from behind the counter. She held two cups of coffee and had menus tucked under one arm. "Where've you been?"

"I've been busy detecting, Hilda. Where else?"

"We were wondering if you ever planned to show up again." She motioned with her head toward the far end of the diner. "Your highness's table is free." She set the coffee down in front of two customers seated at the counter

"Did you miss my big tips?" Laskey shot back as he and Jacob made their way toward the last booth.

"I had to cut my budget in half because you avoided us all last week. I'll be with you in a minute, Hon."

"How's Daisy Mae?" Laskey asked when they'd settled into the booth.

"Every time I leave the friggin' house, she gives me a pathetic look and mews like an orphan."

"She needs a playmate."

"Don't even think of it. One spoiled cat is enough."

Hilda came to lean against the booth on Laskey's side. "And who is this fine gentleman you have with you today?"

"My godson. You remember Jacob Gillis, don't you?"

"That little squirt you used to bring in here? Well, Jacob, like they say, you sure have growed up. So what do you guys want this morning? The special? Two eggs any style, scrapple, hash browns, toast?"

They ordered the special. "And coffee ASAP," Laskey added.

"You probably don't even have coffee in your cupboard, do you?" Jacob grinned. "I remember how it practically took a mule team to drag you to the grocery store."

"Too many choices. It's a pain to choose ketchup from seventeen different varieties."

Jacob leaned closer and, lowering his voice, said, "I found out a couple things."

"Which are?"

"Ama Hunter might have had something someone would want to steal, and John Hunter may have been here in Doylestown the night of the murder."

"*Might* and *may*?" Laskey narrowed his eyes. "How did you come by this information?"

"John's sister."

Hilda appeared with the coffee pot and two cups. "So, Laskey here has been telling me all about your adventures in Africa," she said to Jacob. "I guess that must have been really something. Did you see lots of animals?" She set the cups down and filled them.

"I did a few safaris, but seeing the mountain gorillas Dian Fossey tried to protect is at the top of my list of favorites."

"Wow. I'd like to sit down and hear all about it. Come back sometime when we're not so busy, you hear?" She thumped Laskey on the shoulder. "You can come back a little sooner, too, you old codger." She walked away.

When Laskey raised his eyebrows in a question, Jacob looked down and spooned sugar into his coffee. As much as he loved the man, he found Laskey's intense gaze daunting, as if he saw through all the layers down to where the truth lay, and right now the truth was that he'd lied about who he was with last night.

"John Hunter's sister was the friend you met in New Hope?" Laskey asked finally.

Watching the creamy brown swirls set in motion by his coffee spoon, Jacob nodded. He set the spoon down, lifted the cup and blew on it, even though the coffee probably wasn't that hot. Damn, why did he have to feel guilty over just one little avoidance of the truth? As soon as his eyes had popped open this morning, he realized seeing Kate had been a mistake. He set his cup down too abruptly, splashing coffee on the saucer. "Yes, I had dinner with Kate Hunter last night. She showed up at my house yesterday morning before you did."

Laskey stared at Jacob. "You and Kate Hunter were friends or . . .?"

"No," Jacob said quickly. "She was two years below me in school, and . . . . Well, I didn't really know her that well."

"So why did she show up at your house at that god-forsaken hour if you didn't know her *that* well?"

"They wanted me to be their spokesperson. She and John. They thought that would look better than hiring an attorney." He rubbed his fingers across his brow. "I declined rather abruptly. Actually, I was rude. She called me an asshole, and I guess I deserved it. I thought I should apologize, so I stopped by yesterday afternoon and somehow or other . . . Well . . . . I felt sorry for her. I'm not sure how it happened, but we wound up together for dinner."

Laskey furrowed his brow. "Tell me you don't plan on seeing her again until this is over."

"I don't plan to see her again before this case is over, and I don't plan to see her *after* it's over."

"What did Ama Hunter have that was worth stealing?" "Two triptychs."

"Triptychs?" Laskey's voice rose in surprise. The man seated at the counter nearby turned to look.

"Considering your background, I'm sure you know what a triptych is." Laskey had gone through a rigorous art course at the Barnes Foundation while he was an FBI agent consulting with the arts crime division of the Philadelphia Police. The Foundation, home of one of the world's greatest collections of impressionist, post-impressionist, and early modern paintings, also offered art history courses.

"Of course, I know what a bloody triptych is. But I expected you to say something like a piece of antique jewelry handed down from umpteen generations back, or a long, lost Vermeer from someone's attic, or the secret to eternal life. Where did she get triptychs?"

"Her parents smuggled them out of Poland when they escaped during the Communist regime. They belonged to one of the churches, and the priests were trying to rescue them from the Communists."

"Kate Hunter told you that?"

Jacob nodded.

Laskey sat quietly, absorbing the information. "And what about John being here in Doylestown Monday evening?" he asked finally.

Jacob was puzzled as he considered Kate's disclosure. It made no sense for her to come up with an alibi when her brother refused to. "She said John was supposed to meet Ama at the Cockle Burr Inn to negotiate a financial settlement."

"I guess John can say anything, can't he? He could claim he was in orbit around the moon. But can he prove it? Since he told me nothing, I have to assume he's lying to his sister, although I can't imagine why."

"She said Claude McGonigle from the Reilly Foundation followed John to Doylestown. McGonigle had a meeting there about the same time John headed in that direction."

"And did Claude McGonigle hang around to see if John was still in Doylestown during the time Ama was being murdered?"

"I'm just repeating what Kate told me."

Laskey shifted, rearranging himself in his seat and stretching his long legs into the aisle. "I'll check it out, but the theft of a valuable work of art from a dance studio in Goose Bend, Pennsylvania seems a bit far-fetched." He rubbed his hand across his chin. "That would make Inglehook happy, though. Imagine the mileage he'd get: *Former Member of New York City Ballet Murdered over Art Relics Smuggled from behind the Iron Curtain.* Maybe Inglehook could tie in a conspiracy involving John's former football teammates. He'd really have a show then."

AFTER BREAKFAST, Laskey strode in the direction of the library. No one would question his being there. Even with computers in every office, libraries still yielded useful information so people would simply assume he busied himself with research related to a case. And he *would* be working. There were just some things he preferred not to tell people. For instance, that he liked opera. Nor did he divulge that since the age of thirty-five he'd always had three cats. Never two, never one. Always three. He didn't tell people why he never married. The only person who knew that was the person he didn't marry. Certainly, he would never tell anyone his excellent record of solving crimes had been as much a result of intuition and instinct as of science. He knew perfectly well his instinct was nothing magical, but rather bits and pieces of knowledge that merged into a pattern after floating around his subconscious for a period of time. So far, his instinct hadn't kicked in on this case.

Ten minutes later, he ascended the marble steps of the library, concave from decades of traffic, and entered through double doors into the neon lit main room. He saluted Miss Berry at the check-out desk, winking at her as he passed. She peered at him from over her glasses, put her forefinger to her lips in a shushing signal, and smiled. It was an old joke between them—her shushing him. The joke was so old Laskey couldn't remember its origin.

He passed the computer terminals that had replaced the card catalog, turned right into the fiction stacks, went to the far side, and then made a left turn through nonfiction which brought him to a nook with a small table and two chairs.

He took off his jacket, threw it over a chair, pulled several books from a shelf, and stacked them on the table. Opening one, he placed it in front of where he was going to sit, and then he sat in the chair that he hadn't put his coat on, making it appear that both places were occupied in case someone decided to join him.

He sat down, stretched out his legs, and closed his eyes, resting his interlaced fingers on his stomach. The air was musty. But what did he expect? It was a library. He heard the squeak of a book cart in a nearby aisle and the clunk of books being re-shelved. The murmur of voices coming from the central reading room was barely audible, like something heard in a dream.

He directed his thoughts to the murder. Forensics had given him nothing, and no witnesses had come forward. He'd hoped to learn something from the four phone calls registered to Ama's phone and from the text to the same person. "Looking forward to seeing you soon," she'd texted.

Late yesterday afternoon, he'd gotten through to Marek Molnar, the recipient of the four phone calls from Ama as well as the text, but Molnar appeared to be genuinely surprised and distraught at Ama's death. He claimed to be in Argentina with his dance company. Prior to Argentina, they had performed in Bogota. Molnar admitted to speaking with Ama several times, adding that she seemed very down. They were old friends, he told Laskey, dancing together with The New York City Ballet until he formed his own company. When asked about the text, Molnar said he assumed she planned to attend a performance by his company the following month in Philadelphia. Janis, Laskey's assistant, was attempting to verify Molnar's presence in South America at the time of the murder. He'd also asked her to pull up a picture of him. He was guessing that Molnar was the dancer in Ama's photos.

Laskey opened his eyes. John Hunter's behavior puzzled him — the looks between brother and sister and John's refusal to give an alibi, but Kate's giving one in his stead, hare-brained as it was.

And why was Jacob being pulled in? Spokesperson? What an absurd idea. Or was it?

He thought he'd come to understand Jacob pretty well, but sometimes he didn't understand Jacob at all. He had stepped in after Jacob's father died, spending as much time with the boy as he could, taking him fishing, hiking in the Poconos, and to Phillies games. Once, they went to an ice hockey game, but the behavior of Philadelphia fans was so rude and crude that Laskey decided one time watching the Flyers was one time too many for an impressionable teen. Occasionally, he brought Jacob to his house for the weekend. Jacob had always talked freely to him. He supposed the boy was so starved for fatherly affection he saved up everything he wanted to say to a father for when they were together. When Jacob reached his teens, the topic of conversation included girls, and Jacob was evidently as hot-blooded as any other teenage boy, mentioning dozens. But never once did the name Kate Hunter cross his lips. Now suddenly she was visiting him early in the morning, and they were having dinner together.

He hoped Jacob didn't turn out to be as naïve as his father. George Gillis had been both brilliant and handsome. He never forgot a name, face, or fact. His blue eyes and wavy blonde hair, coupled with a perfectly symmetrical face always guaranteed the admiration of women which he never seemed to notice. He adored his wife and children, and they adored him. He'd been fun, always up for hiking, fishing, cross-country skiing, game-watching, or whatever. George had a passion for what he did, and for what he dreamed of doing. He'd been so sure he could show the country how to make a successful go of organic flower farming that he gave up a professorship at Penn State and was well on the way to achieving his dream when he died much too young. Unfortunately for his family, he'd invested his entire retirement in the business. He was also something of an artist. Not a traditional artist with paintbrushes or pens, but the way he patterned the swaths of flowers on the farm rivaled any painting by Van Gogh or Cezanne.

"Well, well, well," Miss Berry's voice interrupted his thoughts.

Laskey looked up to see her approaching from the 600's aisle, dangling her glasses in one hand.

"Solving crimes?" she asked.

"Trying to." He smiled up at her.

"*Hmmph.*" She reached down and picked up the book that lay open in front of him and read the title. "*The Fifty Most Convincing UFO Sightings.*" She shuffled the other books he'd pulled from the shelf, reading the titles. "I see you're boning up on UFO's. Let me guess: aliens came down from the planet Excanabalis, murdered the dance teacher in Goose Bend, and stole her toenails to carry back to their planet to help propagate a new species."

"You caught me. I thought if I sat here among your fine books, I'd be able to solve the mystery by imbibing the scent of old paper and dusty covers."

"Well, you never know. Just keep it quiet back here."

He watched her walk away. She hadn't been bad-looking before her hair turned the color of slate and her wings started to flutter. Not bad at all. He should have asked her out. He was sorry now, but that's how it was. He couldn't rewind time. If he could, the thing that had set him against women forever never would have happened in the first place.

But he was supposed to be solving a crime, not mourning his past or thinking about Jacob. He blew out a stream of air, leaned his chin on interlaced fingers, and tried to focus. Statistically, John stood a good chance of being indicted for murder, and Inglehook was drooling over the anticipated publicity. The special prosecutor was either an egotist or needed to satisfy some ambition. Laskey would hate to see Jacob do something to screw up Inglehook's plans for a big media event.

A shiver ran down his spine. Where had that thought come from? Jacob screwing up Inglehook's plans? What an absurd idea. Jacob was the closest thing he would ever have to a son and, like parents everywhere, he sometimes worried needlessly. Anyway, he needed to stop referring to him as a boy. "He's a grown man, you old fart," he mumbled. "A grown man."

"DID you verify Marek Molnar's presence in South America?" he asked Janis when he returned to the office. A petite brunette, fiftyish, with a heart-shaped face and a long, sharp nose, he had found his assistant consistently dependable when it came to tracking down details.

"He was there," she said. "A couple people are pissed with me for waking them up to find out. But do we care?"

"Not even a little."

"Marek Molnar directs the company and dances a couple lead rolls. He danced . . ." she checked her notes, ". . . . last Saturday in Bogota, and on Tuesday and Wednesday in Buenos Aires. He performed the role of the tiger in "Dragonetta," whatever that is. One contact referred to him as *that arrogant prick who heads up the company*. The theater manager in Bogota was fuming because a bunch of *bonita chicas* stormed Marek's dressing room after the show and left the backstage a shamble."

"Can you find me a picture of him? Anything else I need to know?"

"Marcus has a couple questions. He jotted them down and left them on your desk. Robert can't seem to find what he's looking for and wanted to ask your advice. And we're running out of office supplies." She held up a Precise V7 Rolling Pen. "This is our last pen."

"Fire off another letter to the purchasing department," he grumbled. "Do they think supplies grow on trees?"

He entered his office, closed the door, and went to stand by the window. The bit about the triptychs was interesting but not setting off any alarms. Technically, the triptychs belonged to the Catholic Church so perhaps the Petrowskys had handed them over as soon as they arrived in The United States. Even if they'd kept them, hoping to return them to the church in Poland someday, what were the chances they were worth much? If they were valuable, and if Ama meant to use them to raise cash, she would hardly have done it from her dance studio but would have gone to New York or Philadelphia. Of course, the improbable sometimes happened: an interested party knowing she had valuable works of art; her just happening to have them in her dance studio instead of locked away in a safe place; someone deciding to murder her instead of paying for them. Rats! Those scenarios were about as likely as his going to Mars for his next vacation or aliens from Excanabalis stealing Ama Hunter's toenails.

He pulled his car keys from his pocket. It was time to get back on the road actively pursuing a killer instead of hoping the answer would float into his brain. It would eventually, but meanwhile, he needed to scavenge for facts.

Chapter Nineteen

Laskey drove between the stone pillars flanking the entrance to The Reilly Foundation and then followed a forsythia-lined lane curving through a shallow forest. Typical of roads in Pennsylvania, the lane was pitted with holes as a result of the state's straddling the freeze-thaw line. He bumped along for half a mile before coming to a meadow. A few hundred yards beyond the meadow, he arrived at two buildings separated by a small parking area and brightened by the glare of sunshine more fitting for August than March. He pulled in beside a BMW, got out, and looked around at the headquarters of The Reilly Foundation.

Gordon Reilly, the never-married and childless owner of Reilly Pharmaceuticals until his death in a plane crash, had left his fortune for the establishment of a foundation providing aid to war orphans, designating his country estate, equidistant between Goose Bend and Doylestown, as headquarters. Like pretty much everyone else in Upper Bucks, Laskey knew the history of the organization. In the beginning, large amounts of cash had been funneled into Tanzania to aid refugee children from Rwanda and Burundi. Later, much of the money went to support orphans in Kosovo.

Reilly's old stone house stood off to the right of the parking area. To the left, the foundation offices were housed in a modern structure of stone, cypress, and glass, and surrounded by beautifully landscaped grounds—a far cry from the original offices in a refurbished barn which Laskey had visited a number of years ago for a charity event.

He followed a flagstone walkway to the entrance of the office building, pushed open the door, and walked into a wide foyer smelling of cedar and leather. There was no reception desk. Because of his yearly contributions, he received quarterly newsletters and knew the foundation had a director, an assistant, a couple secretaries, and several field workers. There was seldom reason for the public to be in the building, thus no reception desk.

He took a few steps farther into the hall. Except for his shoes squeaking on the dark brown Emperador marble, the building was so silent that silence itself became a sound. He took a deep breath, inhaling the scent of liberally spent money. A natural-wood table that he recognized as a Nakashima stretched along the left wall of the entrance hall. Brown leather sofas and chairs, carved mahogany accent tables, Chinese lacquer-ware, and paintings filled the room to his right. As soon as he was done with this case, he'd take the time to check what percentage of donations actually went to help orphans. Not that it would change anything other than bringing his own contributions to a halt. Ads enticing prospective donors were a constant presence in various periodicals as well as the occasional TV spot. "For twenty-five dollars a month," they said, "you can support a child like Henri." Or Mary, or Mohammed. Pictures of wide-eyed, sunken-cheeked children always accompanied the ads.

He let his fingers trail along the surface of the Nakashima table as he made his way toward where the foyer formed a T with a hallway. When he came to the juncture, he stopped, trying to decide which way to go.

A woman stepped into the hallway from a room off the right corridor. "Detective Laskey?" A little hefty around the waist, she had white hair cut in a blunt line and thin penciled brows.

"Yes." He went toward her. He had called beforehand, so McGonigle was expecting him.

She stepped back into the room, leaving Laskey to follow.

"If you'll have a seat, Mr. McGonigle will see you in a couple minutes. He's just finishing up . . . ." Her voice trailed off as she extended her palm toward a deep red leather chair.

Five minutes later, McGonigle entered with his hand out. "Welcome to The Reilly Foundation. Sorry to keep you waiting. I had to finish up . . . ."

"No problem." Laskey stood and shook his hand. "Thanks for seeing me. I just need a minute."

"Glad to be of service. Come on back." McGonigle gave a little "this way" nod of his head, indicating that Laskey should follow him. Slim and well-tailored in his Armani suit and Hermes silk tie, he led Laskey into the adjoining office and gestured for him to have a seat.

Laskey's gaze made a flying trip around the room taking in the burled wood paneling, the Aubusson carpet, the Chesterfield sofa upholstered in the same soft brown leather as the chair he was about to sit in. Despite sun flooding through the expanse of floor-to-ceiling windows which comprised an entire wall of the room, a museum lamp lit an oil painting on the wall behind McGonigle's desk.

Laskey sat down and focused on the director. It galled him to admit that this slick man, with a predilection for expensive things, was fairly good-looking. He appeared to be in his early forties, had a full head of sleek brown hair, grey-green eyes, and a suntan. It was bloody March, and the man had a suntan.

McGonigle settled back, propped an elbow on the arm of his chair, and waited for Laskey to speak.

"Is that a Walter Baum?" Laskey asked, pointing to the painting behind the desk. He knew it was a Walter Baum, but he couldn't resist flaunting to McGonigle that detectives aren't necessarily culturally challenged. Especially ones that spent a year in an art history class at the Barnes Foundation.

"Yes, it is." McGonigle turned to look behind him. "We like to support our Bucks County artists. Actually, along that line, we're having a gala here next month. We've invited every high school and college in the five-county area around Philadelphia to submit their best student work. There'll be a reception when the winners are announced. I have a local artist working on the posters and invitations. I expect to pick them up from her in a few more days. I'll make sure your name is on the invitation list." He paused, apparently waiting for a *thank you* from Laskey. When none was forthcoming, McGonigle pointed to the wall opposite him. "Back there is a Redfield," he said. "The sculpture on the bookcase is by Stella Burke, and the table in the entrance hall is a Nakashima original."

Laskey knew the price for one Nakashima table could support a few hundred children in Tanzania for a couple years. Hell, probably for a dozen years.

"We have several Ranulph Byes in various places in the building," McGonigle continued. "But enough of that." He waved his hand in dismissal. "I can give you a tour later if you have time. Meanwhile, you have questions for me." A half-smile on his lips, he propped his elbows on the chair arms and templed his hands.

"John Hunter was here late Monday afternoon?"

Laskey noted the almost imperceptible twitch on the director's lips as he reached for the humidor on the right-hand corner of his desk. McGonigle pulled the humidor toward him, withdrew a cigar, and held the cigar absently between his second and third fingers as his eyes drifted to the grounds beyond the glass wall. Then, as though suddenly remembering Laskey's presence, he slid the humidor toward his guest. "These are from the Dominican Republic. The finest available. Have one."

Diamond Crown Laskey read on the label as he helped himself to a cigar. He seldom had the opportunity to enjoy cigars of this caliber, so the meeting wasn't a total wash. He nipped off the end with the guillotine beside the humidor, lit the cigar, and puffed, eyeing McGonigle through a haze of cigar smoke. Was the distinguished director going to answer his question, or did he have to pull it out of him?

"No other cigar has a comparable flavor," McGonigle said, his gaze flitting back and forth between Laskey and points on the ceiling, the walls, the window.

Laskey kept his eyes glued to the director.

"Yes," McGonigle answered finally, tapping his cigar on the marble ashtray. "John Hunter was here Monday afternoon. He does the books for the foundation."

"How long was he here?"

"Until a quarter before seven. We walked out together. I had a board meeting in Doylestown at seven." With the fingers of his free hand, he tapped a persistent rhythm on the desk.

"You followed John to Doylestown?"

"No." His fingers stopped moving. "John said he was headed back to Goose Bend. To Ama's studio. They were going to try and resolve their issues."

The man was lying. Laskey could tell by the way his eyes shot off to the right and from the micro-twitch of his mouth. "He didn't tell you he was meeting her at the Cockle Burr in Doylestown?"

"Why would he meet her at that dump? No, he was quite specific. He was going back to Goose Bend."

Laskey could guess why McGonigle would lie about the person who did his books. Even a novice should be able to figure that out by looking around at this building and what it contained, or by adding up the cost of the director's clothes. Was John in on the financial mismanagement going on here? Kate, ignorant of the situation but knowing that John had been with McGonigle, had probably thought she was doing her brother a favor. Yet . . . Unless Hunter and Son Enterprises was in financial trouble why would John stoop to abetting embezzlement? Money for paying off Ama? But that didn't compute. If John was stock-piling his resources in order to pay off Ama, why murder her?

"That's all I needed to ask," he said, rising. Thank you for your time." Then as an afterthought, ". . . and for the cigar."

About to leave, he noticed two pink bags sitting along the wall behind McGonigle's desk, one with a picture of ballet slippers and the other with a dancer en pointe.

McGonigle's attempted laugh hinted at embarrassment as he shoved the bags underneath his desk. "They don't fit the décor," he said and coughed up another mirthless laugh. "They belong to my daughters." A veil of cigar smoke floated up to blur his face.

"Who do your daughters take dance lessons from?"

"Martha and Wendy have lessons from Ama Hunter. Or rather, they *did* have lessons from her. Terrible thing." He shook his head. "I wish we didn't have to explain matters like that to them, but if we hadn't, they'd have heard it from someone else. The whole gory shebang." He brushed invisible ashes from his lapel.

"You must drive them to their lessons since you have the bags here."

"Yes, when I can. There are so many evenings I have to be away. Sometimes I'm away for weeks. So when I'm here, I try to do that little family thing for my daughters, drop them off at their ballet class."

"How nice. Again, thanks for your time."

One thing he totally failed to understand, Laskey groused as he stood beside his car for one last puff of the very excellent Diamond Crown. In tiny towns, people were full to the brim with gossip, yet not a single soul in Goose Bend confessed to having seen John Hunter on Monday evening or to knowing where he was or what he was doing. Only McGonigle claimed to know the whereabouts of John—McGonigle, who lived elsewhere, and who was in Doylestown that evening. Or so he said.

He stubbed out the cigar on the pavement and, after sticking the remains in his jacket pocket for later, pulled out his phone and pressed Bump Herrington's number.

"Do you have anyone who isn't busy at the moment?" he asked.

"I can dig up someone," the police chief answered.

"I have a job for him. I want you to send him over to the Cockle Burr."

Chapter Twenty

The police officer entered the Cockle Burr Inn and, finding no one at the reception desk, walked down the hall to where the bar was located at the rear of the motel. A man in a security uniform was sitting at the bar, nursing a mug half-filled with beer even though it was only mid-morning. Someone in the back was doing something that involved a lot of clinking, clanking, and plopping things down on hard surfaces.

"You the night watchman?" the police officer asked.

"What does it look like?" The watchman patted the insignia on his uniform.

"You check the parking lot every night?"

"That's what they hire me for." He wiped away his beer mustache with his coat sleeve.

"Did you see a silver Lexus ISF out there last Tuesday?"

"How come?" Looking at the officer sideways, the night watchman took a swig of beer.

"Murder investigation."

The watchman's eyes widened. "The one in Goose Bend? Did the husband do it? The paper said it didn't look like no robbery."

"That doesn't mean it was the husband."

"Boyfriend?"

"I'm not at liberty to discuss the investigation. Do you recall seeing a silver Lexus?"

"Well, buddy, I don't remember seeing no Lexus out there, and if it were one of those big fancy ones I would of noticed. Want a beer?"

"I'm on duty."

"I won't tell."

"Guess I better not. Do you have security cameras out there?"

"You kidding? This place can barely keep the toilets in order much less buy security cameras."

The officer reached in his pocket for a card and handed it to the watchman. "In case you remember seeing a Lexus."

"I won't, because there wasn't one."

"John Hunter's Lexus wasn't at the Cockle Burr Monday evening," the officer said into Bump's answering machine a few minutes later. Then he left the same message for Laskey. He supposed both were too busy to answer their phones.

Chapter Twenty-One

Friday, March 7

The wind keened around the corner of the house, waking Jacob. Groaning, he pulled the blankets around his ears trying to shut out the high-pitched scream. A loose shutter on one of the upstairs windows hammered against the stone walls and, from the direction of the pond, the din of geese suggested an altercation of some sort. He wished they'd choose a different venue for their persistent hwaaaanking. Jet lag and murder created an infallible formula for fatigue, and it didn't help that he hadn't run in two weeks. His last few days in Rwanda had been consumed with packing and saying good-by, so the habit begun in high school of rising early for a daily sprint had gone by the wayside.

But like it or not, he had to rise and shine. The funeral began at ten. He blew out a white cloud of breath and threw back the bedclothes. Shivering, he grabbed jeans from the back of a chair, stepped into them, pulled on a T-shirt, and then a brown and black flannel shirt that had been his dad's. As he slipped into his shoes, he glanced out the window to see a gloomy dome of sky settling over the fields and tree branches whipping in a frenzy.

He ate breakfast—a mug of coffee and a fried egg plopped on a piece of toast—while roaming around the house, checking to see what he needed to do before tomorrow's onslaught. Mom, Meg, and Aunt Zuela planned to come first thing with mops, brooms, scouring pads, as well as man-bashing jokes, which he'd learned to take with good-humor. They'd have him fetching and carrying and reaching corners they couldn't reach. They'd ferret out the last traces of dog stench and kill the mold which he still occasionally caught a whiff of in spite of leaving the windows open and freezing his ass off. The smell of soot around the fireplace was enough to choke a lesser mortal, and the odor of lard seeped from cracks and crevices around the stove. They'd fix all that. Was there any army anywhere that attacked with the same ferocity as mothers, sisters, and aunts on the rampage against dirt and stench?

His mother had dictated a shopping list which he planned to take care of after the funeral. Stone cleaner, furniture polish, Murphy's Oil Soap. That much he remembered. The other things on the list . . .. Well, they were on the list. Odor-wise, by tomorrow night he'd have a new house.

His roaming brought him to the mudroom. He set his mug on the floor and crouched beside Daisy Mae who sat on her haunches swiping at a spider web blowing up from the heat vent. "You don't want to get tangled up in that," he said, lifting the kitten away. He wiped her paw, and then ran his hand across the vent, brushing away the remaining web.

"Damn vents got me in trouble once," he said, stroking her neck. Laskey wasn't so crazy after all; it was good to have a creature to talk to. Especially one who purred her agreement with everything he said. If only he could find a woman who did the same. He unfolded himself to sit flat on the floor. Cradling Daisy Mae in his lap, he reached for his coffee.

"I hated that damn Cape Cod," he said to the kitten. He'd been angry at having to leave the flower farm, his tree house, woods where he roamed freely, the spaces between rows of flowers that he used as his private race track, the near-by river that lay in wait for his fishing line. Mainly, he'd been angry with his father for dying.

Shortly after they moved into town, anger still curdling his insides and the hunger to commit mischief in retaliation for his misery eating away at him, he'd snitched a five pound bag of flour from the kitchen. He filled the heating vents, cleaning up the tell-tale sprinkling of white around each with a sponge. A few days later, the temperature dropped. That evening, Meg sat at one end of the sofa, legs curled under her, geography book on her lap. The book was opened to a map as she tried to memorize the rivers of Europe. "Volga, Dnieper, Volga, Dnieper," she repeated, jabbing her finger alternately at Russia and then the Ukraine. His mother, busy grading papers, reclined on the other end of the sofa, sometimes holding a paper up to the lamp beside her to better decipher student scrawls. She let out a little huff each time she finished scoring a failing paper.

Jacob sat at the dining room table where his mother had condemned him to do his homework. "When you show that you can otherwise concentrate, you can sit on the sofa, too," she told him. Due to the small size of the rooms, the dining table stood about twelve feet from the sofa and, thanks to an arch between the two rooms, his mother could see everything he did as well as the things he didn't do. Actually, she didn't see everything. Jacob pretended to study spelling, but instead read a *Magnus Robot Fighter* comic book concealed in his spelling book, murmuring the dialog in the frames instead of spelling out words.

Meg complained of the cold. His mother, agreeing that it appeared to be getting colder, went to her bedroom and came back wrapped in a pink angora housecoat, a gift from Jacob's father the previous Christmas. She suggested that Meg might also want to put on a housecoat or a sweater. Jacob, eyes frozen to a frame where Magnus Robot rescues Leeja from the grasp of a Pol-Rob, stopped muttering and waited. Meg, not wanting to bother going to her bedroom, continued to complain.

"Alright," his mother said finally, looking up from her grading. "Turn on the heat. But let's try to keep the temperature turned down. Philadelphia Electric bills are extortionate." She went back to running her red marker through incorrect answers.

Meg went to the thermostat and flipped the switch. As the heater fan roared on, clouds of white shot into the air. Jacob's breath came out in little snorts, and his stomach convulsed as he struggled to keep from breaking into full-scale laughter. From the corners of his eyes, he watched his mother and Meg staring open-mouthed at the snow storm.

It hadn't taken his mother long to figure it out. His silent laughing. The flour-smeared sponge hidden beneath the kitchen sink. During the two days of scrubbing, dusting, and vacuuming it took him to eradicate the last molecule of flour from furniture, floors, books, and blinds, his mother glared at him, her lips drawn as tight as a fishing line weighted down by a ten pounder.

Daisy Mae rubbed against his arm, purring, jolting him back to the present. "Sorry, but I have to leave you alone again today." What he wanted more than anything was to have an uninterrupted Friday at home. There were hinges to tighten, peeling wall paper to remove, creaky floorboards to map out for a carpenter, and a loose shutter to batten down. Then he wanted to meander down to the river for a few minutes and wet his fishing line. Instead, he had to pick up Aunt Zuela and put in an appearance at a funeral.

———

LASKEY PARKED his Sequoia behind a van with "Springside Florist" painted on the side. The hearse was parked on the opposite side of the street from St. Martin's, presumably so that it would be headed in the right direction after the funeral. The service didn't begin for another hour and a half, but Laskey wanted to observe people as they arrived. Other than the two men who lugged flowers from the van into the sanctuary, no one else appeared to be around. He expected the crowd to start trickling in around nine-thirty.

He got out of the SUV, went around to the passenger side, and slipped into the front seat where he had room to prop his laptop on his knees. He logged on. He'd learned little about triptychs during his course at the Barnes Foundation other than that they were the popular standard format for altar paintings from the Middle Ages onwards, and sometimes painted by such artists as Memling, Giotto, Hieronymus Bosch, Rubens, and Van Der Goes. A triptych by one of these artists would be valuable, but he'd bet a year's salary the ones the Petrowskys brought to America were by a second or third-rate artist.

He typed "triptychs at auction" in the search line. While he waited for the information, he looked up and saw that a police car had parked in front of the hearse. Two officers got out and began placing orange cones a few feet behind the hearse, blocking off enough space for the casket to be lifted into the back after the funeral.

A group of five women, their skirts flapping in the wind, clattered past him heading toward the front doors of the church, two carrying cakes, the other three transporting food containers of assorted sizes. Reception, afterwards, Laskey assumed. Meet, greet, and eat with the mourning family.

When he looked back down at the computer screen, he was surprised. "Damn," he said. "Who would have thought?" In 1969 a Francis Bacon triptych, *Three Studies of Lucian Freud,* had sold at auction for $142.4 million, and in May of 2015, Picasso's *Les Femme d'Algers* sold for $179.4 million.

He typed "Polish triptychs" into the search line. A series of pictures came up, the photos showing large altar piece triptychs, some still in churches, others in museums. Next, he searched for "Polish triptych artists," and a list of a couple hundred artists with unpronounceable names popped up. He recognized none of them.

Sighing, he shut down the computer. Without seeing them, there was no way to know if the triptychs Ama's parents had smuggled into the country were valuable.

Chapter Twenty-Two

"You look glum," Aunt Zuela said, slipping into the passenger seat of Jacob's Rav4.

"It's a funeral. I'm supposed to look glum."

"Not until you get there. Did your order this dismal weather for the occasion?"

"I did. I talked to that sexy babe on Channel 22 weather news and asked her to arrange some funereal conditions."

"Well, let's go get this over with." She fastened her seat belt. "We might have been better off walking. I bet there's not a parking place anywhere near St. Martin's."

She was right. Cars lined the streets for blocks around. By the time they found a spot and walked to the church, a bottleneck had formed at the door. They pushed their way into the crowd entering the vestibule and snailed their way into the sanctuary where a panoply of wreaths arced across the front, filling the church with a banquet of fragrances.

"Shit, it's an open casket."

"Watch your language, Aunt Zuela; we're at a funeral." Jacob cringed at the idea of viewing the dead, but was glad he had Aunt Zuela to lighten the atmosphere with irreverence.

"I hate open caskets." She said.

"So, do I. We can skip the viewing part."

They inched down the aisle until they found two seats near the front. This was the first time since high school graduation he'd been part of a crowd in Goose Bend, and he couldn't resist looking around, searching out old friends, classmates, neighbors. He caught a glimpse of the man with white, sprouting eyebrows he'd seen at Odette's, but still couldn't place him.

When the congregation lapsed into sudden silence, Aunt Zuela nudged him. "I see Mr. and Mrs. Hunter made it back from their cruise," she said.

Jacob looked around to see the Hunters walking down the aisle, eyes straight ahead, faces expressionless, mother and daughter leading the way followed by John Jr. and John Sr, arms clamped unnaturally to their sides. They lined up in front of the casket, John and Kate in the middle, the parents at each end, the four inclining their heads simultaneously, as though having rehearsed the gesture.

The perfect family. But this time the tire had blown out a long way from the service station, Jacob mused, recalling Aunt Zuela's reference. He would love to know what was going through their heads as they stood there together, isolated, feelings masked.

John and Kate had gotten their mother's dark hair and flawless complexion, but fortunately not her disposition. A bony woman with overly bright eyes and the nervous gestures of a frightened bird, Jacob had the notion she nibbled on celery for breakfast, carrots for lunch, and grilled fish for dinner. Mr. Hunter, ruddy-complexioned, puffy, and with a look of having been in the sun too long, didn't look like he fit with his family.

After an appropriate number of moments, the Hunters claimed their places in the front pew. The priest stepped closer to the pulpit, held up his hand for prayer, and was in the process of bowing his head when a ripple of sound began making its way row by row, from the back to the front. Whispers. Scuffling feet. Rattling programs. Jacob turned, craning to see.

"Good lord, why did they bring that woman?" Aunt Zuela hissed. "She probably hasn't a clue what's going on."

He recognized Mrs. Petrowsky from Kate's portrait. Ama's mother sat in a wheel chair, gazing about with a puzzled look as a tall, thin woman rolled her toward the altar. The thin woman, ramrod stiff, and wearing a black felt hat over tightly permed gray curls, focused on the casket ahead as they made their way down the aisle. A young man, looking to be in his early thirties and cursed with a mop of untamed dark hair, traipsed along behind, fixing his attention on the maroon aisle runner and dragging his feet. I'm not the only reluctant one here, Jacob thought. When they came to where the casket rested on the bier, the young man stood by, looking useless and out of place.

Jacob stole a glance at Aunt Zuela. Even *she* barely breathed in the stark silence enshrouding the congregation as the thin woman bent to engage the brake on the wheelchair and then moved around to help her ward stand. A rosary that had been draped across Mrs. Petrowsky's lap fell clattering to the floor, jarring the silence.

Mrs. Petrowsky looked around in confusion until the thin woman put one arm around her shoulders and with the opposite hand directed the mother's attention to her dead daughter. Jacob held his breath as Josephine Petrowsky examined the body.

Suddenly, Mrs. Petrowsky wrenched her arm from her companion's grasp and aimed an arthritic hand at the figure in the casket. *"Jest Charla,"* she cried out in a cracked voice. Then again, her voice rising, *"Jest, Charla."*

Chapter Twenty-Three

"I never witnessed anything like that in all my sixty-five years," Aunt Zuela said as she brushed the crossword section of the paper off her favorite chair and plopped down. Jacob and Charlie had trailed along behind her into the living room. "What a scene. Emergency technicians carting that woman away in an ambulance. Who decided to bring her, anyway? Inez Winters, I guess. Good god, I have a headache. Jacob . . ., do you mind?"

He scurried to the kitchen, searched cabinets until he found a bottle of Tylenol, and then grabbed a glass. While he waited for ice from the ice-maker to clunk into the glass, he puzzled over Mrs. Petrowsky's outburst. Most of those he talked to after the service thought her to be crazy, but he wondered. She seemed to know exactly what she was saying. The riddle of the murder had begun to nip at his heels, and he imagined the labyrinth of possibilities.

As he filled the glass with water, a sudden gust of wind whistled around the corner of the house, grabbed hold of the branch of a Japanese magnolia, and knocked it a few times against the window. By the time he returned to the living room, the wind had died. Charlie sat quietly, watching something, or nothing, through the window, his mind seemingly elsewhere. Aunt Zuela, unable to sit still, patted her thighs impatiently.

"Tell me again the name of the woman who wheeled Mrs. Petrowsky in," Jacob said, handing her the tablet and the water.

"Inez Winters." She slipped off her shoes as she took the glass. "And that Neanderthal following her was her son. She's another one of those crazy people that escaped from Poland with the Petrowskys."

"Why do you call them crazy?" He sat down.

"Well, you saw them." She tossed the Tylenol in her mouth.

"How many crazy people escaped with them from Poland?"

Ignoring him, she took a long drink of water.

"What the devil are you two talking about?" Charlie asked, snapping out of his reverie.

"Ama's parents escaped from behind the Iron Curtain," Jacob answered. "I'll tell you the . . . ."

"What was she saying anyway?" Aunt Zuela interrupted. "*Jest Charla!*"

"You're the language expert." He looked at Charlie. "Wasn't she always the expert? Remember how she used to quote the history of word origins to us from the OED?"

"How can I forget?" He loosened his tie. "So, Aunt Zuela, what do you think? Was it gobbledygook or Polish?"

"Knowing French and German and being able to quote from the Oxford English Dictionary hardly makes me a language expert. I guess you two are hungry?"

"Starving," they answered in unison.

"Well, then, let's move this party to the kitchen."

In the kitchen, she lifted the lid of the crockpot and stirred. "Hope you boys don't mind barbecued beef sandwiches."

"Right," Charlie said, taking the seat he always occupied when he came with Jacob. "How many times did we beg you to make those for us?"

"Best I remember, about twice a week you'd come here and ask for them. Jacob, make yourself useful and find something for the two of you to drink."

He opened the refrigerator and looked inside. "Want a coke, Charlie?"

About to dish barbecue onto buns, Aunt Zuela stopped and studied Charlie. "What are you so glum about? The funeral's over."

"I'm not glum."

"Of course, you're glum," Jacob said, handing him a coke. "She isn't the only one who's noticed."

"Well, for Pete's sake, we were just at a funeral, and our former buddy could have murdered her."

"You think that?"

Charlie shrugged. "No. But that doesn't mean he didn't."

"He didn't." Zuela went back to piling beef on buns.

"How do you know?" Charlie asked.

"I already told Jacob why; John Hunter doesn't have the balls."

"Well, then, I can relax on that score," Charlie said. "But in your vast knowledge of human nature, what do you know about that asshole Inglehook? He's enough to make the sun cry."

"Who's Inglehook?" She added chips and pickles to the plates.

"Jacob didn't tell you?"

"I haven't met him yet," Jacob reminded Charlie.

"Inglehook is the special prosecutor assigned to prosecute whoever they arrest for this murder," Charlie explained. "Assuming they ever figure it out. But Inglehook has already decided John Hunter is the guilty party." Frowning, he wiggled the blade of his knife back and forth. "But I'm going to shut up about the asshole; I don't want to spoil a good lunch." He gave a dismissive wave.

"Is Inglehook married?" Aunt Zuela set the filled plates on the table.

Charlie looked at her in surprise. "What's that got to do with it?"

"Nothing. Just wondering."

"You don't want him." Charlie picked up his sandwich and took a bite. "*Nobody* makes barbecue beef like you do, Aunt Zuela."

"Don't talk with your mouth full, and I've already planned to give you left-overs to take home, so you don't have to flatter me."

"Do I get any leftovers?" Jacob, starved after a breakfast of nothing more than toast and egg, grabbed his sandwich.

"That's what we're having for lunch tomorrow. I'll bet you hadn't even thought of feeding us while we're cleaning and spiffing for you."

"Whoops, I guess I hadn't."

"And neither of you answered my question. Is Inglehook married?" She shifted her eyes from one to the other.

"I believe he is," Charlie answered. "Besides, you wouldn't want to wake up to his 'good morning' every day. He has a nauseating nasal voice."

She took a sip of tea and turned to Jacob. "How come Laskey isn't married?"

"Don't know." He reached for his Coke.

"Is he gay?"

"*Noooo.*" Jacob made a face. The idea of anyone thinking Laskey was gay was laughable.

"If he's not gay, why isn't he interested in women?"

He spread his hands in an I-don't-know gesture. "He just isn't. Maybe he's shy. Maybe he's a misogynist." Judging from the way waitresses fawned over him, Jacob didn't think Laskey disliked women too much.

"Well, I always thought he was a nice man. He's not bad look-ing, either."

"It sounds like you're interested," Charlie said. "Even though you always told us you'd never marry again after . . . ."

". . . after my husband ran off with the charming coed. No, I'll never again do another man's laundry or share my closet. I was just asking, that's all."

Chapter Twenty-Four

Saturday, March 8

Faithful Care Nursing Home stood at the west end of Goose Bend just inside the town limits sign. Laskey leaned against the wall outside Mrs. Petrowsky's room waiting for the attendant to leave. Inez Winters, sitting ramrod straight, had parked herself in a bedside chair, hands crossed in lap, and was watching the attendant fasten a blood pressure cuff around the sleeping Mrs. Petrowsky's arm.

Earlier, he had gone to Mrs. Winter's house and found her son, Pavel, in the front yard fiddling with an old Mazda.

"My mother is over at the nursing home," Pavel told him.

"Didn't they take Mrs. Petrowsky to the hospital after the funeral?"

"Yep. Then they brought her back." Pavel grunted and tried to twist the screwdriver around a lug inside the carburetor.

"So, it sounds like she's ok."

Pavel kept tinkering.

"Where were you the night of the murder?"

Pavel froze. After a few seconds, he withdrew his arm from the engine and turned to glare at Laskey. Then, drawing back his shoulders, he straightened and stretched himself to his full height. "I was home with my mother."

"So you were both here?"

"I was working on the car. Ask the neighbors. They seen me. Mom was inside watching television."

Motives jumped out and surprised him sometimes, Laskey thought as he waited for the attendant to finish with Mrs. Petrowsky, but he could think of no inducement for either Pavel or his mother to murder Ama Hunter.

The attendant removed the blood pressure cuff, rolled up the band, and after a remark to Mrs. Winters, left the room, nodding to him as she passed.

He stepped inside. "I'm Detective William Laskey." He held his ID out for Mrs. Winters to see and then glanced at the sleeping form of Josephine Petrowsky. "I'm told you're her oldest friend."

"We came to this country together."

"From Poland?"

"Yes. Why are you asking?"

"I understand the Petrowskys smuggled out a couple pieces of religious art."

"They didn't do anything wrong." She sounded alarmed. "Tadik's uncle . . . Tadik was Josephine's husband, and his uncle was a priest . . . gave them some things from one of the churches to save from the Communists."

"Does Mrs. Petrowsky still have them?"

"I don't know. She might. She has lots of stuff. Why?"

Laskey walked over to the window and leaned one shoulder against it. "Did Ama have enemies?"

"I don't think so."

He studied Mrs. Winter's face, deciding the look she was giving him was one of bewilderment. "Who were her friends?"

She looked at him blankly.

"Can you think of anyone who would have killed her?"

She drew in a deep breath and let it out in a whoosh. "One of those deadbeats at the hotel."

She said it with such certainty that he wondered if her look hadn't been one of bewilderment after all, but rather something else. "Where were you the evening of the murder?"

She looked surprised. "Why . . ., I was at home." Her hand flew to her neck.

"And your son, where was he?"

"You don't have no right to ask where he was. He has nothing to do with this horrible mess."

"I'm sure he doesn't. That's why I'm asking. To rule him out. It's a question everyone close to Ama gets asked."

"He was working on a car, and then he went to Quakertown to get some parts. He was home before eight. That's when *The Voice* comes on, and I heard him out there banging away while I was watching it."

Laskey looked down at the floor. Between 8:00, or shortly thereafter when Ama's last student left, and approximately 9:00 when Bump found the body, someone slipped up to Ama Hunter's dance studio, shot her, and vanished without a trace. People tended to remember where they were when a significant death occurred, yet either Pavel had forgotten where he was, or his mother had forgotten.

Chapter Twenty-Five

Jacob scrubbed mildew from tile grout at one end of the bathtub while his mother sanded rust from the water fixture at the other end.

"I guess you saw lots of old friends yesterday at the funeral," she said.

She often made this kind of remark, not technically a question but a statement requiring a response.

"Yep, I did. And it seems no one has decided to run me out of town." He scrubbed vigorously at a stubborn spot of black. Downstairs, Meg and Aunt Zuela scoured the insides of cupboards. The odor of Murphy's Oil Soap floated up from the kitchen to blend with the upstairs smells of Ajax, Barkeeper's Helper, and Clorox Antibacterial Cleanser.

"You still blame yourself for the fire." She stopped sanding and looked at him, squinting against the sunlight blasting full strength through the window.

"Of course, I do. It was my fault. Who else do I blame?"

"It was an accident."

"An accident that wouldn't have happened if Charlie and I

hadn't been sneaking around doing what we weren't supposed to be doing."

"Get over it. You have to forgive yourself."

"Have you forgiven Uncle Willard for not reimbursing us for Dad's improvements to the farm? He got a shitload of money when he sold the place to that developer, but he didn't give you one cent." He didn't detest too many people, but Willard Bottom, who had been married to Dad's sister before she died, was one.

His mother tore a new piece of sandpaper from the sheet and, frowning, rubbed at the spigot. She wasn't frowning at the spigot, Jacob knew. She'd been careful not to criticize Uncle Willard in front of him and Meg, but they both knew she felt the same way about the man as they did.

Dad had contracted with Uncle Willard for the use of a few acres of his farm on which to operate a flower farm, as well as for a house on the property which had stood empty for a couple years. Uncle Willard would receive a percentage of the profits from the business in return for the use of the land and house. Jacob steamed every time he remembered that his dad had cashed in his retirement fund and invested the money in greenhouses, seeds, organic fertilizer, a tractor and other needed equipment, and that Uncle Willard had taken it all when Dad died. A few years later Uncle Willard sold the farm to a developer without reimbursing Jacob's mother for any of the expenditures from which he profited.

"You haven't forgiven Uncle Willard either, have you?" Jacob asked, raising his eyebrows at her.

"No." She smiled and gave him a playful pat on the cheek. "So, we're both imperfect people." She sat down on the edge of the tub. "I resented the money at first, but it was his ignoring you that I can't forgive. Had things been reversed . . . .. had it been Uncle Willard who died, your father would have stepped in and tried to be a father to his children. Not once did Willard offer to spend time with you. He never took you to a movie, or fishing, or came to your events at school."

"If it makes you feel any better, I didn't want to go fishing with

Uncle Willard. Or wherever else he might have offered to take me. Besides, I had Laskey, and I liked him a whole lot better."

She sighed. "We all have something to forgive, don't we?"

"You just admitted you haven't forgiven him."

"Right now, I'm talking about forgiving yourself."

Jacob felt his face grow warm. "You really think it's that easy? I screwed up big time."

"Forgiveness isn't saying what you did was right. It means you accept what happened as something that can't be changed, and move on."

"Have I not moved on?"

"I'm guessing you have a ways to go yet." She patted him on the knee. "It used to tear me apart when I saw you hang your head every time the word "fire" came up."

"Mom, you have no idea what it's like to grow up with a reputation."

She squeezed his hand and they sat quietly for a few moments.

"It's terrible, isn't it?" she said at length. "I feel so sorry for the Hunters. You don't think John . . . ."

"No, of course not. There was a lot of bitterness in that family. Between John and Ama. Between Ama and her mother. But I don't think he did it. And you're right about forgiveness. When you can't forgive it eats a hole in you, doesn't it?"

She nodded.

"There's something I always wanted to ask you." He cocked his head sideways at her.

"And that is?"

"Did you move to Carlisle to get away from your reputation as mother of the infamous town arsonist?"

She laughed. "I moved to Carlisle because I thought teaching college students wouldn't be as exhausting as teaching high school kids. But see, I'm right: you're still agonizing over what you did. To use your term: suck it up and get over it. Come on, let's get back to work."

HIS CLEANING CREW left late in the afternoon in a flurry of *Good-byes, See you soons* and summonses for Sunday dinner. The smell of fresh wax and furniture polish had banished the odors of dog, soot, lard, and mold, and the view of pond and woods gleamed razor sharp through newly washed windows. Daisy Mae wandered into the kitchen and brushed against his legs as he savored the view.

A few minutes later, not wanting to mess up his immaculate kitchen by cooking, he was sitting beside his cold fireplace with a *National Geographic*, debating running out to The Silver Spoon for supper, maybe calling Laskey to join him, when he heard a vehicle screech to a stop behind his house. He got to the window in time to see Kate slam the door of her green Subaru with a vengeance and then storm toward his back steps.

"I hate you," she lashed out when he opened the door to her banging. She pushed past, giving him a slight shove, and then turned to glare at him. "You're working for the District Attorney's office. You couldn't tell me that, could you? I had to learn it from that detective. You let me believe you were going to be doing some big deal job with that environmental agency. Hah!"

"I'm helping Charlie with the research for a pollution case. I'm not . . ."

"And they sent you to see what you could find out. You sneak!"

"No, they . . ."

"And now that detective, that . . . . ."

"Laskey."

"Yes, him. He's asking me questions. He . . ."

"Stop." He grabbed her shoulder. "I'm not a spy. I'm helping Charlie with a river pollution case which has nothing to do with anything else."

"You're lying." She brushed away his hand. "You had plenty of opportunities to tell me, but you didn't." Red spots the size of silver dollars burned on her cheeks.

"No, Kate, I'm not lying." A feeling of defeat washed over him. "But believe whatever you like." He turned his back to her, inhaled slowly, and then let the breath out in a long, shaky stream. He wished their paths had never crossed. He understood that having a family member murdered and half the town wondering if another family member did it, would drive a saint to both wrath and insanity, but she was unjustly aiming her anger at him. He had no intention of being her victim. The Hunters—not the brother, certainly not the sister, not even the father—had barely crossed his mind since high school graduation. Not until he moved back to Goose Bend. He could probably safely say they never thought of him either until now when they wanted to use him. He'd have nothing else to do with her. Or John. Guilty or innocent.

"Kate . . .," he said, turning around and lifting his chin so that he looked at her simmering face from beneath lowered lids, " . . . I'm doing research for Charlie as a personal favor, and because it's a case I'm interested in, and because it's one that affects the town." He heard the chill in his voice. The utter coldness. "There, I've told you. If I failed to do so before, I apologize. In five weeks I begin a job with WARFA. And yes, it's a big deal for me. If there were any way for me to make this go away for you and John, I would. Other than wishing that, I can't do anything about it. I think you need to leave now." His heart pounding, he held the door open for her. Scorching him with her glare, she took a quick breath, and then marched past him. Heart racing, he closed the door behind her and leaned against it until he heard the sound of her car rounding the side of the house and then shooting down the lane back to the main road.

Chapter Twenty-Six

Monday, March 10

A ten-minute break, that's all Bump Herrington was allowing himself, and yet he was already on his third cup of coffee at the Pennston Hotel. He'd guzzled the first two in less than four minutes, leaving him six in which to dawdle a bit with the third. Ten minutes, when he needed about three years. His effort to stave off the notion that the son of his long-time friend might have murdered his wife, had pushed his nerves way beyond frazzled. He wasn't sleeping. He was sweating like a stevedore. When he managed to eat, it was on the run, chomping at a sandwich or a chicken leg, leaving a path of crumbs and bending over double from acid reflux.

Cradling the mug in his hands and letting his nose bathe in the steam rising from whatever cheap brand they brewed at the hotel bar, he heard the door behind him swing open and someone step inside. A gust of noise blew in from the street. Voices. Traffic. A baby screaming. Used to, at any given time you hardly found more than ten people out there. Now the block crawled with everybody and his brother. He reckoned Lacy's Mercantile must be the top tourist attraction in the county right now. People, pretending to have an errand on Main Street, parked blocks away just so they could stroll past Lacy's and steal a glimpse at the "Miss Ama's Dance Studio" sign over the door after which they took a few minutes to stare at the upstairs windows. What they thought they might see mystified him.

But the ones that got to him, *reallllly* got to him, were the reporters.

He was downing the last few sips of coffee, when his nose alerted him that Jimmy Q had crept up behind.

"He's out there," Jimmy Q hissed.

Bump twisted around to face the old man. "Who's out there?"

"That man I seen sittin' on the bench that night."

Bump jumped up, threw two dollars on the counter, and bolted out the door.

"Where?" Bump looked up and down the street.

Jimmy Q, slower footed than Bump and just emerging from the bar, wrinkled his brow. "Well . . . ., he *was* over there." He pointed in the direction of Fifth Street. I guess he's done gone."

Chapter Twenty-Seven

"You two look like something the cat dragged in." Maureen looked back and forth between Charlie and Jacob. She'd walked into Charlie's office to hand him a stack of mail. "Is there something I don't know?"

Listlessly, Jacob raised his hand toward Charlie, deferring to his friend for an answer. Charlie, a lackluster expression on his face, thumped his knuckles on the desktop in a lazy rhythm. "Just Monday morning blues."

Jacob tilted his chair back to rest on its hind legs and clasped his hands behind his head. "How was your weekend, Maureen?"

"I bet you really care about my weekend, Jacob Gillis."

"Of course I care about your weekend." He managed an anemic smile. "I guess Charlie and I do look like a couple of bilious crabs this morning."

"My, my. What a vocabulary. Bilious. Well, when you get over your bilious crabbiness, I'll talk to you. Until then . . ." she gave a dismissive wave, ". . . somebody needs to feed the fish."

"The fish?" Jacob shot Charlie a quizzical look.

"You didn't see the new fish tank outside my door?"

"I guess not."

"Maureen wanted an office pet, so she stuck an aquarium out there. Half-way between my office and the one Ingleshit is using."

"Oh . . . well . . ., fish are good. Why do you look like you just missed the pass that lost the game?"

Charlie's gaze floated to the window. "I made a big mistake when I requested a special prosecutor so early. I should have waited. I guess you haven't heard. Inglehook is mentoring me."

"Mentoring you?" With a clunk, Jacob dropped the chair legs to rest squarely on the floor.

"Yep. Inglehook and Judge Blanchard are good friends. Judge B is the one who recommended him. They went to law school together." He frowned. "I would have thought Judge B had better taste in friends. Anyway, Inglehook convinced the judge he's mentoring the rookie DA, and now Inglehook is spreading the word to everybody else."

Jacob let out an uproarious laugh.

"Well, laugh if you like." Charlie's face reddened. "How do you think that makes me feel?"

"Like crap. But I'm not laughing at you. I'm laughing at the idea that Inglehook could be so stupid. You made a name for yourself in some pretty high profile cases when you were working for that Philadelphia firm. What was it the media called you after the car dealership case where you took on the Mafia? The scourge of South Philly? And the censorship case in Whitemarsh when you represented the American Library Association? I've yet to hear Inglehook's name mentioned in the glorious terms the media hung on you. Actually, before last week I never heard his name period."

"I'm guessing that's his problem. Rumors have it he has his sights set on being the next State Attorney General, but he needs to score a few points to secure the party nomination. He gets a half-point for mentoring me. Trying a high profile murder case will give him a whole bunch of points. Think of the media coverage: *Lester Norman Inglehook Prosecutes Rich, Ex-high-school Football Hero for the Murder of New York City Ballerina.* Assuming John did it, of course. You and I know he didn't, but Inglehook doesn't know that yet." He cut his eyes at Jacob in a flitting sign that Jacob interpreted as doubt at John's innocence.

"Was John a hero?" Jacob didn't mean to sound caustic, but anyone with "Hunter" for a last name was not on his list of favorites this morning.

"He did his part for the team. You can't knock him for that."

"Of course not. What I said came out wrong."

Scowling at the picture of Abraham Lincoln hanging on the wall next to him, Charlie wadded up a piece of paper, aimed it at the black and white portrait, and hit the president in the nose. "Sorry Abe, nothing personal. I just need a target." Abe seemed to wink as a shadow from a passing cloud flickered across the room. Charlie blew out a long breath. "Inglehook needs for John to be the suspect. A robbery, or drug-related killing won't get him time on Anderson Cooper or Fox News. He's concerned that I'm going to screw up his trial by dropping a piece of information to John." Charlie rose and paced. "The asshole has been in twice to warn me. Not to mention torturing me with a few dozen phone calls. When I'm busiest, of course." Pacing past his desk, he grabbed another piece of paper, wadded it, and launched it at Lincoln, this time hitting his neck. "*Just wanted to make you aware that attorneys have been disbarred for such infractions,*" Charlie said, imitating Inglehooks's nasal voice. "He told me about some idiot lawyer in Pittsburgh being disbarred for sleeping with the wrong person." Red spots blazed on his cheeks as he sat down again and cocked his head at Jacob. "He's friggin' threatening me."

"It sounds like Maureen picked an appropriate name for him. *Ingleshit.*"

A look of amusement crossed Charlie's face. "Don't know what I'd do without Maureen. You look morose, too. What's up?"

Jacob shrugged. "Busy weekend. My mother and sister, not to mention Aunt Zuela, had me fetching and carrying and scrubbing all day Saturday. *Do this. Do that. Get rid of this. Empty this.* They wore me out. But my house sparkles. Yesterday I tackled some yard stuff." Not even his closest friend was going to hear about his encounter with Kate or his wretched attempts at sleep because of it. It both puzzled and annoyed him how she aroused such consternation and fury in him, yet at the same time all she had to do was come within five feet of him to make him feel like champagne bubbled through his veins.

"Oh, I almost forgot," Charlie said. "Mrs. Petrowsky died early this morning."

"I guess, in a way, that's a blessing. Heart attack?"

"Don't know. That would be my guess."

Jacob stood. It was time for him to do the job he came to do and leave Charlie to his work. Sliding his hands into his pockets and jingling his keys, he looked up at Lincoln's portrait. "Forgive him, Mr. President," he said. "Our friend Charlie is young and greatly in need of a mentor. Eventually our new, inexperienced DA, under the guidance of Inglehook, will find a less revered figure for target practice."

He exited under a barrage of paper wads.

JACOB LOOKED from the office window down through a maze of branches. Sunbeams, passing through crisscrossed limbs, fractured and fell in pieces on the street below like parts of a giant jigsaw puzzle. A breeze swayed the tree limbs, pulling the puzzle pieces back and forth, reminding him of when his grandmother took him to see *Swan Lake* and of the dancers swaying to Tchaikovsky's notes. The overheated theater and the somnolent music had made him sleepy. Eventually his eyelids grew heavy and his head fell back, the upholstery scratching the back of his neck as his eyes closed. A dissonance in the music jolted him awake, and he looked up to see Odile, costumed in black, pirouetting across the stage, trailing evil.

"I thought the good guys were supposed to win," he said to his grandmother after the performance. They were standing in the taxi line, shivering in a cold Boston mist.

"Not always," she replied.

Not always. Jacob leaned his head on the window. On the street below, a dog escaped its leash and ran unchecked, weaving through a stream of pedestrians. The owner chased behind, but each time he was almost close enough to grab the leash the dog darted off in a new direction. Did Laskey feel that way about this case—a feeling of not being able to grab on?

What had Mrs. Petrowsky meant when she yelled out at the funeral? *Jest Charla?* He didn't think it was an outpouring of grief the congregation witnessed, but something else. Fear? Anger?

Laskey had been standing out in the entrance when it happened. In the commotion that followed—the two doctors jumping up to attend to Mrs. Petrowsky, her removal, the ambulance arriving— maybe no one had even told Laskey what she said. It was possible that he thought the commotion was just about Mrs. Petrowsky fainting.

He grabbed his jacket from the back of a chair and headed toward the door. As long as he was passing along the information to Laskey, just in case he hadn't heard, he might as well find out what Jest Charla meant and pass that on, too. He guessed Mrs. Petrowsky's friend, the one who pushed her wheel chair, knew.

<h1 style="text-align:center">Chapter Twenty-Eight</h1>

Jacob pushed open Aunt Zuela's door without knocking and walked in. She was ensconced in her red velvet easy chair, tarot cards spread across her lap.

About to flip over a card, she paused, still clutching the card between thumb and forefinger, and said, "You have a way of showing up at meal times, don't you?"

"I can take you up to the Silver Spoon."

"Never mind. I don't want to bother with make-up." She gathered up the cards, squared them into a stack and set them on the table beside her. "Where was Ama going?" she asked as she stood up. She brushed her hand across her skirt, smoothing the wrinkles.

"What do you mean?'"

"She must have been planning a vacation with all those prepaid credit cards. Ahhhh, but I can tell by the look on your face you didn't know. Well, stop gawking and come on back. How's ham and cheese on rye?"

"You heard that Mrs. Petrowsky died?" he asked as they made their way to the kitchen.

"Of course I heard."

While she put on water to boil for tea and set about making

sandwiches, he sat down at the kitchen table, his mind crawling with curiosity. "What is this about prepaid credit cards?"

Humming, she grabbed a jar of Dijon from the refrigerator and began slathering generous amounts of grainy, yellow-brown onto rye. A dollop dropped to the floor. She wiped it up with a sponge and then threw the sponge in the sink. Jacob tapped his foot impatiently.

"Ama was purchasing prepaid credit cards at the bank every month," she said finally, as she set a plate with sandwich and chips in front of him and another at her place. "She went to the branch over in Pottstown as though she didn't want anyone here to know."

"How do you know this?" He took a bite of the sandwich.

"Are you too hungry to wait for me? Didn't you have breakfast?"

"Sorry." He put the sandwich down. "All I had was a Snickers bar."

She set a cup of hot water and a tea bag in front of him and then sat down. "I'm out of soda. You and Charlie drank the last of it Friday."

Absently, he dunked the bag up and down and then dribbled a series of miniature lakes across the table as he set the bag aside.

"I know about the credit cards because Belinda Castor told me." She crumpled her napkin and reached over to wipe away the tea puddles. "Belinda used to work at Bucks National Bank here, but they transferred her to the Pottstown branch to be the new manager, and she's not one bit happy about having to do that drive every day." She gave Jacob a knowing look. Ignoring her food, she ran her finger around the rim of her cup as she talked. "Twenty-six miles there every morning, and twenty-six miles back every night, and you know what the traffic's like. They could have made her manager at the branch here, but no, they like inconveniencing people."

"The rest of the story, please," Jacob prodded.

"Belinda said she was sitting in her office one day when she saw Ama slinking in. You know how those offices are all half-glass now?

Ama wore a hat with a floppy brim and loose clothes like she didn't want anyone recognizing her. But she has that walk. You know." Zuela jumped up and took a few steps with her toes pointed out and arms lifted in an arc like a dancer. "You can always spot a ballerina by the way she walks." She pranced across the kitchen, her Uggs slippers scraping on the tile, and then, almost losing her balance, twirled around to klutz back to her chair. "What do you think? Could I have made it with the New York City Ballet?"

"You should definitely stick to teaching Shakespeare."

She laid her napkin in her lap and picked up a chip. "Belinda asked the teller about the transactions and discovered that Ama was buying prepaid credit cards. It kept happening. Instead of depositing the dance tuition checks in her bank account every month, Ama was cashing them and buying credit cards."

Jacob wondered if she'd been hiding money from John in order to get more in the divorce settlement, but then as quickly as the idea flashed into his mind, he rejected it. Anyone, certainly a judge, could figure out how much money she earned from teaching. Number of students times fees. Voila. "Did Mrs. Castor say how long she'd been buying the cards?"

"Several months. Funny thing about small towns. We know every bloody thing about everybody, even down to what they do at the bank, yet, someone can be murdered right under our noses, and no one is able to figure it out. Do you think Laskey knows about the credit cards?"

"I don't know. I'll it pass it along."

"Can they trace the cards?"

"I suppose."

"Someone would have to forge her signature on the sales slips."

"I'm sure there're lots of good forgers around." Including one who could forge Diego Rivera's name on a copied painting, he recalled.

"There's something else." Aunt Zuela leaned toward him. "Four months ago, Ama bought a million dollar insurance policy and made it out to her mother."

"A million dollars?"

"Yep. A million dollars."

He considered the implications. But maybe there were no implications. It was probably just a case of Ama wanting to make sure her mother's nursing home care was guaranteed on the o chance Ama met with an accident of some sort. Unless she had some reason to be afraid of John.

"We should set you up with a dedicated line to Bump Herrington's office so you can convey gossip directly," he said as he brushed the last crumbs of the sandwich from his hands onto the plate.

"Don't get smart with me, you little twerp."

He grinned. "I think that expression is outdated, Aunt Zuela. Maybe jerk or asshole."

"Well then, jerk, why did she buy an insurance policy?"

"Do I look like the Sphinx? I don't do riddles." Then he said in a more serious tone, "To take care of her mother, probably. But I'm curious about the credit cards. Maybe she was planning a *get-over-the-divorce* indulgence of some sort?"

"I could have helped her with that; I know how that goes."

"Mrs. Petrowsky's friend . . . I keep forgetting her name. The one at the funeral with the Neanderthal-looking son?"

"Inez Winters."

"Where does she live?"

"The next street over. Why?"

He stood up and threw his napkin down beside his plate. "I'm going to pay my respects. She just lost her good friend."

"You don't even know her."

"I'm going to pay my respects briefly, and then find out what Mrs. Petrowsky was saying at the funeral."

A few strides brought him to the front door, and then out and into his vehicle. He could no longer sit by, listening to gossip, waiting for reports from Laskey. There was no law against him asking a few questions relevant to the crime, was there? "No," he answered himself as he gunned the motor and pulled away from the curb, ". . . no law at all."

Chapter Twenty-Nine

Jacob pulled into the driveway of Inez Winter's bungalow and parked behind an old model Toyota Corolla. A 1960's Volvo sat on blocks between her unattached garage and that of her neighbor's, and in the middle of her lawn, her son, whose name Jacob had forgotten, leaned over the engine of a Mazda sports car that flamed red-orange in the early afternoon sun.

Engrossed, or deaf, or both, the son didn't look up when Jacob got out and walked over and introduced himself, but continued tightening the steel clamps on the radiator. "I'm here to see Mrs. Winters," Jacob said, raising his voice. Then he remembered the son's name. *Pavel.*

Pavel stopped his tinkering and swiveled his head to stare at Jacob for a few seconds before straightening and wiping a hand over his face, leaving a black streak. "And your business is?" Dropping his wrench to the ground, he leaned back on the fender, pulled a pack of Camels from his shirt pocket, and tapped the pack on the back of one hand to extract a cigarette.

"I'm a friend of the Hunters; I have a question for your mother about Mrs. Petrowsky."

"She's in there," Pavel said after an interval, and jerked his thumb in the direction of the front door.

Should any such contest arise, he'd have to remember to nominate Pavel for the *Conversationalist of the Year Award*, Jacob mused as he made his way up the walk to the half-open wooden front door. Reaching through the opening, he tapped on the metal edge of the screen door, rattling it against the frame.

"Come in," a raspy voice answered.

He stepped inside, letting the screen door squeak shut behind him. Inez Winters, dressed in a blue chenille robe and a pair of too-large men's herringbone slippers, slumped in a chair, an orange and black afghan draped over her lap.

"Excuse me for disturbing you. I'm Jacob Gillis. John Hunter and I were classmates in high school. I'm so sorry about the death of your friend." Nose twitching at the smell of licorice, one of his least favorite aromas, he took a step forward. The drapes were drawn and the room lit only by a low wattage table lamp. In spite of the gloom, he noted the abundance of porcelain figurines, collector's plates, cheap souvenirs, crocheted doilies, furniture store art.

She examined him through red-rimmed eyes, one hand fumbling to close the gap between the lapels of her robe while the other held a pipe of black licorice suspended between lap and mouth. A smear of black specked her lower lip. A brown pottery bowl on the table beside her held a couple dozen of the candies in assorted flavors.

"Shut the door," she said at length. "First Pavel, and now you. Don't you young men know how to close doors? I can't go jumping up every minute with my arthritis."

"Sorry." He closed the door. "I returned to Goose Bend recently, and I'm working temporarily for the District Attorney." When a puzzled look crossed her face he realized he should have invented a better introduction; she'd be wondering why someone from the DA's office was bothering her.

She set the pipe of licorice back in the bowl, licked her fingers, and after wiping them on her robe, placed her hand on a worn

Bible that lay on the table beside her. "It belonged to Josephine," she said. After a drawn-out sigh, she motioned to the sofa.

"I wanted to ask . . . ." he said sitting down, ". . . . at Ama's funeral, Josephine Petrowsky called out something I didn't understand. Jest Charla. Or something like that. Do you know what she meant?"

The Afghan fell to the floor as she stiffened.

Jacob swallowed and waited as a steely silence enveloped the room. Apparently, he'd sparked an unpleasant memory.

"Josephine thought it was Charla," Mrs. Winters said finally, her voice almost a whisper. "But Charla's been dead a long time now."

"Charla?"

"We weren't allowed to say her name, and I don't even know why." She looked at Jacob, her eyes wide with incomprehension. "Josephine's mind went bad. She remembered things from a long time ago and got them all mixed up inside her head. She thought it was Charla that was dead."

"Who's Charla?"

"We weren't allowed to talk about her after . . ."

"After what?" He leaned closer.

"I don't know." She raised her palms in bewilderment. "I lived in Baltimore when it happened. I don't know what Charla did. That girl was always a little crazy. Happy wild, and then down in the dumps. Up and down, up and down."

Charla, whoever she was, sounded bi-polar. "Tell me who Charla was, Mrs. Winters." He tried to keep his voice soft, non-threatening.

"Ama's sister."

He blinked. "Ama didn't have a sister."

"There were two girls, Ama and Charla. Now they're both dead. They're *all* dead. Charla, Josephine, Tadek, Ama."

"It's OK to talk about her now," Jacob said quietly. He rubbed the knuckle of his forefinger across his forehead. Maybe Mrs. Petrowsky hadn't been the only one with dementia. Ama had no siblings according to Kate, and Kate should know. Was Charla a cousin? Or the daughter of a different friend? "Which was the older sister?" he asked. Maybe questions would set Mrs. Winter's mind straight.

"The older?" She scrunched her face, thinking. "Ohhhh . . . Yes, yes. I remember now. Charla came first." She drew in a long breath. "That Charla was a mean child. We saw the Petrowsky's three or four times a year after we moved to Baltimore, and she was always bad. Throwing tantrums. Snatching things out of Ama's hands. Tearing Ama's clothes. Hitting her. Once she threw Ama's shoes in the toilet, and . . . ." She gave a little huff. ". . . one time she hit Pavel over the head with a fire poker." She frowned at the memory. "I can't even remember all the nasty things that child did. Tadek smacked her on the behind, but it didn't do no good. Josephine even made her kneel down and pray for forgiveness in front of everybody. *That* was embarrassing." She bent over, picked up the afghan, and spread it over her lap. "Once, Charla latched on to one of Ama's earrings and tore her lobe clean through. That poor child wound up with an ugly scar."

He acknowledged the ring of truth in what Mrs. Winters related. "How did Charla die?"

"They didn't say." She gave him a dismissive wave. "I don't want to talk about it. Leave me alone."

"I think you'd better go." The voice came from the doorway.

Jacob looked around to see that Pavel had slipped in and was pointing to the door.

FOR THE SECOND time that day, Jacob made his way to Aunt Zuela's front door. He didn't want to use the network in the DA's office, and his own wireless hadn't been hooked up yet. Tomorrow, they said. He'd have to use Aunt Zuela's.

If he pursued the history of Charla Petrowsky, and he already knew he would, who would it hurt? Not Ama or her parents. They were all dead. The Hunters, maybe? He imagined their discomfort at being associated with something unsavory, or maybe even criminal. Mrs. Winters seemed to have no idea what had caused the rift in the Petrowsky family, but it had to have been something bad.

The door was locked. He knocked and then rang the bell. Her canary-colored Beetle was parked in the driveway, so she had to be nearby. Mostly, she had to be nearby because he *needed* for her to be nearby. He pressed his nose against a window and, looking through the vee of pulled back curtains, saw the dark shapes of living room furniture and, somewhere in the back, a glimmer of light. He moved to the edge of the porch and searched the street. Maybe she was out reaping gossip. Maybe she'd walked down to the Seven-11. Maybe she'd taken up jogging. He tried to picture her in jogging outfit, ear buds plugged in and a water bottle gripped in one hand while mopping sweat from her brow with the other.

Wisps of clouds floated in a pastel sky, and he breathed in the smell of newly cut grass and forsythia. Across the street, an older woman loosened mulch in her flower bed, arranging it in an even pattern around azaleas about to bloom. The neighbor next door washed windows and, several houses down, a young mother in tight jeans and baseball cap attached Easter eggs to a tree while her toddler waddled around the yard.

He turned back to the door and pounded.

"Good lord!" he heard her exclaim from the other side as she fumbled with the lock. He stepped back as she flung it open. "Are you trying to break my door down?"

"No, I'm just trying to get you to answer. Doesn't your bell work?"

"It works just fine."

"You didn't hear me ringing?"

"I was taking something out of the oven. So what brings you back for the second time in one day? It isn't supper time yet."

Jacob sniffed. A compelling aroma wafted from the kitchen—a mixture of sugar, cinnamon, succulent meat, and other ingredients he couldn't identify. "I thought I might come back for the second course."

"I should have guessed. And I was hoping it might be for the pleasure of my erudite conversation. Come on back to the kitchen. I seem to be using that phrase fairly frequently lately; I should make a recording: *Come on back to the kitchen.*" She reached around him, closed the door, and then headed off through the dining room. "I'm trying out a new recipe for pot roast," she said as they made their way back. "You stuff the roast with garlic cloves and then marinate it in prune juice."

In the kitchen, she motioned toward the counter where a cake with swirling waves of dark chocolate frosting sat on a cake stand. "The chocolate cake is for the Historical Society's bake sale, and since the kitchen was already a mess, I thought I might as well whip up a batch of peanut butter cookies."

"Don't you think there might be too many chocolate cakes at the bake sale?" Jacob aimed his finger at the icing.

"Don't you dare." She slapped his hand. "Go stand on the other side of the room. I don't trust you anywhere near that cake while I'm rolling out cookies."

"You might want to reconsider and take bread pudding. I'm sure Mrs. Garrett and Mrs. Myers, not to mention a few others, will bring chocolate cakes. Isn't that too many chocolate cakes?"

"Give it up, Jacob. You're not getting cake today." She began tearing off pieces of cookie dough, rolling them into pieces, and then pressing the ovals onto the cookie sheet. "Did Inez Winters fill you in on the meaning of Josephine Petrowsky's gibberish?"

"She did."

"And?"

"How about a fair exchange? Information for chocolate cake?"

"How about information for all the meals I've served you up in the past?"

"Actually, I was hoping you'd let me use your computer. My wireless isn't hooked up yet."

She stopped rolling dough. "Does this have something to do with your visit to Mrs. Winters?"

He nodded. "Give me an hour or so, and then I'll tell you."

He saw a flash of interest in her face. "Sure. Make yourself comfortable back there. Jezebel is up and running.

"Jezebel?"

"My computer. I always name my computers."

Before beginning his search, Jacob placed a call to the Department of Vital Records of New York State, identifying himself as an attorney with the Bucks County Pennsylvania District Attorney's office. "I need a copy of a death certificate for a Charla Petrowsky," he said and spelled the name. "Her first name might have been Charlotte, however. I also need a marriage certificate, if one exists. We have a case pending." It wasn't exactly a lie. The DA's office *did* have a case pending. Or would have. Though he doubted a secret sister had anything to do with the case. He gave them the number and then called Maureen to alert her that he might be receiving a fax.

He spent the next hour Googling Charla Petrowsky, but found nothing. Finally, he gave up and followed the seductive smell drifting from the kitchen where Aunt Zuela was just pulling a tray of cookies from the oven. Several batches were cooling on sheets of wax paper. He sidled over and grabbed a cookie.

"Not before supper," she said, slapping him on the arm. "You have to eat your veggies first."

He held the cookie suspended a few inches from his mouth. "Aunt Zuela, you have no idea how I need comfort food right now."

She slipped her hand out of the oven mitt. "You look like you need comfort period. What's going on?"

"Finish taking care of the cookies and then come sit down." He grabbed two more.

"Okay, what's up?" she asked, joining him at the kitchen table two minutes later.

He relished the stunned look on her face as he told her about Charla. There had been very few times when he, rather than she, had been the purveyor of new information.

"*Nooo,*" she said when he finished. "I'm not so shocked at the discovery of a mysterious sister, but that they managed to hide it from everybody. Sounds like she was a naughty one."

"I expect she was a lot more than just naughty to merit the banning of her name." He frowned. "To use your term, I didn't find squat about her on the internet."

"The obituary mentioned the school Ama attended in New York. I'll bet they know something."

"You're right. I'll give them a call."

"Wouldn't it make more sense to go to New York and find someone who knew her? Like an old school friend who is willing to tell all? In person, you learn things people won't tell you over the phone."

"You're right, but . . . "

"I'll go. I bet I can find out all sorts of scandalous things."

JACOB SAW the note taped to his back door as soon he pulled into the backyard. Leaving the chocolate cake in the passenger seat, he walked toward the door, squinting, trying to make out the writing. When he came within a few feet he saw that the words had been painted in burnt sienna with a wide bristled artist's brush. "I'm sorry," the note read.

Chapter Thirty

Tuesday, March 11

"**A**ma Hunter had a sister?" Laskey gave Jacob an incredulous stare.

"There's more," Jacob said. He'd been waiting in front of Laskey's office door since six-thirty. At seven, Laskey finally came strolling up, shaking rain from the sleeves of his Woolrich jacket.

"What the hell. Come inside." Laskey unlocked the door and ushered Jacob in. He threw his keys on the desk and then peeled off his coat and hung it on the coat tree beside the door. "OK, let's hear it." He plunged his hands into his pockets.

Jacob told him about the prepaid credit cards and the insurance policy.

Laskey let the news sink in for a few moments and then sat down. "So, easy things first. I knew about the insurance policy. Ama probably wanted to provide for her mother's care in case something happened to her and John was no longer around to foot the bill. Million dollar policies for women Ama's age aren't expensive, so that doesn't set off any alarms." He narrowed his eyes. "The credit cards suggest she might have been planning a trip somewhere. But why the secrecy? And a sister? I'd like some proof. Even if it's true, it probably has no connection to this case." He frowned then, as though reconsidering. "Well, back to work," he said at length, slapping his hands lightly on the desk. "Let me know when the next round of surprises pops up."

"THERE'S a woman here to see you," Maureen said, sticking her head around the half-closed door of Jacob's office. "I told her you were busy, but she looks like a deranged tigress, and I don't have time to call out the National Guard to rescue you."

"Who is it?" He didn't have time for visitors. He wanted to work four or five hours on the river case and then go home to install shelves in the room he'd chosen as his study. He would have preferred to work in his yard, but since it was raining, shelf installation it was.

Before Maureen could answer, Inez Winters pushed past her, trailing water from her plaid umbrella.

"You can't . . . ." Maureen protested.

"It's all right," Jacob interrupted. "Mrs. Winters was a friend of Mrs. Petrowsky." He rose, curious as to what brought her here and, at the same time, hoping that whatever it was didn't take much time. Maybe she'd remembered something else about Charla.

"Well then . . . I'll leave you alone." Maureen shot Mrs. Winters a nasty look and then disappeared.

Mrs. Winters' eyes radiated a strange and potent force. "You have to stop them." She squeezed the umbrella handle hard, her knuckles turning white. "Yesterday, you told me who you worked for, so I know you can fix it. It's not right, what they're going to do." Her voice had risen.

"Why don't you have a seat and tell me what someone shouldn't be doing." He came from behind his desk, put his hand on her arm, and urged her toward a chair. He needed to be more careful about what he said. Helping Charlie with research didn't constitute working for the DA's office.

"You have to do something now, before they . . . ."

"Please . . . ," he raised his palm toward one of the Windsor chairs in front of his desk.

She perched on the edge and clasped her purse tightly to her chest. The plaid umbrella clunked to the floor.

"They're going to cremate her." Then in a louder voice, "Cremate her." She looked at him defiantly. "They can't do that. The Petrowskys didn't believe in cremation."

Jacob was about to explain that the DA's office had nothing to do with disposal of bodies, cremation or otherwise, but she cut him off.

"Tadek and Josephine were old-fashioned Catholics. Tadek's brother was a priest in Jasna Gora. They didn't believe in any of this new stuff like cremation because our bodies will be resurrected someday." Her words tumbled out, tripping over each other. "Those horrible Communists in Poland tried to steal what was in the churches, but Tadek and Josephine brought some church pictures all the way to America to save them. That's the kind of people the Petrowskys were. True Catholics. And now they're about to do something terrible with her body."

"Who decided to cremate her?"

"They said it's in her will. But I have her will. It was in her Bible. I took the Bible from her room yesterday after she died."

"Who are *they*?"

"Them at the nursing home." Her fingers opened and closed in nervous syncopation on the metal clasp of her purse.

"Did you bring the will with you by any chance? The one from her Bible?"

She nodded, opened her purse, and, with shaking hands, handed him a set of folded papers.

"Wait here a moment," he said. "I want to have Maureen call the nursing home."

When he returned, he unfolded the will and read in a low voice. "I, Josephine Petrowsky, of the Borough of Goose Bend, County of Bucks and Commonwealth of Pennsylvania, being of sound mind . . . ." At some point, Josephine Petrowsky's mind had become unsound. He continued reading in silence. Mrs. Petrowsky stipulated that all her earthly possessions, other than her house and furniture, go to her daughter, Ama Hunter. In the event Ama preceded her in death, they would go to Ama's husband, John. The possessions named in the will consisted of a few government bonds. She left her house and furniture to her *dear friend*, Inez Winters, with the exception of the curio cabinet in the living room, along with its contents, which she left to Kate Hunter.

He looked up. "You're familiar with what's here?"

"She told me what was in it."

"Why did she leave the curio cabinet to Kate?"

"She liked her. Kate drove her around places she needed to go, like the doctor's office or grocery shopping. Ama always pretended she was too busy. I guess Josephine wanted to repay Kate."

"But why the curio cabinet in particular?"

"Kate admired it once. Something about the rosette etched into the glass, and the yellow velvet lining the shelves."

Jacob read further, searching for funeral arrangements. She asked to be buried next to her husband. Other than that, there was nothing about final rites. Seth Lewis had written the will and was named as executor. Seth had been three grades above Jacob. After graduating from Moravian College, he had gone to Dickinson Law School and then set up practice in Goose Bend.

"I have the nursing home on the phone," Maureen said, sticking her head through the door. "They say they have a will, and that it stipulates Mrs. Petrowsky be cremated. The will is dated a month ago."

He checked the one in his hands and saw that it was dated four years ago. "Tell them to do nothing until we've sorted this out. I'll get in touch with Seth Williams." Then a thought struck him, and he reeled. A murder. And on the heels of the murder, the victim's mother dying. A million dollars in insurance money. Two wills. One recent. A new will stipulating cremation? "Maureen, I need to see you a minute." He jerked his head in the direction of her office.

"What?" she said when they were safely out of Mrs. Winter's hearing.

"We have a murdered woman who assigned a large insurance policy to her mother, then the sudden death of the mother, and a very recent will that stipulates cremation for this mother who apparently doesn't believe in cremation. Can you have the nursing home fax over a copy of the will? I'm going in Charlie's office to use his phone. I don't want Inez Winters to hear me talking to Laskey about an autopsy."

Jacob alerted Laskey and then waited in Maureen's office for a response from the nursing home. Within a few minutes, the signal for an incoming fax beeped, and the second will ratcheted out of the machine, inch by ponderous inch until the complete document lay in his hands. He read rapidly over the first few lines, and then slowed. *All the rest, residue and remainder of my estate, whether, real, personal or mixed, whatsoever the same may be and wheresoever situated, I do give, devise and bequeath to . . .* He looked up at Maureen.

"What?" She raised her hands. "Don't keep me in suspense."

Silently he reread the portion that had surprised him and then flipped to the last page. Yes, it was Mrs. Petrowsky's wobbly signature.

"Well, what does it say?" Maureen's hands were still raised in a question.

"All the rest of my estate . . . ." He skipped over the next few words. " . . . I do give, devise, and bequeath to my two daughters, Ama and Charla."

Chapter Thirty-One

L askey strode into Seth Lewis' office.

"Who might you be, and what brings you barging into my office?" Lewis, who had been hunched over his desk engrossed in a document, straightened and looked up with a frown. "Was my receptionist invisible?"

"Either invisible or gone to the powder room." Laskey held out his ID.

"Sooooo, you're the famous detective brought in to solve the crime of the century in these parts. To what do I attribute the good fortune of now having a face to go with the name? Have a seat." He thrust an arm toward a brown leather chair.

Laskey remained standing. "You drew up a will for Josephine Petrowsky. You know she died yesterday?"

"Yes." He gave Laskey a puzzled look.

"You're her executor and responsible for her funeral."

Lewis nodded. "I contacted the funeral home yesterday about the financial arrangements. I thought they would have gotten back to me by now."

"They're getting ready to cremate her."

"They're what?" Lewis dropped the pen he'd been holding and sat upright.

"There's another will."

"Another will?" There was bewilderment in his voice.

"Drawn up by Theodore Samsi. It names Ama Hunter and her sister, Charla Petrowsky as beneficiaries."

"Ama didn't have a sister."

"She had one," Laskey said dryly. "Inez Winters knew about her. Charla is dead. I don't know how or when she died, but for some reason, the Petrowskys disowned her and pretended she never existed. The second will, the one that stipulates cremation, leaves everything to be divided equally between Ama and Charla."

Seth gaped at him. "I'm afraid I've been knocked off my feet here. Have you seen the second will?"

Laskey nodded. "The signature appears to be legitimate."

"I want to see it for myself. Josephine Petrowsky wasn't in her right mind." A blush flamed his skin from clavicle to hairline. "Samsi is an idiot. I have no idea why she'd go to him. If she, in fact, did. The second will won't stand. If there really was another daughter, and if she's dead, as you say, that alone proves Mrs. Petrowsky wasn't of sound mind." He reached for the phone. "I need to deal with this." He nodded toward the chair. "You're making me nervous hovering over me. Can you *please* sit down while I contact the funeral home?"

Laskey settled into the chair and stretched his legs out in front of him while Seth barked at the funeral director. Neither Seth nor the funeral director needed to know that there would be no body to cremate or bury, period, until after the autopsy. They were trying to keep the autopsy secret even though he knew their efforts were probably in vain. For all he knew, word was already spreading like dandelion fluff in a wind storm.

Seth hung up. "I wonder how she even got to Samsi."

"Ama must have taken her."

"Why would she do that?"

"No idea. Does Ama have a will?"

"I have it here." He pointed to a file cabinet. "We wrote it up two months ago. You can read it if you like, but basically it leaves everything to her mother. In the event of her mother's death, every-thing would go to her sister-in-law."

"Kate?"

"Kate gets everything including the million dollar life insurance policy I heard Ama had taken out. Although I guess before anything can be dispersed to Kate, we have to find evidence that Charla Petrowsky, if there really was such a person, is dead." He looked off to the side and ran a forefinger over his lips. "It doesn't make sense that Ama would let her mother construct a will dividing everything between two sisters, but then ignore the sister in her own will."

LASKEY CLIMBED the steps to the second floor of an old office building in downtown Quakertown, found Samsi's office, and entered a reception room curdled in drab shades of beige and smelled of French fries and ketchup. The blinds from one window had detached and lay on the floor in front of the window.

"Can I help you?" Samsi called through the open door between his office and the twelve-by-twelve reception room. The attorney sat behind his desk, shirt sleeves rolled up, top two buttons of his shirt unbuttoned, and tufts of dark chest hair curling around the shirt opening.

Laskey entered the tiny office. The remains of a Big Mac, a large drink, and a super-sized order of fries cluttered the top of a file cabinet. Samsi's red-striped tie created a boundary across his desk, separating a misaligned pile of documents from a stack of files.

"Yes, I wrote a will for Mrs. Petrowsky," Samsi said after Laskey stated his business.

"Someone brought Mrs. Petrowsky to your office, and she told you what she wanted in the will?"

"No, on both counts."

"Explain, please." Laskey crossed his arms and looked down at the attorney.

"Ama Hunter came to my office and told me what was to be in

the will. Then she offered to pay me extra if I took a jaunt out to Goose Bend for her mother's signature. I wrote it up, went to the nursing home, read the thing to the old woman, and then grabbed one of the nurses as a witness, and it was done."

"You're aware that Mrs. Petrowsky had dementia?"

He shrugged. "She seemed fine to me."

"Thank you for your time, Mr. Samsi." Laskey turned and headed for the door. "I appreciate it," he called over his shoulder. "Hope your fee for doing the will was satisfactory."

Chapter Thirty-Two

Zuela clasped the cold metal ring of the knocker, molded in the shape of a lion's head, and banged it for the third time against the scarred door. Taking a break from Shakespeare to play Mati Hari was supposed to have been fun, a nice break in the grinding routine of grading papers and presenting the same, or nearly the same lectures she had for the last thirty years. But while Jacob nestled in a nice warm office, she stood in front of the massive oak door of St. Ursula's freezing her butt off. Glacial rain lashed at her legs and, in spite of her hat, needled her face, while miniature icebergs slid past her collar to float down her back. It was bloody March. Not April. Wasn't it supposed to be windy instead of rainy, and why hadn't she worn slacks instead of the skirt she thought more proper attire for appearing in front of brides of God? Or were they brides of the Church and sisters of God?

She crossed her arms, and tried to warm her hands in her armpits. She'd anticipated sleuthing in balmy weather, followed by lunch, shopping for books at *The Strand*, and maybe rounding off the day with a show. Instead, here she was in Queens in front of a depressing gray stone building, shivering. Jacob was going to owe her big time for this.

Noticing a buzzer beside the doorframe, she slapped her palm against her forehead. Why hadn't she looked for a buzzer in the first place? She bore down on the buzzer a little longer than necessary, then stuck her hands in the sleeves of her Burberry and waited.

The clicking of a key in the keyhole came from inside. *Finally*, someone was going to rescue her. At least if Butterfingers on the other side ever stopped fiddling with the lock. The door swung open, and Zuela slipped past the nun into the warmth of a long hall. A contemporary of the Virgin Mary, Zuela guessed, taking in the layers of wrinkles as the good sister closed the door and fumbled with the key trying to reengage the lock. The nun turned around and her cataract-clouded eyes swept over Zuela from top to bottom, landing on the puddle of rainwater at her feet. She pursed her lips.

"Good morning, how are you? Nasty weather, isn't it?" Zuela said brightly. She was beginning to understand those stories about how Christ's brides had been blessed with a special talent for inflicting guilt in the hearts, minds, souls, and private parts of students. But sugar caught more flies, and all that. She stretched a smile across her face.

"Can I help you?" Fumble Fingers asked.

"Will you direct me to the office? I'm here to see the principal."

"The office is back there." The sister pointed down the hall and then waddled off, leaving Zuela to follow.

"Nice school," Zuela called to her back.

The nun grunted in reply.

"Been here long?"

No answer.

The floors of the corridor smelled of cleaning compound. Once, the nun stopped and, with excruciating slowness, bent to pick up a pink hairband. They passed a trophy case and then the school library where Zuela caught a glimpse of girls in kilts, some actually studying, most not. One applied fingernail polish. Several, hiding their cellphones behind stacks of books, tapped out messages.

In the main office, after interminable explanations as to why she was there, Zuela received permission to enter the principal's inner sanctum. Sister Marie, wearing neither habit nor wimple, sat behind a neatly ordered desk and was engaged in an activity that required an intense frown, a stack of papers, a red pen, and the occasional tugging of her ear lobe. "Have a seat," she said without looking up. "I'll be with you in one moment."

Zuela sat down in one of the two no-nonsense chairs fronting the desk and examined the long, rectangular room. The principal's desk occupied one end, while the other held a small conference table. Unmatched bookcases of varying heights lined the walls. A few had etched glass doors, others, plain doors, and some had no doors at all. A tall case behind the desk had a shelf missing, and the books were stacked horizontally instead of vertically on the shelf below. At the far end of the conference table, a man stood on a ladder beneath a hole in the ceiling, filing at its edges. White plaster snowed down to settle on his khaki coveralls, the rungs of the ladder, the table, the chairs, the floor.

"What can I do for you?" Sister Marie asked finally, putting down her red pen and looking up.

"I'm Dr. Zuela Hay. I'm here on behalf of one of the attorneys in the DA's office in Bucks County, Pennsylvania." She handed Sister Marie the letter of introduction from Jacob. "Mr. Gillis is looking for information on two of your former students."

Sister Marie's brow furrowed as she read the letter. She finished, refolded the letter, and handed it back to Zuela. "According to the date on Mr. Gillis' letter, these girls graduated twelve years ago. The records won't show much other than their grades unless there were some custody issues."

"Mr. Gillis thinks someone here might remember them. He's particularly interested in Charla."

Sister Marie cast a long look at the stack of papers on her desk, sighed, and then pushed herself to a standing position. "There are two older sisters here. I'll get them."

Left alone, Zuela looked over at the workman grinding away at the plaster. He gave one last scrape, dropped his file noisily to the floor, and climbed down from the ladder. He took a smoke detector from a box and re-ascended. Jiggling the device, he tried to fit it in.

When it wouldn't go in, he removed a tack hammer from his tool belt and tapped the detector in an attempt to force it in.

"Damn," he said to the ceiling when the detector still refused to fit. He flitted his eyes at Zuela. "I'm sorry, lady. I didn't mean to curse. For a minute there, I forgot you were here."

"Not a problem." She went over and looked up at the hole. "Not quite big enough?"

"No, it isn't." He kept his eyes focused on the hole as though looking would solve his problem. "But I have to be careful about getting the hole too big."

"I guess you'd have a different dilemma then."

"Yeah. It's a bitch trying to patch over old plaster. They built this place to withstand nuclear war and the Apocalypse, and then they ask me to drill holes in it. I've got twenty of these mother . . .. I apologize. I don't usually talk like that around here."

"Been here long?"

"Yeah." He set the alarm on the top rung of the ladder and nodded to the file lying on the floor. "Would you mind handing me that?"

She passed the file up to him. She heard footsteps approaching through the outer office and turned in time to see Sister Marie reenter followed by two traditionally dressed nuns.

After introducing Sister Teresa and Sister Margaret, the principal dragged a chair from the other end of the room, motioned for them to sit, and then resumed her position behind the desk. She folded her hands and nodded at Zuela, indicating that she should take charge.

Hands concealed behind her scapular, Sister Theresa narrowed her eyes when Zuela asked about the Petrowsky sisters. "Hmmmm," she said. "Petrowsky." Then she shook her head. "There're so many similar names around here, you forget."

"Ama was a dancer," Zuela prompted.

A light went on in Sister Theresa's eyes. "Oh, I know who you mean." She leaned her head toward Sister Margaret. "Remember that girl who danced in the talent show? Cute little thing with platinum hair and big, brown eyes. But the other one, Charla . . .. I don't recollect much about her. Do you?"

Sister Margaret scratched her cheek, thinking. "Didn't they come from Poland or someplace like that?"

Sister Theresa nodded. "I believe they did. But I didn't have either girl in class. Did you?" She tilted an ear toward Sister Margaret.

"No."

Zuela fought to control her impatience. "Can you tell me *anything* about them?"

"I think Mrs. Petrowsky was in charge of the arts and crafts auction one year." Sister Margaret wagged her head, memories apparently surfacing. Then she stopped and frowned. "Well, maybe it was her." A note of doubt had crept into her voice.

Sister Margaret's eyes brightened. "*Ohhhh.*" She clapped her hands together. "Mrs. Petrowsky was the one that made that delicious apple cake for the bake sale. The one with the cream cheese icing. She made a second cake for us to enjoy in the convent afterwards."

Zuela pressed two fingers hard against her temple. "You remember nothing about Charla?"

Sister Theresa shrugged. "Nothing, really. It's funny, though . . . ." she narrowed her eyes, searching the annals of her memory. "I think I do remember now one sister being at graduation, but not the other. Sister Margaret?"

Sister Margaret shook her head. "What with being in charge of the programs, and the caps and gowns, and the flowers, and all that, I was too busy to know who was there."

Zuela tapped one foot on the floor, noiselessly, impatiently. She couldn't go back to Goose Bend without *something.* She was as curious as hell, and she didn't want to admit failure to Jacob. "Did you hear anything about Charla dying?" she asked.

"Nooo. She didn't die, did she? Poor thing." Sister Margaret breathed out a shaky stream of air.

"We would have heard if a student died," Sister Theresa said.

"Do you remember who their friends were?"

"There were so many girls."

Perhaps we can give you an alumni directory," Sister Marie interjected. "The graduation dates are listed, and you can see which students were the same age as the Petrowsky girls and call some of them."

"Great idea," Zuela answered, sighing inwardly at the number of phone calls that would entail.

A FEW MINUTES LATER, an alumni directory tucked inside her purse, Zuela pressed her back against the massive oak door, sheltering in the overhang while gathering the nerve to dash to the subway stop. Rainwater, channeled by gargoyles on the roof, shot down spouts to feed the rivers roiling along the sidewalks. Her shoes were soaked. Her feet hadn't been this cold since she locked herself out of her house one snowy day after taking out the garbage wearing only flip-flops. She pulled her Burberry tighter, preparing to run for it. First, lunch. Then a look at the directory and a few calls. Maybe she'd get lucky and find someone right off the bat who remembered the Petrowsky sisters.

About to dash, she heard the clicking of a key and moved aside. The door inched open, and the workman from the ladder stuck his face through the opening.

"Excuse me," he whispered. His face was still speckled with white plaster. "I pretty much know all the girls that come here; they like talking to me. The name you want is Alice Sieron. She and Charla Petrowsky were as close as Siamese clams."

"Alice Sieron," Zuela repeated.

"Her name's in that directory. Prob'ly married now, but they got both maiden and married names in there."

"Thank you." She reached out to shake his hand. "You've made my day."

Chapter Thirty-Three

Chilled to the bone, Laskey limped around puddles in the cratered sidewalk leading to Kate's front porch. He expected her to open the door and, as she had done before, throw excuses at him trying to postpone yet another interrogation of her brother. *Sorry, but John is asleep. John is in the shower. John has gone out for a walk. He's in the toilet for a lengthy stay.* He couldn't blame her for trying, could he? When he finished with John, he had a question for Kate: Did she know she stood to inherit a million dollars, a curio cabinet, and the things inside?

John opened the door after the second knock. With a resigned look, he stood aside for Laskey to enter. "Come in. . . . I guess. Not that I have a choice."

Laskey noted John's changed appearance. Sporting two days' growth of facial hair and without his Hermes tie and Hugo Boss suit which he'd exchanged for sweats, John Hunter looked more human somehow. "I just want to clear something up," Laskey said.

"Yeah, I'm sure you do." John shut the door and motioned to the sofa.

Laskey remained standing.

"So, how can I help you? What can I clear up?" John crossed his arms high on his chest. "What can I repeat that I've already told you twenty times before?"

"Already told me? That isn't much."

John lowered his chin to rest on his collarbone. His face was thinner, the lines around his mouth had become furrows, and for a few moments, Laskey thought he might be about to cry.

"I didn't kill Ama."

"Why did your sister tell someone you were in Doylestown that evening, yet you refused to give an alibi?"

"I wondered when you were going to ask, and I know who the *someone* was. Somehow, Kate had the misconceived idea that Jacob Gillis might have a magic formula for diverting suspicion from the unfaithful husband. Or what is it people are calling me these days?" He gave Laskey a daring look and waited, nostrils widened, chin up. "Never mind." He gave a dismissive wave. "I'm sure my imagination can fill in the answer to that question. Come out to the kitchen. I was about to warm up left-over Chinese."

He trudged toward the dining room, leaving Laskey to follow. "Kate went to buy groceries and won't be home for God knows how long since she no longer shops locally," John said without looking back. There was a mixture of dejection and cynicism in his voice.

Laskey followed, trying to ignore the flashes of obsidian, hunter green, and cobalt blue that leapt from the frames of Kate's paintings. She was an excellent artist. When this case wrapped up, he intended to ask to see her studio. Depending which way the case ended, of course.

"Sorry, but I didn't eat breakfast. Nor dinner last night," John said as he entered the kitchen. "Actually, I haven't eaten many meals at all lately. Now I'm suddenly too hungry to be polite, and since nothing else is going my way right now, at least I'm going to eat."

Laskey caught the faint whiff of turpentine. An open door on the far wall revealed what looked to be a glassed-in porch converted to an artist's studio. An easel held a half-finished landscape, and several canvasses were propped against the wall, their backs to him.

John, about to open the refrigerator, looked over his shoulder at Laskey. "Want some? Chinese is all I have to offer."

"I'll take a rain check on that."

While John dumped the contents of a take-out box on a plate and nuked it, Laskey, deciding the visit might not be that short after all, sat down at an old round table with wrought iron legs—the kind he associated with the ice-cream parlors of his youth. He rapped his knuckles lightly as he looked around. The walls were emerald green. Glass knobs in an assortment of colors and designs had been affixed to outdated white cabinets, giving the kitchen a sassy look. Plants lined the window sills as well as occupying part of the counter space. Pottery—Peruvian, he guessed—stood here and there. He admitted he wouldn't mind having a cheerful kitchen like this even though there wasn't much room left to cook.

John, arms folded, stared at the microwave until it dinged. The smells of garlic, soy, and seared pineapple drifted out as he took the plate from the oven, grabbed a fork, and sat down. Without looking at Laskey, he began eating. "So, ask me," he said between bites.

"I already asked. Why did Kate tell Jacob you were in Doylestown at the Cockle Burr?"

"Because that's where I was."

"Why didn't you tell me?"

"I had my reasons."

"Which are?"

John let his fork dangle on the side of his plate. "Because my wife has been murdered, and I don't know who did it."

"Sorry, I'm a bit confused. Please explain."

"Do you have any idea what state you're in when someone tells you your wife has been murdered? It's like time stops. It's like you're looking at everything from outside your own body. From up there somewhere." He raised his hand above his head and wiggled his fingers. "When it finally started to sink in, I couldn't connect what Bump was telling me with anything logical, except for . . . ." He pinched his forehead between thumb and fingers. "A few months ago, before I moved out, I told Ama something I shouldn't have. In a weak moment − a really stupid, stupid moment. So when someone killed her my imagination went into overdrive. My first thought was 'hit man.'

Because of what I know. At least what I *think* I know. If someone murdered her for that reason, then . . ." His voice tapered off.

Laskey could guess what John was thinking, but he wanted to hear him say it. "What do you think you know?"

John scraped his feet on the tile; his already sloping shoulders sank further.

"Tell me," Laskey prodded.

John propped his elbows on the table and leaned his head on his hands for a few seconds until, seeming to have come to a decision, he rose abruptly, dragged his chair over to the stove, and climbed onto the seat. He opened the cabinet above and began pulling out bakeware, piling it on the stove except for a muffin pan that clattered to the floor. Reaching his hands deep into the cabinet, he extracted a brief case. He climbed down from the chair, laid the case on the table, and took out two black binders.

"The Reilly Foundation," he said, plunking them down in front of Laskey. "I do their books. Things haven't looked right the last couple years, so I started making copies of receipts for various expenditures and records of transfers. It wasn't easy with McGonigle breathing down my neck, but . . . ."

McGonigle's Rolex, the Hermes tie, the expensive cigars, the BMW, had been churning in Laskey's head ever since his visit to the Foundation.

"I think McGonigle suspected I was up to something," John said. "He kept walking in to hover over me when I was there last week. That was the same day that. . . ." He rubbed his fingers over his brow. "Look, Laskey, I know I was being irrational. But unless you've had someone close to you murdered, you haven't a clue what goes through your mind." He looked at Laskey and waited for a sign that he understood.

Laskey nodded.

"Now that I've gotten over the initial shock, I realize how preposterous it was to think McGonigle would hire someone to shoot my wife . . ." He took a long shaky breath. "If he wanted anyone shot, I'm sure it would have been me."

"Probably. I paid a visit to McGonigle last week. He told me you were headed back to Goose Bend that evening."

"He wanted me to look guilty; that way I'd be busy fighting my own battles and ignore what he was doing. Before you came to the office Tuesday morning, Kate asked me where I was when . . . ." He swallowed. "She knew I'd have to answer that question sooner or later. My mind had pretty much shut down, so I told her, but then I thought better of it and cautioned her not to say anything. She didn't understand why, so we were arguing when you showed up."

"I suspect you might be right about a little embezzlement going on. Actually, a lot," he added, remembering McGonigle's taste for expensive works of art. "Have you seen receipts for items that aren't in the office building?"

"You think he might have bought things for the Foundation and then transferred them to his house? Or sold them for extra money?"

Laskey shrugged. "Just a thought."

John pushed aside the plate of food. He'd barely eaten any of it. "That's what made me suspicious. I saw receipts for paintings, but didn't see the paintings. There were also two smaller Nakashima tables missing. I didn't pay any attention at first, but then I started to wonder where they were. There were other expenditures I didn't quite understand. I asked, but McGonigle was vague. He told me what category to put them in and left it at that. I began to wonder . . ." He shifted in his seat, hesitating. "McGonigle draws up the budget for the foundation without much input from the board treasurer. The treasurer then presents the budget to the rest of the board. I don't think they ever question anything. Mostly, they're on the board because it makes them look good to be associated with the Reilly Foundation. And . . ." He ran his fingers through his hair. "I think McGonigle might be having an affair. I found receipts for a gold bracelet from Tiffany's and a $3150 David Yurman bracelet from Saks—one of those cable bracelets with diamonds like my sister has. There's a copy in there somewhere." He nodded to the binders. "I asked McGonigle about the bracelets, and he put on a big act about his wife's birthday and how he hadn't wanted the receipts left in the house for her to find, and somehow or other they got mixed up in the wrong stack of receipts." John shrugged. "Maybe I'm wrong about him having an affair; it's just he seemed . . . Well, he acted guilty. Besides, I know what his salary is. He can't afford David Yurman bracelets for his wife's birthday present, and I've never seen her wearing one. I'll bet there's a mistress somewhere getting expensive gifts paid for by donations meant to feed all those orphans he goes on about."

"Can I take these with me?" Laskey raised his hand to indicate the binders.

John thought a moment and then nodded.

Opening one, Laskey looked at it absently. He would turn them over to his financial sleuth. He already had him busy finding out what he could about both the Reilly Foundation and Hunter and Son Accounting. So far, his sleuth had been unable to find any hint that Hunter and Son was anything but honest, but The Reilly Foundation was proving to be more complicated.

"Maybe you could find someone who saw me at the Cockle Burr," John said. "I fell asleep in the car while I was waiting for Ama. Didn't wake up until nearly midnight. Guess I was really tired," he added sheepishly. "I got to my aunt's house only a few minutes before she got in from Bingo. I heard her come in, but I was already in bed." He swallowed and gave Laskey an uncertain look. "They check the parking lots in those places fairly often, don't they?"

"Bump sent someone over to question the night watchman. No one saw your car." Laskey closed the binder.

John's cheeks reddened. "The shit head of a night watchman didn't see a flaming red F-2 Jaguar parked right at the front door? Every time I park that car somewhere, half the world comes over to look." His mouth hung open in disbelief.

Laskey stared at him. A Jaguar? "You weren't driving a Lexus?"

"No. I was driving my party car. Kate's junk heap was in the shop. That damn Subaru falls apart on a weekly basis, so she was driving my Lexus." A corner of his mouth twisted sardonically. "Some party it turned out to be."

LASKEY PAUSED on the front porch. Shifting the binders to hold under his left arm, he whipped out his cell phone with his right, and called the office. "Anything on the autopsy?" He immediately regretted the bark in his voice.

"Well, good afternoon to you, too," Janis jabbed back.

"Sorry. Didn't mean to come across that way. Forgive me. Got a couple things under my skin right now."

"No kidding. There's no news from the coroner."

"Nothing?"

"They've got a whole bunch of bodies over there to slice and dice. You have to wait your turn."

"OK. Let me know."

"You really think I wouldn't?"

"No, Janis. Of course not."

"Inglehook called. Wants you to call him back."

"Don't tell me."

"Don't tell you what?"

"That Inglehook called."

"I just did."

"No, you didn't. You didn't tell me anything."

"You have something against the special prosecutor?"

"I don't have time to talk to him." He disconnected and stuck the phone back in his pocket.

He shivered, not from the icy precipitation that didn't seem to be letting up, but from the shadow of a suspicion that skulked in his head. Was there a connection between McGonigle's interest in high end art works and Kate's possible access to two triptychs? McGonigle, Laskey suspected, collected art work not only for the Foundation, but also for himself. There was no legal way for him to get into McGonigle's house to see if he had stashed things. Or maybe be wasn't stashing. He could be selling in order to pay for David Yurman bracelets.

LASKEY POUNDED on the door of the night watchman's apartment until, bleary eyed and dazed, the man opened up. "Need to talk to you," Laskey said, holding out his ID. He pushed in without waiting for an invitation, and then turned around to look at the watchman still standing dumbly beside the door. "Did I wake you?" He doubted the watchman was awake enough to catch the sarcasm.

"Didn't get to bed until four A.M," the watchman grumbled, wiping sleep from his eyes.

Laskey, not in an apologetic mood, ignored the man's ill-humor and asked what he had come to ask.

"Oh, yeah. The red Jaguar. It was parked at the front door. I tapped on the window to make sure the man inside wasn't dead. Had his head propped on the head rest and his mouth open. I guess he was just tired. Must have slept there for three, four hours. Ever' time I checked, he was snoring away."

Laskey showed him a picture, and the watchman identified John Hunter as the man asleep in the red Porsche.

"Thanks, you can go back to bed now."

Laskey drew an imaginary line through John Hunter's name on the suspect list in his head and headed out the door.

Chapter Thirty-Four

J acob slammed on the brakes and swerved to avoid hitting the green Subaru that shot from behind his house. The Subaru squealed to a stop, backed up, and came to a stop beside him.

Kate rolled down her window. "Sorry," she said.

He raised his hands in a question.

"You said I could paint your pond. So I . . . ."

"You were working in the rain?" The weather had cleared only minutes before.

"No. I was here yesterday, but I took the painting home for a few final touches. Today, I was getting rid of the result. I didn't think you'd be home this early."

"Getting rid of?" The vision of her drowning a masterpiece in his pond flashed through his mind.

"I left the painting in your mudroom. The door was unlocked. If you like my pond-scape, keep it; if not, dump it. I did it for therapy."

Sometimes she had a way of rendering him speechless. Was he supposed to thank her for a painting she didn't want?

"The oils are still wet, so don't touch it except on the sides. I suppose I should back up so you can park."

"Yes, you should back up. But don't leave; come inside, I have something to tell you."

She looked alarmed.

"No, no. Nothing to be distressed about." Just astonished, he thought. Hopefully, Daisy Mae hadn't wandered into the mud room and brushed against Kate's wet oils, streaking the painted pond with cat hairs.

HE STARED AT THE PAINTING. She had transformed a prosaic scuttle of pond water into something magnificent. The painting pictured a troubled sky, dark clouds tumbling in from the lower left and rising to the upper right corner, partially obliterating the blue of a happier day. Amorphous forms of navy, indigo, white, silver, and ice-blue mingled in a collage that set his insides singing. The pond mirrored the sky, but in more intense colors.

"This is the most beautiful painting I've ever seen," he said finally, still absorbed in the richness of hues. In the lower left, just above the surface of the water, a bit of fuchsia peeked through the clouds – the same fuchsia as Kate's prom dress. He felt a twitch of surprise. He still remembered thirteen years later? They'd been kids. She, more than him. She had avoided his eyes that evening, seemingly happy with her date, but each time the glint of fuchsia skittered across his line of vision, his attention was drawn away from the kaleidoscope of other gowns, the multi-colored corsages, the blue and yellow decorations.

"I'll hang it over the living room fireplace," he said. "If you have second thoughts, you know where it is. Although I might grow too attached to let you have it back." He reached for the painting.

"Careful. Remember, it's still wet."

He took the painting by the sides and, holding it away from him, carried it to the living room and set it on the mantel. "When it dries, I'll have it framed."

"What did you want to tell me?" she asked.

"Ama had a sister."

Her head gave a little jerk. "What?"

"Mrs. Winters claims that Ama had a sister."

"The woman's crazy. Ama was an only child."

She stared at him with a jumble of expressions—bewilderment, disgust, disbelief—as he related the conversation with Inez Winters. When he finished, she sank onto the sofa, pressed her hands tightly between her knees. "I don't believe it," she said, shaking her head. "But even if it were true, which it isn't, why would they disown a child?"

"No idea."

She frowned. "Theoretically speaking, the sister could have been pregnant and had an abortion which would have made her a murderer in the Petrowsky's eyes. Or maybe it had to do with drugs. Or something else illegal. But that's only theoretical; Ama didn't have a sister. Did Inez say how this Charla was supposed to have died?"

He shook his head. "I tried to find a death certificate, but no luck."

"All those years Ama was married to my brother, all those years she was a member of our family, she lied to us?" Sparks of anger shot from her eyes. "What was so terrible that she couldn't even tell her husband?" She looked at Jacob as though he had an answer.

"I'm going to New York," she said then. "I know where Ama went to school. She probably lived in one of the surrounding neighborhoods, and I'll batter down the door on every house in Queens until I find someone who knew the Petrowskys."

"Let me do some research first. If I don't come up with anything, I'll go with you." He hoped Aunt Zuela had information that would render a trip to New York unnecessary.

"This has nothing to do with you."

"No, it doesn't. I'm just meddlesome and innately curious."

"Do what you like, but I'm not waiting for you. I'm going tomorrow."

"You don't know what you might be walking into."

"I'm leaving on the seven o'clock from Princeton Junction. With, or without you."

JACOB STARED AT THE REFRIGERATOR. He was too wound up over the mysterious sister and too worried about Aunt Zuela to eat. She ought to be home by now, or at least on the train, so why wasn't she answering her phone? Maybe she was on route from the station and had finally realized that driving a car and talking on the phone at the same time was dangerous. Though he doubted it.

He opened the Frigidaire and stared at the carton of eggs, container of hummus, and the steak he'd set out to thaw yesterday and then stuck back in when he decided to order pizza. Two pieces of left-over pepperoni special, unappetizingly curled at the edges, occupied the otherwise empty bottom shelf of the refrigerator. He took out the hummus and a bottle of Dos Equis but set them on the counter when a loud *hwonnnnking* drew him to the window.

A glaze of moon silver licked the pond surface, and the objects outside had darkened to mysterious shapes. He squinted his eyes, seeking out Simon Legree, but it was too dark. Forgetting the hummus and beer, he moved restlessly about, swiping at the counter top with a sponge when the surface didn't really need cleaning; opening a cabinet to see if he had bread but forgetting to take note; checking the beer supply in his refrigerator; retrieving a package from the mudroom that the UPS man had left.

Daisy Mae, who had been lying on a pile of old towels in the corner of the mudroom, stretched and followed him into the dining room, which still smelled of Murphy's. He knew the package contained the collection of miniature African masks he'd shipped from Rwanda, so he set the box on the table beside the stack of photos he'd taken of the mountain gorillas. He'd open the package tomorrow.

He picked up the gorilla photos, looked at the top two, and then set them down again. He wandered back into the kitchen. The house had begun its evening dialog—the knocking of the loose shutter and the clunk of plumbing answered by the creak of old wood settling for the night. The refrigerator hummed, and from somewhere above the kitchen ceiling he heard a squeak that made him look upward, wondering about the source. The evening stretched long and lonely before him. It was too late to go for a run. Too dark to skip down to the river and throw in his fishing line. And damn it! Where was Aunt Zuela?

Resigned to waiting, he grabbed the Dos Equis and settled with the newspaper in front of the cold fireplace. He picked at the contents of the paper, ignoring the beer except for an occasional sip. He'd turned to the comics section and was in the middle of *Hagar the Horrible* when he heard the rumble of a car and saw the flash of head lights through the window. He hurried to the back door, recognizing the sound of Aunt Zuela's Beetle as it ground to a stop.

"Where have you been?" he called, going to meet her. He knew he sounded annoyed, but he'd been worried.

She slid from the driver's seat and swung her purse over her shoulder. "You know perfectly well where I've been. Slogging around New York City in the rain, ruining my shoes, getting soaked to the bone."

"Did you find out anything?"

She dug through her purse, pulled out an index card, and handed it to Jacob. "Alice Sieron Wentworth was Charla's friend. I talked to her baby sitter. Alice will be home tomorrow." She grabbed two paper bags from the back seat. "I brought chicken wings and peanut butter cookies; I'm starving."

"What did you find out about the Petrowskys other than the name of Charla's friend?" he asked when they settled at the card table to eat.

"Mrs. Petrowsky was in charge of the arts and crafts auction for the school one year. She baked marvelous apple cakes for their bake sales, and she made a cake for the nuns in the convent. They enjoyed it immensely. Ama was a cute little thing. She danced in the school talent show. They didn't remember seeing Charla at graduation, but claimed if a student died, they would have known."

His curiosity grew as he listened to the details of her visit. Ama Hunter's life was turning into a story riddled with enigmas—her parents smuggling triptychs from Poland, Ama playing the role of the dying swan queen and then dying herself, her mother dying with two wills, Ama sneaking about to banks in a broad-brimmed hat trying to hide money, and to top it all, the emergence of a secret sister.

When she finished eating, Aunt Zuela tore a section from the roll of paper towels he'd put on the table, wiped her hands, and looked down at Daisy Mae rubbing against her legs. "When did you get the cat?"

"House-warming present from Laskey."

"Well, that's creative. A good mouser, I hope."

"Not old enough yet, but when she reaches the appropriate age, I'll have a talk with her about her responsibilities." A knocking on the back door interrupted him. "It's Laskey," he said, rising, and glancing out the window. The Sequoia was parked beside the Beetle.

"Does he know you're poking around in his case, sending spies to New York?"

"No, and I'd thank you not to tell him."

"Thought I'd drop by and check on Daisy Mae," Laskey said stepping inside. He scooped up the kitten who had followed Jacob to the door and ran his forefinger over her ruff. "Got another one of those?" He nodded at the beer in Jacob's hand.

"Sure. Come on in." Jacob led the way to the kitchen.

"Where'd you get the chocolate cake?" Laskey motioned to the cake sitting beside the bag of cookies.

"The private pre-bake sale before the official bake sale for the Historical Society of Goose Bend."

"I'm not even going to try to understand what you just said."

"After an extravagant amount of begging, haggling, and threats to resort to chicanery, I was allowed to buy the cake from Aunt Zuela for an exorbitant price before the actual bake sale began. She's sitting over there now, as a matter of fact." He nodded toward the card table.

"Good evening to you, Dr. Hay," Laskey boomed.

"And good evening to you, Detective Laskey. You sound very formal this evening. *Dr. Hay*." She had risen and was headed toward where they stood in the kitchen.

"Well, since I haven't seen you in years, I thought maybe formality was in order for a famous Shakespearean scholar."

"Famous? In my dreams." She held out her hand to shake his. "It's good to see you, but I'm going to run now. I had a rather busy day." She raised her eyebrows at Jacob, grabbed her purse from the kitchen counter, and, with a wave of her fingers, headed toward the mudroom. "I'll see myself out," she said.

When the backdoor slammed behind her, Laskey peeked into the bag of cookies and sniffed. "If you had to pay big for the cake, then I guess I should have a big piece along with a couple of these beauties."

Jacob cut an over-sized piece of cake, set it on a saucer along with two cookies, and handed it to Laskey. While Jacob pulled another beer from the refrigerator, Laskey, plate in one hand and Daisy Mae in the other, strolled over to the door leading to the living room. "Since you don't have a fire going, we might as well sit in your living room."

"Are you going to tell me what's happening with the case?" Jacob asked, following Laskey into the room. "There must be something you can share." He handed Laskey the beer.

"Relax." Laskey set the cake and cookies on the coffee table and after setting Daisy Mae on the floor, collapsed onto the sofa. He twisted off the bottle cap and took a long drink. He took a bite of cake, and then munched the cookie. "Five star," he said holding up the cookie. "The cake, too." About to take another drink, he lowered the bottle to stare at Kate's painting.

"Where'd you get the painting?" he asked at length. "It's nice."

"Yeah, it's nice. So tell me what's going on," Jacob said, trying to change the subject. He knew the likelihood of Laskey recognizing the artist was pretty good considering his background in art.

Laskey's eyes narrowed as he continued to look at the painting. "Where'd you get it?"

"It was a gift. Anything on those prepaid credit cards?"

"Nope." His eyes lingered on the pond-scape for a few more moments, until, sighing, he withdrew a cigar from his coat pocket and held it up to Jacob. "Any chance I can light up? Three puffs, then I'll stop. I promise."

"Take as many puffs as you like." Jacob raised his palm in a *be my guest* gesture.

Laskey nipped off the end of the cigar, lit it, and an aromatic fog of cedar floated over to Jacob. He inhaled deeply. He liked the smell. It reminded him of being comfortably ensconced in Laskey's house as a boy—a man's world, not a woman's world. Not that he minded his mother and sister, it was just that sometimes he liked to be away from things feminine.

Laskey flapped a hand at the puffs of smoke curling up from the cigar. "I'm stinking up your house, but I just needed to be indulged for a little while." He picked up a copy of *The Smithsonian* from the coffee table and fanned at the air around him.

"Actually, I don't mind the smell, Lask. All that Old English and Murphy's *clean and tidy* smell was starting to get to me. It's a little too scrubbed and scoured around here to be comfortable."

Laskey munched into the second cookie. "Since you're the one who alerted me to Mrs. Petrowsky's wills . . . ," he said between bites, ". . . you already know that several people stand to gain. It's a bit of a mess. Since both Ama and, presumably, her sister are dead, Kate Hunter gets everything."

Jacob frowned. "If Mrs. Petrowsky's second will is judged invalid, which it probably will be, all Kate gets is a curio cabinet."

"Ama had a will, too. In hers, everything goes to Kate. Which means the proceeds from the insurance policy will also go to Kate since there are no other relatives." He stubbed out his cigar in the empty saucer. "The lawyers will sort it out." He leaned back and, tilting his head to rest on the sofa, looked up at the ceiling and stroked his throat. Daisy Mae jumped up beside him and snuggled into his thigh. "Kate Hunter benefits from all three wills."

"Get serious, Laskey." Jacob felt a flush of anger. "Everyone knows Mrs. Petrowsky wasn't of sound mind when she signed that second will, and all Kate has to gain from the first is a curio cabinet."

"And whatever is inside. Mrs. Winters gets a house and a bunch of furniture. I guess you can say that son of hers stands to gain, too, since he can sell or pawn Mrs. Petrowsky's furniture and buy another broken-down car to clutter up his mother's front yard." He upended his beer and drained it. "Mind if I have another?" He slid Daisy Mae gently away and rose. "I'll get it."

When Laskey returned, he stopped in the middle of the room, his brow contracted in thought. "You're right, the second will can't possibly be valid," he said at length. "What I don't know is . . . ." Still frowning, he paced. When he came to the fireplace, he stopped and looked up at the painting. Then stepping closer, he raised a finger and let it hover over Kate's signature.

He turned around, the color drained from his face. "This is your pond, and the painting is still wet. I can smell the oil. Kate Hunter has been here in the past few days." He took a step toward Jacob. "You're working for the DA, and that office may have to prosecute a Hunter. Surely you realize that?"

Jacob was stung to silence. "I'm not working for the DA," he said at length. "I'm doing research for Charlie because I know more about environmental legislation than he does. Going out to dinner with Kate Hunter just sort of happened. I wasn't thinking about my relationship with Charlie at the time." Jacob felt a red-hot flush burn though his body as Laskey stared unrelentingly at him. "While we were at dinner, she asked if she could paint the pond. I didn't think there was any harm in that. She did it yesterday when I wasn't around, but she left the painting in the mudroom. She didn't want it." His excuses sounded weak and flimsy.

"Do you realize what you've done? You might only be doing Charlie a favor, but you could compromise both yourself and the DA's office by accepting this painting." He walked over to the window and gazed out into the dark. "I could tell you a story . . .," he said in a barely audible tone, ". . . about a young man. Obstinate, head-strong, ambitious. A lot like you. I was . . ." He looked down at his injured foot and flexed it.

Jacob held his breath. Was Laskey finally going to tell him what happened to his foot?

Seeming to change his mind, Laskey squared his shoulders,

turned around, and looked Jacob in the eyes. "Don't get yourself in a mess, Jake. Extrication isn't always possible." He started for the door. "Give back the painting," he called over his shoulder. "And Jake," he paused and twisted around. "Don't ever mistake pretty wrappings for the quality of the gift inside."

Chapter Thirty-Five

Wednesday, March 12

J acob hurried toward the boarding area for the Manhattan train, pulling his wool jacket tightly around him as he maneuvered past commuters. The sun had risen spring-time bright but the temperature had reverted to February cold. He stopped at the top of the short flight leading down to the platform and searched among the passengers waiting at the rails. He saw Kate standing halfway down the estrade, her back to him. Dressed in gray slacks and a bright green three-quarter length coat, she hugged herself to keep warm as gusts of wind whipped her hair into tufts.

He'd struggled half the night and from the moment he woke trying to decide whether or not to go, either choice weighing him with guilt. Defy Laskey? Leave Kate to walk into the unknown? But his back-and-forths kept bringing him to the same place: Kate shouldn't be setting out alone to explore someone's dark past.

"Sorry, Lask," he mumbled, starting down the steps. "I have to do this."

"You came," she snapped, when he touched her arm.

"Obviously." He could be abrupt, too.

"If you're going to be such a jerk, why didn't you stay home?"

He let out a pent-up breath. "Sorry, Kate. I'll behave." He gave her a wan smile. "I guess I'm a little nervous about what we might find." He wouldn't tell her the real reason for his edginess was his regret at doing something Laskey asked him not to do. There had been times, and yesterday evening was one, when it seemed his father looked at him through Laskey's eyes.

"I'm sorry, too, but I'm a bit put off by what you told me last night. Not to mention a severe lack of sleep lately. Imagine that. I've let a murder in the family disturb my beauty rest."

"Understood." Easing his shoulder closer, he tilted his head to breathe in the smell of her coconut-scented shampoo.

"You didn't have to come, you know." A puff of vapor came from her mouth.

"No, I didn't have to." He found himself wondering why they needed to go at all. What did a mysterious dead sister have to do with the more important topic of the moment: Who killed Ama Hunter? Two days ago, yesterday even, curiosity about the sister gnawed at him. He supposed it was Laskey's warning that had dampened his inquisitiveness.

"It looks like I was just in time," he said when the shriek of a train's whistle, followed by the rattling and wheezing of wheels and brakes, prompted them to step back from the tracks.

On board, they settled into straight-backed seats, as unpliable as if they'd been upholstered with wood. A bell announced the closing of doors, and then the train labored away, rumbling and pulsing as it gathered speed. An Amtrak express sped past, jolting them with the sudden compression of air between the two trains.

"Why didn't we take Amtrak?" he asked, squirming to make himself comfortable.

"School teachers on leaves of absence can't afford Amtrak." She combed her fingers through her hair, teasing it back in shape. "And I'm trying to save money." She closed her eyes and rested her head on the back of the seat. "When I've saved enough, I'll stop teaching in high school and get an advanced degree so I can teach in college where they have lighter teaching loads. Then I'll paint for hours and hours every day. You know . . . . No, of course you don't know." She opened her eyes and looked at him. "Last year they invited me to exhibit at the Salmagundi Club. One of my college professors convinced them I was an up and coming artist."

"That's great."

"I declined."

He looked at her in surprise. "Why?"

"Do you know what the Salmagundi Club is, Jacob?"

"No." Obviously, it was some club interested in art.

"It's an organization in New York City. When you're invited to exhibit there, and then join later, your professional reputation climbs a few notches."

"So why didn't you exhibit?"

"I teach school, remember. Eight hours every day, plus preparation. I have neither time nor energy left to prepare an exhibit." She began rummaging through her large shoulder bag. "I brought breakfast." She extracted two muffins wrapped in Saran wrap. "Orange-cranberry," she said handing him one. She set hers on the seat beside her and reached into her purse again, this time bringing out apples and handing him a Golden Delicious. "Before you ask, no, I did not bake the muffins. I don't cook."

"What makes you think I was going to ask?" He stared at the apple.

"Is something wrong?"

"I don't suppose your middle name is Eve, is it?"

"You're not funny." Nibbling at her muffin, she turned her attention to the scenes rolling past the window.

His gaze followed hers as he munched into the apple. The previous day's rainwater lay in fetid puddles on the streets. He saw similar puddles on the flat roofs of hastily constructed box buildings whenever the train raced through elevated stretches of track.

The monotony of steel wheels hammering against steel tracks mesmerized him. He rested his head on the back of the seat and closed his eyes, glad that Kate didn't feel the need to be chatty. Ever since Laskey's ultimatum yesterday evening to not see her, he'd wondered if his godfather knew something. He tried to brush away the hint that Laskey might have found evidence to charge John with his wife's murder, and that he was trying to save Jacob from the hurt of being involved with the sister. Except that he wasn't involved.

People piled on at New Brunswick, and again at Edison and Metuchen. The seats filled, and after Rahway, aisles became crowded. Newspapers rattled, phones rang, and the child across from them asked for the dozenth time how much farther. A man stood over Jacob smacking gum and grasping the back of Jacob's seat to support himself as the train swayed and swerved. His knuckles jabbed Jacob's back where he clasped the corner of the seat. Each time the train lurched, the man lurched, too.

Kate suddenly seemed to remember Jacob's presence after the stop at Linden. "Ama went to St. Ursula's School in Queens," she said. "I looked up the address. We can go there and ask about Ama and this supposed sister, and then . . ."

"That won't be necessary." He told her about Aunt Zuela's mission. "We can go directly to Alice Sieron Wentworth's house."

"Does she know we're coming?"

"We'll surprise her."

"It may be a surprise she doesn't want."

"Hence, the reason for surprise."

The train had become warm. He wanted to take off his coat, but in their cramped state it seemed more trouble than it was worth. Anyway, they'd be at the station soon. "Tell me about Ama," he said, resigning himself to being overheated for a few more minutes.

"What do you want to know?"

"I keep wondering if the solution to her murder lies in her past." At the moment, the Sherlock in him was edging out the Perry Mason.

"She and John met when he was a senior at Lehigh. During one of his wild weekends in New York City, he ran into her coming out of a restaurant while he was going in. He stopped her and worked his magic, persuading her to see him that evening. That's the story I got, anyway. John brought her to meet the family a few months later. When I walked in the living room and saw this gorgeous being with her stage smile, I was totally jealous. And, oh my God, was she ever thin." Kate gave a little laugh. "I decided I'd starve myself until my shoulder blades stuck out like hers. My diet lasted all of one hour. Mom's plans for welcoming her prospective daughter-in-law began with cocktail hour. Ama had a goblet of water. No drinks. No nuts or olives. No cute little cocktail sausages. I followed suit. For dinner, Mom had whipped up a feast. Ama ate three peas, an asparagus spear, and a sliver of roast beef. But not me. Oh, no. After depriving myself of pre-dinner goodies, I'd had it with dieting and went back to my usual eat-everything-in-sight-mode. Including dessert. I think it was crème brulee that night."

"Your figure doesn't seem to have suffered from extra helpings of roast beef and crème brulee."

"You're noble." A thoughtful expression spread over her face. "I don't think Ama was ever happy, but at least in the beginning she tried to smile. A few months after they married, she stopped trying, and when Josephine Petrowsky moved to Goose Bend, Ama put on a frown and never took it off again."

The train had stopped at Newark station, and they turned to look at the throng waiting on the platform, jostling for positions near where the doors were about to open.

"There's another train three minutes behind," a voice blared from the platform speakers. "Please wait for the next train. Three minutes. You can see its headlights now. Please wait."

Ignoring the announcement, people packed the aisles until the closing doors blocked further entrance. The man with the chewing gum was forced backwards away from Jacob. The train grumbled, picked up speed, and headed on toward its destination.

"I think Ama married John in a weak moment," Kate said when the wheels had once again fallen into a steady rhythm. "John charms women like buttermilk attracts flies." She let her gaze rest on the back of the passenger's head in front of her. "Ama was passionate about dancing. When she realized what she'd done, it was too late. The Petrowskys were old-school Catholics, so I don't think it even occurred to her to divorce my brother."

She swiveled her head to face him. "Josephine used to whine about how she and Tadek struggled when they came to this country, and how much she wanted for Ama. Then along comes John – rich, good-looking, charming. An ambitious mother's dream-come-true. My opinion, in case you're interested, is that Ama was confused. She let her mother convince her that marrying the right person was more important than her dancing career." She turned to look out the window.

"Josephine Petrowsky was a master of the guilt-trip," Kate continued after a few moments. "She was friendly enough to outsiders, and she behaved around Mom and Dad, but I was in a position to see what others didn't. John saw, of course. Most people had no idea how Josephine used every trick in the book to control Ama. I won't bore you with all her manipulative devices, but I suppose that's why my sister-in-law hated her mother: she wasn't strong enough to stand up to her."

The wadded-up Saran wrap containing her apple core and muffin crumbs had been lying in Kate's lap. She leaned over and deposited the waste in her shoulder bag on the floor. "Anyway, . . ." she said, sitting upright again. ". . . soon after they married, John enrolled at Wharton. He hadn't told Ama about his plans to go to Wharton until after the wedding. Once John got his MBA, Dad planned to retire and turn the business over to him. The business was John's inheritance. Mine is the house and whatever remains in Mom and Dad's bank account when they pass." She gave a bitter laugh. "Something about this arrangement doesn't strike me as quite right." She looked at him in alarm. "I hope that didn't sound like I'm ungrateful, or that I want Mom and Dad to die so I can have their money. It's just that . . . . Well, John could go to Wharton, but I can't study art. My parents think being an artist is too ragged and radical for a properly brought up young woman who needs to keep her money properly invested."

The arrangement didn't strike him as quite right either.

"It was partially my fault. I kept going on about wanting to run off and be a Bohemian, and they believed me. All I really wanted was to get an MFA so I could teach in college and have enough energy left over after teaching to do my own work, but instead of explaining it nicely, I had to torment them until they got the ragged, radical artist image fixed in their heads. Dad paid John's tuition, but not his living expenses while he was getting his MBA. The Ballet Company of Philadelphia offered Ama a spot, but ballet companies don't pay much, so Ama started a dance school."

Intrigued, Jacob listened to how Ama, after giving up her career, began to withdraw, losing interest in everything, friends, husband, home, isolating herself on an island of bitterness.

"Back in November . . .," Kate continued, ". . . when John moved in with Nancy B and Ama realized she had neither career nor husband, she went way beyond bitter. Sometimes, I even thought . . . ."

Around them, people began folding newspapers and gathering belongings. "We're almost there," the mother in the seat across the aisle said as she took markers and paper from her son and deposited them in a canvas bag.

"Sometimes you thought . . . .?" Jacob leaned closer so he could hear above the racket of detraining preparations.

She shook her head. "Never mind."

The train darkened as they entered the tunnel under New York Harbor. Passengers teetered on the edges of their seats, ready to bolt as soon as the doors screeched open. A few minutes later they rumbled into Penn Station.

Chapter Thirty-Six

By issuing a stream of grunts, shrugs, and noncommittal answers, Laskey had learned to shield information from nosy people trying to ferret out an inside scoop. It was a skill he managed to do on autopilot without interrupting whatever train of thought he happened to be engaged in. Right now that skill was in full deployment as the bartender at the Pennston Hotel moved back and forth, wiping glasses, cleaning the counter, checking his supplies, the whole while trying to gain enlightenment re the murder. Laskey sipped his coffee and replied to the various maneuvers with *hmmmms, ah so's,* and raised shoulders. To direct questions, he answered with, "Time will tell," or "I'm off duty; my mind has shut down." Always on the tip of his tongue was: "It's none of your business." He never said it even though the words practically burned a hole on his tongue trying to lash out. *Keep your bridges up and in good repair,* he kept reminding himself.

His train of thought at the moment had to do with the conversations he'd just had with two members of Kate's book group. The day after the murder, they assured him that Kate had attended the meeting which usually ran until after ten, or sometimes later, depending on how much gossip they had to sift through once the book discussion ended.

Shocked at what had happened, they'd simply left it at that: Kate was there that evening. This morning, they'd amended their answers. "Kate didn't feel good, so she left early," one told him, questions vaulting from her eyes. To the woman's credit, she hadn't asked why he was rechecking Kate's whereabouts on the night of the murder. The second corroborated the first woman's story. Neither remembered exactly what time Kate left except that it was before they served cake and coffee.

The bartender tossed the towel he used for drying glasses over his shoulder and leaned on the counter. "Did Jimmy Q really see someone sitting in front of Lacy's that night?" he asked.

The question jolted Laskey. He struggled to keep his face impassive while bafflement, and then ire, burned through him. No one had informed him about the old man seeing someone in front of Lacy's. "What do you think?" he asked after giving himself a few seconds to regain composure.

"The man's crazy. He invents half of what he says. He hears voices. He prob'ly' sees ghosts, too. But still . . ." the bartender shrugged, ". . . you never know."

"I'VE BEEN police chief here for twenty years, and if there's one thing I know, it's that Jimmy Q Haskell is off his rocker." Bump's face was bright red.

"But you questioned him?" Laskey's voice was a stab of cold steel.

"I did." Bump dabbed at the sweat trickling down his forehead. "I didn't say anything because . . . Well, you were so busy I didn't think you'd want to waste time on an old man that hears voices and doesn't know which end of the week it is."

"Bring him in." He'd seen Jimmy Q pedaling around almost every day, so he knew he was likely nearby.

Fifteen minutes later, Jimmy Q sat at the conference table, a grin on his face, a stench billowing up around him. Bump raised the window and stood beside it.

Laskey sat down opposite Jimmy. "Tell me what you saw the night Ama Hunter was murdered."

Jimmy Q fidgeted under Laskey's uncompromising gaze.

"Jimmy!" Bump interjected.

Still fixing Jimmy Q with his stare, Laskey held up a hand to silence Bump.

"I seen . . .," Jimmy Q began. He stopped, sniffed, and then wiped the back of his hand across his nose. "That man sat on the bench across the street, and I seen a woman leave." He threw a fleeting glance at Bump.

"Tell me about the man."

"I seen him again yesterday."

Bump let out an exasperated sigh, but said nothing.

"Who was the man?" Laskey asked.

"The same man I seen gittin' in a truck a ways back. One of them trucks with a tow thing on the back and something written on the side door."

"Hackett's Garage?" Bump stepped forward. "Is that what was written on the door?"

Jimmy Q scowled up at the police chief. "Didn't read it."

"A yellow truck?"

"Yeah, yeah, it war yellow." Jimmy Q brightened.

"Woodsie Hackett has a garage out on the edge of town," Bump explained to Laskey.

"He war just sittin' there." Ignoring Bump, Jimmy Q had aimed his remark at Laskey. "Didn't see him do nothin'."

"And the woman you saw leaving? What color hair did she have?"

Jimmy Q shrugged. "Couldn't see her hair."

"Why not?"

"She wore a scarf and walked with her head down. Like this . . ." He jumped up, crossed his arms over his chest in a tight hug, lowered his head, and lurched to first one side of the room and then the other before plopping back in his seat with a smirk.

"Other than a scarf, what else did she wear?"

Jimmy Q screwed up his face and thought for a few moments. "Pants," he said finally.

"How do you know it was a woman?"

He gave Laskey a look of disdain. "I know a woman when I see one."

"You saw her leave, but you didn't see her return."

"Nope. I went back in there to watch 'em throw darts."

"What time did she leave?"

Jimmy Q looked at him as though he was crazy. "I don't never know the time."

"Which way did she go?"

"Thataway." Jimmy Q pointed in the direction that indicated she had turned to the right after leaving the building.

"Well . . .," Laskey said, loosening his lips into the semblance of a smile, ". . . thank you for the information. If you remember anything else . . . ." He was halfway out of his seat. "I'm going to pay Woodsie a visit."

***

DERELICT GAS PUMPS, rusted, and with frayed hoses, fronted Woodsie's Garage. The left side of the building consisted of a service area with bays for three cars. A small office occupied the right side. The three people milling around the service area, two in mechanics uniforms, and one who looked like a customer, ignored Laskey as he ambled over to the office and peered through a window, grimy with years of dust, exhaust by-products and oil smudges. Seeing no one inside, he meandered the few feet to the service area, asked for Woodsie Hackett, and was directed to a pair of feet sticking out from beneath a Toyota Camry.

Laskey bent down. "Woodsie?"

"Yeah?" A deep bass welled out from underneath the vehicle, following by a couple of metallic clanks of a wrench on the under-carriage.

"I need to talk to you."

"I don't know who the hell you are, but I guess you must be

blind and can't see that I'm underneath a car, trying to . . . ." There was a grunt and another clang of metal against metal followed by two *shits* and then a series of light taps. Ting, ting, ting, ting.

Laskey squatted. "I'm Detective William Laskey. I'm not blind, and I need to talk to you now, if not sooner."

The tinging stopped. Legs encased in a pair of blue coveralls emerged inch by inch from beneath the Toyota. When the dolly had rolled completely out, revealing an oil-streaked, grease-smeared Woodsie, Laskey stepped back and watched the mechanic sit up and then give him a wary look as he hoisted his six-foot-plus-quite-a-few-inches-tall frame to standing position.

"How can I help you?" Woodsie wiped his hands on a rag dangling from his pocket.

"Might be best to find a quiet place." Laskey swept his hand around indicating the customer and two employees who had stopped what they were doing to listen.

"Come in the office." Woodsie turned to lead the way.

Stacks of work orders, bills, and inventories cluttered the tiny office, and it smelled of lubricant. Woodsie removed a pile of files from a chair and motioned for Laskey to have a seat. Then he collapsed into the desk chair and looked guardedly at his visitor.

Laskey saw the red cowboy boots lined up beneath the window. "You were sitting across from Ama Hunter's studio the night she was murdered." He framed his words as a simple statement of fact, not an accusation.

Woodsie pressed his lips together and nodded.

"What were you doing?"

"I, uh . . . . ." He swallowed. "I was supposed to pick up my daughter from her dance class. Not the last class," he hastened to add. "Janey's class ended at eight. But I forgot. Well, I didn't actually forget, I just got hung up and lost track of time, so her mother had to pick her up. When I didn't show, Janey called her mother."

"If you didn't show up, then how is it you were there?"

"When I realized what time it was, I rushed over, but I was too late."

"So you got out of your truck, sat down on the bench in front of Lacy's, and stayed. For how long?"

"I guess maybe . . . an hour and a half. Or thereabouts."

"An hour and a half? Why?"

"I'd gone up to Allentown to pick up some parts that afternoon, so I called my wife and told her I had a flat tire on the way home."

Confused, Laskey held up his palms. "That was after your wife picked up your daughter?"

Woodsie nodded. "I gave her time to get home, and then I called. I told her my spare was flat, too, to explain why it took so long. Truth is, I was a little preoccupied and needed some time to figure things out. You don't think I had anything to do with the murder, do you?"

"Did you?"

Woodsie's face turned gray. "No." He shook his head violently. "No, no, no."

"What were you so preoccupied with that you sat there for such a long time?"

Woodsie shifted, legs moving this way and that. He ran a hand through his hair and then scratched the back of his neck. "I . . . . uh . . . .. I left work a little early."

"To go to Allentown for parts?"

"I was with another woman." He said it fast and then gave Laskey a pleading look. "I'll tell you what I can, which is just about nothing, but please, does my wife have to know?"

"I'm not interested in your personal life unless it has some bearing on this case."

"It doesn't."

"Give me a minute by minute run-down of what happened while you were sitting in front of Lacy's."

"When I got there some of the students from the class that ended at eight were playing around on the sidewalk, waiting for their moms to stop gabbing. I think the clucking hens group was a mix of moms picking up from that class and dropping off for the next class. Then all the moms left. There were thirty or forty minutes of no mothers, and then they started arriving to pick-up from the class that ended at nine. In between there was lots of whooping and hollering from the hotel bar. Old man Haskell came out and peed two, three times."

"Then what?"

"I sorta fell asleep." He shrugged as embarrassment flushed his face. "I was tired. Sneaking around does that to you, you know? I don't know how long I dozed. Maybe fifteen, twenty minutes. When I woke up, I saw a woman come out the door of the stairwell leading up to the dance studio and walk away."

A current of electricity shot down Laskey's spine. Jimmy Q hadn't imagined the woman. "Describe her."

"She walked fast and wore a scarf. Sorry, but I was too busy making up things to tell my wife to pay much attention. A flat tire and a flat spare weren't going to be enough, so I needed to figure out what to say."

"And did you?" Laskey raised his eyebrows.

"Told her I forgot to pay the AAA bill, and I had to call a friend who took forever getting back to me and then insisted I buy him a beer for his trouble."

Laskey rose and looked through the smudges in the window to where the sun bounced off the concrete like it had summer in mind. "Which way did the woman go?"

"Toward Sixth Street. She crossed over the intersection at Sixth and headed toward Fifth. I didn't pay attention after that."

"You've been a big help." Laskey turned as though to leave, but stopped. "Did you see a Lexus ISF anywhere that night?"

"Sure did. It's hard not to notice one of those. Around here, them with money go for beamers and the big SUV's. The only person in Goose Bend that has a . . ." The color drained from his face. "John Hunter drives an ISF," he said in a barely audible tone. "But he wouldn't . . . ."

"Where did you see the Lexus?"

"Parked down near the Lutheran Church. I saw it on the way in. Otherwise I probly' wouldn't have noticed it from where I sat."

The Lutheran Church was where Kate's book group met. "How long was it there?"

He shrugged. "Can't really say. I think it might have been gone when I left. But I wouldn't swear to it."

Laskey waivered in the doorway for a few seconds. It was a ploy of his, pretending to leave. People usually relaxed when they were about to see his back, and relaxed people coughed up more information. He dug his hands in his pocket and looked down at his shoes, thinking. Kate Hunter was too smart to park the car nearby if she meant to murder her sister-in-law, and she was also too smart to be seen leaving a book group early if murder was what she had in mind. Not that he thought she murdered Ama. But regardless of what he wanted to think, or didn't want to think, he had to consider her a suspect. He shivered. The idea of a beautiful, talented artist shooting her sister-in-law sent a chill down his spine. If for no other reason, he didn't want Kate to be the culprit simply for Jacob's sake. No man should have to endure what he had.

"Sorry about it's being a little cold in here," Woodsie said, mistaking Laskey's shiver. "I turned off the heat a couple days ago."

Laskey swiveled around to face Woodsie. "Tell me again about the woman you saw leaving."

Woodsie lifted his hands in a helpless gesture. "I already told you everything I can. She wore a scarf. She walked with her head down. Seemed like she was in a hurry. Hold a gun to my head and I still couldn't describe her."

"Clothes?"

"Yep, she wore clothes." He made a sound, half sniff, half laugh. "Sorry, that just popped out."

Laskey smiled. "Let me rephrase. What kind of clothes was she wearing?"

Woodsie shook his head slowly. "She might have been wearing slacks, but I can't vouch for that. She had on some sort of jacket, or coat. She was like . . . . huddled over, her head down, her arms hugged across her chest. Sorry, I know that's not much to go on."

"If you remember anything else, even if you think it isn't important, get in touch."

"Will do." Woodsie gave him a send-off salute.

Chapter Thirty-Seven

"Do you think we can get away with this?" Kate looked up at the brownstone.

"Won't know until we try." Jacob touched her elbow, urging her up the steps to Alice Sieron Wentworth's front door.

A few seconds after ringing the bell, the door opened to a slit, and a pair of gold-flecked brown eyes peered at them from over the door chain.

"Alice Sieron Wentworth?" Jacob asked.

"Yes?"

"I'm Jacob Gillis from the Bucks County, Pennsylvania District Attorney's Office." He held out the ID Maureen had provided allowing him access to the materials in the law library. "This is my assistant, Kate Hunter."

Alice jerked her head back slightly. "What do you want?"

"We need to talk to you about a recent occurrence in Bucks County."

"You have me mixed up with somebody else. I have nothing to do with Bucks County. I've been in Pennsylvania twice in my life."

Jacob stuck his foot in the door before she could slam it. He hadn't watched all those detective shows for nothing. "There's nothing for you to be alarmed about," he said, softening his tone and smiling his lady-killer smile. That's what Meg had called it once. *His lady-killer smile.* He didn't believe her, but what the hell . . . . If it worked, why not? He let his muscles go soft, hoping Alice would follow suit, relaxing, and thus more inclined to feel comfortable about letting them in. "We're gathering information. I'm hoping you can help us out."

"Information?"

"Can we talk inside?"

"I don't let strangers in the house."

"I don't blame you. But I really don't want to have to waste a couple hours hanging around while we wait for a subpoena." He smiled again. "Just a few minutes?"

"A subpoena? What's this about?" Her eyes flitted back and forth between Jacob and Kate.

"A case involving one of your former classmates at St. Ursula's, Ama Petrowsky. We only need a few minutes."

Alice let out a barely detectable gasp, and her hand flew to her mouth. "For only a few minutes," she said finally.

"Your assistant?" Kate muttered while Alice closed the door to unchain it. "Not on your life."

He grinned down at her, "You could have been the boss, except I'm the one with ID."

"IKEA," Kate whispered as they stepped inside a few seconds later. "Sleek and cheap."

He noted the modern furnishings made from particle board, the scattered toys, the smell of split pea soup drifting from the kitchen and *Spiderman* blaring from the TV. A boy of around four looked up from where he sat on the floor surrounded by a battalion of military figurines. A toddler, sucking on a pacifier, scurried to Alice and wrapped her arms around her mother's knees, hiding her face. Filmy white curtains diluted the sun's rays, leaving the room in a somber twilight. An open bottle of midnight-blue nail polish, a box of Kleenex, and several wadded up tissues with blue smudges lay on the coffee table.

Alice was dressed in tight jeans and a man's pin-striped shirt with the sleeves rolled up. She raised a hand that still held a nail-polish brush and motioned to the sofa. "Have a seat." Then she said to the boy, "Turn off the TV, Joey."

Jacob and Kate stepped over crayons and Legos, maneuvering to the sofa where Kate pushed aside a stack of coloring books to make room.

"Joey, I told you to turn off the TV." Alice's voice had become shrill.

Joey sat back on his heels, staring at the strangers who had intruded in his messy, noisy world. Changing scenes on the screen reflected alternately light and dark on his face. The toddler, still clinging to her mother's knees, peeked at them.

"Joey!" Alice yelled, at the same time pushing the toddler roughly away.

The boy jumped up and ran to turn off the TV, and the toddler, wearing a dazed look, sat on the floor where her mother's push had landed her. Alice returned the brush to her nail-polish bottle and slowly, meticulously screwed the cap on while avoiding the eyes of her guests. When she finished, she moved over to a chair opposite the sofa and perched stiffly on the edge, color drained from her face. She crossed her arms and shivered.

"You knew Charla Petrowsky?" Jacob asked.

Alice didn't breathe for a few seconds.

"You attended St. Ursula's with Charla Petrowsky. Can you . . . ."

"Not here," she snapped. "I can't talk here." She sprang out of the chair. "Joey, take Mandy to the kitchen. Give her some crackers."

Joey folded his arms over his chest and glowered.

Lunging, she jerked him up by the arm and shoved him towards the girl. "Now," she screamed.

The girl began to howl. Joey, a flash of fear in his eyes, scrambled over, took the screaming toddler by the hand and led her away. Pinching his forehead between his fingers, Jacob glanced at Kate and saw her gritting her teeth.

"We can't talk here." Alice's voice had changed from shrill to bull-frog hoarse. "My husband might come home. He does that sometimes—comes home without warning. He's in sales, and he . . . . Oh, my god." She pressed her hands to her cheeks. "You have to go."

Jacob felt himself digging in, feet rigidly on the floor, shoulders firmly against the back of the sofa. He wasn't leaving. Not until he got what they came for.

"Then we have to talk somewhere else," Kate said. Jacob heard the cold determination in her voice. "You tell us where. I'm sure you can find someone to watch your children for a few minutes."

In a fleeting moment of amusement, Jacob recalled what Aunt Zuela had said about Kate being the one in the family with balls.

"Alfred's Deli is a couple blocks away on Whitfield. I'll meet you there." Alice's words were barely audible. After a brief hesitation, she added. ". . . if I can get my neighbor to watch the kids."

"Oh, but you must," Kate said. "We've come to New York just to talk to you. It can be at the restaurant, or it can be here, husband or no. Your choice."

"HMMMPH, your assistant. Not in a million years," Kate said. They were charging down Whitfield Street in search of Alfred's, Kate in the lead.

"Good lord, woman. You walk too fast to be anyone's assistant."

"Did you expect me to drag along like we're on a Sunday stroll instead of about to solve the mystery of Charla Petrowsky?"

"Do you think setting the Whitfield Street hiking record will bring Alice Wentworth Sieron to us any sooner? Or at all?"

"Oh, she'll come. Count on it."

"Yeah, I think she will. She's a woman with a secret from her husband. Can you slow down long enough for me to take off my coat?" The cold weather had receded like a frightened bird.

"What's the matter, old man? Can't you keep up?"

"I could leave you in my dust in two seconds flat." He peeled off his coat.

"You already did. Thirteen years ago," she said under her breath, also shedding her coat.

Was he supposed to respond to that? He draped his jacket over his arm, pretending not to have heard. Damn her pride. Couldn't she just drop it? She was a grown woman; it was time to let go of schoolgirl issues.

They walked more slowly as they continued down the street. Trees growing from cut-outs in the sidewalk filtered the sun's glare, mottling storefronts with patterns of light and shade, and dappling the pavement to create a moving carpet beneath pedestrians and strutting pigeons. They found Alfred's in the middle of the next block. They nodded at the dark-haired man in an apron cranking out the canopy, went inside, and chose a table near the window. The smells of garlic and candle wax wafted around them.

"Do you drink Riesling?" Kate asked, sliding into a chair.

"When beautiful women who walk fast want it, yes."

"Don't pander to me. I'm not in the mood."

"I noticed." He raised his hand to attract a waiter. He would have preferred ice tea, especially for her after their evening at Odette's.

"You can't possibly know what it's like," she said after he ordered a bottle of St. Michelle and three glasses. She propped her elbows on the table, chin resting on clasped fingers. She looked exhausted.

"You're right. I can't." He felt contrite. The reason for his bad mood was minor compared to hers. Tomorrow he'd set himself straight with Laskey, tell him what he had done today and why, and then promise not to see Kate again. She set every string in his body vibrating, but somewhere, there were other girls who could do that. He just needed to find one and then banish Kate to the back of his mind where she'd been for the past thirteen years.

Meanwhile, he felt her pain. She didn't have the option of ending her hell; all she could do was wait, so he let her be as her gaze drifted through the window, watching people. She flinched each time a woman of the same height and hair color as Alice Wentworth passed. Did Kate ever consider the possibility that her brother was guilty, he wondered. Did he, himself? Charlie seemed to think there was a possibility of John being guilty. Jacob heard it in Charlie's voice, in his hesitations, in the way his eyes drifted away when the subject came up.

Not especially fond of Riesling, he took one sip and then, setting the glass down, watched the human traffic on the street outside. What if Alice didn't come? He couldn't do this a second time. It was either find out today about Charla Petrowsky or forget it. At least for him. Then a thought jolted him. What if Alice called the DA's office to find out if their visit was legit? His claim of representing the DA's office lay somewhere in the realm of stupidity, either completely stupid or insanely stupid. He'd returned to Goose Bend determined to avoid anything that even hinted of misconduct; full and complete redemption was his goal. Yet here he was flirting with trouble when he should have listened to Laskey. Why had he thought for even a minute that Kate was his responsibility?

"She's here." Kate straightened, her eyes on the entrance.

He looked up to see Alice coming toward them, purse clasped hard against her stomach. She'd thrown on a gray cardigan and tucked in the tails of her shirt.

"What do you want to know?" she asked after declining Jacob's offer of lunch, but accepting a glass of Riesling.

"Why did Charla's parents disown her?" he asked and shot a glance at Kate who was watching Alice with a child-like fascination, the look of exhaustion gone for the moment.

Alice looked away. "I don't know what you mean."

"It would be easier just to come out with it. You'll tell us sooner or later."

She closed her eyes and let her head droop. "They pushed her."

"Pushed her?" He glanced at Kate again, wondering if she had the same spontaneous, but unlikely vision of Josephine and Tadek Petrowsky pushing Charla from a bridge or ninth-floor balcony.

"They treated her like a marionette," Alice went on. "*Good children obey their parents. Don't question; God will punish if you do. Do this. Do that. Smile now. Say what I want you to say. Think what I want you to think. Be what I want you to be. My word is law. Jump when I say jump.*"

"What did they push her to do?" Kate propped her arms on the table and leaned toward her.

"What they decided for Ama to be, Ama was ok with. But Charla . . .." Alice's voice resonated like the blade of a whipsaw. "Well . . ., Charla hated it." She picked up her wine, lifted it halfway to her mouth, and then set it down again.

Jacob tried to curb his impatience, suspecting that her reluctance to talk, her edginess, the ill-humor with her children arose because of her complicity in whatever crime, sin, or outrage, Charla had committed. "Alice?" he prodded.

Her eyes glinted. "Oh, the Petrowskys were going to be somebody important here in the Land of Opportunity. So la-de-da that they named their daughters for a queen. Amalie and Charlotte after Queen Charlotte Amalie from one of those countries over there across the ocean. Can you believe it?" She widened her eyes first at Jacob and then at Kate.

One of Kate's eyebrows twitched at Jacob as though to say, "See?"

Alice gave a flip of her hand accompanied by a bitter laugh. "They named their girls for royalty when they were so dirt poor in the beginning they barely had a pot to piss in."

She took a sip of wine. "Mrs. Petrowsky kept talking about how they had to work their tails off to send the girls to a good school and to pay for their lessons. 'We want to give them a foot up in the world,' Mrs. P. kept saying. Oh, they had biiiggg plans for Ama and Charla. Big, big plans. Ama would be a ballerina and Charla a violinist." She gave a little shrug. "I guess where the Petrowskys came from, musicians and dancers were sort of up there on the social ladder. At least the Petrowskys thought they were."

"Cut to the chase, Alice," Jacob said. "Why did they disown Charla?"

Her purse, which had been perched on her thighs, thudded to the floor as she clenched her hands and slid them into her lap. "Charla didn't want to play that stupid violin. She hated it. If they'd only let her dance, too, then she wouldn't have . . . ."

"Wouldn't have what?"

"Danced."

Jacob was confused. "You just said . . . ."

"Oh, Ama was the perfect one. Little Miss-Do-Everything-Right. Pure and white like the swan in that ballet she talked about all the time."

"*Swan Lake.*"

"Yeah, that's it. They told Charla she was evil because she wouldn't practice. Can you believe her own parents told her she was evil? *Why can't you make us proud? Why can't you be like Ama?* They were always on her back." Alice brought her hands back up to the table and began tapping her fingernails—seven painted midnight blue, three still a chalky white.

"Charla danced eventually. But it wasn't ballet." She smiled smugly. "Marek Molnar taught her the basics. Marek was the son of Ama's teacher." She lowered her voice. "And he taught Charla other things, if you know what I mean." She raised her eyebrows at Jacob.

"What kind of dancing?" Kate asked.

Alice rolled her eyes. "The naughty kind. The kind that's an invitation to further activities." She tapped her nails louder. "Ama and Charla both had a thing for Marek. Guess who won? I'll give you a hint. It wasn't Ama." A strange sort of smile played about her lips as she turned to Jacob. "I'm sure you know how a girl earns her income after dancing in those places. But the dancing came later. The other began in high school."

He heard Kate's sharp intake of breath but kept his eyes on Alice who raised a defiant chin.

"She was a prostitute, Mr. District Attorney," she burst out. "A prostitute." Her voice broke. "Look, we were friends, but that was a long time ago. I'm married now; I have two children. Don't mess that up for me. We thought we were just being naughty. Why not do for money what everyone else did for free? If my husband ever found out . . .. For me, it was just a couple weeks."

"We won't tell him," Jacob hastened to say. "How did the Petrowskys find out?"

"Her father went out looking for her one evening. I don't know how he knew where to look. Somebody must have told him. It was either that or just a streak of bad luck that he went to the right place. He found us on Macon Street." She shivered, hugged herself, and then rubbed her hands up and down her arms. "I can't begin to describe the look on his face when he realized what we were doing. He grabbed Charla by the arm—I thought he was going to jerk it off—and dragged her away."

She lifted her eyes to the ceiling and a tear trickled down her cheek. "I went home. For weeks, for months, I lived in fear. I couldn't eat or sleep. My parents thought I was sick and kept dragging me to the doctor. Going to school was hell; coming home was worse. I could barely open the front door for fear my parents had found out, so I'd stand out on the sidewalk shaking, my stomach turned to pulp, while I tried to muster the courage to go inside. Eventually, I did get sick. Mono. But Mama and Daddy never found out about . . . ." She let her voice die away. "My dad would have beaten me to death," she said at length, rubbing one hand hard against the back of the other. "Charla didn't come to school after that. Somebody said she was sick. Ama came late and left early and didn't talk to anyone, but people thought she was just spending more time at her dance classes. As soon as she graduated, the Petrowskys moved to a different part of New York."

"What happened to Charla?" Kate asked.

"She did what she had to do to live." Alice toyed with her fork. "So what has Charla done now?" She looked up, alternating her glance between Kate and Jacob.

Jacob took a deep breath, disappointed that they wouldn't be able to learn the specifics of Charla's death, since Alice apparently didn't know she was dead. "That was the last time you saw Charla? That afternoon on Macon Street?"

"No."

"You saw her again?" Kate's eyes narrowed.

"I ran into her about a year after graduation. Then she started showing up in odd places. I'd be out on an errand, and she'd pop out from a store or an alley. At first, I talked to her. She was so lonely, it was pathetic. Then I got so I was afraid of being s een with her. That was about the time I met Dickie. That's my husband. I tried to avoid her, but she kept finding me. Over the years, I saw her less and less. I suppose she found friends . . . . in her line of work."

"Over the years?" Jacob and Kate repeated simultaneously, looking at each other.

"A few weeks ago, I ran into her over in the park where I take the kids to play."

Kate gasped.

"A few weeks ago?" Jacob's voice had risen, and people turned to stare. "She was alive a few weeks ago?" he asked more quietly, but leaning abruptly toward Alice—aggressively, he realized, when she drew back.

Alice raised her hands in a question. "Yes. What did you think?"

"Where can we find her?"

Chapter Thirty-Eight

Laskey stood in the parking lot of the Goose Bend Police Station, checking his messages before going inside.

"I insist you double my salary," read the first one from Janis.

Curious, he called her. "Double your salary?"

"For hazardous duty pay."

"Are the North Koreans attacking my office? Has ISIS planted a bomb underneath your desk? Have lions escaped the zoo?"

"Inglehook is going to have my scalp if you don't call him."

"Crap."

"I told him you lost his number. Then I explained you were going to be tied up in a long stretch of interviews and meetings, and probably couldn't get back to him right away. Hey, boss, I can't keep covering for you. He was pissed."

"Bloody hell. Tell him . . ."

"What?"

"Crap, I don't know. I guess I have to call him."

"For my sake, make it sooner rather than later. Please."

"It's going to be later; count on it. Go out and have an ice cream sundae and leave your phone in your desk drawer."

"You really want me to do that?"

"Of course not. Just pretend you're out and ignore him the next time he calls."

He hit the "end" button and pocketed his phone without reading the other messages. There was probably one or more from Inglehook, and he didn't want to see them.

Not ready to go inside and face the looks and questions that greeted him each time, he leaned against the fender of his Sequoia. Never, in all his years on the job, had he had such conflicting ideas of who might have done it, or the motives for which it had been done. Nothing made sense. He was starting to think he needed a minor miracle at this point. Bells. A lightning strike. An angel bearing good tidings of truth.

His phone rang. He looked at the caller ID. Janis again. Was she calling to warn him that Inglehook had acquired a couple of bloodhounds to track him down?"

"It's me," he answered.

"Good God, what a surprise; it's you." She paused, and readjusting her voice to somber, said, "The coroner called. Mrs. Petrowsky died of methanol poisoning."

Laskey let his chin sink to rest on his chest. A second murder definitely narrowed the field.

Chapter Thirty-Nine

J acob tried the door of the Mid-Town Gentlemen's Club and found it unlocked even though the sign indicated the club didn't open for business for another four hours. He and Kate entered a small lobby with walls upholstered in purple satin, a floor made from staggered strips of hard tile tinted in various hues of gold, and a chandelier dripping with crystal knobs. A dark mahogany standing desk occupied one corner. Cherry-scented room freshener billowed from a floor vent.

They passed through the entry into the gloom of a large, windowless room, lit only by a small bulb over the stage door at the far side of the room and a row of pocket lights over the bar area located to the left of the entry. The room contained a couple dozen round tables, some surrounded by four chairs, others by six, and a few at the back by eight. Poles were interspersed among the tables, and a stage projected from the back wall.

"A far cry from *Swan Lake,* isn't it?" Kate murmured, examining the gold-flecked wall paper and the yards and yards of fringe decorating everything to be decorated.

The cloying atmosphere made him feel choked, and he regretted his decision to come to New York. Against Laskey's wishes. Against his own better judgement. Hell, judgement had had nothing to do with it; if it had, he wouldn't be here. He hadn't bothered to take the time to think or consider. A feeling so intense he almost shuddered washed over him: he didn't want to be enmeshed in tawdry secrets, in ugliness, in suspicions; he wanted to be outside, in the woods, aboard a raft on the river, on top of a mountain, or any place free of the dark motives of deviant humans.

Kate was watching him, a steeled determination in her eyes, but there was also something else. Expectation? The question of whether or not he was going to turn his back on her and rush off to a metaphorical calculus class again?

The clatter of dishes sounded through an open door near the bar, followed by the clang of a pan being set down and the whirr of a machine or appliance of some sort. The smells of freshly baked bread, roasting beef, and caramelized onions drifted out, along with someone's voice yelling something about crayfish.

"We're closed."

Jacob whipped around to see a man with very large brown eyes and a mop of dark, curly hair holding a broom. He must have slipped in from one of the stage doors. "Ricardo" was embroidered on a white strip above the pocket of his denim coveralls.

"Is the manager in?" Jacob asked.

"He don't usually come in this early. Maybe in three or four hours."

"How we can get hold of him?"

The man shrugged. "Don't know."

"Actually . . .," Kate said, ". . . it's Charla Petrowsky we want to see."

"Don't know her."

"Charlotte, maybe?"

A look of recognition crossed the man's face. "Miss Charlotte. She's not here either. Probly' home resting up for tonight's show."

"Where does she live?" Jacob knew the chances of a janitor's knowing where one of the girls lived was remote, and his confiding that information, even more remote.

Ricardo was about to reply when a mass of muscles in a suit burst through the bar door and strode toward them.

"There's our cliché bouncer," Jacob said softly, nudging Kate. "Thick neck, square jaw, muscles of steel, and a scar on his cheek. Mr. America."

In four seconds the man was beside them.

"Is there a problem?" he demanded, examining Jacob for a split second before shifting his eyes to roam Kate's body. He looked no older than Jacob, yet his short hair had turned gray. "We don't open until seven."

Jacob felt his shoulders tense.

"We can see it's closed," Kate replied in a glacial voice. "If it were open, *I* wouldn't be here. Neither would my friend. We're looking for my sister-in-law's sister. There's been a death in the family."

"Oh . . . ." Mr. America seemed momentarily at a loss for words, as though the idea of family or death had never occurred to him, but then a sliver of suspicion crept into his eyes.

"Charlotte Petrowsky's sister has died," Kate said. "And her mother, too. We came to let Charla know."

Mr. America studied Kate as though trying to decide whether or not to believe her.

"Charla is to inherit some money," she added.

Jacob flinched. Did she know what was in the second will, or had she just made that up to grab the attention of the bouncer? If that was her purpose, she had succeeded. Interest flickered in the man's eyes.

"I can't give out her address, but I'll call and see if she wants to come in. She's been sick, but she might want to hear you if money is to be had." He motioned to the tables. "Sit down. I'll ring her up."

A heavily made-up young woman wearing a terry-cloth lap robe, a pair of untied sneakers, and carrying a stack of red napkins, had shuffled in during the interchange. Jacob assumed she was a waitress who would change later into an outfit more fitting for the venue.

"Hey, why don't you turn on a few lights?" Mr. America yelled at her.

"Fuck you." Ignoring him, she set the napkins down on a long table placed along the left wall and began folding them into triangles.

"Idiot," Mr. America mumbled. "Wait here. I'll give Miss Charlotte a call." He flipped on the lights as he exited through the door to the right of the bar.

"Shall we?" Jacob motioned to a chair.

Kate sat down and leaned her arms on the table. "And now we wait." She frowned at the far side of the room. "That seems to be mostly what I'm doing lately. Waiting." She laid her head down on her arms.

He paced. What he hated about this whole thing, this murder, was that there was nothing he could do. He'd rolled his ankle during the first five minutes of a game once and had to sit out the remainder watching everyone else play. That's how he felt now. He'd managed to hand along a few tidbits from the gossip mill to Laskey, but nothing that Laskey wouldn't have found out from someone else. Except maybe the bit about the tryptics. He would love to discover that Charla Petrowsky had something to do with her sister's murder, but how likely was that?

When his pacing brought him behind Kate, he stopped. Her back rose and then receded with each breath. Had she had fallen asleep?

The urge to touch her, put his hands on her shoulders, and comfort her almost overwhelmed him. He turned away and plunged his hands in his pockets, safely away from her shoulders. On the train, thighs close together, sometimes touching, he'd been on his guard, reminding himself that there were a lot of other women out there who could make him burn with desire—women who wouldn't thoroughly piss him off as Kate had managed to do on a regular basis.

"Ama and I used to come to New York together," Kate said, lifting her head. "We made a pact that if she would come with me to art galleries, I would go with her to ballet performances." She gave a sniff of a laugh. "Ama was bored silly at art galleries. It wasn't much fun with her dragging her feet through the displays and looking at her watch every thirty seconds. Sometimes she made me really angry, you know? I never could figure out why John wanted to marry such a self-centered person. He's a lot better off without her." Her cheeks flushed, and she squeezed her eyes shut, clearly embarrassed at her outburst.

"Were you bored at the ballet?"

"Some performances I enjoyed more than others. Why don't you sit down, instead of hovering over me?"

He pulled out a chair and sat down.

"She never should have married him. Her career was more important than he was and . . . ." she faltered. "To be honest, I guess my brother was no great catch in the marriage department. Ama was talented, but I don't think that idea ever lodged in his brain. Do you have any idea, Jacob, how many men are still living in a different century as far as women go?" She gave him a challenging look.

"Of course. I'm not blind."

"You admit it?" She stared at him in disbelief.

"Like I said, I'm not blind."

"What about your sister? She was talented. Did she give up music because . . . ."

"No. She couldn't afford Julliard. But her husband is great. Now that their two kids are out of diapers, he cooks dinner and does the dishes so she can practice. She's studying with a teacher at Curtis. There are lots of men out there who support their wives' talents."

"What was your father like? I mean, as far as your mother doing her own thing? Or did she have anything she liked doing? Art or music or . . . whatever?"

Jacob's face relaxed in a broad smile. "I can't imagine any man telling my mother what to do. She was, *is*, a strong woman, and my father liked smart women with a will of their own. 'Makes them more interesting,' he used to say." It occurred to him then that he, too, liked strong women. While it was always great to find women who turned him on, the ones he wanted to hang onto after his lust had been sated were the ones with purpose, opinions, and sass.

Otherwise, the relationship was flavorless and bland, like soup with no salt.

Kate retreated into her private thoughts, while he watched the waitress entering and leaving, setting up the buffet table with dishes, glasses. Once, she glanced over at them and asked if they wanted something? Coffee? A drink? Another waitress joined her to help with the set-up. A woman dressed in sweats emerged from the stage door, went over to converse with the waitresses, and then, casting a long look at Jacob and Kate, returned through the door to what Jacob guessed were dressing rooms.

He was beginning to wonder how much longer they had to wait when Mr. America swaggered back into the bar area. "She's on her way," he called over. "I'll be right here." He came around to the front, plopped onto a stool, his back to the counter, leaned back on his elbows, and watched them. A man wearing a white shirt, black pants, and black bowtie—the bartender, presumably—appeared behind him and began setting up the bar area: taking out and arranging the bottles and glassware. The clinking, clanking, and shifting stuff around did nothing to calm Jacob's nerves.

The minutes ticked away until Kate, with a sharp intake of breath, nodded toward the door to the left of the stage, and Jacob looked up to see Charla Petrowsky staring at them. In spite of Charla's Farah Fawcett hair, a curvier body, thicker, darker eyebrows and heavily lined eyes, it was obvious she was Ama sister.

Charla fluffed her hair as she walked across the room to Mr. America, who still leaned against the bar. Laying her hand on his thigh, she whispered something in his ear to which he nodded, and then she turned and walked toward them, her red and white candy-striped six-inch sandals clunking on the black tiles. She wore form-fitting black pants tapering off a few inches above her ankles, a high-necked yellow knit top, and a blue and red paisley shawl draped loosely over one shoulder and tied at her waist on the oppo-site side, the vee of the triangular scarf pointing down her left leg and moving with the leg as she came.

"Hi, I'm Jacob Gillis." He stood and reached out his hand to her and, motioning with his head, said, "This is Kate Hunter."

Kate mumbled something. Charla shot her a glance and then, dismissing her with a twitch of her lips, focused on Jacob.

"What do you want?" She draped her hands over the back of a chair. She had long, thin fingers with black-lacquered nails decorated with silver stars.

"Why don't you have a seat?" Jacob held his palm toward a chair.

She swept her gaze in the direction of Mr. America as though to confirm he remained within protecting distance and then sat down.

She looked back and forth between Jacob and Kate, who was staring, mouth half-open, at Charla.

"You're Ama Hunter's sister," he said finally. Kate had been the one to initiate this whole thing—the trip to New York, the search for Charla, so he'd expected her to take charge of the conversation. Instead, she was struck dumb.

"My sister is Ama Petrowsky," Charla said.

"She married Kate's brother, so she was Ama Petrowsky Hunter." He glanced at Kate, who still showed no signs of helping him out.

"Was?" A snigger of a smile played about Charla's lips. "Did she divorce him? Murder him in his sleep?"

"I'm sorry, but Ama died last week, and on Monday . . . ." He took a deep breath, ". . . your mother died. She'd been sick for a while."

For the span of a few seconds Charla remained immobile, devoid of expression until, in a sudden movement, she threw her head back and broke out in raucous laughter. Jacob saw the others in the room gape in their direction as Charla guffawed until tears ran down her face. Finally, she stopped and ran her hand beneath her eyes, wiping away smudges of eyeliner.

"Two at one shot. I guess my mother, the bitch, must have died of old age. But what happened to my precious sister? The little shit. Did she fall off the stage and crack her skull? Did one of those queers in tights drop her?"

This wasn't the reaction he expected. Come to think of it, he didn't know what he'd expected. But not this.

"Or did she finally get so skinny she dried up and blew away like a dead leaf?" She broke out in another spasm of laughter. "Maybe a drunk driver ran down Miss Goody-Two-Shoes? No, that's not right. Miss-Prim-and-Proper-Ballet-Shoes." She rose and tottered over to the buffet table, grabbed a napkin, and swiped at the mascara that bled beneath her eyes like Spanish moss. After throwing the crumpled napkin back on the table, she waved at the bartender. "Hey, Lucas, can you serve up something to celebrate my sister's untimely death and my mother's timely death? Unless you got a free bottle of champagne, maybe some of that nice apricot vodka." She came back over and sat down. "You guys gon' help me celebrate?" She raised her eyebrows at their lack of response. "Hmmmph, guess not. So, are you going to tell me how my dear sister and my loving mother died, or are we playing Twenty Questions?"

"Where were you Monday evening a week ago?" Jacob asked, surprising himself with his question. It wasn't his place to ask, but it had just popped out.

Her mirthful expression vanished. "Why are you asking?"

"Ama was murdered."

Charla blinked. "Murdered?"

"So, where *were* you?" Kate suddenly sprang to life.

Charla had her chair angled toward Jacob, but she tilted her torso around to glare at Kate. "Tell me again who the fuck you are."

"Ama's sister-in-law. Kate Hunter." Her words snapped like miniature firecrackers. Jacob reached across the table and squeezed her hand in an attempt to calm her.

"A little shit, that's who you are. How dare you come here and ask me a question like that. Both of you. You're shits. My sister has been dead to me for years. My parents have been dead to me for years. They can all go to hell. And you can go to hell, too." She waved them away with the back of her hand, and scraped the chair back, about to escape.

"Wait." Jacob held up his hand. "That's a question everyone connected with Ama has had to answer. Even Kate here." He held his palm toward Kate.

"Well, I'm no longer connected to Ama Whatever-her-name-is. Got it?"

"Hey, you okay over there?" Mr. America called.

"Yeah," she answered without looking at him. Instead, she fixed Jacob with a cold-blooded gaze. "So what happened to Ama? Somebody shot her? Stabbed her? Bashed her head open?"

"She was shot in her studio where she taught dance classes."

Her eyes widened, but she recovered quickly. "Her husband?" She gave Kate a contemptible look.

"No," Kate shot back.

"No one has been charged yet," Jacob added quickly. Dear God in heaven, he'd much prefer to be trekking through the wilds of Rwanda right now, counting poachers' trails.

"So my talented sister taught dance classes? I would of thought she'd been dancing on the stage somewhere. Going along with Mama's big plans. Except, I never saw her name mentioned. Sometimes I looked at the paper. You know, that section where they print that kind of stuff." She ran a fingernail over the table, tracing out something. "I could have been a dancer, too, only they made me play the fucking violin instead. One day I smashed that devil against the fireplace until splinters and strings was all's was left." Her eyes lit up. "You shoulda heard Mama scream, and I thought Papa was going to shit in his pants." She shrugged. "For all I know, he did. They incarcerated me in my room for two months for that little performance, but you know what? It was worth it. So what about Ma? Did she die of old age or of the bitch-virus?"

"Heart attack probably."

Lucas appeared with a tray containing a flagon of vodka and three glasses. "Anything else?" he asked setting it down.

"We'll let you know, Cutie." Charla pinched his thigh. "Hey," she called out in the direction of Mr. America. "Come over her a minute, Honey Bunny." She filled their glasses as Mr. America ambled toward them.

"What's up, Baby?" He massaged the area between her shoulders.

"Want to tell these people where I was a week ago on Monday night?" She grinned up at him.

"Are you sure you want me to?"

"Hell, why not?"

Ignoring Jacob, Mr. America leered at Kate. "After she got done here, she was with me. Want to know what we did?"

"Shut up, you." Charla slapped him playfully on the arm. "Go on back over there to your bar stool."

Giving Kate a final leer, he retraced his steps to the bar.

"Do you want me to call the manager so he can tell you I was here from six o'clock until two the next morning?" She tilted her face to Jacob. "Just in case Honey Bunny's word isn't good enough?" Giving Jacob an impudent look, she dipped her forefinger in her vodka, poked the finger in her mouth, and sucked. "Hate to disappoint you," she said when she withdrew the finger. "But it wasn't me that shot my dearly beloved twin."

"Your twin?" Kate's eyes widened.

"Yeah, my twin."

Something about the divulgence seemed right to Jacob. Sisters hating each other was one thing; twin sisters hating each other was the stuff of legends.

"We look a little similar . . .," Charla said, appearing to enjoy their surprise. ". . . but you must of figured out by now that we aren't much alike otherwise. So there, you got what you came for. You took a gander at the evil sister, and you found out where I was on the infamous evening." Her chair was still tilted toward Jacob. She stretched her legs out away from the table, and with the toe of one foot, pushed off a shoe, letting it clunk to the floor. After following suit with the other, she wiggled her toes and let out a sigh.

Jacob had seen all he wanted to see and had heard more than enough. Good God, was he in the middle of one of those horrible porn novels? He needed to go out running and work up a sweat, or throw rocks. Something normal. He raised a questioning eyebrow at Kate: *Anything else you want to talk about?* He was relieved when she shook her head and stood up. He started to push back from the table but paused.

Charla had propped a foot on the thigh of the opposite leg and was making a guttural, teeth-baring ughhhhh as she massaged the calloused arch, flexing the foot back and forth as she rubbed.

"Occupational hazard," she said when she saw Jacob watching, and jerked her thumb toward a pole. Finished with the one foot, she lifted the other to perform the same ministrations but stopped when she noticed Kate about to stand up. "What? Leaving already? Are you too good to have a drink with me?" She slid her foot back to the floor and narrowed her eyes. "You're not leaving yet. I came all the way over here because there was something about money." She looked at Jacob. "Did Ma have some sort of insurance policy or something?"

"Yes. She had an insurance policy. I need your address and phone number for the insurance agent." He looked at Kate. "Do you have paper and pen there?" He nodded at her purse.

Kate pulled a pen and a small sketchpad from her purse and handed them to Charla. After a brief hesitation during which she looked suspiciously from one to the other, Charla scribbled down an address and phone number.

"The agent will get in touch," Jacob said, taking the notebook.

Kate rose. "We have to catch the train. Are you coming, Jacob?"

"Next week I'm taking off somewhere, too." Charla said with a smirk. She slipped her feet back in her shoes. "South America."

"Really?" Kate's voice dripped with sarcasm. "A tour?"

"A tour of a bedroom more likely." Charla's raunchy laugh rang out again. "My darling sister might have gotten the praise, but I got the man. And oh, how Ama wanted Marek Molnar. He has his own dance troupe now. I'm going to travel with him around South America and wherever else he goes. I'm never coming back to this place."

JACOB WATCHED Kate's reflection in the train window. She'd been silent since leaving The Manhattan Gentlemen's Club, saying nothing during the taxi ride to the station or while boarding the train. Once on board, she slid into a seat and turned her face to the window.

After the train passed beneath the harbor and reemerged into the fading light of what little day remained, she looked at him sideways. "Charla killed Ama," she said. Her gaze lingered on him for a few seconds before she turned again to the window.

Jacob knew the possibility of Charla having killed her sister was remote, but he'd let Kate have her few moments of peace, consoling herself with the fantasy that Charla's guilt proved John's innocence.

"When I saw Ama that night . . .," she said in a near whisper, her face still averted. "I knew something was wrong. She was so . . . nervous." Narrowing her eyes, she looked out at the buildings rushing past her window. "I'm guessing Charla contacted Ama because Charla knew their mother was getting old and might die, leaving insurance money."

He stared at her in disbelief. Not at her theory, although it was absurd, but because she'd just admitted to being with her sister-in-law on the evening of her murder. "What time did you see Ama?"

"After her last class. I left the book group early. But Ama didn't want to see me so I left." She lay her head on the head rest and closed her eyes.

He grasped the arm rests hard and cursed under his breath. If someone saw her there . . . . People had a way of constructing entire dramas from one tiny bit of information, and you never knew when someone might grab at anything just to solve the crime. *I saw Kate Hunter sneaking up to Ama's studio that night. I heard they really didn't like each other. I guess Kate wanted to protect the family money so she could go off and study art somewhere. Kate wasn't like the rest of the family; she was a renegade.*

Then he breathed a sigh of relief. No one had seen her. Otherwise they would have blabbed it all over town. But he had to warn her not to tell anyone else. "Kate . . . ." He leaned toward her, his shoulder touching hers. She didn't respond. "Kate," he said again and touched her hand. But she had fallen into the abyss of exhausted sleep.

Chapter Forty

Laskey examined the contents of Mrs. Petrowsky's locked curio cabinet through its glass doors, while members of his team rummaged through the house searching closets, drawers, trash cans – any place where a medicine bottle tainted with methanol might have been hidden. Another crew sifted through the waste at the nursing home and, yet another, the town garbage dump,

The light oak, curved-front curio cabinet had four shelves. The three bottom ones were filled with bric-a-brac, but it was the items on the top shelf that held his attention. One triptych pictured Jesus on the middle panel with the apostles lined up on the side panels, while the second triptych depicted scenes from the nativity. He didn't need to find the key to the cabinet to see that the triptychs were most likely valuable. The art work had been expertly executed and embossed with generous amounts of gold. As soon as either of Mrs. Petrowsky's wills was probated, Kate Hunter became the owner of the masterpieces.

Unless he had to arrest her for the murder of her sister-in-law and for the death of Mrs. Petrowsky.

Chapter Forty-One

Thursday, March 13

"Coffee to go?" Hilda called to Laskey's back.

"No, thanks. Got to get to work." He exited the diner and headed in the direction of the library. Already keyed up when he swung his legs out of bed, if he had another cup he'd be turning somersaults.

"Good morning, Miss Berry," he said a few minutes later, striding past the head librarian. "I'll try to keep it down back there."

He detoured through the mystery section, stopping a few moments to let his eyes graze over the spines. He'd read hundreds of mysteries, enjoying every minute of trying to figure out the puzzle of whodunit, but he understood that the wages of crime, especially murder, went far beyond puzzles and solutions. The family of the accused and of the guilty suffered major trauma, yet rarely did a book dwell on that. It was always gather the clues, figure out who did it, catch the criminal. Shouldn't some writer, some-where, focus on the shattered lives of the innocent people connected to tragedies? Maybe when he retired, he'd take up the occupation of writer.

He continued through the stacks and claimed his favorite thinking spot in the nook hidden away between the 600s and the 700s. He flung his coat over the back of a chair, sat down, and began scribbling on his yellow legal pad. Writing helped to slow the whirlwind inside his head – ideas, and fragments of ideas tumbling about so fast he sometimes had a hard time grabbing onto them.

The bottle of cough syrup laced with methanol is in the office, he wrote. Found in the bagged trash at the nursing home, wiped clean of fingerprints. Either someone working for the nursing home or a visitor put methanol in the bottle and fed it to Mrs. P.

Yesterday, he'd scooted over to the nursing home within minutes of the bottle being found and spent most of the evening and half the night interviewing the employees. Those who weren't on duty had been called in. None seemed to have the remotest reason for poisoning a patient.

He continued writing.

John Hunter: has alibi (Could have hired a killer. Doubtful.) Motive: monetary gain. No record of visiting Mrs. Petrowsky in nursing home.

Mrs. Winters: no alibi for the time of Ama's murder except her son's word. Visited Mrs. Petrowsky daily. Had access to cough syrup. Motive: inherits a house and furniture minus the curio cabinet. Seems unlikely that she would murder her friend when the friend was probably going to die soon anyway.

Mrs. Winters' son: no alibi. His mother says he was home. He claims he went to get a part for the car he was working on. Neighbors can't confirm either. No one at the parts store can confirm. Motive: he doesn't have a regular job, so he would benefit from his mother having a little extra money. No record of him visiting Mrs. Petrowsky in nursing home.

Conspiracy between Mrs. Winters and her son?????

McGonigle: was at meeting in Doylestown. Could have hired killer. Unlikely that he would have targeted Ama and not John. No conceivable motive for poisoning Mrs. Petrowsky.

Laskey let out a huff. In regard to McGonigle, he was engaging in a wild flight of imagination. Truth was, McGonigle disgusted him. He didn't think for one minute that the director of The Reilly Foundation had anything to do with Ama Hunter's murder, and certainly not Mrs. Petrowsky's, but he kept his name on the suspect list as petty revenge for the man's being a cheat and an asshole.

Nor did the idea of Mrs. Winters and her son conspiring in a double murder set off any tremors in his gut, but maybe his instinct had taken a leave of absence on this case.

There was one more person on the list inside his head. Why did his mind balk every time he started to write her name down on paper? He'd tried contacting her yesterday after his second interview with the book club members but had been unable to track her down. John told him she'd gone away for the day without saying where she was going, and that he hadn't pushed her to tell because he looked forward to being alone. Laskey had woken her up with a phone call at seven this morning.

"I'm working on the timeline for the evening of the murder," he'd replied to her irritated question of why he was calling her at that hour. "Where did you go after you left your book club?"

She blew out a loud huff, and snapped "I was at Rita's Spa in Doylestown."

"You left a book club to make a late evening visit to a spa?"

"Anything wrong with that?"

"No. Do you do that often?"

"You mean do I drive over to Doylestown after eight in the evening for a little pampering?" Her voice had registered the same disbelief his sisters had in theirs when he questioned why they needed new clothes at the beginning of every school year. "No, I don't make many late evening visits to Rita's. But we were discussing a boring book. I had a headache. I was tired of John and Ama's squabbles over money. I was fed up with John's continuous groaning about what a bitch she was. I decided to escape it all for an hour or two."

He called the spa as soon as they hung up. Kate had signed the guest register, the receptionist reported, but hadn't recorded the time. Later, he'd go over to Rita's and try to find someone who'd seen her, but as of right now, Kate Hunter's whereabouts at the time of Ama's murder were unaccounted for.

Gripping the pen, he forced himself to write: *Kate Hunter: parked three blocks from murder scene. Was at book club, but left early claiming she didn't feel well. Went to spa in Doylestown, signed in, but no proof of when she actually got there. Visited nursing home twice during the week before Mrs. P. died, thus could have given her cough syrup or left it on bedside table for someone else to give her. Motive: monetary gain from both wills.* He chewed on the end of his pen. If the triptychs were worth what he thought they might be, she'd do almost as well from the first will as from the second.

What really puzzled him was the second will. Why did Ama have Samsi draw it up in the first place and go to the trouble to have Samsi come to the nursing home for a signature? To calm her mother? Sometimes people with dementia had periods of coherence followed by bouts of anger and frustration. Could Josephine Petrowsky have regretted what happened with the other daughter and gone back in time, thinking Charla was still alive, and that she could make amends in her will? Had Ama gone along just to humor her?

Most puzzling was the cremation stipulation in the will. During the course of the last week and a couple hundred interviews, he'd gleaned that Ama despised her mother. Did Ama hate her mother so much she asked Samsi to include cremation just to thumb her nose at her mother's religion? In the end, Ama had done them a favor by having Samsi add the stipulation because it raised a red flag.

His phone pinged. He pulled it from his pocket and checked his messages.

Charla P still alive.

"What?" He stared at the message for a few moments before noticing that Jacob was the sender. When he clicked on the second message, also from Jacob, there was the address of a club in New York City, followed by the words: *Charla has alibi.*

Laskey laid the phone on the table, leaned his head on the back of the chair and let out a long *arghhhhhhh.* How had Jacob found out? He shouldn't be meddling. Definitely, definitely, Jacob should not be meddling.

His phone pinged again. This time, a message from Inglehook. *See me at 11 sharp! My office.*

What the hell? The man wasn't going to leave him alone.

Annoyed, he punched out Woodsie's number. "Can I pick you up in thirty minutes?" he asked when the mechanic answered. "I want to have you look at something."

Then he rang Jacob. There was no answer. The boy sends him an earth-shaking message and then disappears? Peeved, he stuck the phone back in his pocket, picked up his pen, and added a name to the list.

Charla Petrowsky. Dispatch someone to NYC immediately to check her alibi.

A GUST of wind tore at Jacob's coat as he walked the half block between his parking place and Dr. O'Neill's office. Once again, the day had dawned February cold but summer bright. A few strides later, he swung open the door and walked into a waiting room lined with maroon-upholstered chairs and smelling familiarly of antiseptics, cloves, and zinc-oxide.

"Jacob Gillis," the receptionist called from the check-in window, her eyes crinkling in pleasure. "Remember me? Marcie Miller? Two classes behind you in school? Good lord, man, it's good to have you back in town."

"Of course I remember you, Marcie. I'm glad to be back." He'd repeated that phrase dozens of times during the past week as he ran into people he hadn't seen in years.

"Well, come on back. Dr. O'Neill is ready for you."

Jacob followed her to the hygienist's room.

Dr. O'Neill turned around from where he had been arranging a tray. Sporting an ear to ear grin, he reached out to shake Jacob's hand. "How's our famous quarterback?"

"Great. And you?"

"Still hanging in there. I gave my hygienist a couple hours off so I could do your cleaning myself. It sure is good to have you back. Make yourself comfortable." He gestured to the chair.

Jacob took off his jacket and hung it from a wall hook and then unfolded himself onto the chair, stretching out his legs and draping his arms loosely on the armrests.

"Any good dentists in Rwanda?" Dr. O'Neill fastened a patient napkin around Jacob's neck and then took a dental explorer from the chair side tray.

"One or two that were passable. But they didn't have comfortable leather recliners like this." He patted the arms of the chair.

"Caught sight of you at the funeral last week. . . . Open wide . . . . I tried to catch you, but I couldn't get through the crowd in time." He probed a tender spot, and Jacob winced. "A bit of plaque there." He sat back frowning. "What a terrible, terrible thing. And they still have no idea who did it?"

Jacob shook his head. "I haven't heard if they do."

"People are nervous. They don't know if a killer is on the loose, or if . . . .." he let his voice trail off as he probed Jacob's gums. "I cut a crown preparation for Ama a couple weeks ago and fitted her with a temporary. She was supposed to come last Monday for the crown, but the lab got behind and it wasn't ready. She was pissed. Well, ... more like really angry. I suppose the divorce was taking its toll on her." He blew out a little stream of air and shook his head. "That's one crown that's never going to be used." He put down the explorer and picked up a scraper. "I'm having a hard time picturing her dead when she sat here such a short time ago. And the mother dying right after. But I guess that was a blessing in a way. When your mind goes . . . ."

Dr. O'Neill chatted while he scraped, Jacob nodding occasionally and uttering *uh huhs*, while the scene from yesterday replayed in his mind. He had been surprised at Charla's coarseness which stood in marked contrast to the grace and elegance portrayed in portraits of Ama. Even though she started out as a street walker, Charla had gone on to work in an upscale gentlemen's club, so he would have expected her to have acquired a little of the gloss that came with a classier job. A classier job? He almost laughed at the idea.

Dr. O'Neill retracted the scraper from his mouth. "You ok?"

"Yeah, yeah, I'm fine."

"Thought you were choking there for a minute." He reinserted the tool and bent closer to Jacob's mouth. "I guess you heard about the issues with building the new high school."

Jacob half listened to the saga of how the new school was delayed while tax-payers fought over whether or not to include an indoor pool in the gym facilities.

After finishing up with a brushing and flossing, Dr. O'Neill removed the napkin from around Jacob's neck and sat back. "There, you're done. Have Marcie make an appointment for you in six months. We can't have you going so long between cleanings, now can we?" He followed Jacob to the reception desk, waited while Marci made another appointment, and then clapped Jacob on the shoulder. "Everybody was glad to see you move back to Goose Bend. A lot of kids nowadays go off to college and think they're too important to come back to their home town. But you've gone to law school, worked over in Africa, and now you have an important job in Philadelphia. We're all right proud of you."

His every fiber danced with warmth as Jacob left. People were happy to have him back after all the time he'd spent worrying about being remembered as the town arsonist? The warmth evaporated when he remembered that Laskey had probably started trying to contact him as soon as he got the message about Charla being alive. Jacob hated having to admit that he'd flagrantly defied the request of the person who'd become almost as close as a father. Actually, it hadn't been a request. Laskey had ordered him point-blank to have nothing more to do with Kate.

Chapter Forty-Two

Had it not been such a humorless situation, Laskey would have found Woodsie's edginess and the expression on his face laughable as the mechanic tried to pretend he was someone he wasn't. Woodsie, seated on Mrs. Winter's living room couch, shifted first one way and then the other, crossing and then uncrossing his long legs. Per Laskey's request, Woodsie had scrubbed off the oil and grease and exchanged his mechanic coveralls for a pair of khakis and a blazer.

"Thanks for seeing my assistant and me at such short notice," Laskey said to Mrs. Winters. "We're trying to establish Ama's movements during the last few days of her life. Any help you can give us would be appreciated."

Mrs. Winters shook her head. "The last time I saw Ama was on Sunday afternoon. She promised to come back the next day, but I guess she got busy."

Laskey ran his hand over his neck and nodded as though contemplating her answer. His contemplation needed to be brief, however, so that he could ask enough questions to sound like that's what he actually came for and then high-tail it before the son came home. With Pavel's interest in tinkering with cars, he assumed Pavel would recognize Woodsie. Janis had set up the appointment, inquiring if Pavel was there. Mrs. Winters responded that he had gone over to Quakertown for a motor part, and then asked what Pavel had to do with this whole sordid business anyway.

"Did Ama visit her mother both Saturday and Sunday, or was it just Sunday?" Laskey asked.

Mrs. Winters pressed her palm against a cheek and frowned as she tried to remember. "I can't remember if she came both days, or just Sunday. Is it important?"

"Just trying to pin down what she did that weekend." He shuffled his feet and coughed. Then he coughed again, and pretended to clear his throat. "My throat is starting to get a little tickle. Hope I'm not getting a cold." He sent her an imploring look. "Would you mind terribly getting me a glass of water?"

Laskey watched Woodsie narrow his eyes and lean forward as he observed Mrs. Winters shuffle past on the way to the kitchen, and again when she reappeared a minute later with a glass of water. Laskey gulped it down and then set the glass on the coffee table. "Thank you so much for seeing us," he said, rising. "I think we have what we need." He wondered why she hadn't inquired if they had any suspects. Most did.

"Well?" Laskey asked when they got back to his Sequoia.

Woodsie shook his head. "It wasn't her. Did you notice how Mrs. Winters doesn't swing her legs like most people do when they walk? She bends her knees the way a camel walks. I was watching a documentary about the Sahara the other night and it showed a bunch of camels. They move more from the knees than from the hips." He stepped away from the SUV and took a few steps, illustrating Mrs. Winter's stiff-backed, lifted-knee walk. "Naaah. The woman I saw was all but running."

Laskey would have liked to take Woodsie over to watch Kate, but he doubted Woodsie could distinguish the walk of one young woman from another.

They got in, and he pulled away from the curb. A block past Mrs. Winters' house, he saw a woman emerge from a side street, turn the corner, and march along the sidewalk in the same direction they were going, clipping along like she was out for a morning constitutional. He slowed the SUV to a crawl, pressed the button to lower the window on the passenger side, and pulled over to drive along beside her. She looked sideways at them.

"Dr. Zuela Hay," he said, steering with one hand and using the other to prop himself on the front seat divider while leaning toward the passenger side window. "I thought I recognized you." When she stopped, he tapped the breaks.

She stepped up to the car window and, looking past Woodsie, focused on Laskey. "Shouldn't you be busy detecting crimes instead of accosting women on the streets of our lovely town?"

"Actually, I'm on a reconnaissance mission looking for chocolate cake." He was vaguely aware that Woodsie sat reared back in his seat, swiveling his eyes back and forth between him and Zuela, while their conversation breezed across his chest.

"Sorry to disappoint you. I bake once a year for the Historical Society bake sale and that's it. So, Mr. Detective, you'll have to go scavenging for chocolate cake somewhere else."

"Peanut butter cookies, then?"

"Like I said, once a year." She gave him a dismissive wave and resumed her walk.

He followed, smiling broadly, until she stopped again.

"What do you want?" she asked, hands propped on her hips.

"Just wanted to tell you that was the best chocolate cake I ever had. Bye now."

Chapter Forty-Three

"Is this your new job? Resident ichthyologist?" Laskey stopped to watch Maureen dropping TetraMin Tropical flakes into a fish tank. He didn't remember having seen an aquarium in that spot before.

"Yep. Didn't have enough to do already, so now I'm the official fish feeder."

"Whose idea was the fish tank?"

"Mine. Charlie wouldn't let me bring my labradoodle to work, and sometimes I need a sane being to talk to. Animals are calming when you're angry and soothing when you're stressed. They're faithful. They don't talk back. They make few demands." She flicked fish food flakes from her fingers and closed the box. "What are you up to?"

"His royal highness . . .," Laskey nodded toward Inglehook's door a few feet beyond the aquarium ". . . has demanded my presence. Eleven sharp. I don't have enough to do, so he's decided to sever my day in the middle."

"Let me know if you need a stiff drink afterwards. I'll pull something out of my bottom drawer."

"Yeah, I'll bet. See you."

INGLEHOOK'S DOOR STOOD AJAR. Laskey rapped lightly, and then pushed it open.

The special Prosecutor sat at his desk, his head bent over a document. He lifted his eyes without raising his face, and said, "Laskey." And then nothing further.

Laskey shifted uncomfortably. Was he supposed to walk in? Wait? Bow and grovel?

"Give me a minute," Inglehook said then, his face still tilted down and his eyes up. He stared at Laskey for another few seconds from beneath droopy lids and then focused his eyes downwards, appearing to study the document. He pressed a curled forefinger on his lips in a pretense at concentration. Laskey saw that his eyes glided too fast across the page for him to be actually reading.

Laskey stepped back into the hallway and turned his back. He knew a show of power when he saw one. Shifting from foot to foot, he jingled the car keys in his pocket, and when the waiting became too long, turned around to stare at the bald spot on Inglehook's crown. The special prosecutor's face was long like a horse's and his eyes too close together. Not a handsome man; but an ambitious one. News had gotten around: Inglehook wanted to be the next state attorney general.

Inglehook pushed away the document he was pretending to study and beckoned Laskey in. "Arrested anyone yet?" He leaned back in his chair, and clasped his hands behind his head.

"You damn well know I haven't."

"My, my. Such language. Why haven't you made an arrest?"

"Not enough evidence."

"You have enough."

A spark of anger ignited deep inside Laskey, and at the same time, a premonition. His chest tightened.

"With both mother and daughter murdered there can't be too many suspects." Inglehook unclasped his hands, leaned forward, and began rhythmically thumping his fingers on the desk. "Can you give me an explanation as to why there's been no arrest?"

"I already did."

Inglehook's face went rigid. "Three people stand to gain from one or the other of those wills. John Hunter has an alibi. Mrs. Winters has an alibi; at least for Ama's murder. Kate Hunter does not. And, as it happens, Kate Hunter has the most to gain from the deaths of those two people. What are you waiting for? An engraved invitation to arrest her?"

"You seem to know a lot about what's going on." Inglehook hadn't yet heard that Ama Hunter had a sister, alive and well, who would be the biggest beneficiary.

"Of course, I know what's going on. You can't keep secrets in places like Goose Bend and Bump keeps me informed even if you won't." He lifted his palm toward a chair. "Have a seat, buddy." His voice had suddenly acquired a note of confidentiality, and he attempted a smile.

Laskey sat down. Inglehook would be neither the first nor the last DA who tried to intimidate a law enforcement official into making a premature arrest. Laskey had never had to deal with one, but he supposed it was inevitable that sooner or later he'd run head on into an overly ambitious prosecutor.

Inglehook leaned his elbows on his desk and templed his hands. "What else do you need in order to arrest Kate Hunter?"

"A murder weapon would help."

"We both know the gun may never be found. Wouldn't it be a shame to let two murders go unpunished for the lack of one little item? That isn't justice, is it?" He paused to let his words sink in. "Look, I'll make no secret of it. I have an agenda, and I need to get on with it. I'm on the list of possible nominees for State Attorney General for my party." He seemed to puff up as he spoke. "If I can acquire a nice feather in my cap, I should be able to sew up the nomination. But I don't have much time. The powers that be will decide in twelve months who they'll put forward. Right now, most of them support me, but there's someone else trying to attract their attention. You know . . ." he inclined his head toward Laskey, ". . . there might be something in this for you. I've checked your record, and I'm impressed. I might be able to bring you on as chief investigator in the state office. Once I'm in charge, of course." He sat back and watched Laskey for a reaction.

Laskey didn't flick an eyelid or move a muscle.

"I can call an investigative grand jury. . . ." Inglehook looked away, ". . . but by the time they meet and deliberate, that would add a couple weeks to the process. Right now, every day counts."

Laskey felt a frisson of devilishness. "Ahhhh," he said and rubbed his chin. "I think this might take more time than you have. Maybe you ought to recuse yourself and call in another prosecutor since you need to get on with your agenda."

Inglehook's eyes went cold. "You don't get it, Laskey. This case is my agenda. There's going to be lots of publicity. TV coverage. National news. I'm not letting anyone else get his hands on this. But I need to get the show on the road." He thumped his fist on his desk. "Arrest Kate Hunter."

"Can't do."

"You *can* do. You have motive; she lacks alibi. All you need are a few incriminating statements." His eyes bored into Laskey's. "Get that, and I can prosecute."

"You want me to force or invent compromising words from her, or a false statement from someone else?"

"Call it what you will. You know Kate Hunter did it. What we're after is justice."

"'S'funny. I always thought our justice system was built on the principle that it's better for a guilty man, or in this case a woman, to go free than to unjustly convict an innocent person."

Inglehook studied Laskey through narrowed eyes. "Very well," he said finally. "If you want to play dirty."

Laskey squirmed. What was Inglehook about to spring on him? The dread that had been festering in his insides grew.

"I haven't had the pleasure of meeting your young friend, Jacob Gillis," Inglehook said. "He came to work here about a week ago, I believe?" He held up his palm to silence Laskey. "I know . . ., Jacob is just helping Charlie with research for a case. But unpaid, part-time, temporary, whatever you want to call it, he's still working for the DA's office. Judge Blanchard was over in New Hope having dinner two days after Ama Hunter's murder, and guess who he saw?" There was a nasty glint in Inglehook's eyes. "Your young friend was dining with the person you are about to arrest. Or is that the reason you're not arresting her?"

Laskey reeled. Judge Blanchard lived outside Goose Bend on a country-gentleman property. Most people in Goose Bend and its environs recognized Jacob, thanks to his act of arson and to the pass that won the state football championship.

"I know about Jacob Gillis' past," Inglehook continued. "Gained fame as an arsonist." Affecting calmness, he propped his hands on his belly and twiddled his thumbs.

Laskey grasped the arms of his chair and pushed his feet hard against the floor to contain himself. For a brief moment, the thought had rushed through his head that a jail term for assaulting an acting DA would be worth enduring for the pleasure of smashing Inglehook's head against his desk.

Inglehook pressed on. "How many witnesses do you think we can drag up that will testify to having seen Jacob with this woman at other times? At her house, for instance."

Laskey caught himself before he said it: *Depends on how much you pay them, jackass.* Was Inglehook bluffing? Not that it mattered. If the man was willing to manipulate compromising statements attributed to Kate, he'd be more than willing to find someone to back up his accusations.

"And the big question . . ." Inglehook wore a sneer. "Has Jacob been passing information to her? Things you've told him? Blanchard told me how you stepped in when his father died and more or less became his surrogate father. It would be a shame to see the young man called up in front of the ethics board. Maybe even lose his law license."

Laskey blinked back the burning moisture that threatened to fill his eyes, and tried to imagine ropes tying him to the chair, preventing him from attacking the demon that sat behind the desk in front of him.

"Look, Laskey," Inglehook said, softening his voice and leaning toward him, "Since you don't have a murder weapon and at this point, probably won't, you need to do something else. You don't want this crime to go unpunished, do you?" He raised his eyebrows in a question. "It isn't just one murder, but two. Sometimes you have to be a little imaginative to carry out justice." Inglehook's face hardened. "Take care of it, or . . . ." He looked up at the door. "Right on time."

Laskey turned to see a medium-height, sandy-haired man dressed in khakis and navy dress shirt hovering in the doorway.

"Laskey, let me introduce you to Martin Anser. I decided it was time to bring in my own detective. Martin and I work together at the state attorney general's office. Martin, why don't you tell Detective Laskey what you've learned."

Anser took a few steps into the room. "Jacob Gillis was seen with the suspect several times."

Laskey started to assert that Kate was not the suspect, but rather one on a list of possibilities, but caught himself.

"First . . .," Anser continued, ". . . a news reporter outside Kate Hunter's house saw Jacob going in. That was last Wednesday. He identified Jacob from a picture we showed him. The same day, Judge Blanchard saw them together at the restaurant. This past Monday when the UPS man delivered a package to Mr. Gillis' back door, he saw Miss Hunter's car parked behind the house and her walking up from Mr. Gillis' pond. The UPS guy, who lives down the street from Kate Hunter, said he waved, and she waved back. We know this happened because that evening the UPS man was heard at the Pennston Hotel carrying on about a *little romance* going on between the suspect's sister and the new man in town. On Monday, we're going to dredge Jacob Gillis's pond for the murder weapon."

Sweat beaded on Laskey's brow.

"I also checked shooting ranges in the area," Anser continued. "Kate and Ama went to the range over on Bethlehem Pike where they had a lesson learning to operate a pistol."

"As you can see . . .," Inglehook jumped in, ". . . all I need are statements that show intent. Did Kate Hunter need money? Did she despise her sister-in-law? She was at a book club for a little while that evening, but where did she go after the book club? I'm sure

Jacob Gillis can provide you with something. He's seen enough of her, apparently, to come up with some ideas."

Laskey didn't remember rising, but he found himself on his feet, his face burning like a furnace as he fought to keep from lunging at the man behind the desk. He lifted a shaky hand and pointed at Inglehook. "You are asking me to manufacture evidence. Justice, you say. That isn't justice. That's . . ." Salt flooded his mouth. He swallowed.

Inglehook rose, too. "If that's the way you want it. The grand jury meets on Thursdays. It's too late today, but next week I'll be asking them to investigate and hand down an indictment." He looked at Anser. "Thanks, Martin. Why don't you go hang out in the reception area. I'll talk to you in a few minutes."

Anser nodded, shot Laskey a quick glance, and left.

"I'm calling the bar association ethics committee on Monday," Inglehook said as soon as Anser was gone. "I understand your friend is an environmental legal expert and was going to be working for WARFA. We'll see if they still want Mr. Gillis when the committee is finished with him." He sneered at Laskey. "In view of your attitude, I'd move sooner, but unfortunately, next Thursday is the soonest I can get in front of the grand jury. Since you refuse to make an arrest, they will order one. You have a choice, but if you don't make the right one, your young friend is going down." The words had slithered from his mouth. "Find what you need and arrest her so we can get the show on the road. And need I say . . .," he narrowed his eyes, ". . . I will have your job? If you don't know who my aunt is, then maybe you should ask around. I think you'll find I have a little clout in Bucks County."

"WHAT'S WRONG?" Charlie looked up at Maureen standing ashen-faced in his door.

"I need to talk you." She closed the door, pulled a chair close to him, and sat down.

Chapter Forty-Four

J acob blinked. He'd been staring for so long at the computer he'd lost track of time and his eyes burned. Checking the lower corner of the screen, he saw he'd been in his temporary office for two hours without accomplishing anything significant on the pollution case. Instead, the vision of Kate Hunter filled his head — Kate with her head reclined on the back of a train seat, murmuring, "When I went to see Ama that night. . . .

He logged off and went to the window. Down on the street people were doing ordinary things. Going to the grocery store. Picking up laundry. Walking dogs. Mailing packages. Normal life. What a precious thing normal life was. That's what he'd wanted and expected when he returned to Pennsylvania. Normal life. Not a murder.

He tried to construct a scenario with Charla as the murderess — her arriving in town without the excessive make-up and with straightened hair pulled back in a bun like Ama's; making her way to the nursing home to slink through dark halls after insuring that the nursing and janitorial staffs were occupied elsewhere; slithering down the hall, poison in purse. That taken care of, she would have gone to Ama's studio. And then. Bang! All that remained would be to scurry back to New York and persuade Mr. America to cover for her.

Ama's address was available on the internet along with the location of her studio and her class schedule, so Charla could have timed her arrival at the studio, knowing when classes were finished. The nursing home was a different story, however. Charla wouldn't have known that Mrs. Winters spent a good deal of time at Mrs. Petrowsky's bedside. Or even that Mrs. Winters had moved to Goose Bend.

Or did she know?

Sometimes the failure to grasp the utter stupidity of an act, gave a person the bravura to pull it off. Was Charla brazen enough to chance what a saner person wouldn't?

Something nagged at his memory. Something to do with Charla. He reran the scene in New York again. For the hundredth time. Was it something she said? Something the bouncer said about her? Was it wishful thinking?

"MAUREEN." Inglehook stood in the doorway glowering. "You didn't hear me calling?"

"You called me?" She looked innocently up at him even though she wasn't innocent. She'd heard him bellowing her name.

"Tell Jacob Gillis I need to see him. Now."

Maureen shrugged and turned her attention back to her computer. "Tell him yourself. You know where his office his."

She pretended to examine something on the screen. Without looking, she knew Ingleshit's face had turned apoplectic; she could almost feel heat radiating from it. She heard a huff and then the sound of his spit-polished, see-your-face-in Antonio Maurizi's slapping against the floor as he stormed away down the hall behind her. When the footsteps stopped—in front of Jacob's office door, she presumed—she sighed and tried to focus on work. It wasn't easy. First, Laskey storming out of Inglehook's office. Then after her talk with him, Charlie storming out of his own office. Now, Ingleshit had a metaphorical hatchet in his hand and looked like he was about to scalp someone.

Down the hall, Ingleshit called out Jacob's name. She stopped her pretense at work and listened. There was no response. Jacob must have slipped out. Ingleshit's footsteps retraced their way to her.

"Where is he?"

"Who?" She attempted a look of perplexity.

"Jacob Gillis."

"Oh, him. I'm not his keeper." She began shuffling through a desk drawer as though searching for something.

JACOB KNEW Laskey well enough to understand that when he closed his door it meant *stay out, do not disturb, leave me alone.* He raised his hand to rap, held it suspended a few seconds, and then lowered it. A few seconds later, he lifted it again and tapped gently. There was no answer. Deciding to brave whatever it was that had caused Laskey to hide away, he twisted the knob and inched the door open.

Laskey flicked his eyes at him and then looked away as Jacob closed the door behind him. The lights were off. Strips of light filtered through the blinds, striping the floor.

"What's wrong?" Jacob asked.

Laskey rested his eyes on him for a few moments before looking away again.

"Lask?" Jacob took a step closer.

Laskey wiggled his fingers at a chair. Jacob sat down and waited, his stomach clenching. Of course Laskey would be angry with him; he'd defied Laskey's imperative to stay away from Kate. But didn't what he learned make up for his defiance? Once, Laskey started to say something but then clamped his lips together and let his gaze stray to the far wall.

"I'll be retiring Monday," he said finally.

"What?" Jacob jerked upright. Laskey retiring? In the middle of a case? "Why? Tell me this isn't true."

"All right, I'll tell you it isn't true. I'm not retiring; I'm going to be fired."

Fired? What was he talking about?

"Inglehook isn't happy with me." Laskey flitted his eyes at Jacob.

"He isn't your boss." Jacob felt his face redden. "He can't fire you."

"No, but he pulls a few strings in the good old boys network. I don't suppose you know who his aunt is, do you?"

"Not a clue."

Laskey pinched his forehead between thumb and fingers. "You've heard of Mimi Foxcroft?"

Jacob nodded slowly, trying to recall what he'd heard about Mimi Foxcroft.

"To refresh your memory, she's the widow of Harrison Foxcroft."

"The richest man in Upper Bucks," Jacob said. "They lived over in Tinicum Township."

"Mimi still lives there. Harrison Foxcroft owned a bunch of businesses in the lower end of the county. A construction company, a janitorial service that took care of a whole slew of buildings in Philadelphia, a uniform factory, a hotel, and God knows what else." Laskey's voice was full of dejection. He stumbled over his words, stopping occasionally to contain his emotions. "Foxcroft had enough money and clout to control a few people in high places around the county. His widow is carrying on the tradition."

"But why?" Jacob's voice shook with fury. "You're the best detective around."

"Apparently, not." Laskey looked down at his hands resting in his lap. "He wants an arrest by Monday morning. If not . . . .. I'm gone."

"And who does he want you to arrest?"

Laskey shrugged. "Doesn't matter. All Inglehook needs is someone who looks guilty enough for him to convince a jury. The arrest has to happen so he can commence a trial ASAP, and I'm sure he has a few ropes to pull to get an early trial. He needs to shine for the media before the state attorney general nominations. I must either manufacture evidence to feed his ambition or sacrifice my career."

Unable to find words, or to even think, Jacob felt like he was sinking in mire. Laskey looked at him as though to say something, but then changed his mind.

"Jake," Laskey said finally. "Do you mind leaving? I just want to be alone right now."

Jacob stood up and edged toward the door. "I'm not going to let his happen," he said, turning around. "I'll figure out a way. Charlie and I."

Laskey gave him a half smile.

"We will, Lask. We will."

<hr>

LASKEY CLOSED the blinds and sat in the dark. The physical darkness didn't even begin to measure up to the inner darkness rising from the soles of his feet, consuming him inch by inch. He'd found it impossible to tell Jacob that his career, too, would be over, and *that* was the darkest hell. Losing his own career was devastating, embarrassing, emasculating. But at least he'd spent most of his working life doing what he wanted. Jacob was just beginning. Even if the ethics committee decided to merely slap him on the hand, even if there were no murder weapon found in his pond, a bell once rung can't be un-wrung.

Inglehook could probably manipulate the grand jury into an indictment, but finding Kate Hunter guilty of murder was a different story. The Hunters had the resources to hire the best criminal lawyers, ones who had the ability to rip Inglehook's case to shreds. If Kate weren't convicted people would always wonder if she did it, and they would remember Jacob Gillis as not only the boy who burned down the town, but, *if rumors were to be believed*, the young lawyer who conspired with the artist who murdered her sister-in-law.

JACOB SLAPPED his hands on the frame of Inglehook's office door as though to hold himself back. Every fiber in his body was ready to do battle.

"Aha, the infamous Jacob Gillis appears." Inglehook looked up, his mouth twitching under the intensity of Jacob's stare. One of his hands rested on the desk where he absently flipped the pages of a pad of sticky notes. *Swish, swish, swish.* "Did someone tell you I was looking for you, or did you just materialize on your own?" He stopped flipping the sticky note pages and bent the corner of the pad back to make it lie flat again. "Can I assume you have more sense than your detective friend and have decided to help him out?"

"Help him out?" Jacob heard the scorn in his own voice. He took two steps into the room.

"Didn't he tell you what I need? I think we all know who killed Ama Hunter and her mother."

Jacob broke out in a sweat.

"There's almost enough evidence to arrest Kate Hunter, and I'm sure the remainder will be forthcoming, thanks to you. If not, then Laskey has screwed up this case. In which case I'll have his job. I have enough connections to make that happen." He narrowed his eyes at Jacob. "But what worries me right now is that you might have been passing along information to Kate Hunter detrimental to our case." The pitch of his voice had risen. "Have you? You've been seen with her."

Jacob felt like he'd been hit by a three-hundred pound tackle.

"Everyone knows about your relationship with Laskey." Inglehook's eyes had narrowed to mere slits. "It doesn't take a rocket scientist to figure out you know more than you should, and that you might have passed it along to your girlfriend who is about to be arrested for the murder of her sister-in-law as well as for the mother of said sister-in-law. Fortunately, you were arriving on a plane at the time of the shooting so we know you're not guilty of murder. Or did your plane get in earlier than I thought?" He raised his eyebrows. "Or could the coroner be wrong about the time of death? Maybe it was actually a little later than the time he first suggested. I better have both things double checked."

Clenching his fists, Jacob took another step forward.

Inglehook sprang from his chair and held out his palms defensively. "Hold on. I'm not accusing you of murder, I just . . . .'

"You bloody, fucking idiot."

"Back off." Bracing against an attack, Inglehook pushed his chair away and took a step backward.

After an interval, Jacob loosened his fists and let his hands drop to his side.

Ashen-faced, Inglehook motioned to a chair. "Sit down, and let's talk reasonably."

"No."

"Very well, then. If you want to be difficult, we'll talk standing up." He put his hands on the desk and leaned, straight-armed, onto them. "Both you and your detective friend are in trouble, but you can dig your way out of this hell hole if you cooperate. Kate Hunter must have said something to you we can use. I need one good incriminating statement. Three or four would be better, but one will do. Like what she was doing that evening when she skipped out of her book group. Or why she needs money. Something along that line. Every day counts for me, and I'm tired of waiting." He banged his fist on the desk.

Jacob struggled to breathe.

"Consider this . . .," Inglehook continued. "There are plenty of pretty faces out there. You'd better get over this one right fast, because she's going to be doing time. Or worse." He paused to let his words sink in. "It's going to happen. Count on it. For my own purposes I need it to be sooner rather than later." He gave a sniff. "If you don't cooperate, I will have you in front of the ethics committee, and you can kiss your upcoming job goodbye. Maybe, they'll have you back in Africa," he said with a sneer. "Who knows, you might enjoy spending the rest of your professional life rooting around the jungle counting dead elephants."

Jacob was stung to silence. At first it wouldn't sink in. But then it began to. Slowly. The man standing in front of him was threatening, not only Laskey's job, but his own future as well. And for Kate, something worse.

"Like I told Laskey," Inglehook said, ". . . carrying out justice sometimes requires a little imagination. Apparently, you're too stuck on that young woman to know what the rest of us know. That she committed murder. Even Laskey knows she's guilty. He's just being too old-maidish to take the final step. Things don't always fall into place the way you want them to. You have to help them along." He meandered over to the book case and ran a finger along the spines of an old set of books as though looking for a particular title. "Give it some thought, Mr. Gillis." He pulled out a volume and opened it to a random page. "I'm sure you can come up with something. You can go now." He waved him away.

FROM WHERE HE sat in the law library on the ground floor, Charlie looked up in time to see Jacob shoot past. He checked his impulse to run after his friend. Later, he thought. Later, he'd try to offer some sort of assurance to Jacob. Right now he had to do this. He'd counted the minutes between now and Monday morning, and he needed every single one.

Chapter Forty-Five

J acob barely remembered the drive home. He vaguely recalled walking into his house, picking up Daisy Mae, and then setting her down again. Then he'd added water to her bowl. He'd gone to the refrigerator and looked at the Pils Krombachers lined up on the bottom shelf, but closed the door without taking one. After that, he stood at the kitchen window looking out. The sun, sinking toward extinction in the southwest, bled trails of mauve and violet over the pond. The sun would rise again tomorrow, but would he? Would Laskey? Their careers threatened to go up in flames, and it was his fault.

He should have stayed another month in Rwanda. He should have left the door unanswered when Kate knocked. He should have

. . . .

There had to be a way out of this. He paced, stove to fireplace, fireplace to stove, and back again. He couldn't let the most important things in his life slip through his fingers: reunion with his family; the reputation he'd fought to regain; the reputation of the man who stepped in to love him like a son; the dream job.

When he thought he might explode with the frustration of not knowing what to do, or what he *could* do, he grabbed his jacket from the peg in the mudroom and, ignoring the spattering of rain and the gathering twilight, set out across the patch of crabgrass and weeds that was supposed to be the back lawn. He continued through an overgrowth of higher weeds and brambles toward the pond, stopping a few feet from its shore. He picked up a handful of rocks and hurled them one by one across the water toward the willow at the far side. The geese scattered. He picked up more rocks, threw them, and then some more. His energy expended, he set off toward the darkening woods. Rain drops trickling down his cheeks, he jogged through the stubbly field but slowed to a walk when he entered the shallow forest. He brushed past bushes, scrub pines, and pin oaks, their limbs slapping him in the face and snagging his clothes. After nearly stumbling over a fallen log and sloshing through patches of mud, he arrived at the shoreline. The Pumqua River. The river where his father took him fishing.

The current burbled past. Clear. Clean. Unpolluted. He closed his eyes and inhaled, the smell of skunk cabbage and wet bark almost making him giddy with relief. He'd visited poisoned rivers in India, in Bangladesh, in Nigeria—rivers full of trash, rotting corpses, and chemicals; rivers so rank that technicians wore gloves when they dipped their test vials in. Minnows still darted about in the shallows of the Pumqua, and air bubbles erupted on its surface. When Charlie told him the Pumqua was in danger and that there was a case pending, Jacob had grabbed hold, eager to save the river. Now, because of wanting to do what he thought was the right thing, he was in trouble. He and Laskey.

He heard a splash. And then another. Suddenly, it didn't seem like such a long time ago that his father would step out on the porch, close his eyes, tilt his head back, and take a deep breath. "Smells like a fishing day," he'd say. Or: "Smells like a hike beside the river day."

"What do you smell, Daddy? How can you tell which kind of day it is?" Not that Jacob cared whether it was a fishing day or hiking day. Both were special – any day spent with his father was special. He was just curious to know how his father decided which it was to be.

Dad's reply was always the same. "Can't tell you. That's arcane knowledge. You'll acquire it someday. Well, son, let's get our fishing gear out." Or: "Go find your hiking shoes. Hurry up now. We don't want to waste any time."

Jacob would go running off to grab hiking boots from his closet or fishing gear from the basement, having no idea what *arcane* meant, but the word made his father's ability to decipher the mood of the day excitingly mysterious.

He still missed his father even after all these years. The first time Laskey came for him was three months after his father's sudden death. His mother had moved them from the flower farm to the Cape Cod in town where Jacob, angry and morose, hibernated in his room. His mother, struggling with her own shock and grief, tried to draw him out, but with no success. One day, Laskey showed up.

"Come on," he said, standing in the door to Jacob's room. "We're going for an outing."

"I don't want to," Jacob had replied sullenly.

"Not a choice. You're coming with me."

Jacob got up then and followed Laskey. It was easier to comply than fight. They drove to Philadelphia in silence, Jacob clenching his teeth and focusing his eyes on the dashboard of the Sequoia, refusing to see or care where they were going.

"The zoo," he said with a frown when they finally stopped. "I'm not a baby."

"Me neither." Laskey got out, walked a few steps toward the entrance, and then turned to stare at Jacob, until he finally slid out of the car to join him. "They have mongooses," he said. "Just got them in last week."

Against Jacob's will, a bit of interest flickered. After his mother read "Rikki Tikki Tavi" to him, he'd begged his father for a mongoose, refusing to accept the fact that a mongoose couldn't be had just for the asking.

The zoo had imported five yellow ones from South Africa. He and Laskey watched the creatures scampering around their enclosure, and Jacob forgot his anger and grief for a few minutes. When he reached out to touch the white-tipped bushy tale of one rubbing against the fence, Laskey, ignoring the sign about not touching the animals, didn't stop him.

They spent the afternoon at a Phillies game. Collapsing back into his shell, Jacob refused to enjoy himself. How could he? His father was dead. He *shouldn't* enjoy himself. Not ever again. He felt guilty about forgetting for even a few seconds while they were at the zoo. When tears began to trickle down his face, he quickly wiped them away. But not fast enough. Laskey saw him. "I guess I *am* a baby," Jacob said, pissed that he'd been caught.

"Then that makes me one, too," Laskey replied. "I cried when you father died. Is there something wrong with that?"

Jacob dissolved into tears then. It was the first time he'd let go. Laskey put his arm around him and pulled him closer. The incident had never been referred to again by either of them, but that day marked the beginning of Jacob's climb from despair.

Now Jacob had jeopardized the man who had stepped in to ease his pain. He could probably save Laskey by repeating what Kate told him about going to see Ama that evening, her need for money, her plans. And he would have. Except Kate Hunter was not a murderess.

IT WAS NEARLY ten when Charlie showed up at his back door, bleary-eyed, hair in wild disarray, yellow and gray tie hanging from a pocket of his rumpled suit jacket.

"Beer?" Jacob asked as he led him into the kitchen.

"Got anything stronger?"

"Jack Daniels."

"That'll do."

Jacob grabbed two Old Fashioned glasses from the dish drain and filled them halfway. They tossed the whisky down. He poured two more.

"To oblivion." Charlie raised his glass.

"Agreed." Jacob clinked his glass against his friend's.

They drank the second shots only fractionally slower, and then Jacob shoved the bottle into Charlie's hand. "Let me light the fire while I can still stand."

"I got you in trouble again." Charlie sank into a rocking chair.

"I got myself in trouble. You had nothing to do with it." He set kindling ablaze and then leaned back on his heels and watched the wood chips ignite and the tongues of flame lick at the logs.

"You were tired, jet lagged, and excited about being back," Charlie said, "and I took advantage of you."

"Oh, shut up and drink." Jacob flopped into the other rocking chair and held his empty glass toward Charlie who still grasped the bottle in his oversize hands. "How did you find out?"

"Maureen overheard shithead threatening Laskey." He filled Jacob's glass and then his own. "She was in the hall feeding those damn fish."

"How did Inglehook know about me being with Kate?"

"Judge Blanchard saw you together over in New Hope. He and Ingleshit were classmates in law school."

Jacob suddenly remembered the identity of the man with the white eyebrows. Blanchard lived a couple miles outside Goose Bend and had fifty yard line seats at football games.

"Inglehook brought in a detective from the state attorney general's office to do some snooping. A reporter saw you at Kate's house, and the UPS man saw her here. He delivered a package to your back door as she walked up from your pond." He refilled his glass. "I'm going to bring Inglehook down."

"How?" Jacob tried to swallow the lump in his throat.

"I'll figure it out. Between now and Monday morning." He set the Jack Daniels down on the hearth. "Just curious, who was that friend of Laskey's that went on those bird watching expeditions? You know, the one he worked with at the F.B.I.? I think you told me Laskey went with him to the Dominican Republic once."

"Can't remember." Jacob felt a flash of irritation. The world was about to fall apart, and Charlie was thinking about Laskey's old friends? "You taking up bird watching?"

"Maybe."

Jacob downed the remaining few drops in his glass. He supposed Charlie was trying to distract him from impending catastrophe, but it wasn't working. "Hand over the bottle." He nodded to the Jack Daniels.

Charlie held it up and stared at the bottom. "Shall we split what's left?" He divided the remaining drops between them.

"Oh, yeah," Jacob said after finishing off the whisky. "I remember now. Thunder Ferguson was his name. I met him once."

"Thunder?"

"Because he has a thunderous voice and hairy hands."

"What do hairy hands have to do with it?"

"Nothing. I thought it was sort of weird for a big, loud man with hairy hands to be into bird-watching. He looked more like a bear wrestler. He traveled all over the world with his binoculars and camera looking for rare specimens. Red-headed woodpeckers. Purple gallinules. Whatever."

"*Hmmmph.*" Charlie set his empty glass down on the hearth and looked into the fire.

"Hold on," Jacob said rising. "Whiskey's gone. Time to switch to beer."

Not so steady on his feet now, he brought back two bottles of Krombacher, and handed one to Charlie. The room had started a slow spin. He'd never experienced a black-out from too much drink, but now he longed for oblivion. A log crackled and broke in two. He reached for the poker, prodded the glowing embers to rearrange them, and then threw in another log.

Charlie held out one hand to the flames. "Remember when we thought the Hunters had everything? Money, prestige, good-looks? And how much we despised Mr. Hunter? He was so damned right-eous the way he looked at us like we were vermin."

"Shit!" Jacob cried out. Inside, he was torn apart, shredded, and the fury he'd been trying to contain burst from its confines. He was angry, angry, angry. At everyone. At Mr. Hunter for his part in their lives years ago. At Kate. It all began with Kate, so of course with her. At Charlie. Jacob's life was about to fall apart, and Charlie was talking about bird watching? And he was angry with Laskey, which made no more sense than the anger Jacob felt for his father when he died. He, Jacob, was going to be the cause for Laskey's downfall; Laskey should be the one burning with rage. "Shit!" he cried out again.

Chapter Forty-Six

Friday, March 14

The living room sofa where Jacob left Charlie snoring the previous evening was empty except for a crumpled blanket and a pillow that still bore the imprint of Charlie's head. Daisy Mae slept peacefully on top of a second blanket that had slipped to the floor.

"Feel free to get cat hair all over my clean blankets," Jacob groused.

He plodded into the kitchen. His head pounded; his mouth felt like a cesspool; and the smell of soot and whiskey rankled his stomach. The empty Jack Daniels bottle sat on the hearth. They had drunk every drop, yet there was still the smell. He vaguely remembered yelling shit a few times. A Krombacher bottle lay on the hearth, a puddle around its mouth where the last drops had dribbled out, while several empty bottles stood upright on his side of the fireplace. An equal number of empty bottles, along with his tie, were on the floor next to where Charlie had sat.

He drank a glass of water, and then another. Best thing for a hangover, they said—the infamous "they." Regretting that he hadn't bothered to put Aspirin or Tylenol on his shopping lists, he made coffee. Life began to trickle back into his veins after the second cup. When his body approached semi-functional, he dressed, filled Daisy Mae's bowls with food and water, and headed out the door, shooting a finger at Simon Legree who was creating a fuss as per usual. He slid into his Rav4, and took off.

———

"I WAS afraid you might not be here." Jacob set a large cup of Columbian Dark Roast in front of Laskey. He held another in his hand. The blinds were open, and light flooded the office.

"I'm here until I'm gone." Laskey picked up the cup and took several gulps before putting it down and wiping his mouth with the back of his hand. "And I don't go down without a fight. Nor do you. Charlie told me Inglehook managed to nab you yesterday. You're going to stand up and fight alongside me."

"Damn right."

Jacob sat down, and they fell silent for a few moments as they drank their coffee, Jacob's mood notching up an iota. He almost felt like a boy again, depending on Laskey to come up with a solution to a problem.

"Thanks," Laskey said after an interval, indicating the coffee with a nod. He stretched back in his chair, arching his back and neck for a few seconds. "Guess what I found this morning?"

Jacob shrugged. "Give me a clue."

"A Walther PPK Pistol hidden in a paper bag behind one of the triptychs in Mrs. P's curio cabinet.

Jacob froze. If there were fingerprints on the gun . . .

"I stared at those damn triptychs the other day for God knows how long," Laskey said. "At five o'clock this morning, my eyes popped open, and it finally registered that every item in the cabinet had been arranged in precise symmetry except for the corner of a paper bag sticking out from behind Baby Jesus. I jumped out of bed and went flying out to Goose Bend. And there it was, a PPK hidden behind the savior of the world. At least they won't be dragging your pond now."

"Dragging my pond?"

"Never mind." Laskey waved his hand in dismissal.

"What about fingerprints?" Dreading the answer, a suffocating lump formed in Jacob's throat.

Laskey shook his head. "If someone was clear-sighted enough to wipe prints from the cartridge, you can bet the gun got wiped clean, too, as well as the handle of the cabinet. It's an old PPK. The Nazis left them behind by the thousands when they fled eastern bloc countries at the end of the war. They also destroyed all records of ownership." He drummed his fingers on the desk. "I think it's a good guess that Ama's parents brought the gun with them when they escaped." He took another swig of coffee and then got up and began pacing, head down, hands behind his back. After a few turns, he stopped and extended his palm toward a trove of items and reports lined up on his desk. The picture of Ama as Odile stood upright in the center, propped against a pile of books. "Walk around the room and watch her eyes," he said.

Jacob didn't feel like playing games, but he got up and walked first to one side of the room and then the other, keeping his gaze focused on Odile's eyes. He'd seen paintings where the eyes followed you. The Prado had several. But those were all paintings. This was a photograph, and he had to confess that having the eyes of a dead woman follow him made shivers run down his back.

"So, here you have it." Laskey swept his arm around, indicating the collection that cluttered his desk. "A picture of Odile which has nothing to do with anything except for spooking me. A bottle of methanol-laced cough syrup with no finger prints on it. A list of numbers from pre-paid credit cards that haven't been used. Ama Hunter's cell phone. Her purse. An address book. Cotton balls covered in make-up consistent with that on the body. Thirty-seven plastic bags with strands of hair, all of them belonging to students — the results just in a few minutes ago. Various reports, including fingerprint studies that tell us nothing. Locked away, we have a gun with no fingerprints. And now, a resurrected sister has entered the equation. I had her alibi confirmed by a colleague in New York. I don't think the bouncer's word is worth rot, nor the club manager's for that matter, but even so, I don't see how Charla Petrowsky could have done it." He rubbed his chin and frowned. "There's something we're not seeing."

"What about the source of the methanol? Did you look for that?"

"Of course. We found nothing."

"Lask, you don't really think Kate . . . ?" He couldn't finish the sentence.

"When everyone else is ruled out . . ." Laskey ran a thumb over the nails of his opposite hand, avoiding Jacob's eyes.

"Can you rule out Mrs. Winters' son?" Jacob's voice had risen. "Maybe he had some reason we don't know about. I mean, other than what his mother would have gotten in the will? Or maybe that was enough."

Laskey shook his head. "He was never in the nursing home, for one thing."

"Maybe they did it together. He and his mother."

"And maybe Charla and Mrs. Winters did it together, or . . . McGonigle and John, or McGonigle and . . . . Never mind."

"What are we going to do?"

They looked helplessly at each other.

"Whatever we do, it had better be quick," Laskey said finally.

"I've gotten you in this mess."

"I can always find another job. Or retire early. It's you I'm worried about." He searched Jacob's face. "You really do like her, don't you?" he asked at length.

Jacob closed his eyes and nodded. "I'm scared shitless I'm going to find out I don't know her at all. That everything about her was an act." He paused and swallowed. "There's something you need to know," he said in a barely audible voice. "We went to New York together. To look for Charla and . . . ."

"And?" Laskey's eyes bored into him.

"On the train when we were coming home, Kate told me she went to see Ama that evening. Or she tried, but Ama seemed nervous and wouldn't talk to her. Maybe Ama was expecting some-one, or had something planned, or . . . ." His chest constricted. Had he just put a nail in Kate's coffin? He looked up at Laskey who was studying him intently.

Finally, Laskey blinked and looked down at his watch. "Why don't you go over to Danny's while I finish up the weapons report? Take me five minutes. Order for me. I'll be over soon as I'm done, and then we can talk."

THE WARM SUN on his back and a clean breeze tousling his hair as Jacob trudged toward the diner did nothing to alleviate his misery. He kicked at a Starbucks cup littering the sidewalk sending it sailing across the curb and into the road. Anger ate holes in him, and doubt shot at him from every angle. It suddenly struck him as odd for Kate to come and ask him to be the family's spokesperson. He gave a little sniff of a laugh. Maybe she had some cockamamie plan to get even with him for spurning her as a teenager. And *that*, Jacob Gillis, is a ridiculous idea he chastised himself. No more Jack Daniels for him.

Picking up his pace he came to the diner, but instead of going in he stood near the entrance absently watching customers enter and exit. Each opening of the door surrounded him with smells that normally made him hungry, but for a change he had no desire to eat. Now that he thought of it, he'd forgotten to eat supper the night before.

"Jacob Gillis," Hilda called from behind the counter when he finally ventured in. "Where's your friend? Laskey hasn't gone and gotten too good for us, has he?" She was transferring slices of shoofly pie onto two plates.

Jacob manufactured a half-smile. "He'll be along in a minute. I'll order for him."

"Have a seat, hon. I'll be right over."

The booth in the far corner was free. Jacob took off his jacket, and sat down. Grabbing the menu from behind the napkin box, he looked at it without reading. Yesterday evening with Charlie, when Jack Daniels had freed his mind of inhibitions, a question had plagued him. Had Kate known about Charla all along, and knowing of his relationship with Laskey, enticed him to New York to set up the sister as a possible suspect?

"Coffee, hon?" Hilda propped one hand on a hip; the other held a stainless steel coffee pot.

Jacob pushed his cup toward her. "I guess we'll both have the special, whatever it is, and . . . . Shit!" Then he said it louder. "Shit!"

People turned to look. Hilda's mouth fell open. "Are you all right?"

A sudden vision of something on Laskey's desk had connected with a memory of Aunt Zuela prancing around her kitchen. "I know how she did it," he burst out. "I know how she bloody, friggin' did it." He sprang up, almost knocking the coffee pot out of Hilda's hand, grabbed his jacket, and dashed for the door.

EVERY NERVE and muscle in him tingled as Jacob waited for a response from Laskey who had frozen as if caught in a stopped frame on a movie reel.

Finally, Laskey picked up one of the items on his desk and frowned at it before setting it down again. "Can this be?" he asked.

Jacob nodded. "And I know how to prove it." He explained what had to be done.

"We have to entice Charla here," Laskey said. "Do you think a check for a million dollars will do the trick?" Suddenly brimming with energy, he bolted up and strode back and forth. "We need to do it tomorrow. I'll persuade the insurance agent, but what about . . ."

"I'm betting he'd love to be in on it."

"He'll need a disguise and a new name. Something unremarkable. Brown. Smith."

"Percival Smith."

"*Percival?* Get serious." Laskey grinned. "I've had some interesting moments in my career, but this one, if it works, will top the list."

"It *has* to work."

Laskey nodded. "Yeah. Otherwise . . . ." He rubbed his chin, thinking. "The insurance agent . . . . What was his name? Oh, yeah, Carmichael. Carmichael needs to set it up. He can tell her he wants to clear his desk of a few chores before he goes away on vacation to . . . . ummmm, the Seychelles, maybe. No. Nepal is better. He'll be there for a while on a trek up Goripani, so if Miss Charla Petrowsky wants her check for a million dollars before he leaves, she'll have to hightail it down here tomorrow."

"Shall I take care of *Mr. Percival Smith?*"

"ASAP."

Chapter Forty-Seven

Saturday, March 15

Jacob gave up trying to sleep. Yesterday it had seemed so logical, so possible. But what if he was wrong? What if this turned out to be another day of infamy for Jacob Gillis? Only this time Mr. Hunter Sr. wouldn't be yoking him and Charlie with two years community service, Saturdays only. Instead, he'd lose everything he'd ever worked for. He threw back the covers and sat up.

He looked out the window as he pulled on a pair of khakis and saw that the weather portended to be picnic perfect. Sun coming up bright and warm. March winds taking a rest. Geese quiet for a change. Or maybe the geese had left. He hoped that instead of being in Africa counting dead elephants, he'd be here to greet the geese when they returned in the fall on their southward migration. He checked the time on his cell phone. Six o'clock. Five hours to wait until he found out if he was right, or if he and Laskey were going down.

He set out for Doylestown. He'd stop and have breakfast somewhere, read the paper while he ate, let the buzz of conversation sedate his apprehension. He took the road leading up to Sky Drive, drove past the northern border of Goose Bend, and then turned onto the road leading to Doylestown. When he came to the overpass for the old railroad terminal, he jammed on his brakes, veered to the side of the road, and parked. He got out and walked over to the precipice overlooking the spot where the railroad entered the tunnel. Without thinking, he climbed down the steep bank to the tracks.

He'd come here as a boy. It had been off-limits to pretty much every kid in town, including him, because of the tetanus incident, but it was the perfect place to be alone. The warmth of the sun on his back as he entered the tunnel, faded within a few feet. The smell of rust and rot was overwhelming. He tread carefully on the decaying ties, any one of which could send him sprawling if his foot came down on a crumbling edge. He found the simple, childish act of walking tie to tie calming.

He walked from one end of the tunnel to the other, falling into a rhythm as he went from the morning end to the afternoon end of the corridor. He turned a few feet short of the west opening and started back toward the eastern end. When he reached the middle, he stepped down and stood sideways, his feet on the gravel, one oak slab between left foot and right.

His nightmare reasserted itself as he stared at the mildewed, pock-marked walls of dark concrete. If he were wrong, not only would he be giving the ethics committee more fodder, but Jacob Gillis would be the laughing stock of both the Bar Association and the town of Goose Bend. Hell, everybody in the state of Pennsylvania would probably hear about how the boy who burned down the town had pulled yet another stupid stunt.

Worse, Laskey would go down with him.

Worst of all, Kate would be arrested for the murders of Ama Petrowsky Hunter and Josephine Petrowsky.

He looked toward the end where he'd entered. The sun blazed through, marking out a space of thirty or so feet. He swiveled his head to look at the opposite end which was imbued with a paltry, gray light. He supposed, if he were philosophical or poetic, he'd have something profound to say about the light, or lack of light, at the end of the tunnel, but he felt neither philosophical nor poetic. All he wanted now was to be right about how Ama Hunter and her mother had died.

BUMP HERRINGTON HAD BEEN out for more than an hour trying to walk off his worries, but it wasn't working. Someone he knew was going to be arrested, and, although he wasn't sure which person that was, it was going to hurt. The agonizing, the loss of sleep, the sporadic, hurried meals, or rather lack of meals, had taken a few pounds off his frame since he found Ama Hunter shot to death. He'd also acquired a few more gray hairs.

His walk brought him to the block where Kate lived. The sun had risen high enough to slide over the rooftops on the southeast side of the street, illuminating the fronts of those on the opposite side. On the sunny side of the street, he walked past Kate's house, continued to the end of the block, and then turned around. Retracing his steps, he castigated himself as he had done frequently during the past few days. He was the police chief. An officer of the law. Yet, he had let an old friendship influence his thinking. He'd exonerated all members of the Hunter family from the start because they were his friends. A fine family, he told Laskey. Yet it happened all the time—someone from a fine family doing the unthinkable.

A near stumble on a crack in the sidewalk jerked him out of his reverie. Finding himself three houses away from Kate's, he stopped and studied the old rowhouse. Why, for crap's sake, did she live on a street of half-broken down houses? He would have expected her to stay with her parents. Or at least in one of those new condos that had gone up along the road to Doylestown.

He heard the sound of an engine and turned around to see a BMW creeping along as though about to stop. The car passed him and then pulled into a parking place in front of Kate's. Bump watched a man in a suit climb out and go to her door. A few seconds later, the door opened, and the man went in.

Curious about someone in a BMW visiting Kate early in the

morning, Bump sauntered past her house and then, after fifty or so steps, turned around and sauntered back again. The fourth time he repeated his circuit, the man came out carrying a package wrapped in brown paper. Bump went rigid. It was Claude McGonigle from the Reilly Foundation. Perplexed, Bump watched McGonigle climb back in his BMW and pull out into the street.

What was the head of the Reilly Foundation doing walking out of Kate Hunter's house on a Saturday morning with a package? And what was Kate Hunter doing associating with a jerk like McGonigle? McGonigle had called Bump last Christmas and asked for a couple experienced men to direct traffic and parking during a big event at the Foundation. The hourly wages weren't much, but Bump guessed that a couple of his officers might like to earn a little extra for Christmas. Two jumped at the chance, but after the event when they went to collect their money, McGonigle shamed them into donating their time.

"Think of the children," McGonigle told them. "Poor kids with no parents, no food, no shelter, no Christmas presents. The war wasn't their fault. Surely, you can find it in your heart to help them by donating a little of your time."

When they told him the story, Bump had paid the two officers from his own pocket.

The episode still made him angry, and his neck grew hot as he watched McGonigle's car turn at the end of the street. He ran one finger around his collar pulling it away from his skin. McGonigle could drive a big, fancy car but not pay people he employed?

Puzzled, Bump continued toward his office. What was in the package? Triptychs? A couple days ago, Laskey had asked him if he knew about Mrs. Petrowsky owning a couple. The package seemed to be about the right size. Should he call Laskey?

Bump had been floating along for so many years in a town free of serious crime that he'd become sloppy. He screwed up when he sent someone to check John's alibi at the Cockle Burr. Bump knew John had two cars but forgot that the officer he sent was fairly new in town and didn't know about the red Jaguar. He screwed up again when he failed to tell Laskey about Jimmy Q seeing someone.

Because everyone assumed the old man was crazy, Bump had blown him off. He couldn't screw up again. McGonigle and the package probably meant nothing, but he'd inform Laskey anyway. As soon as he got back to headquarters. He'd grab some breakfast first. A few minutes delay wouldn't matter.

Chapter Forty-Eight

"**E**asy as pie, getting her to come down from New York," Carmichael, the insurance agent, said to the little group gathered in his office. He rubbed his hands in delight. "I could practically hear her salivating when I told her I had a million dollar insurance check waiting. I wish I could see her face when she finds out what we're up to."

"Sorry," Laskey said, looking down at his watch, ". . . but you're going to have to leave now and go hang out in somebody else's office. She'll be here in about ten minutes; you need to scoot."

"And what do I tell them down the hall when I show up to wait while you guys are having all the fun?"

"Hell, I don't care. Talk about the Phillies or Hitler's mustache. Just don't tell them what we're up to, and stay out of sight." He waved him away.

When the door closed behind Carmichael, Laskey studied Jacob. Was he making a mistake giving in to Jacob's pleas to be present? *Don't worry about me. I'll be so calm you won't even know I'm here.* Calm? Jacob was as jittery as a dashboard hula dancer, alternating between pacing, rubbing the back of his neck like his skin was full of ringworms, looking aimlessly out windows, and rearranging the top of the reception desk.

Janis sat at the receptionist's desk reading the sports section of "The Doylestown Intelligencer." Detective Murray, another county detective whose help Laskey had solicited, and who was to act as the replacement insurance agent, lounged on the sofa, head back, eyes closed, long legs stretched out. *Percival Smith* kept checking his wig.

"Cell phones off?" Laskey looked around at the participants.

"You've asked ten times already," Murray quipped.

"Only nine times," Laskey retorted. "You should take your places. Just in case she's early."

"Yeah, right. An early train." Murray opened one eye.

"Miracles happen. The train might be on time and all the lights between here and the depot green."

"And maybe the Easter Bunny will visit you this year." Murray rose from the sofa. "But you never know when the marvel of the century might occur—train on time, lights green, and no traffic." He grinned as he strolled from the reception room into the short hallway that led to the agent's office.

"That isn't an insurance agent's grin," Laskey called after him. All morning they had been covering their misgivings with levity. "A little more sharkiness, please."

Murray stuck his hand behind his back and flipped his finger at Laskey.

"Your wig's fine," Laskey said to *Percival*. "Stop playing with it or you'll give yourself away."

Percival gave his wig one last adjustment, ran a forefinger over his false mustache, adjusted the glasses he'd purchased at Rite Aid, and then jammed his hands in his pockets. "You don't think she'll recognize me?"

"Not for a few seconds, and that's all we need. And Jacob . . ." Laskey turned to Jacob, ". . . . will you stop that infernal pacing?"

"Sorry." Jacob forced himself to a standstill. "Are you sure there's a taxi waiting at the train station? Cabs aren't exactly a dime a dozen in Doylestown."

"Right. My man *borrowed* one, and he knows what Charla

Petrowsky looks like. Anyone else approaches, he'll say he's waiting for someone who pre-ordered a cab." Laskey took a few steps over to where the hall began. "You clear on what to say?" he called down the hall to Detective Murray who had positioned himself at the agent's desk.

"I've got it."

"What about you, Janis?" Laskey turned to his assistant who had been assigned the role of receptionist.

"As long as you reward me for working on Saturday, I'll give you an Oscar performance."

"Right. Next time I buy Cracker Jacks I'll present you with the prize from the bottom."

"You haven't eaten a box of Cracker Jacks in fifty years, you old buzzard. And just so you know, you look smashing in a janitor's outfit."

"Janis, if I weren't afraid of offending a good Christian lady, I'd flip you off, too."

"There's an awful lot of finger activity around here today."

"It all hinges on you," Laskey said to *Percival*. "Remember to keep your back turned and to stay hunched over the keyboard while you're cutting the check. Even though you won't be in the same room, she might decide to look when she walks past."

Laskey's phone pinged. He looked down at the message. "They're on the way," he announced. "Places, everyone."

Jacob slipped into the broom closet that opened into the hall and closed the door to a slit. By moving his head one way, he saw Janis sitting at the reception desk; if he tilted his head the other way, he saw the door through which Charla would enter the insurance office. He'd be able to observe her until she came even with the closet door. Once past it, she disappeared from his vision but not from his hearing. In the office across the hall from him, Percival sat at a desk, positioned so that a person passing saw only his back.

Jacob felt nauseous. His life and career, and those of Laskey, depended on the next few minutes. Willing his heart to slow down, he twisted his head to see Janis at the desk. She folded the newspaper, set it aside, and became engaged with something on the computer. He shifted his vision to see Laskey standing at the entry door, a bottle of Windex and a roll of paper towels in his hands. Laskey tore off a towel, sprayed the panes, and began cleaning. Then his hand went to his breast pocket, and he took out his phone. He frowned down at it, hesitating. After a quick look through the glass door, to check that no one was there, he answered.

"Bump?" Jacob heard him say. Laskey's brow contracted as he listened. After a few seconds, he uttered a barely audible, "Thanks." Phone still in hand, he stared toward where Jacob hid. Then, his face wreathed in frowns and one palm stretched out as though he didn't know what to do, Laskey stuck the phone back in his pocket.

Jacob stirred uneasily. Something about the phone call bothered Laskey. He watched as Laskey set the Windex down on a table next to the door and start toward him. But then Laskey whipped around and took a step back as the door swung open and Charla entered.

Jacob's breath caught.

"Miss Petrowsky?" he heard Janis say.

Charla nodded. She wore black pants and a leopard print blouse with three-quarter sleeves. The blouse was belted so that it ballooned around her torso. An over-sized purse hung from her shoulder.

"He's waiting for you," Janis said. "You can go on back to the office. Can I get you a cup of coffee?"

Jacob leaned closer to the slit. Charla didn't seem to know what to do with her hands. She ran a finger over her chin, and then rubbed the back of one hand over the other. Laskey, appearing to have composed himself, sprayed a mist on the door glass and set about cleaning it in wide swipes.

"No, thank you." Charla bit her lips and started toward the hall.

Jacob stopped breathing as she approached. Only when she stalked past, trailing the scent of grated citrus peel perfume, and then disappeared from his vision did he dare take a sip of air. He heard the knock of her heels against the slate floor as she continued into the office. Then the footsteps stopped.

"You're not Carmichael," Jacob heard her say. His stomach lurched.

"No, I'm Robert Smith," Detective Murray said. "Carmichael told you he was leaving this afternoon, and that he'd be here for you this morning, but as it turned out he wrote down the wrong time for his flight. Fortunately, he noticed his mistake last night."

Jacob's neck tightened. Was the whole plan going to crash because she sensed a rat right off the bat?

"I work for the same company, only down in Warminster," Detective Murray said. "We cover for each other when things happen. Have a seat. It'll only take two minutes, and then you'll be out of here. I just need to have you sign a couple things. The check is being cut right now. In fact, he's probably already done."

Jacob heard the scrape of chair legs as they sat down. Laskey had moved on to the glass top table next to the door, spritzing it with Windex, wiping.

In the office, they were talking about the papers Charla needed to sign. *Print name here. Signature there. Initials on this line. Date it here.* Detective Murray had done his homework, using insurance speak as though he'd been spouting it for years. Then finally, the moment they'd been waiting for.

"Hey, Janis," Murray called from the conference room. "Can you see if that check is ready?"

"It's ready. He's bringing it in right now," she called back.

Check in hand, *Percival* came out of the office, glanced briefly at the slit behind which Jacob stood, and then went to join Detective Murray and Charla. Jacob held his breath. Laskey appeared to be doing the same, the hand that had been wiping smudges from glass frozen in mid-swipe. They both knew that the rest of their lives depended on Jacob having been right and Percival proving it.

"Check's ready," Jacob heard Percival say.

"Thanks," Murray replied. "Miss Petrowsky, this is Percival Smith. He's our CFO. He personally cuts the larger checks."

Jacob couldn't restrain himself; he pushed the door far enough open to crane his head around and see into the conference room. Percival stood to Charla's left, holding the check in his left hand. Charla put out her hand to receive her fortune, but the check receded as Percival bent over her.

"What happened to your front tooth there?" Dr. O'Neill, AKA Percival Smith, asked.

Her hand flew to her mouth.

"Ah, I see." Before she could protest, Dr. O'Neill brushed aside her hand, pulled back her right upper lip, and squinted at her teeth. "I have something that belongs to you, Mrs. Ama Hunter. I was afraid that crown I cut was going to waste." He let go of her lip and pulled off his wig.

Jacob collapsed against a wall of the closet. Ama Hunter had murdered her sister and stolen her identity.

***

"YOU ALRIGHT IN THERE?" Laskey opened the closet door.

"I'm ok." Jacob had no idea how long it had taken them to revive Ama Hunter from her faint, arrest her, and then cart her away. Wrung out, he had sunk to the floor, wrapped his arms around his knees, and sat there in a near trance. "I'm just . . . ."

"Yeah, I know."

Jacob rose and stumbled out. "So . . . , it's over." A tidal wave of exhaustion washed over him.

"There for a minute, though, I thought we'd blown it, and that one of those conspiracy theories might be true after all," Laskey said. "Bump called to say he saw McGonigle coming from Kate's house early this morning with a package in his hand. A package the size of the triptychs."

Chapter Forty-Nine

"How did you know?" Charlie asked Jacob. His feet were propped on his desk.

"Puzzle pieces suddenly fell together." Jacob wondered what Charlie was doing in the office on a Saturday. Maureen was there, too.

"What pieces?"

"Charla's feet," Jacob answered, looking at Charlie's. "Is that a proper posture for a district attorney?"

"Nope. But what about her feet?"

"Kate told me how Ama rolled her feet over coke bottles to maintain high arches."

"That doesn't sound pleasant."

"Everything about Charla seemed overdone. Her make-up, her clothes, her actions. Like she was trying too hard at playing a role. Everything except for her feet. She was stumbling around in a pair of FMPs. When she sat down, she slipped them off and started rubbing her arches. Then I remembered Aunt Zuela prancing around her kitchen with toes pointed out like a ballet dancer. Charla had a clumsy walk. It occurred to me that she, or rather Ama, was trying to keep from walking with her feet pointed out which would have been a dead giveaway." He paused to steady the beating of his heart. Ever since the arrest, his adrenaline had been pumping full force.

"Go on."

"Charla, or rather Ama pretending to be Charla, had been out sick a few days. If she showed up at work, she risked someone catching on that she wasn't Charla. What finally clued me in were the cotton balls they found in the trash can in Ama's studio. Somehow, Ama got in touch with Charla and persuaded her to come to Goose Bend and then shot her. Since Ama wore very little make-up, she had to wipe away Charla's. At some point, maybe the preceding weekend, Ama put methanol in her mother's cough syrup bottle. She expected to show up in Goose Bend as Charla, collect a million dollars, and then join Marek Molnar. She probably hoped John would be indicted for her murder."

"Talk about revenge." Charlie removed his feet from the desk and sat up straight. "You don't look so good. I thought you'd be jumping up and down for joy. What's wrong?"

No, he probably didn't look so good. He didn't feel so good, either. He felt like crap, as a matter of fact. McGonigle, of all people, coming out of Kate's house early Saturday morning. What a fool he'd been. Chalk Jacob Gillis up as one big, friggin' idiot. For a few minutes he'd imagined that Kate actually cared for him. "I'm ok," he said at length. "Just a little strung out, I guess."

"How did Mrs. Petrowsky know? The body in the casket looked like Ama to me."

"How well did you look?"

He shrugged. "Not very. I don't like looking at dead people."

"You didn't notice that the corpse had tits?"

"Of course I didn't notice. Who looks at tits on a dead woman? I suppose Ama stuffed her bra with toilet paper for your and Kate's visit?"

"Possibly. But to answer your question, maybe Mrs. P noticed the tits. Or the absence of a scar on her ear. Mrs. Winters told me that Charla once ripped an earring from Ama's ear and when it healed the wound left a scar."

Charlie looked over Jacob's shoulder toward the door. "Are you eavesdropping, Maureen?"

"You're damn right. If you'd invited me to the powwow then I wouldn't have to eavesdrop, would I?" She walked over and handed Charlie a large envelope. "Do you think Ingleshit has heard the news?"

"He has. I made sure of it."

Maureen had a gloat on her face. "Fool that he is, I'll bet he's sitting somewhere right now celebrating with a glass of champagne, thinking he's about to prosecute the most sensational trial Bucks County has ever seen." She moved her hands around as though weaving a tale. "He's imagining the headlines. *"The Great Ingleshit Prosecutes former New York City Ballet Company Star Masquerading as Twin Sister after Shooting Said Sister through the Heart."* What do you think of that, Mr. Jacob?" She punched him playfully on the shoulder.

"I think that's a bit long for a headline." At the mention of Inglehook knots had formed in his stomach. Would he still call the ethics committee?

"Isn't going to happen," Charlie said.

"What isn't?" Jacob asked.

"Ingleshit won't be prosecuting. Charla's arrest isn't the only thing I made him aware of." He raised his eyebrows and waited for Jacob to ask, but Jacob just stared.

"It has been buzzed about town," Charlie continued, ". . . or I guess I should say buzzed about the state, that the great Ingleshit has, from time to time, resorted to reshaping evidence." He patted the envelope Maureen had just given him. "Remember the case having to do with bundling funds for that federal judge election? You were out of the country, but you might have heard. Anyway, Inglehook prosecuted the case. Rumors were that the state suppressed evidence and sent witnesses for the defense on lengthy vacations."

"You can prove this?" Jacob straightened, hope fluttering in his stomach.

"I got some help from Laskey's bird-watching friend. Thunder twisted a few arms, did a little snooping. Besides, I don't have to prove it to get rid of shithead. I left a voice mail last night telling him I was pursuing the matter. Just got a call a few minutes ago from his secretary in the state office. I guess she works Saturdays, too. He's recused himself. Seems Ingleshit's mother suddenly became deathly ill, and he needs to fly off somewhere to be at her bedside. Somewhere out of the country, for all I know. But . . . ." Charlie interlaced his fingers across his stomach. ". . . it isn't going to end there. I'm turning the information over to Laskey. He'll know what to do. Instead of the headline Inglehook was dreaming of, there's going to be one that will haunt his dreams for the rest of his life."

Maureen broke out in a laugh. "Couldn't have happened to a nicer person. Oh, yes, I almost forgot," she said, looking at Jacob. "There's someone in your office waiting to see you."

KATE WAS STANDING beside the window, gazing down at the street below.

"I didn't expect to see you here." Jacob knew his voice was as chilly as an Arctic winter, and that was exactly what he intended.

"There's something I need to say." She moved away from the window.

He would have thought she'd be delirious with happiness now that her ordeal was over, yet she looked dejected. Maybe it hadn't sunk in yet. But if her sad sack look was because she wanted to tell him she was involved with a married man and had only been toying with him . . . . Well, there was no need for her to feel any remorse about that. He didn't care.

"I realize how much I annoyed you in high school, and probably lately, too. It's true; I've been chasing you since I was fourteen. Or younger. I don't even know when I decided you were who I wanted-ed." She wiped a forefinger across the bottom of an eye. "I'm sorry. I've been too stupid to accept the fact that you will never care for me. My haunting you is going to stop now, but before I . . .. Well, I wanted to tell you that being captain of the football team wasn't the reason I liked you; I never thought of you as a feather in my cap." She frowned. "You didn't do me much credit by thinking that. That's not the kind of person I am."

"So, tell me . . . What kind of person are you?" He knew his sarcasm probably screamed out his hurt loud and clear.

"I'm the kind of person who wanted to be like you."

He couldn't put a meaning to her words. What part of him, his personality, his achievements or lack thereof, did she refer to? Or was she toying with him again?

"Oh, don't look so puzzled, Jacob. Surely, you must know what I mean."

"I don't have a clue."

She let out a huff. "It never registered with you that someone growing up with parents who required cleanliness, sensible investments, and proper behavior twenty-four-seven might admire someone brave enough to not care what people thought?"

"You thought I didn't care what people thought?"

"You always seemed like a free spirit."

So, that was it; she'd been a rebel even then, attracted to him because he didn't fit in with what her parents considered proper. All she wanted was to rile her family, and who to do that better with than the lowly town arsonist?

"A free spirit? That's the reason you annoyed the crap out of me in high school?"

She rolled her eyes. "You're really dense, aren't you?"

"Apparently."

"No, Jacob, my admiration for your free-spirit sparked the flame and then chemistry took over. Mine, of course, not yours. When I heard you were coming back to Goose Bend, I was ecstatic. It was my idea to enlist you to help John. But I've been wrong about everything, so I have one more thing to say. " She paused to collect herself.

He didn't care what she wanted to say; he only wanted her gone, and he wanted, once and for all, to strangle the see-sawing sentiments he had about her, one minute thinking he really liked her and could overlook who her father was, only to be followed by knowing he could never forget who her father was, and that he didn't want to anyway.

"I've come to think too highly of you to keep pretending that I can somehow trick you into loving me," she said. "So, I'm going to cut the thread. I'll never bother you again, Jacob Gillis. My family owes you more than we can ever repay and leaving you alone is the only way I can even begin to make restitution for that debt. I suppose we'll see each other occasionally in passing, but we'll be nothing more than old acquaintances. So . . .., goodbye." Pressing her lips together, she turned away and brushed past him making her way to the door.

He grabbed her arm. "Was that a bunch of crap, Kate? Because you're interested in married men now? Or were you just selling triptychs?"

Her mouth fell open. "What are you talking about?"

"McGonigle."

"McGonigle?" She jerked her arm from his grasp and raised her hands in a question. "I can't even begin to guess what you mean."

"This morning. . . ."

"Ahhhh." Understanding glimmered in her eyes. "I see. Spy report. For your information, Mr. Gillis, McGonigle came to pick up the programs and posters I designed for his fucking art show. Did you think the package that contained my posters and programs were triptychs?" She glared daggers at him. "And as for those triptychs, if it's true they're mine, they're going to the shrine at Czestochowa where they belong."

JACOB PLODDED toward Laskey's office, heavy-footed, heavy-hearted. Heavy everything. What had he done? Being around Laskey would make him feel better. A little bit, anyway. It was late afternoon, and he'd had neither lunch nor breakfast. Laskey probably hadn't either. He'd offer to take him out.

"Hey, Lask," he said, pushing open the door of his office and walking in. "You didn't have lunch, did you?"

"Nope, my friend, I didn't." He was standing in front of the window, using it as a mirror as he knotted his tie.

"I could take you down to Arnold's. Or anywhere you like."

"Sorry, I can't this evening." He finished tying his tie, and began to slick back his hair.

"You've been working too many hours lately. You need to take a couple off and eat."

"Who said anything about working?" Laskey turned from the window and grabbed a blazer from the back of his chair. "Maybe tomorrow evening, if you like. Sorry, but I'm going to be late. Have to talk to you later." He strode from the room, stopped outside the door to wait for Jacob to exit, and then locked up and hurried away.

Jacob dawdled on the sidewalk outside. Thanks to his own stupidity, his heart had just been shot full of holes, and he wanted someone to keep him company in his misery. He pulled out his cell phone and punched in Charlie's number.

"Hey, what are you doing for supper? Want to grab something?"

"Sorry, but I have a date. I didn't tell you about this girl I met a couple weeks ago. She's an attorney over in Lansdale. How about tomorrow?"

"Have fun," Jacob said and ended the call.

He could pop over to Westchester and see Meg. Maybe spend the night. That was probably just what he needed—a little time with family, some home-cooking, gin rummy with the kids, an argument about politics with her husband. He tapped in her number. After eight rings he hit the end button.

"Buck up," he muttered "You've just been given the brush-off by someone you were falling for. Won't be the last time. Get over it. Get a hamburger and then go home to Daisy Mae."

He headed toward the center of town where there were several restaurants, trying to forget the grand mess he'd made with Kate, directing his thoughts instead to wondering if he'd put food out for the kitten before he left? Or water? He stopped, trying to recall. He'd been so keyed up about what was, or was not, going to happen today, he couldn't remember. But he'd be home soon to take care of Daisy Mae. It wasn't like he had anything to do this evening.

He'd walked only a few steps when he heard his name, the recognition of her voice sending waves of delighted relief through him. Maybe he wouldn't have to spend a lonely evening after all. He turned to see Aunt Zuela gaining on him.

"Aunt Zuela. I'm glad to see you." He took a step toward her. "I was just about to get some dinner. Want to join me?"

"Sorry, not tonight." She came even with him and stopped. "Isn't it sort of late for you to be down here? Thought you'd be home by now, ploughing the fields, or planting roses, or whatever it is you do out there on your estate. But I have to toodle along. I'm late." She patted him on the cheek and left him staring after her.

Where did she have to be on a Saturday night? Meeting friends for dinner? She wore a bright red dress and silver chain necklace. Like it was a special occasion.

A few minutes later, he stood outside the entrance to Beggar's reading the menu posted on the door. When he saw that the entrees were mainly barbecue, he moved on. Finally, settling on Talleyrand's, he circled through the revolving door and made a beeline to the bar where one could sit alone without being looked down on for being alone. About to slip onto a stool, his gaze swept the rear where people were seated at tables. He stopped short. What, the . . .? Aunt Zuela was there. With Laskey. They were on a date. A bloody date. And judging by Laskey's laughter and the way she was gesturing with her hands, they were thoroughly enjoying themselves.

He snuck out, tail tucked between legs. There was a McDonald's on the way home. Tonight, while everyone else had someone, he'd feast on a Big Mac and greasy, over-salted fries, and damn it, why not go all the way? He'd order the biggest friggin' chocolate milkshake they had. Screw healthy eating.

Before pulling out of the parking lot, he sat for a few moments, thinking. What a fool he'd been, worrying about people still holding the fire against him when he was the one who needed to get over things. Maybe Mr. Hunter really was an asshole, or maybe he wasn't, but either way, what Mr. Hunter was or wasn't had nothing to do with who Jacob was. He'd stubbornly held onto a grudge, and his stubbornness didn't affect Mr. Hunter one way or the other. It had only affected him, Jacob Gillis.

Making a sudden decision, he backed out of the parking space and barreled out of the lot and onto the road to Goose Bend. There was something he had to ask Kate.

He made Goose Bend in record time, screeched into a parking place, and bounded up the steps of her house. Please, he implored as he leaned on the doorbell, don't let John be here.

The door opened a slit. "Why are you here?" The snap in her voice sounded like the crack of a whip.

"I want to ask you something."

"Well, ask and leave. You're a jerk, and I thought I made it clear I won't be seeing you for any reason other than a chance passing. This is not a chance passing."

"You made that quite clear. But I need to ask you something. Can I come inside?"

"No."

"I really don't want to play out this scene on the front porch with your neighbors watching."

"I thought you had a question. If it's a scene you're planning, go away."

"Oh, come on Kate. I have one quick question, but I don't want to stand out here on the porch to ask."

She hesitated. "If I let you in, you'll ask and then leave?"

"I'll leave the instant you tell me to."

With a little huff, she opened the door all the way and waved him in. "So, what do you want to ask?" She crossed her arms tight across her chest, but dropped them when he took a step toward her.

"Will you go to the prom with me?" he asked.

"What?"

"I asked, will you go to the prom with me?"

"Jacob Gillis, you're crazy as a loon."

"No, I'm not. I'm inviting you to a prom, and I want you to say 'yes'."

"What prom?"

"The one I'm inventing just for the two of us. I'll raise a tent in my backyard, engage a caterer, hire a string quartet, and buy a case of 'The Prisoner.' You can wear that fuchsia dress you wore for the high school prom."

"You noticed?"

"Of course, I noticed. You were the most gorgeous girl there."

She stared at him for a few moments and then burst out laughing. "Sure," she said. "I'll go to the prom with you."

THE END

Acknowledgments

I am deeply grateful to all the people who helped me with this first novel in the Bucks County Mystery Series. Many, many thanks to my readers: Mary Allen, Jesse Sisken, and Julia Pezzi (to whom I'm also thankful for listening – much too often! – to my ranting and moaning, and for convincing me not to hit the "delete" button on several occasions.) Members of Bluegrass Wordsmiths gave me input on several chapters, so thanks to Sharon Thelin, Anne Peschke, Mary Allen, Pam Brinegar, and Jane McCord.

Attorney Mark Wohlander helped me with legal issues in the plot and contributed several great ideas. One of his remarks also gave me the idea for the title.

Several people tutored me on issues in the novel: Seth Dix gave me a short lesson on firearms and suggested the Walther PPK Pistol. Dr. Evelyn Clark DDS walked me through the dental issues. My grandson, Jon Pezzi, is my go-to person on all things related to sports. I thought a "Hail Mary" had something to do with counting prayer beads; I had no idea it was also a football pass. Zuela Hay of Louisville, KY graciously allowed me to use her name for my off-the-wall Shakespearean scholar. Zuela of Louisville is not like my character in the least; I just happened to like the name.

Ken Cooke did a super job on my Bucks Country Mysteries website, and my granddaughter, Karina, did an equally super job posing as the dead ballerina. Thanks to Frankie Stallard for her website photography, and to Elisa Baxt for allowing me to use two of her photos.

Special thanks to Glen Dishman, one of my tennis friends, for telling me the story of the senior class in an eastern Kentucky school where the male students really did decide that all the girls should be invited to the senior prom, and where they really did have a poker game to see which boy would invite which girl. Kudos to the guys in that class!

No book can be finished without a great editor. I was lucky to have Chris Hemingway Jones perform that job.

The marvelous cover was designed by Nat Jones. Nat, who is also an actor, created the audio-book as well.

And a really big thank you to all of my family for just being there: Julia, Stephen, Jim, Erin, Kyle, Jonathan, Karina, and Addy.

The Lady

"This isn't a good book; this is a GREAT book."
ABNA Expert Reviewer
The Lady was a semi- nalist in the 2012 Amazon Breakout Novel
Contest.

South Georgia, 1956: When Quincy Bruce's beloved Aunt Addy is
accused of being the inspiration for Nathan Waterstone's infamous
novel, *The Lady*, Quincy sets out to learn the truth and prove her
aunt's accusers wrong. Instead, she discovers other secrets which
place her own future in jeopardy.

Call Me Mara
The Story of Ruth and Naomi

The Hills of Moab, oil painting by Julia Pezzi
Book Cover not yet available
The beloved three-thousand-year-old story of the love between a
mother and her bride-daughter comes to life in the novel, Call me
Mara. Set in Bethlehem and Moab, the story follows Naomi as she
leaves her home in Bethlehem to travel with her husband and sons
to the land of their enemies and then, after a series of misfortunes
and disasters, returns to Bethlehem bringing Ruth, a Moabitess,
despised by the Jews.
Available November 2018 Sign up for publication announcement at
http://www.callmemara.com

GOSSART
PUBLICATIONS

About the Author

Judy was born in South Georgia where she grew up playing baseball, reading, and taking piano lessons. To pay for her lessons, she raised chickens and sold eggs to neighbors. She attended Mercer University for two years, and then Baylor University from which she graduated with a BA in German. She received her MA in German literature from The University of Michigan. After teaching German for several years, Judy decided to become a librarian and earned a MA in Library Science at Kutztown University in Pennsylvania. Judy's life took an exciting turn when she left her teaching job in Pennsylvania to be Head of Library at the Learning Center School of Qatar Foundation. She lived in Qatar for eight years, traveling during every vacation, and enjoying the experience of living in a different culture. Recently, she returned to the United States and lives in Lexington, KY. Judy has two children, Julia and Stephen, two children-in-law, Jim and Erin, and three grandchildren: Kyle, Jon, and Karina.

For more information or to sign up for my mail list:
www.judyhigginsbooks.com/
judyhigginsauthor@gmail.com